DRY HU$TLE

DRY HUSTLE

Sarah Kernochan

WILLIAM MORROW AND COMPANY, INC.

NEW YORK   1977

Printed in the United States of America.

1   2   3   4   5   6   7   8   9   10

Library of Congress Cataloging in Publication Data

Kernochan, Sarah.
    Dry hu$tle.

    I. Title: Dry hustle.
PZ4.K41214Dr   [PS3561.E615]   813'.5'4   76-50918
ISBN 0-688-03149-8

BOOK DESIGN   CARL WEISS

An Incantation to Promote Bleeding

(*From the Latin*)

The stupid man went into the mountain

The stupid man was amazed

I beg you, oh womb,

Be not angry!

PART

I

GIRLS GIRLS GIRLS.

DANCING DANCING DANCING.

NEED A FRIEND?

HAVE A DANCE

START A ROMANCE

GIRLS WANTED INQUIRE WITHIN

NO EXPERIENCE.

Kristal nabbed me in the dressing room. "Hey . . . Randy, is that your name? You want a laugh?"

I nodded, not looking up. Yes, she got my name right. No, a laugh might go down the wrong pipe.

"I have to tell you," she yattered, "Olive is spreading around how you're a sex change, because you don't shave your legs, so she says you're a man." Laughing, she nicked a chip of black eyeliner from the corner of her eye and hiked her frosted wig to the left, then noticed my stricken face. "Don't worry," she said gently. "*I* know who you are. You're just a hippie. . . ."

I had already scanned the dressing room for a back door or a trapdoor or a storm drain. Or, if I tried to make a break for it back through the ballroom, I'd have to trample seven dance-hall hostesses, one elderly gangster who ran the place, and a bartender, a cashier, and an Argentinian fairy who sold admission;

and then once up the stairs and onto the street I'd have to face the rest of an army of zombies who could not die because Times Square had better places for them to hang out at night besides the grave.

I just didn't want to go back in and face Olive and the other six girls. It was my first night, and already I'd lost my first customer. They knew I'd blow it. It was easy to see I wasn't slick. *I didn't know how to entertain men.* This secret belonged to them. It was highly classified and probably horrible.

Then there was my figure. Olive had told me, "With your shape you ought to be a high-fashion model!" She said it without a trace of envy. After all, my shape could never be a source of income for a Times Square dance-hall hostess, unless a man should want his company tall, blond, and terrified, and narrow. A narrow means of support, with my frankly long bones, all hooks and eyes, too narrow for a working girl at the Royale Ballroom.

Olive herself could advertise as a fat bonus: a great, gleaming pudding of stuff. Only her ankles and wrists had bones. I hated her with an honest hatred. While the rest of us sweated honest sweat under the red lights, she swabbed peanut oil on her waist-length tits and sweated some kind of *eau de farm.* Cause she had seniority. She'd worked the Royale for about thirty years.

"Don't cry," Kristal sat down beside me.

But the humiliation was already splashing down my cheeks with salt-water mess.

I was dying to know the secret of entertaining a man.

I wanted to stuff those fifty-dollar tips between my tiny knockers. I wanted to have my own regulars. I wanted them to picture me while they were balling their wives. I wanted to demoralize and rape and pillage. Besides, you have to be somewhat mature to be a high-fashion model.

"Olive's just jealous," Kristal urged on, "cause you're young and pretty and she gets bored at night. She has her one or two degenerates, her regulars that come in during the day to get jerked off and then she doesn't want to go home at night to a lonely bed. That's the lowest—the day trade. They're persons the street pukes up. It goes around to the customers when a woman is a pig. Even the pigs don't want it. They could have pigs for free, you know? . . . Anyhow, Olive's a schizo. In and out of mental places. Honest, she thinks she's the best-looking girl here!"

She whooped. My face was drying off but I still couldn't look at her.

"Randy. Want to open Olive's locker? She's got a big black dildo she always carries around. She locks herself in one of the stalls and fucks herself. I swear she couldn't work without it."

I smiled and blushed. I must have looked so dumb.

"You'd better get back out there now," she said.

"I don't want them to think I'm really stupid," I said. Then I flashed on my whole life so far. "I'm tired of always being the one who doesn't get the point."

"What do you wanna be, super-fotch femme fatale overnight? You're only eighteen, you told me. Well, so what happened with that guy in the white suit that picked you?"

"We went to a table. Then he said that last week he gave . . . fifteen dollars . . . to Nita. For helping him. He said."

"He means jerkin him off." Kristal started briskly narrating my thoughts. "Look, I know what you're thinking. It's your first night and Frank said all you had to do was talk to these guys and dance with them and get them to buy as many tickets as possible and that's all. And now, you think you're not gonna make any money unless you do what all the other girls are doin which is pullin their dicks under the tables and fuckin'm after work, but—hey Randy. *You.* Look at me."

I finally looked at her. She looked like a whore.

She knew, too. "I know I look like a whore, I've always looked like a whore ever since I was a baby. But I make more money than anyone else in the joint and Frank knows it, and listen. I don't touch the guys' dicks. Never. I don't even necessarily dance close. I don't go never mind to first base. Shit, I don't even know how to give a handjob cause I never have in my whole life, I don't care if you believe me."

"But what," I demanded, "do you give them?"

"Oh . . ." Her voice drifted off. "I tell'm stories and crap. . . ." She snapped back. "Listen, I don't give nothin of myself away. What's myself is *mine*. They only think they're gonna get a piece. See, I'm a dry hustler."

She paused, waiting for my eyes to stop queering.

"You take that clown you were just with. I guess you told him, 'No my goodness to betsy, I won't yank your thing for no money.' "

"I told him I had to go to the bathroom," I said.

"Here's what you should have done. He says, fifteen bucks. You say: 'So Nita took fifteen bucks. Then you should know I get twenty-five cause I'm a four-star.' Let him imagine whatever that means.

"He hands over the twenty-five. Now it's yours. You don't need him anymore. He's bought an hour's worth of tickets so Frank doesn't care what you do with him—talk, dance, kiss the customer's nuts—so long as it's under the table.

"Anyway, your guy is grinning like the cat that's just eaten shit and he says, 'What do I do now?'

"You say, 'Whatever you like, it's a free country.'

"He says, 'Should I take it out now?' and starts for his fly.

"Now. You straighten up, real shocked: 'You're going to take out your *thing*—in a *night club!*' like you're a lady, and he's being very low-class.

"This will get him embarrassed because he's wearing that expensive white suit and he wants you—a low-life cunt—to think he's rich and has class. So you *sigh*. Well, okay, if he wants to be an animal.

"Okay, you say. 'I'll do you if you want, but inside your pants.'

"Then suddenly you admire his taste in clothes. 'Wow, isn't that a beautiful suit!' and 'How much did it cost?' . . . Now he wants you to know he's strictly high-class top-drawer genuine leather, so he says, 'Four hundred dollars.'

" 'Four hundred dollars!' Now you get very concerned on his behalf. You say, 'Oh, it's so beautiful and white and you might not be able to get it clean after I get through with you. I mean, that stuff is not easy to get out, and the color white in particular is sometimes never the same. *Then* you excuse yourself to go to the bathroom.

"You go to the can, spend about ten minutes Meanwhile, his head is full of cleaning bills and never mind what he's going to look like when he walks out of here. So when you come back to the table, I promise you he would be gone."

I was suspicious. "What if he comes back tomorrow night in some old jeans?"

She looked amazed. I'd missed the point again. "Think of a new game, of course. I just made that up for the guy you were just with cause he had that white suit on.

"I mean, you can't repeat yourself exactly. Every man is different. They're just like any other person, they're all different. That same guy can come back ten times in ten different disguises and give you a fortune in tips but you'll never have to jerk him off if you play him. When he finally figures it out he'll be too prostated with shame to bust you, so either he'll stop coming around or he'll start picking one of the other girls with the fifty-cent handjobs. And so happy New Year for them."

I ached to applaud. Kristal was musing about something else already. "He didn't have to pay Nita even fifteen bucks to get off," she said at last. "That chick would have done him if he'd just promised to marry her. Nita still thinks she's gonna meet her future husband here. For twenty years she's been believing that. She's a dance-hall brat."

A girl named Inez opened the door and called in, "Frank is pissed. . . ."

"We got to get back to that disgusting playpen," Kristal grinned, and leaned close, and whispered, "I'll teach you. You won't have to touch it. You won't even have to let them feel you. . . . I trust you cause you're a hippie and you remind me of a cute little mouse standing on its hind legs."

The Royale Ballroom looked evil on account of the ceiling which stretched dark and low and dirty like a malice . . . over the bar, over the dance floor lined by tables for two, over "the pen" in the center of the whole room. We all breathed quietly up and down in the pen like some kind of special organism set apart. The Royale kept the place spitting hot so the girls could wear scanties and the men would order much beer and get drunk fast.

There was me, and Kristal, and Beth and Fernie, Cricket, Olive, Nita, and Inez. It was ten o'clock and no customers coming in. We got the loose flake off the street while upstairs the street-walkers worked on the hard-to-get-at grime in the cracks of the sidewalk. Which is not entirely true; we also got a lot of respectable men that would surprise you.

But this was my ignorant first night. "It never catches on til after midnight," murmured Kristal at my side. Fernie, a gargoyle who had not seen better days, was on the nod again, sitting bolt upright asleep in a black bra and girdle, kept straight by a rod of constipation that ran up to her tonsils.

Olive had placed herself under the beam of a white spotlight so she could read her tip sheet for the races tomorrow.

The sturdy Filipino fox named Cricket ate quickly, so the brisket sandwiches wouldn't get cold and the ice cream wouldn't melt. "Look at her, she doesn't know she's pregnant," Kristal whispered again.

There were only four men. Frank had shut himself in his office.

At the cashier's booth, Stan counted tickets and sipped from a paper cup of Scotch lightly tinted with Coke.

George, the waiter-bartender, shuffled back and forth changing the positions of ashtrays. He was a demented Quaker. To look at him you'd think that mad scientists would give up disturbing the peaceful sleep of the dead and quit trying to bring corpses back to life where they were not at ease.

The fourth man was Jimmy who always sat at a table in front of the bar facing the pen, drinking beer and snickering at us. Once in a while Olive would yell, "Come over here so I can bite it off!" and pitch a styrofoam cup at him.

On the other side of the pen was the dance floor and beyond

that, in thick pitch blindness, were tables where you would take the customers to do what you did. The only light in this area was a nasty fluorescence from the jukebox which seemed to play only "Rock Me Baby" and "The Theme From Moulin Rouge."

The pen was bounded by walls, about to the top of the thigh in height, built in a strange pattern similar to a rat maze or an obstacle on a miniature golf course. You had to take a few corners before you got out. I think the design was so if a dangerous type wanted to storm the pen he'd be slowed by barking his balls on a wrong turn and by this time Frank would be out of his office pumping him full of cavities.

The door buzzer went off: a man came in. Fernie jerked awake. We all rose as one: one asp coming up, hauling itself out of the basket, swaying forward to the wall of the pen, the singsong wailing wall: "Come on, sexy, pick a girl, hey handsome . . ." we joined in weird husky voices. By now I'd learned the opening prayer by heart.

The man walked past us, smiling shyly, and went to the bar. He bought himself a beer and sat at a table. I soared inside myself. This man was going to be mine. He was young, nicely dressed, good-looking, with table manners, lonesome, and sweet. He would be wanting the company of some girl of the same upbringing and hygienically safe.

When a customer passed up on the wailing wall and sat at a table, we were supposed to strut out of the pen, one girl at a time, and try to get him to buy time with us. Sometimes he was too nervous to choose right away and wanted us to make up his mind for him. He'd let this single-file sweetheart parade go by til he saw or heard something he liked. Then he'd pick that girl and she'd lead him to Stan's register to buy tickets, at a ten-dollar minimum for half an hour. Sometimes the man wouldn't pick anybody: he just liked being hustled, or he wanted to get stoned before he decided.

Fernie was the first one to descend on him. There was an unspoken courtesy in the pen allowing one of the old-timers—harpies like Beth, Fernie, or Olive—to go first so they wouldn't feel their existence on earth was pointless. They didn't hurt anybody's business anyhow because most men would take one look, get all choked up, and shake their heads energetically.

Fernie was turned down and returned to her warm indentation on the bench, and nodded out again.

Cricket was second up, as usual. The girl really loved making money, hand over fist, and besides, mainly, we knew she was pregnant and always hungry. Most customers bit on Cricket's line. She was pretty in a sly, exotic way, with gold skin and shiny black hair, and getting plump in her bikini where a teen-ager gets plump, and when she'd stand over a table she'd deliberately make her thigh muscles romp around her crotch. Also her English was incomprehensible so a man knew he wouldn't have to talk to her when she got him in a dark corner.

The man refused Cricket.

Now I knew for sure he wanted a nice girl. I jostled with Inez to be third at bat. She stood aside, since I was the newcomer and needed the practice. The young man watched me draw near.

"Hi. Would you like some company?" I asked. I cast down my eyelashes. I was positive I looked demure. All that I lacked was pigtails and a squeaky swing. I began to even wonder what a nice girl like me was doing here, but I'm saving that answer for later.

He shook his head.

Stunned, I retreated to the pen. Inez struck out with him, too.

Olive was next, jugs bumbling around her short nightie. Instantly the man got up and followed her to the ticket booth.

Remember, this was my second humiliation of the night.

"Why did he pick *her*?"

I must have said it out loud.

"He wants a mama," Kristal explained. "Goin back to the womb."

"But it doesn't make sense."

"So what?"

"Men are funny," offered Nita.

The bell went off: a customer was coming in. The girls turned

((16))

their heads, sized him up, and didn't move. Fernie did not even wake up. I stood to go to the wall.

"Don't bother with that guy, he don't have no money," said Inez. "Hippie scum."

"It's my boyfriend," I said.

At the wailing wall Murphy stood grinning through his big beard and waving his fingers howdy.

"Go away," I hissed in his ear.

"This place is far out!" His teeth twinkled from smoking grass. "It looks like a foreign movie!"

"I'm not allowed to talk with you unless you buy tickets," I seethed, "you're gonna get me in trouble."

Then Stan planted himself between us. "You going to pick this girl?" he menaced, wobbling on his feet.

Murphy sucked in his cheeks to keep from giggling. I wished him dead of an overdose. "No," he answered, "I was just rapping with her."

It was the juicehead staring down the pothead. On either side their eyes were pink and wriggly. I turned my back on them and sat down.

"You can't stand and talk to the girls unless you buy tickets," said Stan, "so go over and sit at a table or leave."

"Okay, man," I heard Murphy say. "Sort of a depressing point of view you got there, but I'm sure you really believe in what you're doing—"

"You want trouble?"

"Nice gig," Murphy added, nodding, and left.

The women were staring at me as if I came from some famous nut farm.

After a long silence, Inez advised me tactfully, "Frank don't like boyfriends and husbands coming in."

"Who pays for his reefer, you?" laughed Olive.

"He's a Ph.D.," I said.

"Don't get defensive. Lots of girls support their boyfriends," Kristal said. "Jesus, do you cry easy."

It was my third humiliation of the night.

* * *

Some twenty hours earlier, at about 4 A.M., Murphy and I had been standing in Times Square for the first time in our lives.

We had swallowed our last crumbs of hashish on the bus that rolled us in from Denver. Murphy left me at the Port Authority Terminal.

"You're dawdling," he said.

At that, I came to a standstill, fascinated by a pay phone with no dial. Murphy knew it was risky to try to demagnetize someone's head in a strange bus terminal. He put the phone receiver in my hand and told me to listen to the ocean roar for a while til he could come back and fetch me. I think he considered me less conspicuous standing still and hallucinating peaceably, since I was carrying half a pound of cocaine hidden on my person.

He had to pick up a key from a friend, unlock a loft on Forty-fifth Street, and deposit our luggage there. We were going to sub-let the loft for a month, long enough for him to clear thirty thousand on the dope deal. The other half pound was in one of the suitcases.

He got back hours after midnight. By then I was fine, leaning on a wall outside the ladies' room and calmly reading a candy wrapper. He said he was planning to sell the half pound I was wearing right away tonight. He had already made a call to meet some guy uptown, check out the cash, and then he would dial me at a pay phone in a coffee shop to come up in a taxi with the coke. After that, we could spend the rest of the month in the loft while he sold the other half pound off slowly, ounce by ounce, for maximum bucks.

Murphy had a more different slant on things than a lot of people, it was his nature. It excited him that he didn't know what the hell he was doing. In the past, in San Francisco, Murphy never dealt anything but marijuana and pills to support his hobby, which was to lose on the stock market. He also had a regular job at a university, teaching a course listed for five years in the catalogue as "NEUROPHENOMONOLOGY. Experimental psychology viewed as a religious event produced by psychoactive agents. We will consider arguments for faith and phenomena as a recognizable element of science" I think it meant: seeing everything as extremely funny. Funny ha-ha or funny weird, depending on what sort of dope you'd softened your brain with. Anyhow, the college discontinued the course at last and Murphy decided to close his house.

He had been running a teen-age runaway convention in his backyard garage, and that was how I met him. He let us sleep there and taught us how to forage for food. At night he could sit in his house and watch the garage skylight glow a faint ultraviolet from the lights we set up over our pot plants which grew while we slept and balled. He said he was studying us but I think he just found us extremely funny. However, he kicked us out when his course at the university was canceled and some kid's case of crabs made the impossible trek across the driveway and into his short hairs.

Some said I did it. By this time I had made it into the big house and could call myself his "old lady." When they split, I stayed.

He was impressed by my aptitude for learning. "You're a wise-ass," he said. "Now, if I can wise up your face to match your ass, then I'll fall in love with you." That's what I wanted, too: to wise up, and to have someone smart fall in love with me. I didn't see much else action to be interested in.

I smoked weed and read a lot of books and grew two inches taller than him, and I started a diary. On its flyleaf, I tried the many ways of writing my name, which I was not so crazy about since discovering I was adopted.

I liked Murphy. He was full of good cheer and different slants and odd persuasions. Now that he was unemployed, he decided he wanted to see the Third World. "The First and Second you can learn about in any seed catalogue," he maintained. I didn't care. The nice thing about fanatics—and parents, I guess—is they make all the plans for you.

Sometimes I could be bitter. He kept hiding my birth control pills because he wanted to see if the baby would be tall. He had some very stupid ideas.

So Murphy cashed in all his stocks and bought a pound of blow to sell in New York City. He told me it would be a major caper in the criminal sense. We would make enough money to travel around underdeveloped countries for a long time. "You mean ride on *dromedaries?*" I panted. We were fucking standing up and he fell off the telephone book at one point.

But we had never moved cocaine before. Riding across the country to New York, we held ourselves in some kind of dead man's float on top of the steady tide of adrenalin panic.

We walked to Times Square. According to legend you could get a close look at a sunken city there. Actually, we wanted to be around other crooks.

Murphy halted on the corner of Broadway, closed his eyes. He sniffed and nibbled at the air. "Let me guess what's in it," he said. "It's a combination of . . . sulphur . . . garlic . . . cat come . . . greasy sneakers, Negroes, caramel . . ." He opened his eyes again. "I know! This whole place smells like your under-pants!"

Just then, some one of the citizens appeared out of the steam of manholes and tried to sell Murphy a hot pocket calculator. We steered clear and found ourselves a diner.

Murphy had written down the number of the pay phone on the wall to take with him. I was sitting at the counter nearby so I could pick up when he called from uptown.

My cozy doper visions faded an hour later, and now I stared unprotected at the flabby stack of pancakes in front of me. I thought of wadding one up and bouncing it on the floor. My stomach scowled. I tried looking instead into the mirror and daring to glance at other people on the stools, feeling shy around these fancy street artists, bums, rakes, hookers, junkies, derelicts, all celebrities to me.

Then I felt some inside tubing give a twist and the first blood came down. My period was starting. The nameless wiggy hot women's dread swole in my belly. Then I flooded all over with the worser terror: I was bleeding onto a sanitary napkin packed with eighteen thousand dollars' worth of cocaine.

I don't remember how long I sat basting this illegal hammock between my legs. I lost all nerve when in the mirror I saw the revolving door whirl, and four cops invading the restaurant.

I pitched myself off the stool into the ladies' room, and hurled open a stall door. I was shaking so hard my eyelashes jingled. As my hands scrambled to unfasten the sanitary napkin from its belt I wondered which I should do first into the toilet bowl, throw in the coke or vomit.

The bloody pad landed in the bowl first. Then I spun open the plastic bag and dumped the coke. Then I threw up on it. To cover the evidence. I pushed the handle, the water blubbered, and my masterpiece began to wheel around in the eddy.

"Hey *moron*," said a voice behind me.

I turned to see a girl smiling with kitten teeth, tight black eyes, a wig of red curls, and a lavender-dyed rabbit coat. I didn't know if she was a tasteless narcotics agent or a hooker or both.

"Don't ever tear off like that if you see cops," she spoke fast and firm. "Now they're waiting outside for you because you jumped off the stool and ran like a freak. Those guys are just the pussy posse, out busting whores. They wouldn't have bothered you if you hadn't freaked. You don't look like a whore. Whores don't wear granny dresses and love beads around here." She peered past me at the coughing toilet. "And also that stuff is not goin to flush."

She pulled me out of the stall, went inside and locked it, then crawled back under the door. "Now nobody will find it for a while," and she stood up. "When the janitor comes in he'll probably snort the whole stinking mess and lick the bowl. That's a lot of speed you trashed, by the way. Not that I care. I don't like speed. I prefer diet pills."

I could hear the pay phone ringing outside. I knew it was Murphy calling. "God *damn*. God *damn* . . ." All I wanted was a fresh clean rock on which to bash my empty head.

The girl put her arm around my waist and stopped me swaying. "Shit, you're tall. Now keep shaking all over like that when we go out and you'll make a good impression." She opened the door.

The restaurant was minus about ten painted ladies who had been there before. Two cops had stayed, impatiently waiting for my comeback.

"Get my sister-in-law a thick milkshake," my companion called to the counter attendant as she sat me on a stool. "She's in her third month and the baby just sent back your deadly pancakes. Gimme some extra napkins." She made a big deal about wiping my face and cooing. "What are you horny sons of bitches staring at!" she snapped at the two patrolmen. "She's young enough to be your daughter!"

They ducked their heads and vanished out the door.

The girl planted a straw in my mouth: "You must have milk. Come on."

The sweet vanilla crept into my mouth, and with it a great calm.

The pay phone rang again. I tried to get up but the girl grabbed my elbow.

"Is that for you?" she demanded.

"Yes—"

"What's your name, I'll take it."

"No, I have to—"

"You're too fucked up. Quick, tell me your name."

"Randy."

She walked over and picked up the receiver. "Yeah, you looking for Randy? . . . Sure she's here. . . . No, you'll have to come get her, she's been throwing up again. . . . Yeah, she barfed. . . . Look, quit hollering and just get over here, you bastard, if she's lost the baby it's your fault, if you get my meaning, so goodbye." She hung up.

"What an asshole," she whispered to me. "He doesn't even know me from Adam and he's yelling, 'Where's the coke, what happened to the shit.' "

I said, "He's not used to this. He's a teacher."

"What kind of creep are you involved with who screams on the telephone at a stranger and uses a baby like you to carry coke? That's a serious bust if you're caught."

"I don't know but I think he'll kill me," I groaned.

"How much money did you just drown in the john?" she persisted. "A couple ounces?"

I shook my head, clamming up.

"You'd better talk to me. I'm trying to get you out of a jam. Look, my name is Kristal and I'm your friend and I know a lot of things you don't. That dude was mad, he might want to come and hurt you."

"He's my boyfriend."

"Oh. Does he love you?"

I couldn't follow the question, it was so funny on the ear. Does? He? Love? Me? "What?"

Kristal rephrased. "Does he love his dope and his money, or does he care more about you?"

I was stuck for an answer.

"How much money did you flush?"

"He paid twelve and was gonna get eighteen," rushed out of my fool mouth as I sank my face in my palms.

"Oh. Are you in the middle?"

I didn't understand.

"Are you two just in it for yourselves? Nobody else to pay off?"

"Yeah, just us."

"Well, everything's all right then. Whoo. My darling, there are easier and better ways to make a couple ten gee's without this fuss and bother. Pushing dope is a life sentence in New York, number one. Number two, a sweet baby face like yours is a gold mine in many other safer kinds of businesses. And number three, nobody, but nobody, *needs* to go crazy, just for some cash."

She paused as if expecting a response.

"Do you have any Tampax?" I asked at last.

As she rummaged in her pocketbook, she continued: "You have to decide right now if you're a stupid person, because if you are then you're like most people that just keep shittin rope to hang theirselves with. But you don't strike me as the stupid type so I think you should just get rid of your nerves . . . and think about how you don't need no pain, you don't need no extra grief, you don't need to sell your ass in this life or the life hereafter, and you don't need to tell your boyfriend because why? Because nobody needs to know the truth half the time because it's gonna be a pain in the ass for somebody if they do. . . . There's other ways of . . . Here. All I have is Super." She handed me the tampon and followed me into the bathroom.

I sat on the toilet lid in the stall next to the locked one in which my contraband swam. As I labored to force Kristal's Super up my Junior-sized nook, I listened to her talk through the stall door, spreading wide open my junior mind.

"Here is what we'll tell your boyfriend," she began.

It was a normal pussy raid. Randy slipped into the ladies' room but there was no stopping Officer Dan once he spotted her. Dan is a crooked cop and his nose is out of joint from smelling out dope where dope abides. For his own pleasure Dan prefers the gentle reefer but when he deals shit he deals only the finest coke and scag.

Now, I was taking a pee in one of the stalls when I heard the evil bastard come in after your girl friend.

He was shaking her down. He had her dress over her head and located the cocaine easy. If I hadn't made my presence known he probably would have made her suck his dreadful dick too.

However the moment I unlocked the door and showed my well-enough-known face, Dan knew we would reach a quick arrangement whereby everybody might come out ahead without much fuss and felony and whatever have you.

Dan, I said. As far as I am concerned you are raping a young girl at gunpoint and I will start screaming bloody hell in another minute. Then you will have to arrest her and confiscate the coke because your buddies will hear the noise and come in here. However again, you may walk out of here with the coke as a secret between the three of us, if you will agree to cut us in on your future profits. Yours sincerely, signed, you know fucking well who I am. Kristal Belle, the Hungarian Tempest.

((24))

P.S., 50 percent of your take on the coke belongs to us and may be delivered once a week during our working hours at the Royale Ballroom between 8 P.M. and 4 A.M.

Failure to deliver will result in me sobbing my eyes out to Frank, proprietor of the Royale and favorite son of the mob, and who is like a father to me and all my problems are his problems. Fifty percent is a reasonable figure and my last offer.

Dan says, twenty-five.

A deal, I said.

You cannot split hairs with a serious motherfucker or he might become emotional.

It's certainly lucky we were all three dishonest people in the same john. Instead of losing the whole stash and going to jail, Randy only has to come work with me every night in this perfectly safe dance hall a few blocks from here, so she can collect from Officer Dan whenever he happens to drop by.

Of course you don't owe me anything. People have always told me I could be rich beyond belief if I didn't have such a big heart, but what can you do.

"What about when I don't come home with this Officer Dan's money every week?" I asked.

"You will. You'll make plenty of money at the Royale if you learn to hustle. Your boyfriend doesn't need to know how you got it."

She tipped her head—broad, oversize like a child's head, with a child's expression, at once idiotic and cunning—and it came to me that there was enough room in that head behind the brain for a crumped-up piece of paper, no bigger than a fist, a piece of paper containing all the answers. All the answers smuggled under a cap of sleazy red curls.

I'm always on the lookout for someone who has all the answers.

"It's all real complicated," I hesitated.

"So is modern art."

*   *   *

((25))

When Murphy arrived we all went out on the street and Kristal ran down the story. She had opened her coat. Murphy was staring down at her chest in a sort of meek fashion, never interrupting except to murmur "oh, wow" now and then.

Now, looking back to remembering his face, I know this look to be the hundredth some-odd level of awareness the self enters when exposed to the sight of tits like that floating into view, over her neckline's horizon, like alien zeppelins or indecipherable omens.

She finished by berating him: ". . . if you really loved your baby you'd never put her ass out on the iine for no fucking lame-shit deal in this world because she is a lady, and not dirt."

The dawn had broken, a pink shade. It suited her.

After she sped off in a cab, I walked with Murphy to the loft.

"I think she's a some kind of neurophenomenon," I suggested timidly.

He didn't know. Words failed him.

So here I am, next night around midnight, in a swimsuit and high heels, and mad at myself. I grew up in a good neighborhood. I went to good schools. Even after I ran away from home I was good at panhandling. So if I couldn't score pennies off a man on my first night in a dance hall, I must be a fuck-up beyond my wildest dreams.

A new customer sat down at a table. I shot out of the pen like a sex monsoon.

"Hey there, lover," I bent down, "you want some fun? We can talk and dance and . . ." I was running low on ideas. "And get acquainted, if you know what I mean."

For a moment he said nothing, just stared ahead with coated eyes out of a thin, dark face. Then I heard him say, "I am yours to command," his voice echoing softly as if we were in a vault. "Do with me what you wish," he says.

He had a faint Indian accent and was tucked up sort of limply in his chair. He gave me the quakes, so I turned right around and went back to the pen.

Kristal stood ready to go for him; none of the other girls had budged. "This guy's a masochist," she said under her breath as I passed. "They're a little hard to handle, but it's more or less my specialty. Well, here goes."

I watched her go over, and couldn't hear exactly what she said, but it had some kind of distinct rat-tat-tat rhythm. I assumed it was abuse. The man accordioned up even more, then followed her in this crouching position to the cashier.

"I'm glad Kristal was around to take care of him," said Sheba. "Psychos scare me." Sheba had got into work late that night. Kristal had confided to me that she was "one of the original jerk-off artists. And a lover of dogs."

"These bones are killing me," Sheba wrassled with her black lace support bra. It was wired like fry baskets and squeezed over the scoop neck of her purple leotard for display purposes. "You have to watch out for these masochists, because they're also sadists," she continued sadly. "They'll flip over to being sadists the minute they get tired of being masochists. Just like that, *boomp.*"

"Scumbags!" Olive hooted, and threw her paper cup at Jimmy.

"We had one in here a lotta years ago," said Sheba, "that was a German, pink eyes . . . wanted to pay two hundred dollars to come to a girl's apartment and clean all her shoes. That's all he wanted. Kristal was working here then before she went into stripping, and she kept telling and telling the new girls not to do it, but one of them liked the money and he seemed like such a hopeless little toy poodle. So she lets him come over to her place. She gets the money up front. He spends three hours on all her shoes and slippers and mules and what have you, while she lays around on the bed counting her money and ragging him. Which is what you're supposed to do. But then when he finishes the last pair, he comes. *Boomp.* Now he's a sadist. He beats her up so she can't work for a week she's such a case of black and blue. Pshew, it's not worth it. Look . . . that's Benny! He wants you. Hey, he's good for a sixty-dollar tip!"

Benny turned out to be a whippersnapper type. At forty he still had the looks of a ballsy kid with plenty of the green moxie to show sprouting out of his wallet. He immediately bought me eighty dollars' worth of tickets, four hours' worth, which meant I was his and his alone til we closed at 4 A.M.

Really, the machinery was very smooth in that place. In a matter of minutes there I was sitting across from my next assignment.

I mentally reviewed Kristal's first-night pointers she'd given me earlier in the dressing room, in that soft airy chaste voice of hers, the way she sounded most of the time, like some kind of Bo-Peep. "Remember this," she said, "they all tell you in so many words what they are lookin for. Remember they are like imbeciles because they *need* this crap. Listen, it was the customers that taught me how to dry hustle. They'd set it up for me to trick'm. That's why whores call them tricks. Either they're playin dumb or they really are that dumb—sometimes I can't tell."

George trudged up with beers for me and my Benny. While he was paying I tried to size up my quarry. So far, I knew he was in automotive parts, he was divorced with two kids, and he was so full of bounce and mischief that he regularly scampered around Times Square establishments of all kinds, storing his nuts in his cheeks I guess—

"—my business associates have no conception what I do with my nights," Benny grinned. "They think I'm off hitting the singles bars. I like to think I lead a double life. . . ."

My attention left him for a minute as I tuned in on the conversation at Kristal's table nearby.

"How dare you dirty my boots with your filthy tongue!" she lashed at her masochist.

"Yes, mistress," answered the voice of the tombs.

Benny's hand closed over mine. My flesh didn't crawl, so I decided to let him. "Do you have a lot of fantasies?" I asked him. I hoped this topic would make the next fours hours race by.

"That's a good question," he replied, as if he'd never thought about it. "How about you?"

"I'd like to go to the Third World."

"Hmm." He looked blank. "I've been to Hawaii many times now."

"Yeah? This is my second day in New York City."

We heard a whack and turned to see the masochist on his knees. "Now get out," Kristal snarled, "and don't come back, son of a donkey!"

Her customer disappeared like a crab under a rock.

"Go, Kristal!" Benny cheered. "Hey, how are ya?"

She came over, jaw tensed. "He told me to smack his face, so I had to. One more minute and he was gonna be a hassle. He was having himself a litt-ul . . . *too* much of a good time." She threw me a smile with tiny glittering teeth. "This is my baby girl. Benny's a good person, he'll take care of you," she petted my hair and turned to Benny. "This is a very sweet, innocent girl, you hear, you know how beautiful that is? Her sister's a stripper in the city and she was putting Randy through a college in California cause Randy is just the apple of her eye. It was Randy's first year, dean's list and everything, but her sister was just put in the hospital for a radical mastectomy, so Randy had to come here to work for both of them, poor lamb! We're all trying to chip in so she can bring her sister a nice present and also meet the rent—oopa-doop, I gotta scram now. That guy's for me. Benny, you treat Randy nice."

After she left Benny slipped me a twenty towards flowers for my stricken sister with her boob in a sling.

An hour later he'd had enough beer to forget about my tragic condition. I was very sleepy. I thought he was quite nice. It was nice, him stroking my arm, droning on about his fantasies. ". . . then I have this one which really puzzles me, because I'm definitely a heterosexual. I'm not attracted to men at all. But when I'm having sex with a woman sometimes I pretend I'm the woman, and she's the man . . . what's so funny?"

"I wasn't laughing."

"You did this with your eyes." He rolled his eyeballs upward.

"I was just thinking."

"You're a very pretty girl." He was getting restless. "Hey, let's dance. I'm feeling terrific."

I stood up with him.

"Wow, you're a tall one," he said, stealthily passing me a ten

((29))

spot. "I couldn't make up my mind when I first saw you whether you were a sex change. Nita said if she ever caught me dancing with a sex change she'd bite my head off. The only way I can tell is when they have small feet, then I know it's a girl."

The jukebox was playing fast numbers, disco beat, with a lot of this thudding and gasping and silky violins on top. . . . I couldn't believe what we were doing on the dance floor. This is what I watched.

The man's pelvis goes around and around, see. It circles, snapping every time it comes forward, like a rubber-band ball on a wood bat.

He hooks his arms around his neck.

My hips chase his hips as if they are snagged together, circling and snapping like that. Our bodies don't touch.

My hips are getting the edge on his hips. Looks like my hips are going to whip his hips. At this time it's a dead heat. We are not touching.

My face is the hollow-eyed mask of prostitutes.

Below, all is voodoo. Fantastic tantrum. Hissy-fit.

Inside the mask, my brain and eyes are being sucked down through the funnel of my neck into the mixing motion of the hips. Down goes my heart and vital organs. Everything is hooping around my hips.

I was doomed. Nobody was there peering over the rim when I went down the drain that night.

Kristal calls this experience "getting the bug for the hustle." She got it when she was fourteen. She said, the word goes out: get them. "You stir up so much shit inside, it eats you."

My hips have cornered his hips and are prepared to shoot if necessary.

Then BOOMP—Benny suddenly clamps my right leg between his legs and fastens his boner on my thigh.

((30))

He has another voice now, very far off, sweet, and wailing, it curls into my ear: "Oh, oh, oh, fuck me, baby, take off my bra . . . oh, oh, oh, spread my legs yes baby, shove it in my cunt now . . . fuck me, fuck me, oh, oh, please. . . ."

Benny's first voice returns. "Pant in my ear," he directs.

I manage a strangled sort of puffing, what might conceivably excite a beagle.

The second voice is back: "That's right, oh, oh, you're so big . . . take me, fuck me now. . . ."

My working hours ended the way a fever breaks. You wonder which parts happened and which parts you made up of what happened were just some kind of fever gumbo.

"How much did you get offa Benny?" Kristal asked.

"Tomorrow," called Sheba, "brings promises of financial reward for work well done." She finished the horoscope and folded the paper, glancing at the headline. "Whoops, that was for today. I better get the morning edition up on the corner for tomorrow's . . . I'm all mixed up. G'night, ladies." When she left the dressing room, me and Kristal were alone.

I unhooked the top of my bathing suit and my tips fell to my lap. Kristal smoothed each bill out and counted.

"Sixteen dollars?! You had him to yourself for four hours!"

"Wait, I got a twenty in my panties," I apologized.

"New money he was carrying, too." She handed it back. It didn't look like any other cash I'd ever earned or begged. Stiff as romaine, loaded with nutrition, moistened with the sweat from between my breasts, but it made a mean scoffing sound when I handled it.

"You should have done better, with all that sister in the hospital horseshit I set you up with. Remember all these men are morons."

"I'm not even sure if they're *men*, now," I whimpered. "First I'm a sex change, and then Benny thinks he's a woman—"

"Oh, Benny's fulla stories, tonight he's the bearded lady and tomorrow he's a foreign agent. Your job is not to get confused."

((31))

She laughed, hooking up her lavender fur coat. "You're right, they're not men. I'm glad you fart around with these Ph.D. guys, you really have a way of making me rethink things."

"I think they're neurophenomenons," I muttered.

"Who? Hurry up, let's get out of here."

"These men. I don't even think they're mammals."

"They the ones with no backbones? Ha, see? I took tenth grade, too!" She looked at me with interest, then disapproval. "You ain't been in it long enough to get bitter, candy-face. You were the one lettin him rub up against you like that when you didn't have to. I was watching."

"Does it matter?"

"Suit yourself. *I* don't like to be touched," she said.

"I don't have to come back," I was stuffing the money into my jeans.

"You're not smart enough to stay away."

When people say things a certain way, I believe them. It's my big mistake, no one else's.

As it turned out this time, she was right. That was the voodoo, the heartbeat, the bug of the hustle: *larceny*. And tonight I discovered I had a little larceny in my heart, stuck there like a tiny burr. "And if you keep playing out there," my foster mother used to yell, "pretty soon you've got stickers all over you and nobody will ever touch you ever again!"

I strutted up and down the loft for Murphy's benefit as he rolled around laughing. He'd made me put the swimsuit and heels back on because he said it turned him on.

"And then what happened?" He paused, gulping for breath.

"Then he told me to take off his bra."

"WHAAAW!" Murphy hurled himself onto the bed, hysterical all over again. "Did—did—he have one on?"

"Of course not," I dragged on a joint, happy with my saving grass in the 5 A.M. "He was an average businessman. Automotive parts."

"STOP!" He was going into dry heaves from laughing. "Whaa-haw-haw—then what?"

"He wanted me to pant in his ear. . . . Kristal said I should have just played along and told him he had a tight pussy and huge tits and how hard he was getting me, and then demand twenty-thirty bucks for saying this garbage." I kicked off the shoes and seesawed the bathing suit down over my hips. "Catch," I threw it at my boyfriend, whom I didn't care for in his current attitude.

Murphy was different. I knew when I came back from the Royale, when he opened the door, that he'd made some kind of decision regarding the importance of greed in his life. His face had some new crass pointy parts like a weasel, and the glass face of the handmirror on the bed sported regimental white lines of cocaine.

"My favorite B-girl!" He'd ushered me in, thrust the mirror and a cocktail straw under my nose. "Have a hit, dear."

"You're supposed to be selling that coke, not honking it."

"I'll cut it with something, these rock stars will snort dandruff so long as it's overpriced. Have a toot on the naked city."

"No, I want a joint."

"Well, par-*don*." He blithely flipped the mirror over and I saw my evening's tips worth of coke settle into the floorboards.

"What's the matter with you?" I quailed.

And he laughed softly. "I'm a dealer in *hard* drugs now. I get to read a whole new set of lines. Yeah, whole new script. I like this city, fuck Afghanistan, fuck all those other places. I want to learn how to be a rotten motherfucker. I'll just keep you around to turn the pages."

"I got cramps, let's go to bed."

But he wanted to see me in my outfit and tell all about my customers and how much money they gave me.

I tossed my tips at him; they floated down on top of my wilted bathing suit. "It's just play money," I said. "Silly money. Funny money from funny men."

Murphy gazed at my nude self. "Come here." He beckoned me onto the bed. "Come here, teen-ager, so tall and so tough. Well,

((33))

you may be tall but you're not so tough. You can stop the tough stuff now."

His arms slid around me like a favorite shirt.

My father's naval uniform in a dark closet in Virginia.

That was the hold Murphy had over me. He knew when I was tired of always having to be older than I am, and every day having to get a little smarter than I want to be. He'd just say, "You can stop acting tough now," and the curse would go away.

I don't know from love. But Christ, don't you know that a good hug opening up and closing around my head is what I always lived for. There's a song goes with it that doesn't rhyme but sounds like it ought to: "Hold me close. Just hold me. I'm a long way from home and everybody has to sleep somewhere. . . ."

Them arms, them arms, them strong strong arms. When I was a baby and just barely alive I'd crawl and mew my way across the mighty living-room carpet just to get from one pair of arms to another pair. I'm a big girl now with ideas, but if some mutt set of cock and balls wants to come snuffling around, dipping its swollen nose in my damp patch, man, rolling its spine in a warm lotion ditch, well I don't care what-all commotion goes down in the holler so long as up the hill, honest arms will cradle me.

Murphy was nudging my head down to his hard-on.

I closed my hand on his hearty stem and rubbed the cap. What's wrong with you, I chided myself, you know you love men. What's softer than a baby's foot—why, the fat cap on a man's cock. I scrubbed it with my tongue and bounced the cap off the back of my throat. And not just men, I thought. We'll all of us poor sweet babies.

My father's voice welled up again, as it often did in the silence of other men's bosoms, the voice of the last time I spoke to him, three years back, calling him from a pay phone around the corner from my house. Poor sweet baby, his weak fretting wail: "You've got a family here with me, why do you have to go find somebody else. . . ."

"Liar," I yelled, "I saw the agency papers. You're not my father and that bitch Inger's not my mother and now you've got to tell me whose kid I am."

"Honey, I raised you, I'm your mother and father, I love you and that's all that mattters, isn't it. . . ."

"Liar," we both wept.

Get him, I thought, two small vicious words that spit out of nowhere, and suddenly I squeezed Murphy's joint at the base and wrung his skin up and down, and he bolted in my mouth and poured out his brew. "Good girl," he sighed, "the nurse will give you a lollipop."

"Hold me," I begged. "I don't want to go back to that place." Murphy hugged me. "I know, I know. But you've got to get the bread off that cop, that Officer Dan. I can't afford to lose my investment. Come on. You're tough enough."

Then I realized how intricate Kristal's lie was. That's the worst part about a great lie. They like it so much better that they wouldn't believe the truth.

I woke up the next afternoon hearing a strange man's voice.

"Fucking Redondo *Beach,* man."

The blinds were all pulled down in the loft, a long echoing room with no partitions and not much furniture. The photographer who owned it was away on a remote assignment. Rolls of white, pink, and gray seamless paper backdrop hung from the ceiling; parasol lightstands, empty hangers on dress racks, a kitchenette, an oak table where Murphy was sitting across from the stranger, and by their intense faces and deft motions I guessed they were cutting the coke. I closed my eyes again.

"He moved out to the beach and he had shopping bags full of heroin. Like, I just wanted a little kiss from whatever he had. And he brought out *shopping* bags. Like, it wasn't cut or anything. I said . . . 'Larry? I like you.' The guy was very strung out. His dog was hooked, too. When Larry went to jail, the dog had to kick."

On the pillowcase beside my head were faint red blooms, imprints of blood from Murphy's rioting nose. I looked back at the table to see him set aside a sieve, dip a knife blade into the mound of powder, and jack a hit up his nostril, snuffling briskly. The stranger watched the scale teeter between the weights and a small hill of white blend.

I shivered in the January chill, wrapped the top blanket around my body, and wandered over to the table. Murphy jerked around. "The Big R! She's showing signs of life! D'Piro, this is my old lady. Hey, old lady, come get your wake-up before d'Piro and me turn it into—"

"—cream of wheat for fuckers of Wall Street," bopped d'Piro, snapping his fingers. He had tiny bones, sallow skin, and fast eyeballs. To my credit, I despised him instantly.

The knife blade was heading for my nose; I held a sleepy finger against one nostril and inhaled the big white heap up the other. Gale winds blasted the clouds from my eyes and I decided to run for President.

"This your old lady who's topless bottomless?" d'Piro cackled. "Hey, you know Roxanne with the red beaver? Reddish-brown?"

"No," I managed, through clenched teeth.

"You got to. She's bad."

"This runt knows people in high places," Murphy commented.

"—way too high places, look like a turkey run when the coke comes through—" d'Piro was checking a list and corking little vials.

"There's an extra bagel for you on the dish rack," Murphy got up. He drew me over to the sink, and whispered, "I lucked out on finding d'Piro. He was hanging out in that apartment uptown when I called you night before last and he said he'd do the running for me on the other half pound. He's a record salesman, so he drops off little presents for people on his route, stores around the Stock Exchange and Soho artists and then back at the record company. He says all they ever want to buy is a couple grams at a time so he can get up to eighty dollars per gram and he takes a commission. It's a perfect setup. Now we don't have to worry about running the shit by ourselves, we just sit back here and hold

((36))

out our hats for the money. He's even going to get us free albums," his nails jagging in my skin at every emphasis. "This is a *karmic* type of diversion. We got hit by the heavy bad-news storm front when we got here, but now it's turning around and coming back on us with the reward money. All we have to do is keep on doing what we would do normally, and all this craziness will fall into place."

"Does that mean I don't have to go back to work at the dance hall?"

His eyebrows snapped down like those tricky black umbrellas. "What the fuck do you think I'm talking about? You have to stay there and tough it out. I'm telling you, the shit will come through for us solid. It's all *happening.*"

Sure enough, he did sound like a hard-drugs dealer. He had me fooled. He was jumping around me so much I was seized with panic: all up and down my neck there were miniature brushfires signaling danger . . . invasion . . . national security . . . mass confusion . . . a boyfriend's mental condition . . . and I'd never seen a bagel before. "Can I have a joint?"

"We smoked it all. D'Piro'll bring me a couple of lids tonight." He whipped back to the table and resumed business with his eelly friend, who was saying, "Pshew. I was up the last three nights at fucking *press* parties."

I was wondering about the answer to some question Kristal had asked me. "'Do you love me?" I said.

Back of Murphy's head says: "Don't bother me, I'll rape you later . . . Weird kid."

"Weird *City!*" d'Piro breathed, watching the weights.

I lifted the bagel to my mouth and considered the long and festive chain of rapists in my life so far. There were good rapes, bad ones, mediocre. . . . I suppose I could have fought off most of them except the first. I didn't know who my natural parents were, so I imagined that was the first rape and I was its sorry fruit.

Then when I was sixteen I ran away from the home of my foster parents when I found out they had raped me of the pride of legitimate beginnings. I ran to the Navy who after a year's service in the WAVEs proceeded to rape me of the chance to ever hold a good job by trying and expelling me "under honorable conditions" with the mark "lesbian" on my civilian record forever neatly describing one night of adolescent loneliness.

So I ran to the road, and thumbed a lift which introduced me to the cavalier young rapists of my own generation, and I wish I could remember the first, the one who pricked my cherry and passed it onto his thread, but I can't because marijuana raped my caution and made me foolish of time, names, and remembering.

Then came Murphy, who didn't hear my question, the one about love. And anyway he had raped me of romantic notions. He said it was no use my finding my identity because I'd discover my error the next day and be depressed.

He explained, "The main directive is to have faith that, scientifically speaking, your future is being handled by a phenomenal force that cannot be checked, or be chemically or conceivably under*stood,* and therefore must be simply *with*stood. . . . This will insure you a maximum of happiness and also permit you to laugh a lot." He was responsible for my educated way of speech.

"Stop!" pleaded one of his students who had dropped by and was paralyzed in one corner of the room, to a twelve-hour squat by the might of windowpane acid. At the time, I was puffing on a joint and trying to match socks from the laundry by "blue vibes," "brown vibes," and "black vibes," and I considered Murphy's idea about equally with any other idea I had.

Then after Murphy I was abducted by Kristal, who was going to teach me how to rape back. I had thought this was physically impossible, but she raped me of alternatives.

Every morning I expect to roll over on my pillow and see someone I thought I knew well, staring at me with apologetic eyes and telling me they won't harm me if I don't scream.

In a life so rich with perpetrators, I think the only persons who never raped me were the firemen. The volunteer firehouse was about eight blocks from my home in Virginia, and every time I ran away they would hide me in a spare bunk, dress me up in slicker and galoshes and red hat so I could scream off to the big blazes. They'd get my face all smeared with grease from the Thursday night crab sauté's, and my head foamy with beer. Sometimes they'd have a new volunteer, a real doofus, and send me over to grab his balls so he'd freak out. Then when lights were out they'd ask me all about feminine secrets, things supposedly bundled in riddles by their wives and girl friends.

"How often should I eat it?"

It was dark. My voice was deep and gruff from two days among men: "Hell, three times a day after meals, and brush your teeth first!"

They loved it. I didn't know what the hell I was talking about. They were so sure women were a mystery. Women had it all worked out what they wanted from birth, and then they just acted dumb or mysterious while the men chased around trying to find out what the women wanted, which they'd never find out, unless once in a while some stray skinny tomboy slid under the fence and ratted a little. They didn't dare rape me, these honorable firemen. I knew too much.

Maybe there is some other word I should have chosen besides rape. I have to go by what it felt like afterwards.

As my teeth sank into the bagel my jaw ached from last night's blowjob. I guessed if I worked in a massage parlor I'd be taking my breakfast through a straw. I chewed, and chewed, and chewed, until finally the bread fell apart enough to swallow.

MY DANCE-HALL DIARY

(WEDNESDAY)

NAME: CHARLIE. AGE: 60's. DESCRIBE: Silver-haired, lean. A tall, yielding birch of a man, eyes dark and tragedy-smoked around the edges. BACKGROUND: Public relations. FANTASIES: One particular story. When he was about 20 he almost raped a girl. He was courting her in the slow and tactful pace of his era. At each step, he would press, she protest! and succumb to his greater strength. He has a sweet nature and to use force pains him terribly but he desired her so much . . . and then at the moment when he was to possess her, she was so piteous a victim—yet his passion was sweeping him over her feeble battlements—he went crazy—just as the hinges were about to desert the frame and the door to tumble to his battering ram, her one last cry of outrage stopped him cold. The guy has been racked by merciless lust for months and then dashed to pieces on the rocks of his destination, but he manages to scrawl his epitaph in the sand: A GENTLEMAN WAS HERE.

Turns out this was a worthless recommendation because the lady was very disappointed that he backed down. Turns out that every time she said *no* she really meant *yes* and thought he understood this language of lovers.

He tells me he was destroyed, and ever since then he can only have relationships with women if they take all the initiative. They must tell him what they want and what he should do about it. He says he has never told anyone else this story, but I don't look as vulgar as the other hostesses. Then he asks me to lick my lips slowly while he sucks on my fingers. He says: "I'm imagining your body. It's better that way.". . . Before he leaves he asks, "Will you remember me for the kisses I wanted to give you, but didn't?"

ADD'TL THOUGHTS: Unbelievably sad and sweet. The girls say he always sucks their fingers but I can see why.

TIME: 2 hrs. TIP: $10. TOTAL: 2 hrs. commission @ $7 tickets + tip = $24.

BILL. Late 30's. Hungarian Jew with accent. Thick-trunked, hands shaking with nervous energy, chain smoker, bleak face cragging down like a gulch, the massive rock shifting as he grinds his teeth. One of Nita's regulars. Waited an hour but she hasn't shown up. Finally picks me and we sit over by the jukebox. He says, "Say something. Anything. I go crazy at a table alone." I say how hard it is to find real friends for conversation and not just sex. He agrees: "I'm a romantic. If I see a girl I like I'll do anything for her, I kill myself if she loves me." Turns out he's a soccer trainer and masseur. Used to be a player but had a spinal injury in an accident. He unbuttoned his shirt and showed me the surgical truss around his waist up to his shoulder blades.

He can't sleep some nights, electrified by frustration, his muscles racing haplessly around the site of his toppled spine. There are other problems. "You understand, I can't get hard enough to have sex. I can only be with a woman who does French."

(NOTE: Kristal calls Nita "the compactor—the garbage pail—she screws for tickets. She won't take cash. She gets them up to her apartment, and after the free ride she starts up with the princess act—how she doesn't take money because she's a lady and not a prostitute, and how she can tell he's a warm kind human being and how nice a couple they make and how people shouldn't be alone—then out come the casseroles and the marriage hints—all in the same night, mind you! Some guys say it's not worth the trouble even though it's a free fuck.")

I pretend I don't know what French means and even if I do I don't do it, so Charlie lets small talk, weary sighs, and haunted silences fill up the rest of the hour. Then he goes back to his table in front of the bar and waits for Nita. No tip. TOTAL: $7 commission on tickets. ADD'TL THOUGHTS: He had a kind of sweetness and I was glad Nita would French him.

GRAHAM FINCH. Mid 30's. British store designer flown over for a job by Bloomingdale's. Only been in New York a week. Short. Soft enough to look like he's just floating along on good cheer and the puffs of little cellophane bags of "sweets" he fondles in his pockets. Light brown hair in a tidy trim, with bangs that he tugs on whenever he is mildly amazed and delighted.

I didn't finish the "GRAHAM FINCH" entry that night because I'd drunk too much beer and my writing was poor. Usually, between customers, I'd go into the dressing room and make notes and then reconstruct the whole scene in my year-old spiral-bound diary the next day at the loft. I confess the gothic style of the entries was due to my last two years in high school, when I fell into the arms of the intellectual charisma of Mister Wilder, an English teacher who thought I had "certain glimmerings of the literary soul" and who proceeded to shovel heaps of romantic novels onto my head. I read *Return of the Native* and two days later I began to menstruate for the first time. For almost a year I suffered volcanic periods, intensely painful, sometimes erupting every two weeks and lasting ten days. Often I was unable to walk. I stayed at home in bed with a heating pad, a bourbon-and-honey concoction Inger made to shut up my groaning, and the volumes of Thomas Hardy, Jane Austen, Emily Dickinson, the Brontë sisters, the Dumas guys, Henry James, George Eliot, and Dashiell Hammett. I remember the odor in my bedroom that year was like a rich compost—my blood, molten and thick with egg, and the whiskey, and the book pages with their damp layers of plot and counterplot, a dark thriving mulch of intrigue, and the dead language like dead leaves pasted over the monstrous heaving surface of carnal urges—"If you want to live like a slob, that's your business," said Inger. "I'll just tell the company that we're having over that we installed a swamp in here and watch out for snakes in the hallway."

The following year, my menstrual flow ebbing, I gave all my passion to book reports, attempting to transfer to those weekly assignments some of the glory I had gorged on and now needed to disgorge.

And two years later my pencil is staggering over the pages of my diary like a crosseyed hobo.

At this same moment, two years ago, I am doubled over a notebook in my bedroom in Arlington.

All ten of my fingers smart at the quick, and ten severed fingernails finely ground are sailing to digestion. I'm ornamenting the final paragraph of a book report past the point of coherence, so as to avoid doing my math homework.

The door bursts open. It's Inger. Major gods have been turned to stone upon gazing at her profile.

I used to call her "Mother." The name pricked her, all right, but she didn't bleed. By my pre-teen years, familiarity had matured into a ripe contempt, and I started calling her by her first name. I had been planning all along to revert to "Mother" if she would only take me in her arms and repent—for calling me "you bastard!," not only an obscenity but also a peculiar one for a girl, at the dinner table whenever she felt like it—and repent too for lavishing all her attention and pride with a quite impressive motherly love on my sister Ginny.

Then I found out that she hadn't given birth to me in the first place. I could never call her "Mother" again. I also found out that Ginny had been adopted, too, and therefore had just as much right as me to be tormented by Inger.

But the only person capable of legislating fairness was my father, and he was usually away at the naval base. There he was kept safe in his strange sort of senility by the bosom of the Navy, which prefers its officers to have a warped sense of world affairs. Besides, he had his own anguish worth living for, as he swung down the sky in a parachute and watched his brother's face demolished by the Japanese in a sudden air attack, and descending with the headless body, the two of them like leisurely kites on a Sunday, swinging down the sky to the singsong of groundfire, they were pendulums slowing down time and with it slowing down certain abilities of the mind to grasp world affairs.

So he drifted around our household from time to time, forever awed by our live whole faces and ignorant of their purpose. When he was not at the base, he stayed with his mother in Baltimore. Since his brother's death, she had a chronic cough. "Mama's boy," Inger explained to us. Mostly he was gone, vanished like a ghost, leaving behind empty uniforms and suits I used to try on. Inger and Ginny would be out shopping and I was supposed to be doing my math. I'd jilt the lock to his study, open the closet, climb into the arms of a white jacket, paw through his drawers, then remove a brace of books from the shelf, get out one of the guns from his enormous rifle collection, and fire a bullet into the exposed paneling. Then I'd replace the books. His favorite gun was a World War I snubnose, the "nigger killer." He loved to describe how the bullets explode on contact into a spray of shrapnel. Once, he rolled back the rug to demonstrate the gun on the floor, and he saw the scars of the many times I'd pointed the snubnose there myself.

"Sit up straight, noodle!" Inger sweeps a T square off my desk and shoves it down my back, under my waistband. She and Ginny are going to the movies. "I want your algebra looking neat and pretty by the time we get back."

My "father" believed I had a "mental block" against math. At the beginning of every school year he tore the answers out of the back of the workbook and locked them in his file cabinet.

Now I am opening my algebra workbook. The symbols are a treacherous code that could spell the end of the world as we know it, or a fresh beginning, or they could mean my ass if I don't solve the questions before Inger gets back. The empty house gurgles fitfully.

I take my geometry compass along with me to smash open the lock of the file drawer. Inside, I find a folder marked, simply, "R." In it are the answers from the back of my math book, and my adoption papers.

I felt so foolish for thinking so long that I had inherited Inger's complexion and my false father's sea-scanning blue eyes.

No: two strangers coupled my face.

Before leaving the house I called my English teacher at his home. Mrs. Wilder answered. Here was another shock, another impenetrable coupling.

"I'm going to an orphanage," I told Mister Wilder evenly. "Please don't worry. I'll be all right, if God wills it. I'm sending you my book report anyway. I went over the word limit, I think, but there's nothing to be done about it."

"As long as it's pithy," he replied, strangely ill at ease.

"I want you to know I'll keep reading literature. Everything is cool. I have no parents now. There's no turning back."

"Randy? Have you taken something?"

Now I pelted tears into the mouthpiece. "Listen, I'm a bastard! A bastard! I've never known any love in my life! Tell me where there is any love anywhere in this world, just try and tell me!"

"What did it look like, Randy? Was it a tablet, or a capsule? A sugar cube?"

"Could I come over?"

"Randy. Are your parents there?"

"Fuck yourself," I choked, and hung up. It's the kind of thing a smart-ass will say at a time when they are filled with pain and confusion. I walked to the firehouse.

"Of course you're gonna get maudlin when you drink that much beer," Murphy said.

"Well, this Graham guy stayed with us all the way til closing and he kept ordering more beer."

"Who's us?"

"Kristal and me. He picked me first, and then she came up alongside and told him he'd have to buy two of us. It was so sudden, I didn't know what to say. She was rapping in this great Hungarian accent like Zsa Zsa Gabor: 'Dahlink, vhat a vahndervul vahndervul.' She says it adds some class when you're bullying someone."

Murphy dipped the corner of a matchbook cover into his bed-side bag of coke and snorted. "You want a one-and-one?" I shook my head. "So then?"

"Can I have a joint?"

"D'Piro hasn't come back yet. I don't know where the fucker is." He looked murderous.

"So then Kristal says he can't buy me alone because she's my sister-in-law. My brother's her husband and he works nights. He doesn't want me to be alone in the apartment because I'm so innocent and he's insanely protective and there are 'nigger junkie molesters' in the neighborhood. So Kristal has to bring me to work with her so she can keep an eye on me. He has to buy her too, because there are a lot of nasty men around Times Square and I'm a virgin. Now, that puts a different complexion on things. See, he's obviously very nice, well paid, and a tourist, that's the way she spotted him. So now he's going to be relieved to hear that he's going to meet a nice, *good* girl who's a real virgin, instead of a funky Forty-second Street vampire. He paid eighty bucks for two hours with us."

"What did you all do?"

"I danced with him. We talked a lot. Not me, I was too embarrassed. I mean, I was *supposed* to be shy. Now, every time he hints that he would like to take me out, to a discotheque or shopping at Bloomingdale's or dinner, Kristal jumps in, says, 'Vhat a vahndervul idea, dahlink' and goes on and on about how happy it would make me and what a gem I am for company, how intelligent I am once you get me to talk—then she stops herself. Whoops. She keeps forgetting about her husband. My brother. He doesn't trust any man around me because I know nothing about life."

"So?"

"So, Graham can't take his eyes off me."

"I don't get what it's leading up to."

I grinned triumphantly. "You don't? I must be getting more experienced, cause *I* caught on right away. He thinks I'm a rare find. A captive princess. Like Rapunzel. Shit, I forgot the part where Kristal told him my brother was planning on marrying me off to a rich old garment-district Jew. Well, she knew that he must have to deal with those kind of men every day at Bloomingdale's, and being English he's probably anti-Semitic, so a worse fate he can't imagine for a rare young flower like me. He's therefore determined he's going to be the man good enough, and rich enough, to get me away from this family of mercenary maniacs. Kristal didn't even hit him up for a tip. She says he'll come back and he'll get so involved in the story that we'll get some kind of big money off him."

She also said Graham Finch would fall in love with me and ask me to marry him inside a few weeks. I didn't tell her that the idea excited me out of all proportion. I was going to be courted and wooed by an old-fashioned man with manners! While she was away from the table to go to the can, Graham and I stole glances at each other. With compassion and conspiracy in his voice, he murmured, "Are you happy, my gehl?"

"I don't know," I blushed. The answer was an honest one and didn't require any acting.

"Don't you ever get jealous?" I asked Murphy.

"Huh?" I was halfway grateful to see him look amused, just like old times. "Have you got some sort of romance going that I should get jealous about? Here's an old man who sucks your fingers and wants you to invite him home, and a soccer cripple who wants you to give him head, and some Lord Goon Esquire who wants to take you shopping, and you're sitting there in a bathing suit in January in a basement under a lot of red lights waiting for a dope payoff from a corrupt peace officer. Period."

"I thought all the men were kind of sweet, though. . . ." I was desperate for a joint.

"Very romantic. I'm all twisted up with jealousy and sinus problems. Where the fuck is d'Piro?"

MY DIARY

(THURSDAY)

JIM. 32. Insurance. Just lost 73 lbs. Still fat, but less fat than before, and not used to freedom of movement. Not ready to try out the rig on straight women so he practices seducing whores, is my guess. Lurches around the dance floor like a turd in a flushing toilet. Waiting for Misty (tiny blond pleasant chick from Brazil, married to painting contractor with bread, no one knows why she works here). Finally he offers me $25 cash and a check for $100 which he says Misty would take if she were here, for going to a hotel. I refuse, Misty shows up, he tips me $5 to get rid of me. TOTAL $12.

ELI SMALL. 50's. Born in Latvia, arrived in U. S. 1939, started fruit stand. Now a steel parts salesman. Married with 2 kids. This is a great country, he believes in the 10 Commandments too. Wants to "cuddle" me. I find out he's only here over-night from Detroit and staying at the LaGuardia Sheraton. I say I'll meet him in his room if he gives me $ for taxi and champagne and a babysitter. He does, and leaves to get some sleep before I show up at 5 A.M. after I'm through work. When he wakes up it'll be morning and he has to take the plane back. All this Kristal's idea. TOTAL $72, for 1 hr.

BUDDY. 42. Irish, works for father, electric golf carts. Flashes money. Resents father. Insults me nonstop for ½ hr. All women are jive, he's paying me so of course whatever I say is jive, sees through everything, he's so bored with chicks' shit they give him, they're too stupid to know he knows they're shits, and I wouldn't be in this place if I was honest, so don't think he doesn't know whatever I say is shit. Finishes, happy. Tips me $10. Talks about ships. Calls them "she." Cruise freak, pulls out a lot of tourist agency pamphlets and shows me deck plans. Wishes women were ships, or ships women. TOTAL $24, 2 hrs.

GRAHAM FINCH. Again. Brought me a bottle of perfume. Kristal tells him the garment district elderly Jew came over to our house to propose marriage in person today, but I had refused to come out of my room.

"Her brother my husband is benging on the door! Beng beng beng: 'Unlock the door, you beggage, you tremp!' Vhat should I supposed to tell him? To explain? 'The girl she hess vell in loff with von of the customers'? . . . Look at her! She's in loff vith you!"
I leapt up and fled the table.
In the dressing room, I quickly changed into my civilian clothes and tried to banish Graham's woeful smitten eyes from my mind. Kristal strode in. "That was beautiful what you did! Perfect!

((48))

He's practically a *pool* of wet pants he's so in love with you and he thinks you're just dyin over him. That's right, take the rest of the night off. I'll tell Frank you got food poisoning."

"I feel sorry for Graham." I was buttoning my coat. "I feel sorry for him and all the others, too."

"But so do I," she protested. "They keep settin themselves up for a hustle and they never learn. It's sad, you're exactly right. . . . I'll see you tomorrow night, okay? Here, don't forget your perfume; you left it at the table."

The next day Murphy bought a miniature cassette recorder. During the day he planned to use it to monitor the phone, which didn't ring. D'Piro was still missing, along with fifteen grams, and Murphy was beginning to suspect he was a narc. At night, at work, I was to hide the recorder and tape any exchange between myself and Officer Dan if he should happen to fall by.

It behooved Murphy to snort a lot more coke, so there would be less gone to waste if a bust came down.

I had gone so long without a joint that, in its place, reality was a pill I swallowed. There was an awful dawn in my bloodstream as it began to run clean, and nothing could now reverse my plunge into the nightmare world of sanity. My poor head was invaded by new responsibilities wickedly dancing with common sense. I heard the voice of reason, and realized it was mine.

"How could you," I stamped around, "spend all that money on a tape recorder? And where am I supposed to plant it, in my belly button?"

"It goes in a shirt pocket, like a cigarette pack. Will you please lay down? You'll wear a shirt tonight. So what if you're a little less naked than the other girls?"

"I can't get no customers that way."

"*Any* customers that way. You're starting to sound like a hustler."

"Well, you're starting to sound like a coke dealer! Except you're not even dealing it. You just sit around and snort it and gnash your teeth—"

"How'm I sposed to move it when I can't tell whether the

heat's onto me or not? I've got to lay low til I know that this Officer Dan isn't closing in on the rest of my stash with d'Piro as his ratfink bellboy, right? I have to sit around here trying to remain *smart,* girl, so we don't get fucked over. Now if Officer Dan comes into the dance hall and makes a drop while the tape is going in your pocket, then we'll have evidence of graft and something to bargain with if he's indeed behind this whole thing fucking us over. That's what I mean by smart. Who else is looking after you, kid?"

I couldn't very well tell him that Officer Dan didn't exist. My voice of reason said I was born with a neck, so I should save it.

"Lose that dude," advised Kristal as we changed in the dressing room and I described my homelife.

"It's not that bad," I said, a little jolted. "He's going through this paranoia thing. . . . But usually we're really cool together. We never fought before."

"He doesn't love you."

"Well, who else is looking after me?"

"That Graham guy, for one. By the way, act real uppity toward me tonight, around him. Act like you're getting ready to rebel against me and your brother and sneak off with him cause you're head over heels for him."

I ignored her. "Murphy's a really, really sweet person. In a little while he'll have done up all the coke and we'll be back to normal, stone broke, no more expensive drugs."

"You hippies are such winners," she sighed. "Well, you can't wear that shirt with the tape recorder in that pocket like a third tit, you look like a fed."

"Then I'll tell him I couldn't pull it off, it made Frank suspicious."

"Let me see." She took the recorder and dropped it between her breasts. It disappeared like a tooth under a pillow. Kristal had a fit of giggles. "Let me try it out just once with a customer. We'll get a little something on tape to entertain your Ph.D. daddy!"

* * *

Listening to the tape is like a foreign language record, if you should ever want a quick home course in all-around useful phraseology for a dry hustle.

MAN: What would you say if I said you turn me on.

KRISTAL: Well, thank you, I'm really gettin to like you, too. You're just about the nicest person I've met in years. Here I've only known you one hour, or what has it been, and I feel like I'm close to you.

MAN: I mean in a sexual way.

KRISTAL: Well, thank you, I'm enjoying talking to you.

MAN: Do you work here all the time, or do you take some nights off?

KRISTAL: I've got to work. It's tough. I got three kids to support after my husband was killed and I go to school during the day.

MAN: What kind of school?

KRISTAL: Law.

(Deafening surflike noise here as Kristal's tits jostle the tape recorder: during a session with a customer she is constantly fussing with her tits as if they're bothered being cooped up, so she's gradually working them over her neckline, leaning forward, breathing deep, and other distractions.)

MAN: Do you like sex?

KRISTAL: Sure I believe in it, but I have to like the person. You don't meet so many people to like, you'd be surprised.

MAN: What would you say to eighty dollars for going out with me tonight when you get off work?

KRISTAL: You're offering me money, to go out with you?!

Listen, I would go out with you for nothing because I sincerely like you. I'm *very* disappointed. I thought you were a nice man, but—mister, I'm not that way. I do not work like that. I'm insulted you think I'd give myself to any man for money, I don't care if it's a Wall Street panic!

MAN: But we were getting along, and you were dancing close to me, and I thought—

KRISTAL: —This is a dance hall, not a whorehouse. I've got other people waiting if you don't want my company. See that guy, he's been waiting half an hour for me to get through.

MAN: Don't go. You're so good to look at. I'd like to touch you right here—

KRISTAL (smacks his hand, gets up): You go pick yourself a whore, the place is full of them!

MAN: Hey, don't go, I'm sorry—

KRISTAL (sits): Behave yourself. I'm a woman, you know.

MAN: I can see that. I love to see your breasts hanging out like that.

KRISTAL: Which one you like better, the right or the left one? Listen, I'm quite a woman.

MAN: That's why I picked you. I said, that's a lot of woman there.

KRISTAL: Then treat me like one. Or go pick another girl. For fifteen dollars you can get whatever you want here, including the clap.

MAN: No, I want you. I really love a woman who acts like—

KRISTAL: Women do not know how to carry theirselves. That's the whole trouble right there. Ladies don't know how to *carry* themselves and they're *not honest*. Let me tell you one

((52))

story. This friend of mine, she was married and she had a fight with her husband, so she was drinking in this bar and she met this redneck, you know? . . . You don't know what a redneck is?

MAN: Uh . . .

KRISTAL: A farmer, a truck driver, a—a peasant from North Carolina or West Virginia, the ones with a drawl. You-all this and that, you know? Anyway, she was just talking to him about her problems with her husband, and this guy bought her four drinks. Two dollars! Now, if it had been me, I would have said, "Get away from me, I can buy myself fifty thousand beers." She had the money, too, but she figured she'd let him pay for it. She bought nothing but trouble. This guy thought that for two bucks, four beers, he had a right to do whatever he wanted. See, ladies do not know how to carry themselves. . . . You know what happened to her? He took the car out to one of those lover's mountains and raped her. But that's nothing. He had six brothers. They were in the other car, following. They all got her, too. Oh, she *cried*. . . .

MAN: My God.

(Kristal always manages to tell at least one "cream-their-drawers" story about "somebody I know" in a session to turn the thermostat way up in a short amount of time.)

KRISTAL: Live and learn. Well, I'd rather live and never learn stuff like that! Men have to respect me. That's why I didn't get married til I was twenty, because I waited for the respect.

MAN: I didn't mean I don't respect you. I'm sorry I offended you.

KRISTAL: I'm sorry, too, because I like you. Oh, you're so sexy. I don't think that I would like you if you didn't have the moustache. Moustaches gives you class.

MAN: You like this? I've just had it for about six months.

KRISTAL: You know, I would go out with you, but I have to know you respect me. I've only been with two or three men in my life to make love with, and if you don't believe that you don't have to.

MAN: Don't do that.

KRISTAL: What, you want me to cover myself up? Poor boy, I've got you so horny. *I'm* horny now. I'm going home and get out the old vibrator!

MAN: I think you are so warm . . . and intelligent, and you are so honest with me that I can be honest with you, and we have fun talking. . . . Would you like another beer?

KRISTAL: Only if you got six brothers and they all look like you!
            (they laugh)
Seriously, I wish I could believe you. Listen, I'll tell you the truth, I'm just really upset tonight. My little daughter's birthday is tomorrow and I don't think I'm going to be able to afford her a nice present.

MAN: I understand. Let me do something for you, please. To make up. Here. Tell your little girl a nice man wishes her happy birthday.
            (hands her twenty-dollar bill)

KRISTAL: That's so sweet. I'm not gonna say no. I'll get her a dress like I wish I had when I was little. I'll worry a lot less now, thank you.

MAN: I'd still like to take you out, if you still like me.

KRISTAL: Watch out, it's gonna be expensive for me to like you!
            (they laugh)
Really I do like you, that's why I was so hurt when you

thought I was a wrong kind of woman. Like some people see my titties—

(more heavy tape noise from tit motion)

—next thing I hear is, "How much?" Don't offer me money. Flowers, or a bracelet, or a *momentum* of some sort . . . that's what I like. Like that cross around your neck. I've been lookin at it, it's so beautiful. I love gold like nothin else.

MAN: I get it cheap in Puerto Rico when I go visit my mother there.

KRISTAL: I live with my mother and father. They take care of the kids, but they're very strict with me, like I'm still a little virgin. That's why I couldn't take you home tonight, for instance.

MAN: I could find a hotel room.

KRISTAL: Oh no, I'd feel awful. It's been such a long time for me since I could feel something for a man, a hotel room would be the worst place. . . . I rent this other apartment just to be alone in, but I'm behind on the rent and the doorman would stop me if we went there.

MAN: How much rent do you owe?

KRISTAL: One-fifty. Have you got it? Cause then you could meet me after work and we could go there tonight. Oh, what am I saying. There's too many problems, we'd better forget the whole thing. I wish I'd meet someone like you some time when I don't have so many worries. We'd go to my apartment and I'd make love to you like I want to and pretend that I wake up to you every morning.

MAN: I think I've got enough, let's see, hold on, don't give up hope.

KRISTAL: What a gorgeous wallet. Is that hand stitching? I don't know which I want more, your money or your gold cross!

((55))

MAN (laughs): Here, see? It's all cash, you can just hand it to the doorman.

KRISTAL (palms $150): You'd better stop getting me so horny, I'll end up costing you a fortune! Can I ask you a personal question? Are you big?

MAN: Well . . . not too—

KRISTAL: —Good, cause I can't take it too big. I'm very small. I like at most six and a half inches.

MAN: Well, that's about what I am, I think.

KRISTAL: Seven's too big. Six and a *half*.

MAN: You know how I'd like to do you? Sixty-nine.

KRISTAL: Oh, I love it. You can eat me all you want. Listen, we'd better stop this kind of talk. I haven't had a man in seven months.

MAN: I'd eat you *all* up.

KRISTAL: But first I'd steal your gold cross!

MAN: Well, it's pretty new, I wouldn't mind giving it to you.

KRISTAL: You do that. I'm very religious. I'm a gold digger and I fear God. When I come all over you I come gold. Hot melted *gold*. Oh God, I've got to stop gettin so worked up over you.
(he hands her the cross and chain)
My God, the man was serious! The man's nuts! I didn't know you were serious about giving me that. Oh, I'm so excited, I gotta run into the bathroom and show my girl friend! You wait right here.

Back in the dressing room, Kristal gravely listened to a bit of the tape I played back for her. "Hey, I sound pretty good."

"I guess you'd better go back out to him. You've been in here ten minutes."

"Hell, no. He's a P. R. . . . God damn spic can wait. All I got more to tell him is a phony address for this apartment I supposedly rent."

"But if he comes back tomorrow night all pissed off?"

"If he wants to come back for me, I'll give him more. Quit buggin me, I got a headache."

She'd been drinking a lot of beer and her face had a venomous cast that would become more familiar to me in good time.

"Boy, am I burned up. This place is really gone downhill. Did you see what Frank had in here tonight workin? Did you see that nigger chick, real pretty one? Real slick? Frank ain't never had no niggers in here before as hostesses. All the dark-complected ones are sposed to stay across the street at the Pony Ballroom, his other place. He must be gettin senile."

The only reminder I could see of the old days was a framed list of regulations dated some time in the fifties, hanging by the sink: ". . . Language not becoming to a lady will not be tolerated . . . No dresses may be slit above the knee. . . ."

"You're the one better get back out there," she carped. "Graham should be showin up around now."

Graham had brought me a hundred-dollar gift certificate from Bloomingdale's. When I danced with him he took great pains not to brush his hard-on against my stomach.

"Do you really love me, my girl?" he whispered, and pressed my head into the crook of his neck. "Don't be afraid. I wouldn't hurt you for the whole world. Is it true, dear?"

What was I going to say? "No"? His jaw was trembling. Kristal was getting drunker at the table and pretending to glare at us.

I closed my eyes and let myself be rocked. I had this pang for him now; a little core of hot was born underneath my breastbone.

The jukebox changed to a fast number and Graham politely released me to pony up, the favored Royale uptempo dance step. I saw Kristal had left the table. She didn't return, although Graham kept buying tickets for both of us the rest of the night. Then I let him kiss me.

I wish his mouth hadn't of gushed. If Graham hadn't been so gruesome a wet kisser, this whole story might have turned out different.

When I got back to the dressing room at closing time, Kristal was sitting hunched over the makeup counter in front of the mirror, and glowering at nothing much. "Hi. I left a message for your boyfriend on the end of the tape while you were gone," she said. "Tell him you got Officer Jack or whosis to talk, and then play it for him." She smelled slightly of vomit.

Alone in the cab going back to the loft at 4 A.M., I played back her message. Her voice began out very affectionate but got rowdy later on.

Hi, remember me? This is Kristal. Your hair looks really nice, Murphy, I hope you didn't wash it just for me. Except there's a smudge under your left eye doesn't look so hot, you'd better wipe it off. . . . That's it, much better. . . . Now listen, I just don't want you to think bad of me, that I'm a homewrecker or anything, but I'm not sure you've been Mister Do-Right by your old lady recently which is not my fault, because we left work early and she gets me up to my apartment on the pretext of looking at my furniture or whatever have you, and all of a sudden I see her legs is shakin and she's beggin me to eat her cunt and let her squeeze my tits and she's cryin like a sonofabitch so I had to just get down there and help her out, so now she's already come off twelve times and swears she never wants to see another dick in her life. And I'm worried she's going to go bald down there if she makes me keep this up—RANDY! OH! OH—

I switched off the tape because the taxi driver was peering in the mirror and my own cheeks were pink and straining against the pressure of rapidly accumulating giggles. I never did play the tape for Murphy.

* * *

((58))

I woke to see Murphy bent over a flour canister with a butter knife, cocaine thundering up his nose. He was in a rage such as an archangel behaves when his credibility is took in vain. It was the third day d'Piro hadn't showed.

"And I can't even call up the record company to find out if that greasy bugger even really works for them! And you know why? Because today is fucking Saturday! You know why else? The *phone* is suddenly and mysteriously out of order! I can make calls out, but no calls can come in!"

"How do you know?" pulling a sweater over my head.

"Because I called some friends yesterday I haven't seen since med school who live in the city—they're coming over tonight. I called them back again today to rap and two of them said they'd tried to reach me and got a busy signal and I *know* I wasn't on the line, and the phone company said they couldn't fix it til Monday. You know what *that* means?"

"What?" I zipped my boots up over my jeans.

"I don't know." He kept pinching the skin between his eyes. "He lied. He *lied*. I don't believe what this city does to people. It means something is going to mean something *very soon*. Could you make some dip or something for these people when they come over tonight, before you go to work?"

I nodded, buttoning my coat.

"Jesus, Randy, I'm worried. If I just had a hint or a hunch or a clue. Because there's a pattern starting to happen. . . . First, there was Officer Dan whose last name and actual rank I don't even know, and second there's d'Piro whose first name—where are you running off to?"

"To Bloomingdale's," I said, quickly opening the door.

"I'm going out, too."

We cantered down the stairs together, and took opposite directions when we hit the street.

I used Graham's gift certificate to buy a warm calf-length sheep-lined coat for myself, a set of pink floral sheets for me and Murphy which wouldn't show up his nosebleeds so bad in the wash, and a small ivory tusk on a gold charm for Kristal. I hadn't planned on getting her anything, but when I saw the sharp little charm I pictured how it would look next to the gold cross on her neck.

Murphy went shopping in a bad neighborhood and bought a gun.

"You don't look like you belong here. . . . What's a nice girl like you doing in a place like this?"

They still say this line, except now they serve it up like some kind of cynical joke they just invented.

This man was a stockbroker. Manicured and coiffed and cuff-linked, with raised cheekbones very shiny from superior shaves. He was staring languidly about the Royale, dusting me with occasional remarks, but his innermost mind was preoccupied by superior conundrums. Things that I, a night scruff, could not be expected to grasp. Well, he had some fascination for boring sex emporiums. Or, in my opinion, he was fascinated by his boredom for everything, even flesh parlors. Anyway, about twice a year, usually following dinner with a client, he would succumb to this fascination, or this boredom, and hoot-owl around Times Square: "Just out of curiosity . . . to see if anything's changed. But you don't look like you belong here. What's a nice girl like you doing in a place like this, heh heh."

"I'm putting my parents down," I answered coolly. "To them, this is the dirtiest thing on earth."

The stockbroker had asked the most leading question a lucky little hustler can get. I'd only memorized one or two extensive lies from Kristal, but already here was my chance to tell "the sophisticate story."

His eyes snapped into focus on my face. "How old are you?"

"Twenty. I left Bryn Mawr a couple of months ago. Majored in political science. I got tired of straight A's and following in my father's footsteps just cause the cocksucker didn't get a son like he wanted."

His mouth curled smugly. "So I was right. I knew you didn't fit in."

Kristal had said: "Always use the truth as much as possible or you'll lose track of what you're doing. Also, total horseshit *sounds* like total horseshit, so go for about eighty percent horseshit, tops."

"My father's a naval officer," I continued. "I can't mention any more because he's very important. But he made my mother an alcoholic and then he turned around and tried to make me into a nervous wreck of a yes-daddy ass-kisser with a Ph.D.

"What does he think of what you're doing now?"

"I'm havin a ball! I've run away before, but I always came back. So he doesn't bother to come after me anymore. He doesn't know where I am. . . . But this time I'm not going back. I've had it with the father complex, I've had it with the intellectuals and the trust funds. I left with no money. I don't need him. I can support myself here better than you can imagine." It wasn't hard to act the sorority fugitive with the right amount of bitterness, so long as I pictured my foster father in Virginia. The cocksucker.

"I admire your guts," said the stockbroker. "But do you really enjoy having strange men grope you down here? If I gave you ten dollars like any other customer, would you do for me whatever the other girls here do?"

I managed an enigmatic smile. "What does a lousy ten bucks *usually* get you, sir?"

He fell to gazing about the room again, hunting for a clever answer. Oh, he was playing, all right, and enjoying himself.

The silence was another lucky break for me because I had stone run out of cleverness: I had no instructions on how to hustle beyond this point.

"Or better yet," I joked, "what would *you* consider doing for a lousy ten bucks? And while you're thinking, please excuse me cause I've got to answer a call of nature."

I beckoned Kristal out of the pen and she followed me into the dressing room.

"What's the matter, kiddo?"

"I did it, I did it! I got him!" I jigged on the balls of my feet and crowed. "The guy is really loaded with money and he fell for the sophisticate story!"

"Which one?"

I got bewildered. "*The* one . . . you know. . . ."

"You thought there's only one?" She laughed. "Shit, if I told the same story over and over I'd put myself to sleep! At least have yourself a little *fun* with a hustle. How the hell do I know which story you told him?"

"The one where I'm rebelling against my father's authority and left college and I'm kicking dirt in his face. But now I don't know what to say to get the money off of this dude. I got the rope around his neck but I don't know no knots or anything." My grammar was being shot to pieces in this place but my metaphors were improving.

She turned her back and sat down in front of the mirror, toying with the cross and the tusk on the chain around her neck.

She had been so touched when I gave her the present. "Fourteen karats! Look at the little gold swirls. What's the thing in it, a fang?" I told her it was a wild boar's tusk and the saleslady said it was the latest in vogue for good luck. Kristal liked that.

The saleslady had told me if I wanted to get technical it was probably a pig's tooth.

Kristal looked up from the chain and into the mirror. Her eyes batted back and forth between her face, my face, her face . . . mine.

A worldly woman with a black gypsy-shag wig and black paint caking her eyelids at a wicked slant is studying an eager overgrown girl with long straight naturally blond hair and clear peach-influenced cheeks.

"I don't like myself," she said.

Concerned, I sat beside her and hugged her shoulder. "What is it?"

"I'm startin to have strong feelings for you. I don't have any friends and I never have wanted any. But you're like a friend to me now, and I don't like what I'm filling your head full of.

I think you should cut loose, go home, tell your boyfriend whatever, and forget this whole experience. Just chalk it up. You should have a nice life. Not what I do."

"No, no," I urged gaily, "you've got to tell me what to tell this guy next. I *want* to know."

She shook her head. "I've watched you, okay? You're not made out for it. You haven't got the—the cruelness. I'll take a man for his last fifteen dollars because I don't care. But you're gonna break your heart feeling sorry for them because you always find some way to like these guys—"

"I know, but I *want* to do this one. I don't like him. He thinks he knows it all."

She lit up, then. As if a smile was a kid you hoisted onto your shoulders to wave at the clowns, she lit up a smile and let her little nippers cheer at me. "Yeah," she said, "those are the ones I really get off on hustling, too."

As we came out of the dressing room, the buzzer went off and Kristal's Puerto Rican gentleman from the night before walked in. His countenance was quite stormy. He was planning to fly into a rage but Kristal got there first.

"You bastard!" she shrilled. "I waited up two hours for you and you never showed!"

He was stunned. "I waited for *you,* one hour, in the freezing cold, and there was no doorman, not your name on the bell—at Two-thirty-four East Forty-fourth Street—"

"I told you Two-thirty-four East Forty-*fifth!* Oh, darling, do you realize we were waiting for each other and all that time we were only a block apart? Do you know I even prayed on your little gold cross that you hadn't been killed in a car accident?"

"You can't talk to the lady unless you buy tickets," Stan intervened, tottering.

"Of course the man's buying my tickets, we're in love!" Kristal hooked into the man's arm and led him to the cashier.

I sat back at the table with my stockbroker. I knew he had his lines ready on account of his subtle air.

"So?" I says.

He rearranged the arrangement of his clasped fingers. "I find you very attractive. And unusual. Frankly, I came in here to look at whores—"

"—I'd be out on the street selling my ass," I interrupted, "except I have too much respect for myself. I want to punish my old man, not myself. I just couldn't take cold cash and fuck somebody. I mean, I can assure you I'm no prude"—here I threw in my 20 percent or so of truth—"because the first thing I got rid of, the first time I ran away from home, was my virginity. But somehow money doesn't go natural with sex. Maybe it's my upbringing."

"Everybody's got a price," the stockbroker informed me. That's another verse you keep hearing as if they just invented it, and another easy cue for a dry-hustler understudy.

"Well . . ." I appeared to wrestle with mathematics. At last, "No. I still couldn't do it for a flatout *fee*. Now, if someone wants to pay my rent which I owe, or help me out with my clothes allowance!" I tittered. "But still, even then. It couldn't be just any man, like a trick. The man would have to be clean, good-looking, a successful type, an older man, someone who can appreciate where I'm coming from. Most of the guys we get in here are just atrocious slobs."

I was getting tired of his predatory grin.

I took him for two hundred dollars "rent money," gave him a phony upper East Side address to go to at 4 A.M., and let him think we were two well-bred mutually bored eccentrics playing at tricks-'n-hookers for a one-night lark. It takes a lot to titillate a sophisticate.

I even let him dance close to me before he left. "I'm an excellent lover, by the way," he murmured in my ear.

"If that's true," I kidded him, "I'll give your money back afterwards. Cause I've been acting tough with you but I'm so horny I'd pay, myself, for just one night of good loving. I'd even break down and have my father wire me the bread!"

I was also getting tired of all the slow songs on the jukebox, particularly "Strangers In The Night."

I was too tired to wipe the eyeshadow-mascara "fotch" off my face or to change back into my street clothes that night, so I just stuffed my jeans and sweater into a paper bag and wrapped myself in my new coat for the taxi ride home.

I forgot Murphy had invited company over until I was turning the key in the lock and heard voices inside the loft. It was 5 A.M. There could be only one nasal decongestant keeping them awake.

Murphy and the four University of Michigan med-school class of '68 graduates were sitting around the oak table, consulting a jigsaw arrangement of cocaine in the middle of a handmirror. One prematurely bald and bulky man was organizing the white debris with a dental spatula. Another man, his partly-buttoned safari shirt revealing furry tits, took the butter knife from Murphy, swabbed some residue off with his finger, and vigorously rubbed it into his gums. They stopped talking as soon as I stepped inside. Under the bare light suspended over the table, their faces were all likewise pearlescent, haggard, and prosperous; and they regarded me with the silent approval of doctors who have been delivered a brand new dead body. They estimate that decomposition set in about six days ago. A week, to be on the safe side. Or, they regarded me with the silent consent of cellmates, cause a guy who had done time in the joint once told me that when a death-row prisoner walks through the yard, someone calls out, "Dead man walkin. . . ." And everybody shuts up and divides, opening a deserted aisle to "let the dead man walk through."

I was so tired. "Hi." I took off my coat and went into the bathroom. As I closed the door, their derisive eyes reminded me that I wasn't wearing nothing but an orange bikini. I opened my legs and yanked the string. My tampon was snow white, so I flushed it away, thinking about those academic assholes out there.

I felt the soul's cramps of alienation, as if, in a week's time, I had been forever fenced off from these fine upstanding civilized

((65))

folks who eschew and condemn indecency and support themselves by their well-gotten gains. Jesus, at least I still had Murphy for company; he was an outlaw now too.

I reached for a protective towel.

Fuck the towel, I thought, and walked out of the bathroom the same way I came. Now they were laughing.

Murphy had started off the jokes: "See what you turn into if you don't stay in school and get a high school diploma?"

"I thought you were kidding!" said the well-born blond friend to his right, the one with the dirty collar.

"Do I lie? Did I? Okay, handjobs on the house for all my buddies! Saturday night!"

"Down, boys," cautioned the fourth friend with abundant gray hair and huge hands. "The girl looks somewhat peak-éd and I don't think she appreciates this line of humor."

I threw a blanket around my shoulders and poised my rear over the radiator near the window.

"Sorry, Randy." Murphy was pressing a Kleenex to an infuriated canker under his nostril. "I was just telling them earlier that you were apprenticing as a lady of the evening."

"I'm a *dry* hustler," I retorted. "There's a big difference."

They all looked interested.

"Is that like dry hump?" asked the dirty collar.

"Professionally, I can make a guy come without *touching* him."

"How?"

"She's just being a smart-ass as always," said Murphy, astonished and embarrassed.

"How?" I snorted. "How much did you have in mind?"

The bulky one jumps in. "Twenty-five bucks, for instance, that's the going rate for the West Side-Times Square area."

I drew myself up to my full height, which is good for a sensation. "You must think I'm really cheap. Shove your lousy twenty-five bucks up your nose, mister. I happen to be a respectable person."

"She's having an unusually bad menstrual period," Murphy apologized.

But ole Bulky was keen: "Allright, let's say a hundred."

"My period was over this morning," I said to Murphy, "so now I don't have to give you head for another three weeks."

BULKY: "I want to know what this dry hustle is! Everybody quiet!"

MURPHY (at me): *"Suck my dick, girl!"*

BULKY: "Let's say a million dollars. Now—"

ME: *"You* suck your *own* dick!"

BULKY: "One oh-oh-oh, comma, oh-oh-oh. Okay. What does a customer get for a million dollars?"

I shined him on. The look I gave him belonged to Kristal, and my response was a fair rendering of her favorite motto. "Empty promises," I said.

A high shrill electronic note sang out. The gray-hair pulled a walkie-talkie out of his jacket pocket and spoke with his paging service. Some one of his patients was in labor.

"The phone's on the blink, but you can make outgoing calls," said Murphy.

As gray-hair busied himself with the telephone, I tucked myself into bed. Murphy put a fresh scoop of coke onto the mirror for his remaining three colleagues and excused himself to come over and whisper in my ear before I fell out from exhaustion: "That was un-fucking-called-for. If my friends weren't here I'd smack you. After they leave, I'm going to smack you for that, in the morning."

"Just try it," I slurred into the pillow. "Don't forget I'm workin for some Italians now who don't like their girls showin up for work with lopsided lips."

My boyfriend was very overamped and nervous from exerting himself all evening as a host and a drug pusher. And I guess I can't blame him for not recognizing the different person I was becoming. He had to wait a beat before he could reply. "And we saved a whole big doobie of Colombian for you. You're not getting it now. We'll go right ahead and smoke it up."

"I don't want to get high, anyway," as I drowned off to sleep, "it's not cool no more. . . ."

* * *

I woke up at five the next afternoon. I never got used to this waking up to begin a new day at night, in the dark. It was worse than when I was thirteen and my foster-mother would make me go to bed at seven-thirty. In the spring and summer, it would still be light out and even the birds weren't ready to pack it in. I read a lot of books then, til twilight.

Here in New York, my whole sense of time had shuttled up tight like a roll windowshade that is broke and just keeps snapping back up every time you try and ease it down into its rightful place. You begin to get scared of everything.

I wanted to go home, and hide. But Inger used to be fond of locking me out of the house if I came home late. I had to wait for all the neighbors to go to bed so no one would see me crouching in the pachysandra bed to pee. I'd try to fall asleep on the porch divan but I couldn't bear the fear of sleeping alone, so I'd run off to the firehouse.

Outside, Forty-fifth Street was dark, the sidewalks were ribbed with frozen sleet, the full moon was fraying at the edges, the news headlines snaked around the brow of the Allied Chemical Building without ever stopping, and everything scared me. Like, a man was sitting alone at the oak table and staring at me waking up. Then he reached up and twisted the light bulb on. It swayed slightly. His face was thin and ashen, smooth, his cranium a stark astro-shape because the hair was cut so short. I knew it was Murphy, but recognition scared me more.

He smiled kindly. "I'm scared, too. I cut it myself. Whatever you do, don't look at the sink. But it was time to do it. They don't expect me to get tricky," his voice was soft and measured, "although I had no idea that getting rid of all that hair would make me feel even more exposed. . . ."

He looked at once calm and stunned. His eyes had ballooned out of their lids to accommodate phantoms, new arrivals with pressing business. He was seeing in 4-D.

"You haven't been to bed." I was torn between being scared

((68))

of him and being worried sick about him, but I wrapped a blanket around me and bravely came closer. "Have you had breakfast?"

"Oh, sorry. There's no food in the house. I can't go out."

"Let me run downstairs and get some eggs and milk. Let's get straight today. A whole bunch of vitamins and some protein, cheese and—"

His adam's apple shriveled at the notion. "No, really, I'm not hungry."

"You can't live on coke, you'll get sick. All you've had to eat in the past two days is that onion dip last night and Fritos."

"What dip? Oh, right, what they were eating. They said to tell you it was good, too. Listen, stop with the food crusade and sit down, because we must have a talk before you rush off to work again."

"It's Sunday." I sat. "I get one day off, honey, I'm not rushin off anywhere. Tell me what's wrong."

"Nothing's wrong. Because at last I have figured it all out." His tongue clacked against the bone-dry roof of his mouth. "And I think I'm going to make it through all right."

I waited.

"I am amazed," he said at length, "at the genius of these people. I wish there was some token of my admiration I could give them, but I might end up having to give them a token of my appreciation instead, regrettably." He opened a magazine on the table to show the pistol hid in the pages. "I know this scares you, so I'll cover it up again." He closed the cover over the gun again. "All right. I'll give you the answers in a simplified, condensed form. Now, up til this morning, all I thought I knew was that on Monday Officer Dan ripped off half the coke, and on Wednesday d'Piro ripped off fifteen grams more, and on Friday the phone broke, which I didn't discover until yesterday, Saturday. And I thought that Officer Dan and d'Piro were really narcs setting me up for a bust, right?"

"That's right." He seemed quite lucid so far, and he hadn't smacked me, which he would certainly have done if he actually had figured it all out.

"But then I thought: how could they bust me when they already have most of the shit and they know there's not much left, and anyhow I would beat the rap because of entrapment. Because they were the ones that talked me into giving the coke to them. If they'd really intended to bust me legally right off the bat, Officer Dan would have done it right away on Monday, thrown the both of us in jail, and gotten a search warrant to open the loft and confiscate the other half pound. Right?"

"Right. Won't you at least have a little tea?"

"No, sit tight. I'm trying to be brief, because there's not much time left. The real story is this. Who ever heard of a cop calling himself Officer Dan? It's right out of the silent movies! Right?"

"Right." I was going to get smacked after all. I began to weep quietly.

He pulled his chair next to mine and put his arm around me. "Hold on, baby, I know it's scary, and you're too young for this. I'll tell you what I'm going to do with you, but later on. Right now, you must pay attention. Now. What are Officer Dan's initials?"

Oh, Christ. "O. D."

"Right, which we all know is the fun alphabet-soup game when we were kids, if you get a spoon that says O and D, it must stand for overdose of H. D., for hard drugs. . . . Come on, laugh at my lame jokes, I can't stand to see a tall woman cry. . . . So, Officer Dan is a fun little code name. He *is* a narc. A narcotics agent brilliantly disguised as a crooked policeman. He's worked a long time at gaining the confidence of the pushers in his area by posing as a dishonest cop, until he can map out a way to get close to the big pusher. He's never around for the real busts, oh no. He lets all the other narcs and cops make the arrest while he puts up a big show ripping off dope from the small-time hicks like me who run solo. He passes on the identity of each serious dealer to the regular narcs, who make the bust. For years he's been working his way up to the Big Snowman. And he probably is still years away from getting him. But 'O.D.' is a patient man."

I stopped crying, but I still was not finding the story as entertaining as it was.

"Of course, d'Piro is in on it, but not like you'd assume. Remember, he disappeared; and then the phone blew. All this is calculated to scare me, because I'm an amateur and inclined to paranoia. But, notice the two-day intervals: Monday, Wednesday, Friday. And today is Sunday. Phase Four!

"This means that sometime tonight d'Piro will show up with all the money he owes me. He'll say he was busted, but the cops let him go if the two of us use the bread to buy another pound from a bigger source and let them make the bust *then,* while the sale is going on, so they can get the big guy and in return they'll let us off scot-free. That way, they can't be accused of entrapment, because it's not one of *their* men made the buy, it's 'these two scared amateurs doing a little playacting to save their stupid skins. The mob will probably snuff these two bozos the next day.' (D'Piro will assure me that we're too small-time for the mob to be bothered.)

"But, it's a lie. Great story, but a lie. The cops'll bust us *all* at that meet. And guess who will conveniently escape? D'Piro. Because he's not on the force. He's *not* a narc. If he was, it would still be entrapment. But, he's not the law. He's a freelancer. For hire! He moves all over the country, even the world maybe, so his face doesn't get too well-known, and anyway he plans to retire early. Because his price keeps going up. He'll infiltrate anything, whatever anybody wants, and for whatever side offers him the most money."

"Far out." I was starting to seriously consider the part about d'Piro although I knew Murphy was way off about Officer Dan.

"Oddly enough, they seem to want to keep *you* out of it, maybe because they're not sure you're not a minor. Which is fine, because I want you out of harm's way, myself. Because I'm going to stand my ground and not buy d'Piro's story and not take the money, so when the shit starts coming down it could get dirty—what?"

((71))

"I said, Murphy. Please throw the coke away. Please please."

He shook his head, a bit sheepish. "Frankly, there just isn't very much left, I've tooted up so much of it. In fact, I only have enough to keep me together enough to handle my scenes in this incredible script for another four or five days, and I need all I can get, to maintain a clear head round the clock. Not only that, but there's not much money left. Well, the first thing I have to do is get you out of here, but I can't afford to put you on a plane or in a hotel or leave you totally alone."

"No, no."

"But I've figured this one out, too. You see, the only person we know who has been a consistent ally is your friend Kristal. I thought maybe she was in on it, but I don't think she's smart enough to be working with these complicated people. I think she is what she seems: a very savvy neighborhood hustler, who really doesn't know what Officer Dan's twisted game is. Don't you think so? That she can be trusted?"

"I think, yeah, she's nothing more than a hustler."

"I meant, would you feel safe staying with her?"

"Today?"

"Would she mind? You'd have to make up some little lie to tell her. Tell her we had a fight last night and I'm coked out of my head and you've got to get away from me til I cool down. Would she fall for that?"

"Sure." It was a likely story.

"Now, we're going to need the bread, so you might as well continue working at the dance hall, since you don't seem to mind it that much anymore."

"Hell, I'm havin a ball. I'm rebelling against my parents, they think this is the dirtiest thing on earth. . . ." I muttered.

"I know, this has been my insight all along, but I didn't want to lay it on you because I didn't want to bum you out. At any rate, being a bit wiser than you by dint of twelve more years' experience in being alive, I can inform you that it's just a natural phase and you'll get over it after you've got all your hostility out and over with. Okay, now, get Kristal on the phone and do your act."

((72))

"Now?"

"Got to be now. Honest. I know what I'm doing."

Now was fine with me. Everything scared me. But at least I could be with Kristal who was my one remaining friend and moreover was suspected by me of having all the answers.

"Why the hell couldn't you have given Officer Dan a last name, or some kind of name with different initials than O.D.?" I questioned Kristal.

She was laying back against the headboard on her bed and spooning herself pistachio ice cream from a half-gallon carton. "Because then he could have found out the cop doesn't exist just by phoning up the precinct, of course! I was trying to protect you. You said, quote unquote, 'he'll kill me'! So? You're in no trouble, what do you care."

I was so drunk I didn't feel like being scared. There were many things to be scared of, more now than ever, but I didn't care. Not just Murphy was scary, but if I'd felt like it, I could have been scared of Kristal's apartment. It was three rooms in one of these rent-by-the-week hotels for middle-income transients. As soon as she opened the door, she handed me a glass of Courvoisier and I was run over by a titanic Great Dane whose flapping nipples were being pursued by four puppies.

Then I could hardly get past the door because there was so much living room furniture in the living room. Two sofas, one red vinyl and one peach crushed velvet, were jammed belly to belly to make room for a labyrinth of recliners and ottomans and at least three coffee tables. The mother Dane, Petunia, had this room staked out as her race track, and since there wasn't really any place to sit, we passed through to the dining room, which contained a formal dining room set and a less formal dinette set, all pushed against the wall so that we could get into the bedroom.

"I didn't have any sheets for your bed," she said, "so you can use my electric blanket to wrap around you."

The bedroom was simpler: two twin beds with white and gold French Provincial frames and headboards. Kristal's bed had a white fake-fur spread and white satin sheets, but my mattress was still encased in the plastic it was sold in.

"Finish your drink," Kristal commanded.

The whole place had a certain air of not being lived in.

"I've got the most gorgeous king-size bed set arriving tomorrow you ever wanna see. It's Mediterranean. I'll have the manager store your bed and some of this other junk down in the basement so there'll be room for it. I bet this is a lot nicer style than you're used to living in, with that hippie drug-addict boyfriend of yours." She patted her blue electric blanket over my mattress, sat me down, and refilled my glass.

My memory of the rest of my first night with Kristal is not very thorough. I do recall deciding to tell Murphy the whole truth.

"Are you crazy?"

"No," I said. "Not me. He's the one gonna be real crazy, real soon, and all because of me fuckin up and throwin the dope in the toilet."

"He was going to get a coke habit sooner or later whether or not you fucked up, honey." Kristal knocked back another double brandy, without ever seeming to swallow it. I think she just knew how to open her throat correctly.

"It's time to get the truth out," I declaimed. "Otherwise, I'll never be able to go back to him."

"Do you want to go back to him?"

A mental block prevented me from solving this problem.

"Well," she expounded, "are you in love with him, ding dong the bells and everything?"

"The truth is . . ." I was remembering the shaven spectral stranger who switched on the light bulb earlier this afternoon. "The truth is . . . he's different from what he was. I don't like him. He's weird."

"The truth is, if you tell him the truth, not only do you not like him but he is definitely not going to like *you*. . . . Don't roll your eyes up like that. Don't look up there, no one's gonna help you. Nobody home."

"Who else is looking after me?" I lurched over to get the bottle and fell on top of her. It was lucky she had finished the ice cream and shoved the soggy carton under the bed, otherwise we would have made some sandwich.

"Jesus Christ, get your big bod offa me! Quit holding on, I told you I can't stand to be touched!"

"I want to go home," I sobbed. Then I said some messed-up things I don't remember, about home . . . Home in the cleaving of the jumbo bosoms of the fierce avenger. There I was safe, and while I slept the streets would run scarlet with my enemies' blood. Somewhere, my natural-born mother was rocking by a fire, hugging her vacant womb, chanting for her tender angel blond baby to be delivered back unto her jumbo bosom so that she could fiercely avenge me. She has the ya-ya of the centuries and the know-how of witches. Revenge is her rocking chair. Until I find that home, I'll be "dead girl walkin." Let the dead girl through. Her bones are buried in a plot, a wicked plot to keep her from her home, from her right mother, from the jumbo bosom—

"All right, that's enough, hush. You're just loaded." Kristal stopped rocking me. "Get back on your bed. You're getting snot all down my private parts."

I woke up for a little while the next morning when the king-size Mediterranean bed set was delivered and Kristal made me change to the other single bed so that mine could be carried down to the basement.

Then I woke up in her satin sheets, in the late afternoon. It was dark outside. Kristal was eating copious scrambled eggs from a plate on a newly arrived butcher-block table. She was watching a game show on a TV perched on the formal dining table. "Choose Curtain Number One!" she lashed at the television. "Where do they find such stupid people? . . . Your boyfriend called a couple hours back, he said he'd call again. . . . See, I was right. Number One had the Toyota."

I had seen others cure a hangover by drinking a little more alcohol the next day, so I fixed myself a screwdriver. It was a dumb mistake, but didn't matter. I extracted a dinette chair from the stack in the corner and sat with her.

"Finish these," she pushed her plate toward me, "or I'm going to be sick again. I gotta stop being hungry."

I had a mouthful of the woolly yellow food, and sipped my vodkaed orange juice, which dissolved my nerve endings on contact. I wasn't scared cause I couldn'ta cared. Less. The phone rang.

I had to take the call in the living room. "Can you hear me all right?" asked Murphy's voice.

"Yeah." I sat in a leather chair and it instantly reclined, the noise of adjustment more mighty than a demolition ball. Suddenly my feet shot up on a leather tray. They looked bony and maybe cold.

"You don't hear anything strange in the connection?" he said.

"No. Where are you?"

"At the loft. I can't figure it out."

"What?"

"Well, they just fixed the phone. Without even sending a repairman. They just called up and the phone rang and they asked if I was now getting incoming calls. I'm going to call you from pay phones after this. How much cash have you got on you?"

I had saved Saturday night's tips. "About two hundred fifty dollars."

"Great, I'm coming over to pick it up. I'm going to need it to buy an antibugging device. They're selling that nowadays."

Kristal wouldn't let him come in. She slid the cash under the door. "Sorry," she called. "My dog attacks anything that's a man. Because of her puppies, til they're full-grown."

After a couple more screwdrivers, I arrived for work with no zip and head hung low. Business was light, so I bought myself a few beers to make the pen seem more homey.

I was completely unprepared to see the stockbroker, my customer of Saturday night so long ago, come into the Royale and beckon me up from my seat. He bought an hour's tickets and two beers, just as casual as you please.

"That address you sent me to was a hardware store," he began.

I couldn't remember even vaguely what address I'd told him, so I just lowered my head even lower.

"You owe me two hundred dollars, cunt," his voice still with the matter-of-fact kind of cadence.

I started to cry. It was so depressing. "I don't have the money anymore."

"Of course you don't, you fucking scummy whore. I'm no stranger to depravity. I've gone to bat for worse specimens than you, when they've wound up in court for selling their own babies for—spare me the tears. I suppose the two hundred dollars went toward your pimp's threads."

I shook my head, "No, the truth is—"

"No? Then let me see your arms." He overturned them and examined the soft pale creases for needle marks. "Then if you're not a junkie, somebody else is. Whose habit are you supporting, you clever little cooze, I suppose it's your sister who's a junkie—"

"She's a paraplegic!" I spat. I had stood enough insults. "I have to support her, because she put me through college—until the accident!" I glugged on my beer and resumed weeping.

"Good god." Mortification was setting in. "Why can't you work at a more respectable job, then? Does she know what you're doing?"

"Yes, yes! But I promised her I would never do anything wrong or become a prostitute. I had to have a night job. I never got my degree, because she was in the car accident last year, when I was just a sophomore. She was a brilliant musician on the piano, very high-strung, and she sleeps at night and can't stand to be alone during the day, but she's too proud to see any of her friends because of her condition. . . . She keeps a diary and she gets me to tell all the stories the men tell me every night so she can write a book one day. That's why she didn't mind me taking this kind of a job. I had to work at night so I could be with her in the day, and I make good tips here because many of the customers know my story and they are sympathetic, and the tips are cash so I don't have to declare it as income, because I have to pay for the rent for the apartment and the piano—and she can't even work the pedals because she's paralyzed from the waist down!"

The man thrust a fine handkerchief into my limp hand and made soothing sounds. "What an incredible story. It explains why I originally thought you didn't seem like you belonged in a place like this. Poor girl, you must have no life of your own to yourself."

"I do everything for her," I blew my nose and ejaculated a ton of mucus into his handkerchief. "She's a genius, you see. It should have been me that was crippled instead of her. If I could only afford payments on an organ or an electric piano, something she could play without having to use her feet—"

And so forth. Don't ask me how come it came out, or how much money I got off him. Ask me why I did it. I hated him with an honest hatred.

Graham Finch presented Kristal and me with personal invitations to "A Tea Party," the champagne opening of the new boutique he had designed for Bloomingdale's on a special commission for the Bicentennial. "The British Are Coming! The British Are Coming!" the engraved cards cried.

For Graham, the party signified the end of his work in New York, and so he was hastening the courtship of his dance hall sweetie.

Kristal: "How exciting, dahlink! I vill make up some kind of silly story so ve get avay for your party."

I was plastered, so I just sat there silently at the table and hung my head lower than my neck could permit.

"No, *nichta,* it von't work," Kristal said. "Look at how sad she is. She don't have nothing to *vear.* My husband her brother he dresses her in nothink but bleck, bleck, bleck. Like she is a nun! So men von't look at her. She cen't vear bleck to your Bloominkdale's party, she vould *die,* sooner."

Graham passed her some money for a new dress.

"Oh, vhat a vahndervul fella! How vould you vant to see her— in a pink? Like a beautivul seashell from the seashore?"

Graham looked at me and nodded fondly. My eyes were pink enough from crying to suggest it might be my best color.

"But vhat cen ve do for shoes? She cen't vear the bleck nun shoes vith the pink dress—"

And so forth. After the shoes were paid for, there was the matter of a purse, and then a hat, and the hose, and the corsage, and then when Graham's wallet began to look somewhat desolate I excused myself to go to the bathroom.

"I did that scam on a customer of mine who was a Senator, when I was about sixteen," Kristal remarked, in the taxi back to her apartment. "Except in reverse color coordinates. I said I had to go to a funeral the next morning and I didn't have nothin black in my clothes. I'd get so worked up about believing I was going to the funeral I'd start crying. Every time it would occur to me that I needed something else in black—shoes, veil, wreath, whatever have you—he'd go to the john and open his shoe. He kept all his money in the heel of his shoe! . . . He was really— I loved the hell out of him, he never tried anything funny with me at all. I was his little girl. Every time he was in town he'd come by, and I'd keep calling him 'Daddy' by mistake, which he loved, and he'd ask me, like, if I'd been eating my vegetables. And I'd say, 'I haven't eaten in three days.' So back to the john and off comes the shoe! Once, on New Year's Eve, he talked about getting me out of the dance hall and putting me through school, and he bought a *thousand* dollars' worth of tickets, and I tried to make him dance so much he'd have to take his shoes off, but he didn't. I didn't know much about him, only that they all said he was a Senator."

"Who gives a shit," I grumbled.

"Cause I was impressed he would be a big deal in Washington, and one of my regulars! You don't have to believe me, I don't care. You're in a rotten mood. I'm going to make you drink some coffee directly when we get back."

The coffee only made me scared all over again. I didn't know where in the world I was: not the whereabouts, nor the time, nor my identity, nor the identity of my boyfriend, nor who in hell was this woman with the coffeepot.

"I know just what you're feelin," said Kristal, eating peanut butter and drinking cognac. "I don't have a home anymore, myself. My mother died a couple years back, and my dad just passed away only a month ago. You'd feel better if you knew where your real mother is, so you'd have someplace to go home to."

"How'd you know about my real mother?"

"You told me the whole story last night when you were drunk. I guess you don't remember." She giggled. "You're in luck I have a heart of gold or I'd have chucked you out the window down seven stories, cause you were a real slob. You finished up all my Courvoisier. Well, I know just what you're goin through. You wonder what the fuck you're doin here."

"Well, how the fuck did *you* get here?" I was wide awake and needed to know.

It will probably shock you that I'm from gypsy blood. Even the gypsies can't tell, because I'm so light-skinned. That's why I was so freaked the time that this little old shrunken-up fortune-teller grabbed me at a street carnival, back when I was one of the paid strippers on a yacht cruising the French Riviera resort spots. She grabbed me and started screaming in Hungarian. How did she know I spoke Hungarian?

She's screaming, "Do you know who you are? Do you know who you are? You're the reincarnation of Cleopatra!" She drags me into her tent and drags out a big historical volume and shows me a life or death mask, whatever, of the god damn Queen of the Nile, no less. We did look a little alike.

She's shaking her finger and acts very pissed off: "You were put on this earth to manipulate men! You have all the power! You could have anything you desire, penthouses, precious stones, rich men at your beck and call! But you are foolish. And you will not use your power. You obey your stupid heart instead. So you will never be rich."

She was right in one respect. The only difference between me and Zsa Zsa Gabor is a few million dollars. I just never could get married for money. What for, so I can get up at six in the morning, cook the cocksucker's breakfast, wash his drawers and keep his house clean, and also suck his cock? Even if I had a maid, I wouldn't suck a cock.

I have to be my own boss. No one is on my ass but myself. I make just enough money to keep *me* satisfied.

Anyway, if I'd been a *gadgo,* which is gypsy lingo for a non-gypsy person, I would've shit green paying this fortune-teller money to find out what else she knew about me. That's why they're called fortune-tellers. They make fortunes telling you this crap. It's the most superior hustle the gypsy women have handed down through the ages.

But I'm talking about the *tziganye* gypsies. They are the people that are considered gypsies by the rest of the world. They lie and cheat and steal and move from place to place constantly. The *olah tziganye* are very much looked down upon by the other gypsies, who are like the aristocrats of the race. King Stefan, who became a saint, took the gypsies into his court of Hungary and made them his royal musicians and artisans and converted them to whatever religion was happening then—this was around 900 A.D. And anyone descended from these honored gypsies is usually an artist of some sort and makes an honest living by it.

That's why I know only a few gypsy words. My father was descended from King Stefan's good gypsies, and they speak only straight Hungarian. Pop's whole family was musicians. He himself was a child prodigy at age nine, on the cimbalom, which is the national instrument of Hungary. It looks like a big dulcimer, with strings you can pluck or hit with mallets.

But my father wasn't becoming a child prodigy fast enough to support his family. He was the oldest of ten sons, and when he was seven years old his father got shot in the head and had to stay in the hospital for four years.

Now, my Dad's mother was slick. She found out he had some psychic powers, so she used him as a child medium. She'd bring him around all these gypsy families who had lost kin during the World War One bombings. She'd charge a fee to hold seances wherein her child would describe the location of the unmarked grave where their dead was buried. Since the place was unmarked, it didn't matter what he said, because he was so convincing.

My father was terrified all this time. He really was talking to all these ghosts, and they would lay cold hands on his shoulder at the dinner table. Not only that: he hated playing the cimbalom.

His mother was *real* slick. She even hustled our passages out of Budapest after the 1956 revolution so we could get to America. But she stayed. She was always mad at my father after he married my mother, who was one-half *gadgo*. Mother was a coloratura soprano, very stuck up, and had made up her mind to marry the best musician in Hungary. You should hear *her* sing "Somewhere Over the Rainbow."

I put a lot of value in my mother and father.

When I was born, in 1946, my father threw the cimbalom across the room and broke some heads. He had wanted a boy. But then he grew to love me, and Peter was born two years after.

When our little family came to New York, we settled in the Little Italy section. By this time, Pop was raking in pretty good money. He was the world's foremost cimbalom virtuoso, so he was forever touring with this orchestra, guest soloist with that orchestra, playing with his own gypsy band in the high-class nightclubs. . . . We lived very well. Whatever I needed, no matter what price, he'd give to me. I never had to worry about money. That's why, to this day, nothing has a value to me whatsoever.

Dad was so scared of his gypsy upbringing, he'd never let us go near any of them. He never let me be psychic. He would spend any amount of money on me, but if I fell on my head he'd say, "She can learn this way." He would leave me to pick myself off the floor.

My mom raised me as if I was the Queen of England. She made my clothes then, with lots of frills and handmade lace.

I had a nice, solid figure, but the way she dressed me I looked plump, fat, not sexy at all. How many people can claim, that are adults, though, that they can go home and their mother will set them on her lap and sing them lullabies? Like right now, I weigh about 150, but right up til she died, she'd do this for me, if I was sad or drunk. She also told me there was nothing worse than a man's cock. "If he lays down, step on it." So I was afraid of having sex.

She had one main fault. She was very punctual. Even by the time I was fourteen, she would put me to bed at seven sharp every night after I'd finished my homework; and at nine, sharp, she'd open the door a peek to check that I was asleep.

She'd close the door at 9:01 sharp, and out the window I'd go, down that skinny tree, out onto the streets, which were so full of life, and adventures, all the chaos. . . .

Soon I fell in with a bunch of thieves who were peddling hot wigs and dresses to all the dance halls and whorehouses up in the midtown area.

Frank was running the Stardust Ballroom with his wife Mary. Mary was the brains, and she knew how to run the joint straight up and jelly tight. Mary wanted everything on the up and up. Believe me, she always kept up one thing: "If you're not a lady, I don't want you in the place." Somebody who dresses and acts in a proper manner, she meant. Like, your skirt had to be below your knees.

The minute Mary spotted me, she starts giving Frank the elbow and fussing around in Italian: "Will you look at that girl, look at the long black hair, those big boobs, we'd make a pile of money on her." I understood some Italian because of the neighborhood I came from, so I interrupted her and asked her what the deal was, and that I was the tender age of fourteen and what was my family situation.

So Frank suggested that I continue climbing out the window at nine, and work in their establishment til four, then climb back in the window and go to school in the morning. I have never been a big sleeper, because I don't dream, which is a waste of time in my opinion.

Anyhow, the deal was that I'd make a lot of cashola in a glamorous nightlife of nonstop parties, and for sweeteners Frank would get me a fake ID and a cabaret card. He was in the mob, so I knew it was safe.

In those days, a dance hall hostess was an appealing profession. They had live bands, fancy decorations. Mary really knew how to dress the girls. The gowns were slit up the side and long to the floor, with five tons of stuffing in the bosom, by Conchita, the dressmaker. I was the only girl who did *not* require no falsie excelsior.

If you were caught meeting a customer after work, you were out. What you did on the side was your affair. Mary didn't want to find out about it. That way, a customer never knew what he was going to get for his money with the girl he picked—he wouldn't know who "did" and who "didn't," unless he became a regular. Mary was smart about the importance of the tease aspect.

Now, naturally, all the customers assume any girl will do any fucking thing, because mostly it's true. The blame is, the massage parlors have up-surped the business.

Mary and Frank were my second parents. They got me out of jail a few times . . . after they put me in! Some stupid hostess would be selling pussy out of the place, and if she fit my description they'd throw *me* to the cops when they were after the other chick. Frank and Mary knew I wouldn't say nothing stupid. The first time that happened, it scared the shit out of me; they didn't bother to tell me what the scam was, and here I was in jail for the first time for dis-con and soliciting. But five minutes later, the lawyer arrived and got me out. I'd get one hundred dollars every time I did that.

I remember my first night and my first customer. He was a Chinaman. We danced and he kept saying, "Now after dance we go fucky-fuck." I was petrified, but Mary kept signaling for me to keep him dancing, for ten minutes, at which time he couldn't demand his ten bucks back. I never knew when the dance hall was ever "a dime-a-dance." Tickets used to be twelve-and-a-half-cents, and then you've seen the ones now are thirteen cents, but it was always the same bundle they had to buy: six-fifty for the half hour and twelve dollars the hour.

There were a different class of men in those days. Certainly a more generous class. But this was fourteen years ago.

My best trait was always my baby face. It still is, except now it looks slightly older. No matter how much of a whore I ever looked like, I could also look innocent and act insulted if any man wanted to fuck me.

If a customer thought I was a whore when he picked me, it was his own lookout. Television has made everybody think that cops, doctors, lawyers, whoever, do their jobs straight. Even a whore they expect to do their job straight, if they are wearing the uniform of a whore. It has never been so. I'm about 80 percent honest, and that is enough to satisfy me. Any less than 80 percent and I might have shame. Or something bad would happen to me. Gypsies are very superstitious. For instance, when I'm making up a story I always try to invent a sister, because I don't have a sister. I'm afraid if I was to use a brother in a story, something bad would occur to Peter, my brother in real life.

The head hostess who sold tickets was a very ugly lady, to be quite frank. She weighed two hundred fifty pounds, wore glasses throughout her whole life, never had any men, she had a double triple chin—her nails were beautiful, though. That was her prettiest point. She kept them four inches long, polished and manicured regularly. But even though she was so very ugly, people liked her, the customers especially. She had such a friendly manner. She would get them to spend money when they didn't want to. She's who I learned a lot of lines from.

I got very proficient. Within five minutes I could spot a man's weakness and zero in on it. It's somewhat like being psychic.

I had one problem. I couldn't spend all this money I was making every night, because my parents would ask how I got it. When I was fifteen, almost a year after I started at the Stardust, my mother discovered the dolly-clothes box full of seventeen thousand dollars in cash under my bed.

The first number they pulled was call the doctor. He came downstairs afterward and said, "Yes, your daughter is still a virgin."

"That doesn't tell me she didn't suck their dicks!" That's my father, with the dirty mouth. Every time, four times in all, he had the doctor racing over and approving my cherry, Dad never believed I was pure. I swear, I was a virgin right up til I got married!

My father moved us out of the neighborhood directly, out of the city, away from the criminal influence. He used the seventeen thousand dollars to buy us a home in Connecticut, and then he enrolled me in a reform school.

My parents didn't know they were putting me in a reformatory. They got the grand tour, and all they saw was the nuns, the discipline, the swimming pool, the beautiful statue of Mary, the uniforms and the chapel every morning . . . but they didn't speak much English, so they didn't understand that the House of the Sacred Shepherd was supposed to be for delinquents. So they signed me in voluntarily.

After six months I escaped, went straight back to the Stardust. I had the bug: I loved having men fall all over me.

Back and forth for two years—I'd run off, my dad would bring me back, I'd go back to school, I'd run off, back to the Stardust, my dad would drag me back, I'd go to beautician's school, I'd run off. . . . It was hard on him, since frequently he'd be out of the country on tour with some symphony and wouldn't learn I'd split til he got back.

Already the Stardust was changing. It was no jerk-off fruitstand, no under-the-table misbehavior, but the place was wall-to-wall whores, because Mary wasn't around so much as before. The hemlines went up overnight. I moved into the America, where most of the other hostesses stayed. I used to have copies of their room keys made and sell them to customers. I'd say my name was the other girl's name and give the guy her room number and key. He'd pay me in front, at the dance hall, then show up at the hotel room expecting to fuck *me*. And the other girl would open the door, take him in and fuck him. She'd thank me, even. I sold their phone numbers, too. They didn't mind. They were *whores!*

When I was seventeen, Mary fired me. I was too proud to go back, so I started stripping on the burlesque circuit.

I never came back til three weeks ago. I saw how the Stardust was closed, Frank and Mary had split up, and he was running the Royale and the Pony with the girls who had stuck around.

Whatever I was doing or wherever I was, I would always go back home to my mother and father whenever I got lonesome or scared. Like, you can be away from home for years, but when you go home Mother still has the same chair sitting in the same place. The dining table still has the same damask cloth on it. She's still got the knick-knacks all over the piano, the fireplace is full of pictures of everybody. . . .

Home is someplace you return to to have it the same. The only place you can do that is when you go home.

I always went back, up til a month ago when Pop died. He was disappointed in me, I know. You know how kids say they want to be a doctor or a fire chief? When *I* was little, I opened my moron yap and said I wanted to be a international lawyer. Dad always had it fixed in his mind that some day one of my tits would have a blowout or something and I'd go back to school to learn how to be a international lawyer. And I'd help him get some of his relatives over from Hungary.

My mom didn't like the way I turned out either. She would have disputed with that gypsy fortune-teller. She used to say, "Her *heart* is good. Her mind is what is stupid."

But my brother turned out a worse fuck-up. Once, he slammed the door on my mother's hand by mistake. The

((87))

reason for this was he was in a hurry. He was lifting her purse so he could run away from home!

He is a most gorgeous sonofabitch. I'd show you his picture, except he don't look too good behind bars—Randy? RANDY! You're a god damn derelict, get back over on your own bed and get under that blanket. You're not going to sleep on my new kingsize, and I'm not going to carry you to bed. I turned the blanket up to five so it's nice and toasty for you. Say good-night. . . . All right, don't say good-night. For someone whose parents didn't spoil her, you sure have no manners.

Kristal got me up five hours later at 11 A.M., and wouldn't even let me have a Bloody Mary before we took off for Bloomingdale's. Graham's party wasn't until two, but we had to buy the pink rig.

I dogged after her in the store, with my facial expression sagging somewhere between a sulk and a threat to retch up. She ambled from aisle to aisle on the main floor, until she found a counter that was crowded: one saleslady to four women all trying to buy gloves. Kristal stood in line and gazed patiently over their shoulders.

"I been waiting twenty minutes," I whined when she returned, "and you didn't buy any gloves, we don't need no gloves for this party and it's twelve o'clock already—"

"Don't say numbers at me when I'm tryin to memorize numbers, you're confusin me! Just shut up and stay shut up until I say so."

We went to the credit department.

"I'm such a nervous wreck," she confided breathlessly to the credit representative as we sat at her desk, "my sister here has to buy a trousseau and get married today because the Navy is sending her fiancé to Budapest tomorrow, and I know my charge card isn't lost but I simply could not find it this morning because I have so many purses it could be in and I was in such a hurry to get the girl dressed and married and out of my *life* that I'm a total nervous wreck—"

"You want a temporary authorization to charge merchandise, is that it?" the woman smiled, calmly pulling out a white slip of paper.

"Oh, thank you, I didn't know the word for it, I'm so hysterical. I can even tell you my account number by heart because I shop here so often. It's 071-33-141 and it's under the name Mrs. George Oesterman with an O."

"I'll find your file. What is your address?" Bloomingdale's ran a pretty tight ship here in the credit department, and their people were trained to cover all bases.

"Oh my God," Kristal heaved a sigh. "You probably still have the old address at the Carlyle Towers. I've had about four addresses since then and I don't know why I never notified you. I drive the post offices crazy forwarding my mail because I'm on my fourth marriage! It's my little sister's first one at four o'clock today and I hope to sweet Jesus she never finds out about alimony like I did! I should hire an armored truck to take my monthly income to the bank!"

I groaned an honest groan. Fortunately, Kristal always gave me plausible parts to play. The woman cracked up, and when she returned from the credit check she corrected Mrs. Oesterman about her address on file.

"Oh yeah," Kristal grinned, "I'd almost forgot Two-fifteen East Sixty-fourth Street. That was husband number two, and I divorced him right after I got him to give me a lifetime Bloomingdale's charge card! No wonder I never gave you my new address— I never even got the bills. That sucker's still getting my bills on Sixty-fourth Street and paying them in hopes he'll win me back!" The woman had filled out the white form and handed it to Kristal to sign.

"Now all I'll need is your driver's license to verify the signature," she consoled.

"I'd remarry my number two, if he bought me a villa in France! Oh, yeah, the signature. Oh dear, I might as well update you completely as long as we're sitting here. My new married name is Mrs. Beauregard Pace. That's what I better sign here." She had her license out to prove her identity. Mrs. Beauregard Pace

was the same name I'd seen on her mailbox, and Kristal dupli-
cated the exact same signature that was on the Connecticut license.

"You'd better get a completely new card," advised the woman.

"Could I have it by Friday? I'm going on a round-the-world
trip on Monday, and that would mean I could use it to buy my
wardrobe on Saturday and I won't have to look through all those
purses for my old card."

"Certainly. I'll rush it personally, Mrs. Oesterman."

"Okay, here's my new address." Kristal gave out her actual
address at the apartment building.

My stomach flamed and my hands shook, chilly with sweat, as
we left the credit office. "But Graham gave us plenty of money
for the clothes," I whispered.

"I never pay cash for anything unless I have to," was her terse
reply. "Just keep shuttin up. First we do the dress. I think something on the order of long and youthful and ruffles. Like a com-
munion dress, only in pink. I bet I know where we'll find it right
away, too. We're goin to the bridesmaids' department."

By one-thirty I was wearing a long pink voile pinafore affair,
with a wide-brimmed rose-ribboned pink felt hat on my head,
white vinyl boots on my cold feet, and over my arm a big straw
handbag containing my jeans, sweater, and sneakers.

"You look putrid," said Kristal. "Like a Shirley Temple magazine. Graham's gonna turn to a god damn jelly when he sees this
innocent creature. I'd hate to be wrong, and have him not go
back to England penniless. Hey, we've got half an hour and I
want to go to the furniture department."

She went nuts over an antique armoire with gold trim. "Could
it be delivered by Friday?" she asked the salesman.

"We need ten days for delivery."

"But it's a floor sample."

"Well then, a week, at the very least. It's impossible before
next Tuesday to have it for you."

"Oh. . . ." Her voice trailed away wistfully. "By the way,
is that real gold, all this scrolls and stuff?"

"Gold? You mean gilt. It's gilt detailing."

"Oh. Gilt's gold."

"No, gilt *paint.*"

"Well, fuck that." She turned on her heels. "I don't want it, then."

As we rode the escalator down to the floor where Graham's boutique was opening, she said, "I love gold so much because of my mother. She had all her money in nothin but bracelets and necklaces and heirlooms—twelve bracelets of nothing but gold coins—"

At that moment I realized she wasn't wearing a wig. For the first time I was looking at her real hair, wild thickets of blue-black curls gnarling past her shoulders, and I knew how all that furniture in her apartment had gotten there, and I heard the tribal violins over the clinking of gold coins clasped round hasty ankles fleeing, and I almost saw the gypsy sneak into her lair, but she was quicker than the eye.

I wasn't sure whether I should sprint through the store, out the door, and onto the street to hitchhike to some town where they have a couple of stores spelled "shoppes," and sleigh bells, and no history of vandalism; or whether I should lose myself in awe and admiration for this perfect thief. She was Cleopatra, believe me. In some one of her trashier reincarnations; but still, Kristal held the Nile seed of cunning under her tongue. . . .

Since I was on a moving escalator, I decided not to run for it and allowed myself to stay put, descending by motorized design, getting lost in admiration.

"My dear lovely gehl, you look like a fairy sprite off to a straw-berries-and-cream picnic!" Graham was charmed by the artlessness of my pink outfit. Everybody else thought it was a riot, especially how it clashed with the "Redcoat" motif of the "The British Are Coming!" Boutique. People of fashionable persuasions thronged in and out of the small red and criss-cross white room, while Graham proudly shook hands and escorted me around his creation. Under the banner "To Arms! To Arms!" I was relieved to note that the bouquet of truncated mannequins' arms displayed bracelets made out of red lucite, not gold.

Graham was getting looped on inferior champagne, and confided that he had lied: "Actually, I'm really Australian. It's something to be ashamed of, living in London, so I avoid telling it to people who don't pick up on my accent. . . ." Kristal had warned me to drink only the tea, like a good virgin, but she then disappeared to raid the luggage department, so I switched to the plastic goblets and hosed down my empty stomach with a lot of Cold Duck.

Instead of being pissed when she saw me and Graham swaying and chortling and clinging to each other, Kristal took control of the situation by somehow maneuvering us down a few blocks on Lexington Avenue into this quaint little jewelry store. The owner was out, and his daughter was not very expert about the merchandise.

"Vhat vahndervul rinks!" Kristal cried out. "Now, I vant something to metch my eyes; some days they are black and some days green—"and the poor chick stared at Kristal's eyes, while the sticky gypsy fingers flew around the ring trays on the counter. She ungummed a forty-dollar price tag on a rhinestone ring and switched it with a three-hundred-forty-five-dollar tag on a spray of rubies.

"I think they're dark brown," said the girl, after assessing Kristal's eyes gravely.

"Like the mud?! I change my mind! Ah, ah, ah, look at this red rink here. Only forty dollars for such a beautivul costume jewelry you'd think they vas real rubies here—are you sure these are not the real rubies, sveetheart?"

"It says forty dollars," the girl agreed, "so I guess not." She shrugged.

"I vant it! I don't never vear fake gems but it is so beautivul I von't tell no vun if you don't."

"It's a little too big for you. If you're in a hurry, my father can probably have it fitted by tomorrow afternoon."

"No vittink, I vear it on my thumb. I have too many rinks so there is only the thumb left anyhow to vear nothin. *But.* I don't pay you yet, because we gonna need another rink for these loffbirds over here vith the arms around their little vaists—they vant an engagement rink for this vahndervul day of days—"

"We do not," I said hotly. "We are not engaged."

"Wait one bloody minute, ladies," Graham beamishly waved his hand. "You're my sweetie and I would rather like to buy you something as long as we're here."

"But you bought me all those clothes!"

But Graham had spotted a shy little diamond, set in silver, which didn't look too official and was a perfect fit for the third finger on my right hand, while Kristal slipped an enameled brooch into her pocket and interrupted to inquire the price of a gold Bicentennial coin charm, which would soon take its place on the chain around her neck beside the cross and the pig's tooth.

Graham ended up paying cash both for my ring and the gold coin. Kristal then changed her mind and wanted to buy the ruby ring fitted for her pinkie. The girl took the measurements and then couldn't find the ring anywhere on the counter or in the trays.

"Never mind, you're just so convused and you find it soon. Ve're in a big hurry so you look for it in peace and kvi-et after ve leave and I come pick it up tomorrow, okay dahlink?"

Okay, and so forth.

After cocktails and a sumptuous dinner with Graham, Kristal and I went back to her apartment. I stretched out on my bed, more ready to be mummified than to go back to work at the Royale Ballroom in an hour.

"That guy is just so nice," Kristal purred. "You really oughta marry him. Look at the way he let us order at that restaurant—nuts to soup, the whole number. Now, the dudes that don't make that big kind of money, they always order for you."

"Is all this stuff illegal?" I asked, gesturing around the room. "You didn't pay your own money for any of it?"

"What's the matter, you aren't happy on satin sheets?"

"Is it all hustled, like you did in Bloomingdale's?"

"One way or the other. . . . It depends on the store the way you do it. They all have different policies. I can't wait to get my credit card on Friday! Why, you wanna learn how to interior decorate from me?"

"You'll go to jail, that's all I'm worried about."

"You wanna make a bet right now on that?" she shouted contemptuously. "How much?" The sound produced heavy reverb in my skull. "How much you wanna bet," she repeated in a more quiet and firm tone.

"I'm not going to bet with *you*."

"That's right," she said, very pleased. "You couldn't afford it. Look at how I'm a most terrible person. You're my friend and I just tried to hustle you! Cause I ain't goin to jail for none of this job, kiddo. I've never been to jail in my life, except for five times, and never overnight. There was the three times Nick and Mary threw me in the joint, which I got paid for afterwards, remember? The fourth time was Nineteen Sixty-four in St. Louis when my agent had me and Ladyfingers Love arrested for sleeping on park benches so we'd get a lot of newspaper publicity and photos to promote our strip acts. And the last time was in Sixty-seven: 'suspicion of being in a place where marijuana is being smoked'—ha! That charge was of course thrown out because it isn't even a law. And I never smoke grass anyhow, it makes me flip out. Wait— there was one time more. The last time was in Sixty-eight when I got busted for mayhem. That makes six puny little busts. And you have the balls to worry about me goin to jail for *hustling?*"

I closed my eyes. "Don't pay any attention to me, I just work here."

"You certainly got more sass than I gave you credit for, bitch!" In a minute, she softened up. "I like that. I mean, that you were worryin about me. Listen, don't worry, just believe in me. I've got this seventh sense. The gypsy sense. You get born with it, I dunno. I always . . . get a feeling, when I know the shit's comin down and it's time to move on and get the hell out. . . . I know, cause my left tit lights up!"

Before I could cough up a giggle, the phone rang. "That's your boyfriend," she said. "I got a eighth sense about phone calls."

When I picked up the receiver in the living room, the din of rush-hour traffic made Murphy's voice almost inaudible.

"I can't afford to talk loud," he said, "this is important. I couldn't find a phone booth with a door on it. Listen to what I found out this afternoon. Where were you, by the way, I called several times."

"Bloomingdale's."

He paused, as if he didn't believe me. "Hell of a time to shop, when we're stuck for bread."

"I didn't spend no money," I yawned.

"*Any* money. Listen to what I learned. I called d'Piro's record label and spoke with the sales division. Seems he does work for them, or he *did* work for them until right before I called. They fired him because he didn't show up for work on Monday, and then he came into the office this morning so wrecked on . . . the white powder, you know . . . and, um . . . other things. Well, I can't talk here, but d'Piro was so wired that they canned him. So now I know . . . what happened to my *laundry* that he took to the cleaners. You understand? They gave me his home phone number, but it's been disconnected."

"Far out."

"Far out is a euphemism. My whole scenario is blown now. I'm back with the same strange puzzle pieces. Now what I have to do is find out Officer Dan's real identity and what he's pulling on me, and make some attempt at retrieving the other half pound . . . of my laundry, you know? The only person who can help me is Kristal, so put her on the phone."

It was my pleasure. I reviewed Murphy's case with Kristal and then went back to bed while she took over the show in the living room on the phone.

I was vaguely conscious that I was passing out.

Kristal returned and reported, "I told him I didn't know Officer Dan's last name but that he had clearly fucked up this time, so I would make good my threat and have the mob snuff him. I told him I'd get Frank to arrange for it but that he probably wouldn't never see his cocaine. Anyway, the asshole is cooled out for now. He said you should come back as soon as 'O. D.' is offed, because he misses you."

I couldn't seem to surface for a goodbye or a thank you. She pulled the blanket over me and set the dial. Mother, make my bed, for today I am for a-dyin. Make mine a shroud.

"Don't come to work tonight," she soothed. "You've been trying too hard lately. You've been slaving yourself to the bone."

The apartment door slammed at 6 A.M. and Kristal stomped in and sat on the edge of her king-size bed. She had saved me from a dream that was about to turn into a nightmare of punishment. The electric blanket was set too hot and I was being sentenced to hang by the neck until dead.

I propped myself up to watch the sky get light outside the window. My dress was pasted to my sweating chest and the skirt creases were brittle like a stale pink crust. Kristal's chest was heaving up and down, her hand diving in and out of a big bag of French fries: she was trying to keep her mouth busy so she wouldn't blow up.

"I am *shocked* and *abhorred*," she burst at last. "I'm just so . . . *abhorred* at Frank."

I didn't bother to correct her.

"Do you know what he's started working in that place as of tonight? Fucking *sex changes!* One of them looked like a model. The straight black hair, the high cheekbones, great big violet eyes —violet, mind you, like Elizabeth Taylor—long black lashes, six foot three. That was the first sex change I ever saw in my life that didn't wear nothing but mascara and lipstick. God, she was beautiful. She was a man, and she made us all look sick.

"She got picked! She's French and doesn't know English, and all she knows to say to the customer is bend down and say, 'You sock my tee-eetty, you eat my poo-o-ossy. . . .' Of course the guys ran right after them with *that* fuckin line. And, they walk around with their tits out. And they didn't have nothin but enlarged nipples. So now all the other girls are pulling out their tits, the whole boob, right over the top of the leotards. What filth. Here was eight or nine girls, and none of em made any money but those two fuckin sex changes."

"Far out."

"The other one is French, too, and she translates for the one with the amazing face. The only thing was, her *manner* is ugly. When she opens her mouth you can see she's a cocksucker. You know what I mean, with the loose lower lip—?"

"Ubangi."

"That's it. I'm just so abhorred. That place has gone to rack and ruin. Frank just sits there playin the horses and Cricket's givin him head and his brain is goin soft, you can see it happening. It makes me unhappy. I like to feel respectable when I work."

She stayed awake, and I sat up with her, both of us silent, for another hour. It was more than the sex changes keeping her awake. She drank Courvoisier and ate French fries. Her eyes were narrowed to slivers, as if she were on top of a mountain facing into a steady powerful wind and she were eating to gain the extra weight needed to stand fast, immutable, immune, impenetrable, against the power.

"I wish these fries weren't cold," she said once.

It was the chill factor. The wind had blown up suddenly and might not die for days, and no estimate of damage could be made until the force passed.

I was glad I was born without the seventh sense, because I'm too skinny to stand my ground.

I had the early morning all to myself in the dining room. I ate toast, and wrote "Jan. 28" in my diary.

Around nine o'clock the phone rang.

"Randy," Kristal yelled from the bedroom, "that's about the dogs. Pretend you're the maid and tell anyone who's interested they should come around here at three, and don't wake me til two!"

I picked up the phone in the living room. "Mrs. Pace's residence."

A lady inquired about this morning's ad in *The New York*

Times, in which four fully pedigreed Great Dane pups had to be sold quickly at the bargain price of $150 for each of the three males and $100 for the female. The woman wanted more information about the pedigree, but I said Mrs. Pace wasn't home, however she would receive any interested buyers at three this afternoon.

These calls kept coming in the rest of the day. At noon, Bloomingdale's delivered boxes of new clothes and a complete set of leather luggage, soup to nuts. Two of the boxes were addressed to me, c/o Pace. One box contained a dress from the "Young East Sider" department. It was long, had a V neck and high waist, long bell sleeves, and was made from a slinky gray-blue fabric with paste-diamond buttons all down the front to the ankles. The other box contained blue patent-leather sandals in my size.

It was the first grown-up dressy dress I'd ever had. I hid the two boxes in the living room closet, without trying the stuff on.

Later, Kristal took on ten dog hunters arriving in shifts. "Excuse the godawful state of the apartment," she chattered. "When I divorced my husband two months ago I was so angry and hurt that I took half the furniture and simply plunked it down in here even though there was no room, never mind rhyme or reason for such behavior. I was so mad, you know, cause he was allergic to my Petunia, and when he heard she was pregnant and that I'd bred her behind his back, he threatened to divorce me, so I called his bluff and divorced *him!* But now we are suddenly in love again, like two children. See the beautiful ruby ring he gave me yesterday for the engagement? But we're moving into the Sherry-Netherland on Friday after the wedding, so I have to sell my precious doggies before then, even though they're only two months old. Yes, I promised him I would not be so unreasonable anymore; my little sister here is taking Tuney and I don't care what money I get for the little ones; that's why the price is so cheap, cause all I want is for them to quickly find good homes with loving parents. Money means nothing to me, even though these pups are descended from champs. The sire was King Stefan Burlinghouse VII and the mother Tuney is registered as Wilhelmina Donna Blitzen. I'm such a nervous wreck I can't remember the rest of the bloodline and I couldn't find the papers today, though I know they're here somewhere, but I'll have found them by tomorrow. You look like you're falling head over heels in love with the darling pup over there with the cute little pecker on him! He's my favorite, too. No, I won't take a check, you come tomorrow with the cash, and I'll have the pedigree papers by then. If I take a check, see, I'd have to deposit it in our joint account, and I'm not letting that bastard get his hands on the money I made bringing up the litter alone in a divorced home, all because dogs give him the hives. Come tomorrow around four o'clock, so I can spend the morning to take them to the vet for shots, and kiss all their little faces a last goodbye."

She'd told me once that the litter had been born in a Great Western Motel. Knowing her, the puppies were probably sired by a pony.

The Royale was empty of customers even by midnight. The usual four men were present: Frank, Stan, George, and Snickerin' Jimmy.

Olive was home with the flu.

Nita sat at a ringside table, writing letters to relatives in Brazil, confident that one of her regulars would walk in soon. She didn't desire to sit in the pen along with that black girl, Carla, and those three sex changes.

The third one, Brandy, had been newly hired tonight. She was built like a polevaulter, had amber-tinted bouffant curls, and wore spike heels, bikini underpants, and a yellow turtleneck sweater over her huge boobs. Kristal was outraged that Brandy's tits were bigger than hers but were obviously false.

The other two sex changes gabbled in French. Antoinette paused to explain to Kristal that Pascale was disappointed in the dance-hall business. "Pascale is use to make maw-nay ay-nor-*moose*. She do the factoree for lunch, sometimes thirty types, one day, working at close five dollars each man. One hundred and fifty dollars by three o'clock is not bad in France."

"Oh my God," said Kristal. She turned to me, "Don't they have to take it up the ass? They don't have twats, do they?" I had no idea. "But Antoinette, didn't she get tired of fuckin that many guys every day?"

"Fuck?" Antoinette giggled and translated to Pascale who rolled her lovely violet eyes and dropped her slackened jaw and haw-hawed deeply. Then she shook her head: "No-no." She shaped her hands around an imaginary cock and slid them back and forth at her mouth, making vile rubber slopping noises with her lips.

"Have you ever heard such filth?" Kristal whispered to me. "She goes to the factory to give workers blowjobs on their lunch hour . . . she had them all, for lunch! No wonder her trap's hangin loose."

"I wish it would rain. Then we would have more customers come down off the street." I was surprised to hear Beth speak. I'd become so accustomed to the sight of her sitting quietly, hugging her blue mohair shawl around her shoulders, over her gown with its faded exotic-bird patterns. I had never seen a customer pick her. But she always came to work promptly, her yellow hair always in a fresh Irene Castle bob, and sat down at the mirror to put fresh blue eyeshadow on her ancient lids, rimmed her doleful eyes with a freshly sharpened black pencil, and spat clean spit onto her cake of mascara. One could see that she had been, thirty years back, desirable, and had a gentle carriage.

Sheba slipped in beside her with tomorrow's early edition of the paper fresh off the stands. She turned first to the horoscope. " 'Stop putting off a decision on that all-important problem that's been nagging you. Have dinner with close friends tonight.' That's me, Pisces—anybody else want to know tomorrow's answer?"

"I'm Aquarius," I said.

The buzzer went off. We all leapt to our feet and crowded at the wailing wall. The French sex changes rubbed their nipples energetically, while the real women beckoned and invited at un-usual volume.

The customer was jovial at all this attention. "Which one wants to go for a ride in my taxi tonight?" He didn't know we were so bored that any new face was a fun face, even if it belonged to a bedraggled cabdriver.

Kristal finally was the one who gained his ear. "Sexy, over here! I gotta secret you gotta hear! . . . I gotta secret to tell you!"

"Okay, what's the big secret," he grinned, leaning close to her mouth.

"Listen, everyone else is on the rag!"

The zipper on his army jacket tinkled as his pot stomach quaked with laughter. "Okay, sister, I'll take you, then."

The rest of us curtsied back and sat down again. Kristal and the cabdriver danced by the pen a few times. Once, she pointed me out to him. He winked. I went to the bathroom.

Ten minutes later, Kristal came in. "Get off the toilet, you can get crab poisoning if you sit there too long. I got us fifty dollars for a hotel room, so twenty-five's yours. He thinks you and me are horny and want to party together with someone as a three-scene, so he's driving his cab by at closing time. He really liked you. I told you I was right about wearing that dress. You're the only girl now who looks like a decent human being in that pig pen."

She had forced me to admit that the blue dress and sandals had arrived in the Bloomingdale's delivery. She sensed that it was critically necessary for me to have "class" tonight.

I came out of the john.

"Fifty bucks is shit," she frowned, "and this place is turned to a latrine. At least we know Graham's comin in."

"Graham dahlink person," Kristal hustled him to a table and sat between us, "there is very bad news. Big trouble. My husband her brother has vound out all about this romance business! He has saw the rink on Randy's hand and he vants to know how come. I *told* this stupid-head girl here not to vear the rink in the house, but she cried her eyes and von't take it off. So now I hev to lie a little and tell my husband Randy is engaged to a wery rich and respectvul man that she loffs. But my husband look at the size of the tiny diamond and say, 'How can he respect my little princess if he buy her such a cheap rink for engage?' instead of the old Jew who can buy, vhat my husband say, 'the Grend Cenyon diamond instead of this lousy pebble!' Then Randy opens her pretty mouth, and for the virst time, ever, she curses her own brother up and down. Now he is wery scared. She has a dewil inside! No, I get mix-up, I mean *devil*. He reads these stupid books about devils that people read. So he is gone today to Connecticut to buy a house we move to as soon as god's speed, so she can get fresh air and a good nun school. Tonight ve sneaked out before he comes beck, so ve can talk, all of us, and decide vhat to do. I think maybe it is time to call kvits between you two."

"The man is undoubtably demented and should be committed," Graham seethed. "I would never jettison a meaningful relationship"—he glanced at me, who looked strangely more grown-up tonight, more proud and classy—"because some *Nazi* makes nonsensical threats and assumptions—"

"No," Kristal begged, "he is just so scared his little sister vill run off and give avay her honor before marriage, like all the young girls are doing every day. He must be sure the man she loffs is serious, you understand."

"I want to think this over," he answered intently. "I can't explain what I'm feeling. But perhaps if I go back to the hotel alone, and call up a few friends whose advice I trust, and consider what has happened . . . I'll come back at four. We can all go out for breakfast and talk. By then I'll be prepared to respond to this sudden climax of events and emotions."

The cabdriver was promptly waiting for us in his warmed-up hack when we emerged, with Graham, from the Royale at 4 A.M. Kristal grabbed me by the wrist and darted around to the driver's window.

"We can get another one, he has his 'off duty' light on," Graham called in vain.

"Hey," she hissed to the driver, "our brother just showed up out of the blue, so we can't make it tonight. He just got out on parole and the crazy man is already packin a gun. You better drive us to where he says and we'll party with you on Sunday, after he leaves town. You're free Sunday?"

He nodded apprehensively and switched his "free" light on.

"He's gonna take us, let's get in," she yelled to Graham.

"RANDY! RAAAN-DEEE!"

Everyone turned toward the unholy howl. I recognized Murphy, half a block away, racing toward us, passing under a streetlight which gave us all one second's image of a man who has recently realized that he was framed and who cannot feel charity toward his enemies, and whose nose was running. Every time he spewed my name it made clouds of steam like brimstone. "RAAAN-DEEE!"

"Ai-ee!" Kristal blenched. "It is my crazy husband! Go, Graham, take her home and I vill stop him from harm's vay—!" She shoved us into the cab, slammed the door, and tore off to intercept Murphy.

Screeching into motion, the cabdriver didn't even bother to throw his meter on. When he'd gotten up enough speed I found enough breath to gasp out the address of Kristal's apartment building.

"How you must be frightened," said Graham, stunned, his voice hushed so the driver wouldn't hear. "Your brother had the appearance of an absolute ghoul. Are you sure it's safe for you to go home? Will your sister-in-law be able to calm him down?"

"I don't know," I stammered. "Up until now she's always found a way to keep him away from me. . . . I don't know. I have to trust her."

"My uncle was a dangerous psychotic in Brisbane. The only way to treat these people is to have them committed, no matter what their relationship has meant to you in the past. Sweet Randy, I had all these plans for us, but I didn't grasp how utterly *mad* your brother is. I thought I could reason with him."

"Forget it," I said, my mind on other considerations.

"I can't. I wish there was more time. You see, I have to leave for England on Sunday, by boat—"

I gave him his ring back.

It was an honest gesture and an honest mistake. Graham thrust the ring onto the third finger of my *left* hand and went all the way: "I can't leave without you. Don't be heroic and think you can spare me from becoming involved in your life. I'm already involved. Do you understand what I'm saying?"

The taxi had stopped in front of the address and now the driver was watching us in his rearview mirror. Graham tried to kiss me.

"Get out of my cab, you perverts!" the driver shrilled. "Don't pay me no fare, just get the hell out!" He was under the illusion that we were brother and sister exchanging lizardly incestuous tongues on his back seat. We sprang out and let him disappear in a poof of righteous monoxide. I took my door key out of my purse.

"Will you be at the dance hall tomorrow night?" Graham pleaded.

"No."

"Yes, of course not. You can't go back now."

"Please go." I wrestled with the lock.

"Poor sweetie, you look like you'll perish from fright. You're too young to—" I closed the glass door between us and dropped his ring back outside through the mail slot. It bounced off his shoe but he ignored it, and crouched down to the slot to speak one last vow: "I won't let you let yourself be abandoned. Promise to call me at the Warwick. I love you, dear. I don't care what hour of the day or night—I know you'll call."

"I'll try," was all I could manage, and I ran away, to the elevator.

Kristal unlocked the door barely ten minutes after I got into the apartment. I was feeding the dogs because somebody had to do it. That was Cinderella's big hang-up, too.

"That's it," she announced. "I'm splitting this city this weekend. I knew it last night but I'm positive now. Don't look like that! It's not just the hassle with your boyfriend. I just know *all* the shit is gonna start comin down by next week."

"What was the matter with Murphy?"

"Oh, he hung out all hours at that coffee shop where I originally met you. He talked to all the hookers and finally met a couple of'm that was there the same night, and they said there was no such Officer Dan. They know all the names in the Times Square pussy squad, and they said none of the guys is a Dan. So Murphy decides that you and me had lied, and kept the dope to sell out of the Royale. I was really insulted! He thinks we're holding all the money!"

I was hurt, too. "How could he think I'd deliberately screw him like that?"

"I said it was pe-prosperous. I said, 'The mob controls all the hard-drug trade in this neighborhood. You were crazy to think you could just breeze into town on your own.' I said, 'The guy Randy was climbing into the cab with is the same guy who intercepted your cocaine for them. We spent two weeks gettin this mobster to fall in love with Randy, and you came screamin up and almost blew the whole hustle. We had to lie to you so you wouldn't interfere with our plan to get him to give the dope back for you. He thinks Randy is gonna marry him. We had to shut you out, cause this is *women's* work.' . . . I didn't want to stand around jawing with him all night, so I said, 'Listen, you better make yourself invisible right now, in fact—Frank will be up on the street any minute to close the joint and he's got murderous connections you'd better believe.' So Murphy says, 'I don't believe you've given me the whole story,' but he's scared of Frank showin up. I told him to call tomorrow and we'd explain the whole thing to his complete satisfaction."

"What'll we tell him tomorrow?"

"Nothin. I ordered the phone to be disconnected tomorrow morning. I told you, I'm gettin out."

"What am *I* gonna do?" I followed her into the dining room.

"Why ask me. Go back to your boyfriend. Tell him I was a bad influence on you when you were too stoned-out to know any better. He'll fall for that. I'll be out of town, so he can't get at me." She was testing me.

"No."

"You're a little smarted up, I'm thrilled to notice." She poured herself some Courvoisier and opened a bag of Taco Chips.

"I'm not smart enough to know what to do next, after you go. I know I wouldn't stay on at the Royale. I'd lose my shirt."

"In no time *flat!* Ha ha," she choked. "Get the joke, flat-chest? Well, it wasn't funny. You'd do all right at the dance hall, you got a little technique now."

"Not enough, and I hate it."

"Rome wasn't built in a week, either, so don't be hard on yourself." She poured another shot, and thought. ". . . You and me could work as a team, and hustle enough bread at the Royale by Friday to get you a setup, before I leave. Then you can settle back to bein a hippie. You people know how to live on practically nothing. Just a mattress on the floor, and some candles, eat roots and berries and whatever have you, and work in a psychedelic shop for tourists."

"I want to know, where are you going to go to?"

"Never know. It'll come to me when I'm driving. I gotta score a car by the weekend, reminds me. Tuney has never been in a airplane and she'd probably hemorrhage her ovaries, what with all the pressure she'll be under after losing her babies. . . . What are you getting at, anyway? You want a lift to get out of the city? You could marry Graham, and go to Europe. But listen, if you do that, plan the wedding day for when you know you'll get your period, so that he'll see the blood and go on thinking he's married a virgin. I'm not jokin, either."

"I don't love Graham."

"Then you're stupid, like me. Because Graham's very nice, and he's rolling in money. . . . Well, you can come with me if you want. Don't be afraid to ask. Come along with me, sure, I'll show you the sights! Get away from my Courvoisier, piggie, I bought you some beer in the icebox. You can't hold your hard liquor so good."

I popped the top off a cold beer. "I can't make up my mind tonight. I been up since six this morning. That's yesterday morning. I'm wasted and I don't have no seventh sense."

"If you're nice, some day I'll give it to you as a present. . . .

((106))

Anyway, you don't have to make up your mind til next week. The rent's paid through Tuesday and you can stay on here. But don't answer the door starting Monday. It might be some hyperemotional employee from Lord & Taylor's, or J. C. Penney's, or B. Altman's, or Korvette's. By today those stores have gotten their bills back unopened that I wrote DECEASED on the front of."

At 11 A.M. the apartment bell rang. Kristal plummeted out of bed to buzz the ground-floor door open. I got up too, determined to bring daylight back into my life.

She opened the neck of her bathrobe and opened the door for a used-furniture dealer. "Mr. Aaron, hi. Have you got your truck downstairs like I asked?"

"Yeah," he was surveying the living room decor. An intelligent smile played amongst his other features.

"Okay, three rooms of stuff, like I said, at a good price if you can take it all now."

He walked through to the bedroom and back again to the front door. He placed his hand on the knob. "Eighteen hundred."

"Can you give me a check for that amount right now?"

"Uh-huh."

"Then take it away, man."

She sent me out to a Staten Island bank to cash his check, while his crew started removing the furniture. By the time I got back, after a queasy round trip on the Staten Island ferry through a rapier wind, the living and dining rooms were void, and Mr. Aaron's truck was expected to return shortly for the last load-up from the bedroom.

Kristal counted the cash I'd brought. "That guy's makin about three grand in profit. I had to take his first offer. You can't barter with these people. They take one look and they know exactly what you've been up to."

The cash-laden puppy purchasers arrived and had to tango around the living room to gangway for the men removing our beds. One by one, Petunia's spawn departed for new homes. They would grow up with their true pedigree forever a mystery.

"My god, the papers!" Kristal lamented each time. "I found them last night and put them in that roll-top desk which the movers took away this morning when my back was turned! So now the papers are at the Sherry-Netherland suite. I'll go straight over there tonight and Xerox them in the morning before my wedding and mail them to you. Just give my sister your address, please, I'm too disorganized with all this fuss and commotion. Tuney, stop barking. No one will hurt your babies."

I still have the four addresses in my diary, the only available paper to write on in that confusion. If I ever want to look up some enemies in New York City and get torn to pieces by their Great Danes, I've got their number.

Business boomed that night at the Royale. The temperature dipped to twenty-eight degrees with fourteen-mile gusts, which was better than rain for luring men down into a red-hot basement. Also, there were barely enough girls to go around. The two French sex changes had defected to a massage parlor, and the flu had claimed Olive, Fernie, Cricket, and Nita.

"Now I'll give you lessons in stacking dates," said Kristal. "Only when one is about to leave town can one afford to be so reckless. The object is to get as many guys as you can to meet you after work, each on a different corner. You tell them you can't meet them in front or you'll get fired. That's a big rule here, Frank will back you up. Matterfact, that's why I got fired thirteen years ago. Anyhow, this is faster cash than convincing them to go to phony addresses. They think you aren't tricking them because if they're standing on a corner within eyesight of the door, they'll see you come out and you can't give them the slip. But all the corners have to be *blind,* so you can split without running into any dates. That means don't drink no beer tonight: just tomato juice. Once when I was seventeen, I was Champaling it up and I got my flight patterns mixed up. Somebody told me I had three guys waiting for me at the Seventh Avenue exit, and I knew there was two more guys at two other stakeouts which I couldn't remember to save my life. So I busted into the janitor's closet and put on his big overcoat and sloppy hat, with the mop and the pail, and I tried to get out of the building in this preposterous disguise. It was just my luck none of 'm recognized me! . . . Like, last night was a fuck-up. I was all switched around wrong in my head. I forgot that it's the Broadway door, not the Seventh Avenue door, that Frank locks at closing, and I had told the cabdriver to meet us on Seventh Avenue. So there he was, and we couldn't avoid him because the Broadway side was the exit what was locked. So remember, tonight we got to be all clear on the *Seventh* Avenue side."

By 2 A.M., we had some kind of a rendezvous chart. We'd recruited four manly volunteers to guard various corners along Broadway.

No. 1 was assigned the southeast corner at Broadway and Forty-ninth. He was a supermarket manager from Long Island. We were two horny sisters who wanted to "party." But we lived with our parents. We had a girl friend who would let us use her extra bedroom, but we owed her one hundred dollars. It would be embarrassing to ask her for a favor if we couldn't pay her the money when we came over.

No. 2 had the northwest corner of Broadway and Fiftieth. His face was familiar. He was a middle-aged character actor, in New York for a few days' location shooting. We were a gay couple, and were willing to give him a "show." Kristal described this terrific leather-and-fishnet costume she had at home in Queens, which she could fetch before closing if she had the twenty dollars for cabfare. We'd also need another twenty dollars for the babysitter, another lezzie, to stay overnight. Another seventy dollars to buy from same sitter an incredible three-speed vibrator "cause a vibrator is the only way Randy comes off. I'm the one who likes to have her pussy eaten, and Randy can teach you methods no man has ever known about the correct way to lap a cunt."

No. 3 got the plum spot, the southwest corner of Broadway and Forty-eighth, directly opposite the door which Frank would unexpectedly lock at 4 A.M. He was a masochist, and he wanted more abuse from Kristal after sampling her talents. She commanded him to fork up two hundred dollars in front, and one hundred dollars more if, as a bonus, I came along to jeer at him. She told me that masochists were used to paying top dollar for abuse, "cause a good sadist is hard to find."

No. 4 waited at Forty-seventh Street on Times Square itself. He was one of Nita's regulars. A real snap. Nita only takes big tips, to support her two kids, and then fucks for nothing after hours, looking for that husband. We said we were her approved replacements. Since there were two of us, the tip came to $150.

No. 5 was another one of those overnight tourists, a Japanese sales representative for rotary engines. He was put on hold at his hotel at Kennedy Airport. We asked for the usual: twenty dollars for cabfare, fifteen dollars for the babysitter to stay overnight, thirty dollars for two bottles of champagne.

"Whoo. I think we'll do over a grand tonight if this keeps up," said Kristal, during a breather in the pen, "especially when Graham comes by for breakfast and we nail him for something really big, like a bigger diamond to get you two properly engaged. Look, even Beth got picked tonight!"

Sure enough, Beth was absent from her normal place. "She's not good for a handjob. She wasn't brought up that way. She's been a hostess all her life. Got no place else to do with her time. All she does when she gets a customer to a table is try to hustle him for cab fare home."

"Why does she always have that shawl on?" I asked. "It only makes her look older." Like a grandmother, rocking and warming her hands on the embers of a dying profession.

"To hide some awful mark a customer gave her, long time ago. Some man beat her up, I don't know what the story was."

"I've never seen Fernie get picked either."

"And she's ugly! Beth at least looks like she used to be pretty. Tell you a story. Fernie had one customer back in the old days: Smokestack Magee. He was a TV wrestler and weighed four hundred pounds, though they billed him as six hundred. He always wore overalls and got Fernie to sit at a table so he could tell her how ugly she was, and laugh, and torment her. *One* time, good old Smokestack wanted to fuck. A Jewish girl. Sheba had just got married, so she was out. I was the only one left over fifty who passed for Jewish, so he wanted me. Fernie needed the money, so she took her commission, sent me over to his table without a word, and goes back to the pen and nods out. I knew she's set me up in some way, but I couldn't fool around with Smokestack cause he was a regular. He says, 'Your place or mine?' I said, 'My place.' And gave him Fernie's address. The next day Fernie came in with a black eye and one tooth gone. She's so ugly no one noticed the difference, but she never screwed around with me again."

"Hey Kristal," Inez scurried up, "ain't you a widow?"

"Who wants to know?"

"I got a customer that's a Turkish student needs to get married or he'll be deported. He wants to be a U. S. citizen quick. Him and his three friends have been all over the Square trying to find a girl who'll do it for less than three thousand dollars who they can trust. It's got to be all legal, and they'll pay for the divorce. I can't do it, you know I'm married."

"Tell'm I'm a widow, okay, and I'll talk bargain if he buys an hour's tickets." Inez went back to the table where the young man sat. His friends were drinking beer at the bar and vigilantly observing the due process. "This is bingo," Kristal exulted. "Bonanza. Keno! *Lay Jews Saunt Fate!* . . . These citizenship deals sell for up to five grand, and they take about a week's work during the day for the blood tests, the ceremony, the lawyer, the divorce—so the chick gets no less than three grand up front. But we're in a hurry, so I can get a grand at least out of'm to get you married."

"*Me?*"

"Just shut up, is the best cure for you," she snapped. "Of course you're not gettin married. I wouldn't sell you *that* short. You're just the type that would ordinarily get the highest price.

You're the type they make a deal with and then fall in love with you—so the divorce would be a higher settlement, cause you'd let him have his wedding night! Fact, we'd fake your cherry . . ."

The approaching student motioned Kristal to come to the cashier. He had handsome, elegant features and his blue corduroy suit was clean and modest. He might well have come from some one of those ancient cultures that revere cherries. Oh well, he was getting off easy.

"Go to the dressing room and get out your ID, for when I call you," she said as she rose from her seat.

Before leaving the dressing room with my purse, I sat in front of the mirror for a moment and absentmindedly rubbed red gloss into my wind-chapped lips.

I felt so guilty about Murphy. All along, I hadn't done anything wrong to him, nothing that could be called malicious. But I knew he'd feel definitely betrayed by me when he dialed Kristal's apartment and got the disconnect recording: ". . . that number has been changed to area code 213, 853-1285." If you're calling outside of the 213 area, any 853 number will get you a recording: "We cannot complete your call as dialed. . . ." Even if you called an 853 within the 213 Los Angeles area, all you'd get was was another recording: "—at the tone, the time will be—" Murphy would flip. I could see his admirable imagination promoting me to chief counteragent in a convoluted conspiracy to make him shave his head and renounce all his worldly marbles.

And what would I say, if I could tell him the truth? I couldn't even remember the exact original version of the lie *or* the truth, it was so far behind me. And as for lies, I was no expert in right or wrong. Anybody who told me so was not one either—

Kristal snipped off my twisting thought: "Let's go, I want to clinch this deal before Graham arrives. I told the Turk kid my price was four grand, but that you were new, two weeks out of San Francisco, unattached, and naive enough to agree to the marriage for one thousand dollars. His friend is gonna buy your tickets for two hours til closing, so there'll be four of us at the table. The kid's not sure of himself, so he wants his friend there.

You let me do the talking, and you just relax and be yourself, all innocence."

She spoke very slowly and distinctly, since neither Turk had mastered the language very well. "She will do it only if you get married tomorrow night after work. After four o'clock the morning. She flies back to San Francisco on Saturday for her father's funeral. She needs the thousand cash money for black dress and airplane back to New York on Monday. Then you get divorce."

Handing me back my ID, the wiser friend interrupted: "Not possible tomorrow night. The justice of peace is not open, and also is forty-eight hours of waiting period for blood test."

Kristal waved him aside, "I know that. It's the same law every state except Maryland. South. Drive four hours. You come with car, thousand cash four A.M., and we go to *Maryland*. At Maryland, marriage is possible any time, night or day, with no waiting period. The justice of peace charges extra. You don't understand 'charge'? . . . Little more money, like fifty dollars, because Maryland is the only state for this marriage."

They whispered together in Turkish. I whispered to Kristal, "But Maryland's the same as every other state. They changed the law about fifty years ago."

"No kidding. So what? If I didn't know what, why would they know? They're *aliens*. All they need is a little encouragement from you, so they can trust you. They don't really trust me. They'll fall for it if you do something sweet. C'mon, it's a thousand."

The foreigners broke camp, and nodded to the deal.

"Oh, thank you," I gushed, and laid a hand on the groom's arm. "Now you are a citizen, and I can go to my father. Welcome to America."

At four-fifteen we hailed a taxi at the Royale's Seventh Avenue exit, and made a smooth casual getaway with $725 in cash tips. Kristal was disgruntled. "We could of made more, if Graham had showed up at four. I just don't get it. He's usually johnny on the spot for you. He better not be gettin nervous now of all times. What'd you say to him in the taxi last night?"

I told her everything.

She wasn't put out. "So you can call him any hour at the Warwick, good. In fact, that's better. We may need that."

"I never take long to make up my mind." Kristal lit into a fresh bottle of Courvoisier and finished her liverwurst sandwich. "I get the feeling, right when it's time. If I decide to do something, I figure it's predestiny."

"I don't believe in destiny." Even when dumbest, I have always resisted belief in any one thing, if I'm not certain it can provide me with a generous set of answers.

"Well, if you decide to come along with me, be my guest. And I wouldn't offer it to just anybody. I've just never had, like, a girl friend before, to be close friends with. I don't get into most people. They're so fucking phony. And you better believe they don't get into *me*. Because when I confide them the story of my life, they say, 'That chick is fulla shit. She can't be for real.' They avoid me like the plague. . . . But here, you trust me, and you worry about me, and you don't horn in on my privacy. It's fun. Must be what it's like to have a college roommate. I always sort of wanted one."

"I'm still considering," I called, bringing some food to Petunia in the living room. The buzzer from the ground-floor door went off. I automatically pushed the intercom. "Who is it?"

"It's Murphy." The cheap speaker distorted his voice. "If you don't open the door down here, I'll shoot it open."

Kristal's hand slammed my thumb off the response button. "You knucklebrain! If he can't get in the building we're safe. Shit, if the phone wasn't unhooked we could call the cops."

Several minutes later we heard him right outside our door.

"He must have pressed all the other buzzers til someone let him in," she whispered. "Get away from the door, he's got a gun."

"Randy!" he bellowed. "I know you're there! You better open

the god damn door or you'll never be able to leave this apartment alive! I'll kill you!"

I waited, preserving my breath. Kristal held Petunia's muzzle shut with both hands.

"CUNT! I hope you've got enough food in there to last a year, because I'm just going to wait out here til you decide to talk to me!"

Kristal muttered a Hungarian description.

"HEY, CUNT! YOU'RE A CUNT! THAT'S ALL YOU ARE! CUNT!"

A man who lived down the hall shouted through his door: "Whoever the hell *you* are, quit that racket or I'll call the police!"

Lowering his voice, Murphy pressed his face against the door and hissed, "You'd better let me in, Randy, because I know you sold my dope. If you come across with the real facts this time with me, we'll have a chance to work something out. You *cunt*, thinking you could shake me off so easily—I've never hurt a girl before but if you don't open the door I'll mend my ways—"

"AAAACK!!" Kristal shrieked at full lung. "HELP! SOME-BODY CALL THE POLICE, HE'S GOT A GUN!"

Then she rammed me into the living room closet and locked the door. I landed on a heap of shoes, and something slimy fell on my face. It was my new blue dress. The emptied hanger swung, creaking, on the rod. I chewed on one of Kristal's plastic curlers to keep my mouth from revealing my hiding place. I couldn't make out what was going on outside. It sounded like Murphy had changed his tack and was imploring with Kristal.

I could hear more clearly when Kristal opened the door, "Oh, *ovvicers*, dahlinks, I'm so heppy to see you. My phone is not installed yet so I could not call the police by myself."

Murphy: "For God's sake, Kristal, I'm perfectly calm now—"

A cop: "It's too late for that, unless you can produce a license for that pistol. Also you've been disturbing the peace, if this lady wants to press charges—"

Kristal: "Most certainly of course, I am wery—*very* vrighten of this man I don't know vrom Adem. I just move in here this

place today—and look, you can see. No vurniture . . . my luggage . . . my dog barkink you hear I hev shut her in the other
room so she don't vake the neighbors—"

Another cop: "You've never seen this man before?"

Kristal: "I svear! He vas yellink for some 'Ren-dee," and vords
I von't repeat, and vas all ready for shootink down the door!
Maybe this 'Ren-dee' vas the previous tenant in this apartment."

Cop (to Murphy): "All right, let's leave the lady in peace,
we'll go downstairs, and I'll inform you of your rights."

Murphy: "I know my rights by heart. I won't tell you anything, and I'll make my one call to Legal Aid, when we get to
the station—"

The door closed. Kristal unlocked the closet. "Sorry. I thought
if he shot down the door and saw you, he'd shoot you, too. Hell,
now I've got to get out of town tomorrow instead of the weekend.
Your boyfriend will be out of jail by noon or so, and the good
fuck knows what he'll do next. I'm gettin out of this address before noon, and I'll be on the road by the early morning, after I
settle some loose ends at the Royale—"

"—I'm going with you," I announced in a standing position.

She looked at me abstractly. Finally, she snapped her fingers.
"Graham! The car!"

The air had hunkered down another three degrees, to 25. I froze
obediently outside the phone booth while Kristal dialed the
Warwick Hotel. Dawn was hours away.

I'd been too shook up to pull off the call to Graham myself.

Kristal had set her jaw. "Then I'll do it. He's never heard
your voice on the phone, and without my Hungarian accent he'll
think I'm you."

I'd do any damn thing. No choice. No destiny. Only a breathing out and a breathing in above sea level and 98.6 degrees kept
constant at the core. Easy to assemble. Easy to disassemble.

"Graham," Kristal panted, "my brother just got killed in a car
accident in Bridgeport, Connecticut—and I have to get there. I
don't know what to do. I'm supposed to pick up his belongings

and his remains and I don't have a car and Kristal is sick because the doctor had to give her a shot to make her sleep when she went into shock—I feel so alone and I don't know where I'm going to get a station wagon from—Yes, it's six-two-eight-eight-eight-one-nine. I'll be waiting."

She hung up. "Come inside, it's a little warmer." We huddled inside the doorless phone booth until Graham rang back. He promised to meet her (me) at a car-rental agency and sign the papers for her during his lunch hour. Kristal blurted out that she'd fallen in love with him, it was true. "I've never said that to any man, and whatever happens and wherever you go I hope you'll remember that I said it. . . ."

"Well, you just got your first marriage proposal," she told me after hanging up. "Too bad you couldn't hear it. When we meet him at the rental agency he's going to give you a first-class steamship ticket—he's scared of planes—so that you can run away and meet him in England after the funeral."

There was no point in trying to get any sleep. There weren't any beds. And Petunia kept unearthing these heartsick moans from some deep region that missed her children. Kristal packed up her new luggage. She was folding a skirt, when out of the pocket fell the enameled brooch she had pinched from the jewelry store. She turned it over to examine the price tag. "Fifteen bucks. You want it?"

I shook my head. It was cold outside, but I had enough hot merchandise in my one suitcase to keep me nice and frantic through the winter.

She opened the window, letting in sounds of the morning rush hour, and tossed the brooch out. "Might kill somebody. Sometimes I get lucky and hit the head!" Her laugh died early. "No, that's not funny."

I did any damn thing she said. She accompanied me to the rental-car agency so that Graham would feel inhibited about public displays of affection. She turned away when he slipped the steamship ticket into my pocket and kissed my ear: "I love you. There's cash in the folder, too, with my address and phone number in London. Wire me if you have to miss the boat for any reason."

I drove along the waterfront in the rented station wagon, searching for the main office of this Polish ocean liner, where I could cash in my ticket. I had a legitimate passage in my pocket. I could go to England, and choose my course from there.

But the ship's doctor would say, "Whatever happens, don't leave her alone. If she's left alone she might be dangerous to herself."

I was so exhausted that my conscience was unpacking itself hopelessly wrinkled.

"It's not as if you don't have no choice!"

The cry bounced off the walls of the opposite shore and came back in echo, with the double negative ironed out: "It's not as if you have a choice!"

That night, Kristal chose a secluded space for me to park the station wagon while, no hands, she squeezed the last few drops out of the final hard-on at the Royale. She wouldn't permit me to come to work because Murphy might show up. I fell asleep curled in my sheepish coat on the front seat. In the back loomed the dark cliffs of Kristal's luggage and the humungous profile of Petunia.

At 4 A.M. I jerked awake. Kristal was drumming desperately on the frosty car window.

She slid in. "Drive! Quick! Peel out!"

I yanked the choke and the throttle out, and gunned the wagon into life.

With Kristal screaming directions and Petunia barking, I managed to lose the pursuing Turks' car.

Halfway through the Lincoln Tunnel, I inquired: "Where are we going?"

"I don't know," she scowled. "I'm not a magician. Jesus, I had about seven or twelve hustles all going, and I couldn't keep track of which streets I should avoid to get to the car when I came out. I ran into a big jam-up with two different guys I hardly remember, they were jumping on me, plus your fucking beserk boyfriend, who by the way could pass for the son of the werewolf, and then the Turkish fleet was after me—boy, it burns me. We shoulda got about three hundred dollars' worth of commissions on tickets if we stayed til Monday payday."

"But where are we going?"

"I don't care, just go. Here's the New Jersey Turnpike. Don't wake me or I'll murder you."

Soon she was dead to the world. Occupant temporarily DE-CEASED. Petunia slept also.

I was saved again, by the silence, just when I needed it. I was able to concentrate on remembering how to get home.

PART

II

It was midmorning when I skirted Washington, D. C., and drove into Arlington. Drizzle began to erase the already sketchy sun; Virginia's red clay soil, banking the thruway, clotted in the cold. Even the finest lawns in the neighborhood went all shabby; the red brick colonials looked damp as mudhuts.

I parked across the street from my home. In the front yard a small oriental girl was playing on an alien swingset. The name of the occupants was "WOO" and the brush-stroked letters were drooling whitewash down the side of the mailbox.

Kristal opened her eyes. "Where's this place?"

"Arlington. Virginia."

"You going back to your foster parents?"

"They don't live here anymore."

She hiked up and peered out the window at the yellow invasion across the street, turned her back to it and hunched down into her sleep again, snarling, "You must be permanently insane."

I rolled down my window, opened the car door softly and climbed out. Neon spores flashed in the film over my eyeballs. My legs wobbled so I had to hold onto the door handle a minute before I went around to unlock the tailgate. I unpacked one change of clothing and some toiletries from my single suitcase, stuffed them into my sleeping bag, rolled it up and tied it to the aluminum frame of my trusty old backpack. Petunia watched me lovelessly. After tossing the car keys onto the driver's seat, I walked to the firehouse, taking my old route, cutting through backyards, my head feeling like a globe off axis.

I knocked on the panel in one of the enormous garage doors. Inside, a bolt slid back, and gentle Lieutenant Dexter opened up. "Well, now, Randy Bates. Aren't you the sneaky one. Jeez, you've growed every whichway."

Dex used to put so much greasy tonic on his black hair that when I'd be passing dinner rolls at the firemen's long table, I'd come around and sprinkle salt on his head, and after I sat down we'd all rag him about his dandruff. For a whole year he thought he had scalp rot. Now the white flecks in his hair were real from age, he was fatter, and I could look straight into his sweet oyster-color eyes, instead of up at him. I glanced at his new stripes. "Hey, Dex, good buddy, I see you made Captain," I slapped his buttocks. That didn't use to make him jump a foot.

"Gettin too old for the hanky-pank . . . don't you look the cute little tramp, where're you stoppin in from? You come from down Florida? Your cheeks is nice and pink."

"No, New York." My face had stoked up a bad flush when I stepped inside the heated garage. The smell of fried bacon was so thick I had to sit down on the gleaming bumper of one of the giant "Viva LaFrances." "Where is everybody?" I asked, swallowing repeated alarms from my stomach. "Where's Sergeant Wayne-o? He still married to that old broad that won't put up?"

Dex laughed nervously. "Yah, he ain't changed, he'll be in tonight. Guess you'll miss him. Otherwise it's a whole new crew. Everyone's left is a bad bunch, murderous, raunchy, and mean. We're having breakfast upstairs in a few minutes, otherwise I'd stay and jaw with you. . . ." He grew anxious as I let my backpack slide off my shoulders onto the oily floor.

"I'm not hungry, I just need sleep bad. I didn't know my folks had moved, see. Do you know where they went to?"

"Nope. Didn't even know they'd left town til the wife and me wanted to go on a cruise last month. Sara called up the travel agency and they said Inger wasn't running the show anymore, she'd sold out and moved. West somewhere, I think. Listen, Randy, you remember we're not allowed to have girls upstairs, otherwise I'd let you snooze, but—"

"Oh c'mon, Dex, you used to let me sleep over all the time," I begged, turn down the flame, my brain is melting like a record in a car trunk.

"Aw, baby, that was a couple years ago. You passed for a boy, then. Now you look like a real doll, and there's guys here who can't get any sleep nights with a pretty girl in the next bunk."

"I can still pass for a boy. Tell'm the long hair is cause I'm a hippie. I'll even cut it right now crewcut. I just got to lay down, Dex."

He lowered his voice. "We also got some new boys that are real weirdos walkin around with Bibles. Baptists. You can't even get away with a can of beer at supper—"

"I'm gonna faint, good buddy, no shit."

He tried to help me up. "Come on, Randy, you can make it. I just bought a Lincoln that's outside. You can use the back seat."

My eyes rolled up to see the pleated trap in the ceiling open around the brass pole. A voice called, "Cap'n Dexter! They're blessing the chow up here! You'd better shimmy on up and grab a seat."

"Reet!" he shouted. "Hold on!" The trap closed again, as my eyes continued to roll backwards and I collapsed.

The fever rose to high tide, driving at me in cupped white-cap waves, my frail white cells sucked down in the virus undertow, the bile battering the ribs of my rowboat—I had to make it, haul myself up onto the bow-bone and bail out—

"I know she's here!" I heard Kristal's treble yell. "And I'm going to ride around busting every alarm box I see if you don't let me talk to her!"

I could see a halo of electric light through a woven cloth fog, and fought toward it.

Dex had laid me out on my sleeping bag inside the lifeboat for flood emergency, then he'd snapped the tarpaulin cover over me, all except one corner. I tore at the canvas, the snaps gave way, rat-tat-tat, I reared my ghastly head over the side of the boat and, in front of everyone, heaved forth. Kristal hopped aside so my puke washed past her boots and lapped at the tread of a towering LaFrance tire. I fell back into the boat and gasped.

"Thank you, gentlemen," Kristal said, as male hands dragged me out and hurriedly packed my gear. "Jesus, Randy, every time I run into you you're barfing for some reason. . . . Just prop her up in the passenger seat, I'll take care of her from here. It's some kind of Chink flu goin around New York. Makes you horny. I guess that's why she ran out of the hotel room while I was napping and came over here, to be with all you gorgeous men."

Doors slammed, and the motor started. "I knew the fireplace was the place you'd go," she said. "Scared the shit outa me, wakin up in the afternoon in the car with the dark coming on. It's five now, I hope we can get a doctor at this hour."

"Where's Tuney," I muttered.

"I sold her. One hundred and fifty bucks. Don't worry, I'll get her back."

"Where's my parents."

"We'll find out. Hush. I'm tryin to remember where I saw that Holiday Inn."

I'm missing a Saturday, Sunday, Monday, and Tuesday, in Room 128. I have some impressions from this time, for instance Kristal and the doctor talking. "No, I never catch the little things like flu," she was saying, "only the big stuff like hiatal hernias gets me. Lemme ask you, could you also give me a prescription for a diet pill for myself? I just got a call from my agent that I got this movie part where they want me to lose thirty pounds. See this picture? Sure this was me, the Hungarian Tempest, when I was stripping, just eight years ago. That's what I should look like now if I lose weight. My titties always stay the same. Listen, I have this cold, doctor, that's why my chest is always swollen! . . ."

Then Kristal on the phone, near my pillow: "Hello, room service? Is the bar still open?"

((126))

The TV was always on. Talk shows, old movies, morning newscasts, game shows, medical dramas, provided eerie subplots for my dreams. Even when the volume was off, its shrill subliminal whine wasn't silent, and added to my coma the torment of high-pitched videotone. Sometimes I heard Kristal talk to the screen: "Stupid twat, pick Door Number Three! The god damn Datsun's behind Three!"

I woke once when I heard a glass bottle shattering. Then glass scraping on the tiled bathroom floor. Being swept up. Another bottle nearby, the wheeze of the twist-top opening. Kristal on the phone near my head: "Hello? Coca-Cola? My sister just drank a bottle of Coke with some glass splinters in it! I'm just so hysterical—" Later, I heard a man's voice. Kristal whispering urgently, "The doctor said she'd recover but I'm crazy with worry. I wonder if a piece of glass doesn't stay stuck in you forever. I wonder if I should get x-rays or call my lawyer, you know? Could you call me after you examine the bottle and advise me what your company does in these cases?"

Sailing back and forth to the bathroom, on Kristal's helpful shoulder. Being rolled onto her bed while maid service changed my sodden sheets. Washcloths rowing back and forth over my forehead. Room service came and went, came and went. Tea, Coke, orange juice for me. Food, coffee, and cognac for Kristal, ugly heaps of potato salad, foul pie, plates on which an escaped orangutan had left furious yellow finger paintings in egg yolk, and, tossing to the opposite shore of my bed, I'd look down and retch neatly into the plastic Holiday Inn ice bucket.

I don't know if Kristal ever slept, or if I was the reason for her round-the-clock watch. One morning she said it was Wednesday and that I was much better.

In the wake of delirium and the body's afterglow, I grew desperately horny. My hands found a permanent home in my crotch. Nothing seemed to relieve the continuous matinee of dreams involving anchormen, game show hosts, family doctors, Negro comedians, and garish radioactive creatures. I was eating some solid food now and I writhed with energy, my legs making slow cantering motions while I slept.

Kristal decided to clean me up. She sat me in the bathtub, turned on the tap, and left to answer a phone call. The water gushed into my lap. When the level reached my hipbones, I adjusted the faucets to get a narrow skittering stream, kicked the door shut, and lay back. I slung one lengthy leg over the edge of the tub and braced the other leg against the tiles over the tap. My emaciated mons rose like a dormant volcano above the water, the blond bush matted and twinkling as the stream perked around my clit.

I started working on one of the better fever fantasies. A game show host was humiliating me. "No, I'm afraid that's a wrong answer, Randy, so I'll have to ask you to slip off your pants and spread out on our penalty table over here. . . ." He cast away his mike, bent me back onto a green felt table, forced my legs apart, and went down on me. I could see his contemptuous eyes over the ridge of my mons, as his tongue flashed around my cunt. The sound of the tap water was drowned out by the studio audience which screamed and booed and cheered, with the off camera emcee blaring: ". . . yes, this whore can be yours for nothing as she reclines bucket seats calfback GT-7 motorama pornographic cunt-sucker from the famous penis catalog this girl will do anything, even in front of millions of you viewers at home she's so disgusting she can't help herself"—the host slickered at my clit with lightning nudges, my hips bucked—"she's coming now, she's going to come did you ever see anyone so horny you people, what a cheap bitch absolutely no shame, but that's the game and that's how we play it—look at those thighs shudder, her eyes rolling back in ecstasy, fucking herself to the last fucking—" my clit kicked, my body sprang apart, as I came, floundering, live from studio city, and the waters closed over my head.

Kristal was laughing her head off in the doorway. "I had to hang up the phone, I thought you were being attacked in here! Did you come off good?"

Hung limply over the side of the tub, I hacked and sneezed bathwater onto the mat.

"You better not start spittin up again." She shut off the tap and sat on the toilet lid, swigging Courvoisier. "Nothing to be ashamed of, silly. I started when we were little kids in Budapest. We used the rocks people had for doorstops, we'd sit and rub our pussies on'm. I never tried it with the faucet. I usually just make up a story, and right at the right time I grab hold of it and come off in three seconds flat. . . . I heard from chicks who've had to do a lot of time in jail that the shower or the tub's the only way, though. They call it 'Daddy Water,' honest to God. Look at you, your hair's all wet from dirty water and you're gonna catch cold."

She wrapped me in towels and tucked me in bed, where I sweated the last sweat. "It's most certainly not worth it to drown yourself, just to get a climax," she scolded.

When I woke, the virus was over. All the goblins had split, the fading sound of their vicious gossip whisked about my inner ear. Room service knocked, arriving with my toast, hot chocolate, and jello as per Mrs. Pace's orders. Kristal herself was gone. The waiter said it was ten at night.

I woke up about five hours later. "I'm hungry." Kristal was sitting on her bed and counting cash.

"You're all better," she said, quickly stuffing the money into her purse. "I brought you a Egg McMuffin in the bag there near your nose. I'm going to sleep til I get a wake-up call at three this afternoon. We're having an early supper with some of my girl-friends."

"This is an Italian joint we're going to, but you can order, like, a side order of plain noodles with butter oughta be easy for you to keep down," said Kristal, steering the station wagon expertly around roads of my childhood neighborhood.

"I didn't know you had any friends around here." I was weak and cranky.

"I been picking up some easy bucks managing a massage parlor and I ran into someone I used to strip with. D. C. is cleaning itself up for the Bicentennial so all the customers have to come out here to the suburbs to get their rocks taken care of. This is *the* time to make a fortune. You'll see."

* * *

((129))

"For sure, honey, we get a lot of dignitaries now cause they closed most of the massage parlors in the capital," nodded Daiquiri, swabbing up red squid sauce with her bread.

The Joytown Spa & Sauna's manager was in the hospital, so when Kristal took over she changed all the masseuses' names to liqueurs. The other girls at the table, Kahlua and Saki, were very young and pretty, while Daiquiri more resembled a whore, like Kristal. They all seemed experienced at changing their names frequently. Kristal dubbed her old friend Daiquiri "cause she's a butch! she's a great big bull dike-ery! But she ain't frozen. She proposed marriage to me last night, but I told her she wasn't rich enough. I'm savin it for prosperity!"

"She wouldn't even let me look at her pussy," Daiquiri mourned.

"That guy I had last night in the English Room was plenty rich. He was some big dignitary or lawyer I think, and very in-peccably dressed. He had me pour *tabasco* sauce in his enema, and he kept cryin, 'Mommy, Mommy, I promise to be good,' then he came all over himself, put on his suit, and was all . . . busi-ness as usual! He put two hundred dollars on the books and gave me a hundred dollars' tip. I'm really impressed at the overall class of gentlemen we're getting."

"We're real glad you're around to do English," said Kahlua. "I can't handle those dudes. I start crackin up and ruin the whole mood. They never ask for me again."

"I'd keep a straight face," Daiquiri advised.

"About the only thing straight about you!" said Kristal. "En-glish is pure gravy, seriously. Not only do they pay the best, but if you know what to do, they can be very useful around the place. You order them to mop up the floors and clean the toilets and whatever have you. Then when they get hard, you just 'command' them to jerk themselves off."

"You don't even give them a local? For that kind of bread?" Kahlua gasped.

"I only take the customers I don't have to touch. That's where

((130))

I'm at, that's it. If a guy says 'What now?' I answer, 'Take the situation *in hand*.' "

"You really have to know what you're doing," Daiquiri cautioned. "Like, if you untie them too soon, all of a sudden he slings the rope around your neck, and then you're screwed. There was a girl in the Shower of Gold got killed that way."

"Wow," said Saki, who was Chinese. "Incwedible."

Daiquiri sized me up. "Sandy would do very good at Joytown."

"Her name's Randy," said Kristal. "I was tellin her what a ball you and me had, stripping at the Pink Slipper, all the scams we had goin."

Daiquiri grinned affectionately. "You and me and Felice. So much has changed. The Slipper's closed six years ago. All the old burlesque clubs are gone, you know."

"Bullshit," Kristal retorted. "My agent just sent me a wire and I'm opening at the 402 Club this spring—get your hand off my leg!"

The two friends punched each other's arms and waved steak knives. "Let's get thrown outa here like old times," Daiquiri giggled. "What became of your little friend Felice, anyhow?"

Kristal put away her knife. "I haven't the vaguest," she answered, in an odd stony voice. "Hey—miss? Get me another double Courvoisier and a Coke."

"You were so right to get off the circuit way back then," Daiquiri sighed. "All the bookings really started dryin up after you disappeared. Nobody at the Pink Slipper knew what happened to you. I put money on it, I said, 'With her brains and her build she'll come waltzing back any day from now married to a rich old millionaire celebrity. I still can't understand why you didn't marry that architect that worshipped you."

Kristal's mouth tightened. "I'm so mad at myself. He was seventy-four. He'd made a mint designing bridges, his previous wife was dead, no family or nothin, and all I had to do was play daughter and get him to eat his vegetables. He was just so nice. Boy, did he want to marry me. . . . And he died of a heart attack a year later. I wouldn'ta even had to wait the year. I'd have fucked him on his wedding night til he had the heart attack!" All the girls howled. "Well, it's not funny. I was young, I was stupid. Shit, I was a virgin, you know? I wanted to save myself for somebody special, not some old fart."

I kept sneaking looks at Kahlua. Her face reminded me of someone unpleasant but I couldn't place who. It didn't make me any more sociable. Here I sat, barely six miles from where I grew up, twirling slimy pasta on a fork, in the company of four women from a life my stomach disapproved of. I wouldn't have to sit through this odious discussion if not for Kristal. I grew very irritable, and fed up, with her and her stories and her new choice of career. Now she was yakking about some famous Washington socialite she'd hustled for a Mercedes nine years ago. "... She was the daughter of the famous Russian writer Checkoff." She turned to me for confirmation. "Right? Her name was Darya Checkoff and she had a guilt hang-up, because she'd had a illegitimate daughter, so she was into S & M. Not really heavy, for example her cat o' nine tails was for God's sake *nylon*—"

"—Chekhov didn't have a daughter," I interrupted.

"What do you mean?" She was horrified. "That's who she said her father was, somebody Checkoff." Everyone waited, suddenly uncomfortable with my presence at the table.

I rolled my napkin and inserted it into its ring. "Anton Chekhov didn't have no children. I did a book report on him. I remember my English teacher telling me that."

Kahlua looked down at her lap and flicked her napkin significantly. "Believe me, Randy would remember *anything* about *Mister Wilder*. I always wondered, did you give the baby up for adoption?"

If I hadn't just recovered from being sick, I would have thrown up. My mouth was all for it, dropping into an open position. *"What?"*

"Maybe she lied," Daiquiri consoled Kristal.

Kristal: "Who?"

Daiquiri: "Darya Checkoff."

Kahlua deposited her napkin in the remains of her canneloni. "I was in the same grade as you at George Mason. I remember your mother made a big, big stink and got Mister Wilder fired. She said the reason you ran away from home was because he got you pregnant. She didn't let up until the school deep-sixed him. I was only asking you, what happened to the baby?"

"It's not true!" I hollered.

"Oh, okay, forget it. I was only curious because I was pregnant, too, when you ran off. You want to see a picture of my little girl?"

"How could anybody believe anything Inger said? She's a fuckin alcoholic! I'd like to murder her. Do you have any idea where my folks moved to?"

"Uh-uh, didn't know they'd moved. I live in Pleasant Valley now. I only work around here."

"I remember you, but I forget your name."

She smiled tartly. "Well, I wasn't a blond then, and my name sure wasn't Kahlua. Anyway we never hung out with the same crowd. You and me was never formally introduced. You were one of the rich snotty bookworm types."

"I wasn't rich."

"Maybe you didn't get no allowance, sob sob. Your mother was rich enough. Even if you always dressed funky." She lit a cigarette and resisted throwing the match at me. "So, are you coming to work at Joytown?"

"Maybe," Kristal jumped in. "She worked the dance hall scene up north like you wouldn't believe."

I inadvertently flicked a stray bread crumb at Kahlua. "I made enough money to keep traveling and visiting friends as I please, til I come into my enormous inheritance."

Kristal kicked my boot under the table. "Randy always gives in at the last minute. Wait til she sees with her eyes how much money I made last night."

"Incwedible," said Saki, spraying Binaca into her yawn.

"I hope it lasts," Daiquiri brooded. "Lately they're busting even some of the massage parlors in the suburbs for the Bicentennial and the elections."

((133))

"Not while I'm manager, hell no. We've already got a sauna, and I'll just score a couple of exercycles to make it more like a health joint. I never got busted. I'm so clean it's a shame."

"At the Stardust they make you take a polygraph test before they hire you. Can I borrow your spray?" Kahlua asked Saki. "I always taste that stockbroker dude for a whole day afterwards, even after all this garlic. His come is so acid. I think he must have a drinking problem."

"I'm gonna keep calling you Sandy," Daiquiri smiled at me warmly. "You look like a Sandy."

"Jesus," Kristal breathed as she drove us back alone, "now I see what you mean. Your foster mother was some bitch. And here what's her name, Kahlua, thought you had it so good."

My attention was elsewhere. No friends came to mind for me to visit, since most of my friends were Murphy's, but my boast was an honest boast in that I probably had enough cash rightfully mine, from the northern hustles, to keep traveling. How much, I had no idea. I'd never bothered to count.

"Kahlua's a very lower-class person," Kristal prodded at my silence. "You know, her idea of a hustle is blowin the guy behind the counter at the Seven-Eleven to sell her a six pack after hours on Sunday night." (I could remember Kristal handing me my share of the profits in New York. Then I'd folded it up. And put it somewhere.) "I had to tell them we'd come to work at the Joytown. They woulda gone beserk if they thought I wasn't going to show up tonight. Hello?"

"Don't quit on my account." (And put it in the pocket of something.)

"You're in a hell of a mood. I only took the job because I thought you were gonna settle down here, in your home. I didn't have no place else to go, I don't make plans for myself." (Rolled in the sleeve of the slinky blue dress in the suitcase I left behind in the car on the morning I walked off to the firehouse. I'd walked off without a cent.) "You were sick, in case you forgot, kiddo. I wasn't about to leave you stranded. I like for someone to need me. Managing is a good gig. . . .

". . . I don't blame you for being turned off by the business, it's certainly sicko," she continued chattering after we got back to the hotel room. "The women don't behave properly and so the customers have no respect in their treatment of them," she called from the bathroom, where she was styling a wig. I'd found my money and was quickly counting the thick bouffant of bills. ". . . I really have to change my way of life, that's what I'm thinking. My whole problem is, I stop and bend over and pick up the easy buck if I see it layin in the street, even if there's a truck comin at me." I was astounded, reckoning my total at $1,836. ". . . No more massage parlors, no more dance halls, I don't need that shit. I'm a lady. I have always carried myself that way. So from now on, everything first class." She came out of the bathroom before I could put the money away. "Oh, by the way. I owe you five hundred dollars from your half of marrying that Turk." She rustled in her handbag and licked a finger through her own cash account. "One hundred, two, three—you know where I was going to drive to, if you hadn't dragged me down here? Las Vegas. Ever been there? Oh, you got to come. Vegas is like . . . just the most beautiful plushest magic dream city, if you like action day and night, someplace where you can cut loose, at the shows, the casinos. . . . I'm going to triple quadruple my money there so I won't have to work for a year. Why don't you come along? I'll give you a lift. It's on your way to Los Angeles."

"Why am I going to L. A.? Thanks." I collated the five hundred-dollars bills into my stash.

"I thought you wanted to find your foster parents, to get them to tell you who your real parents are." About to snap my suitcase shut, I froze. "Guess you don't know where they are, oh wise-ass teenybopper." I turned. She ignored me, dialing room service. ". . . Double shots, two of'm, right. And some hot chocolate for my bratty little sister. . . . Yeah, she's much better, just needs more sleep and some heroin. Do you serve peanuts?" I waited until she hung up. "What're you starin at me like a wounded mouse for? I told you I'd take care of everything for you, didn't I? When you look at me like that, I wonder what the hell I do it for. For an ulcer, right?" She huffed into the bathroom and closed the door halfway. I heard her unzip her slacks, sit on the john. She called, "When I sold Tuney I talked to one of your old neighbors that knew your mom—your foster-mom. Inger told her your foster dad was transferred to some naval base near L. A. Now, I know that's gotta be Long Beach, cause my old man and me used to live near there on this ranch—listen, call Long Beach information and see if your folks are listed."

I obeyed. The operator, muffled by the Pacific surf, reported a Bates, Mrs. I., in Long Beach, but could not give out an unlisted number.

"You can still find them easy," said Kristal, as if she already knew, as she emerged from the bathroom. "You drive south from L. A. to the naval base and look for your foster father. If you're in a rush, you could catch a plane to L. A. tonight."

A rendezvous with my former family gave me a certain dread. I needed more time on the lam. I needed to gas up on good times.

"Or you can drive west with me. We'll have tons of fun. It won't cost you a nickel if we stay in the same hotel rooms." It occurred to me that if I had over $2000 Kristal must have seven times that. ". . . Strictly first class. Hiltons, the whole way!"

"Okay." My head began to sing off-key until I sank it into my pillow.

Kristal draped a blanket over me. "Poor mouse. It's your first day out of bed. You can't go anywhere anyway."

Kristal rolled down the car window and whistled, softly. "Tuney!" The voice echoed in the early morning vapor. "Petunia!" not too loud, in the 7 A.M. chrysalis of a suburban Saturday.

Her chain taut, the Great Dane galloped in place, spraying driveway pebbles back. She panted. Laurel leaves dripped.

"Here, girl." Our station wagon puffed at the curb, on the edge of a lawn. Long morose barks bowled from Petunia's throat. A window shade inside the red brick house lifted.

Kristal tromped on the accelerator, and we took off for the thruway without the dog.

"I told the lady not to chain her up! I never had any trouble getting her back ever. I've had Tuney since she was a puppy. I'm the only one she loves. Usually she can break the collar. . . . Aw, fuck." A deep and spreading shame seemed to foul up her sight, and she switched on the windshield wipers as the sun dawned uselessly on the Pennsylvania Turnpike. "Reach behind you and get rid of her blanket. It smells up the whole car."

Maybe we'd been too merry, when we checked out of the Holiday Inn that morning, after staying an extra day for the goodwill settlement check from Coca-Cola to arrive.

"Eight hundred thirty dollars!" Kristal had whooped. "That's two hundred more'n I ever made off a soda company! Must be the—which are we in, the recession, or a depression? Or inflation? All of'm, right? Well, it's cause you were so convincing. Normally I have to play it by myself: 'Hello? R. C.? Seven-Up? I'm sick, I'm dyin!' . . . But with you doing the sick act I didn't hardly strain myself. That Coke rep was so petrified we'd sue—remember? . . . No, course you don't, you were busy dyin." She skipped off to cash the check, and returned with loads of packages from Sears. "I'm still a size nine! I lost five pounds this week!" We went to bed early.

Tuney's plaid blanket ballooned away, and snagged on the center strut.

"How come you're so depressed?" Kristal scowled. "It's not your dog just got stabbed in the back."

"The woman you sold Tuney to, that house . . . she was my gym teacher in grade school. She was the only gym teacher I ever had who didn't hassle me."

"You didn't like gym class?"

"I couldn't do anything. My legs were so tall I couldn't even touch my toes in warm-ups."

"Listen, I couldn't do jumpin jacks, I'd just get so embarrassed. My titties'd flop around."

"That's nothing," I grinned, "I could never climb all the way up those ropes that hung from the ceiling. Every time, halfway up, I couldn't get my legs to grip, my thighs felt all funny, and I'd have to stop. I'd hang there going 'hee hee hee,' and it took me about five more years to figure out why my underpants were so wet after I came down. I mean, I knew I hadn't gone to the bathroom in them—"

Kristal was giggling, out of control. "Oh, oh, stop! I'm flippin out!" The car hulaed in the center lane. "You're a real freak, you know? Gettin off on gym ropes, bathtubs . . . Watcha got hid in the sleeping bag? A slice-it, dice-it machine?" I reached to steady the wheel as we both tossed with laughter.

"I guess I've dug orgasms since I was born," I said, calming down. "If I wanted something out of my fa—my foster father, I'd hike up my crinolines when I sat on his lap, and squirm a lot."

Kristal asked curiously. "Do you get climaxes with dudes when you screw?"

"For sure." I was somewhat surprised at the question. "I never come the first time, if it's somebody new. I have to get used to the guy, his style, whatever. Sometimes it's important I get to like him."

"Hm. I always thought hippies didn't give a fuck."

"Sometimes all I have to be is horny. Like lately. See, I'm used to getting laid every day, with Murphy"—she gunned the motor and punched cleaning fluid onto the windshield—"and it's been three weeks since I balled him, or anyone in fact, and blowjobs don't count because—"

"—I was good at running," she said. "I had to be fast because my father's favorite sport was waitin for the god damn streetcar to take off and catchin up to it when it was a half-mile down the block. I remember one time I hit my brother over the head with a alphabet block and Pop chased me all over Budapest. But I beat the shit out of him. At the House of the Sacred Shepherd, the nuns couldn't believe I was so fast for someone so chesty. The school taped my boobs with a ace bandage so they wouldn't jog up and down, and I'd win all the competition races. You know how? I'd make believe my father was chasin me!"

"I wish that was my problem. I hate being flat."

"My tits would look wrong on your type build. You can wear a whole different kind of sexy outfits than me, cause you don't have to wear a bra ever. Look in back of your seat, there's a shopping bag. See it? I got you some presents from Sears yesterday. I wasn't going to lay them on you til we got to Detroit, but what the hell."

"Detroit? Shouldn't we keep south to avoid snow?" I started opening one of the three cartons from the bag.

"I want to stop off and just get a quick look at some of my old stomping places, say hi to some people. How do you like that navy blue gown?"

I didn't want to be utterly truthful. The material was a synthetic nylon, slippery and cheap. There was a smarmy little red heart over the left bust dart. "It looks like what a fourteen-year-old virgin would wear to an open-house party."

"That's the whole effect." She was excited. "That's the kind of clothes you should wear to attract men. I wear the more smutty slutty stuff because I'm buxom. I attract men with money. You attract the type that will fall in love with your sweetness 'n light." The smallest box contained a curly brown dynel wig. "That's a gypsy shag look. Sometimes you'll want to look more exotic." It was beginning to sound like she had some kind of morbid designs for me. "The wig goes with the other long dress in there, the jersey one." This last dress had a low-cut tight green bodice with candy stripes down the skirt, and it shocked my hand, due to static in the air.

"Thanks," I murmured. "Only I wish you wouldn't keep spending your money on me."

"I didn't pay for them. I used my Sears charge card. There wasn't no Bloomingdale's branch in D. C." I didn't bother to ask how she got her Sears credit card. "That dress there will show up your titties perfect. Cause you've got a nice pair. They're not pointy like most small ones. They got a nice round shape. Like those golden delicious . . . nectarine things. . . ."

"I wonder if guys spend as much time rapping about their penises as girls talk about their busts," I put the presents back in the bag.

"I should sincerely hope not," Kristal retorted, squinting at an overhead sign. "What a repulsive idea, couple of dudes lounging around admiring each other's peckers. Unless they was queer. Even then, I'd rather hear a bunch of dykes sit around comparing dildoes."

"Not if you met the ones the year I joined the Navy."

"You ever make it with chicks?" Kristal turned to me.

"Just once. I was drunk. They caught me in bed with a lieutenant. It wasn't fair, so I ratted on all the real stone lezzies in the corps. The investigation committee gave me a general discharge, but the bitches put 'homosexual' on my civilian record. That's why I can't ever qualify for any secretary or government jobs—the firemen are allowing female volunteers, and I can't even apply, and I swear I've never been gay."

"All it takes is once."

"I don't count that. I don't think it counts if you're closing your eyes and pretending the other chick is a boy."

"God damn it! I gotta pee like gangbusters." She swerved. "Crunch up all that tissue from the boxes, so we can throw it out at a gas station next exit. And you take the wheel afterwards." She frowned at the signs and gnawed on her upper lip til her front teeth went pink with lipstick.

We checked into a double room at the Detroit Airport Hilton at 9 P.M. There had been snow flurries that morning. I went straight to bed and Kristal went down to the Hangar Dining Room.

The room phone woke me up a few hours later. "It's crawling with businessmen in the bar here," Kristal's voice cooed. "Get your ass all sexied up and come down!"

"I'm asleep."

"Listen, these guys are all here on conventions, they're all fucked up on jet lag! They hallucinate that any girl who isn't a waitress is gotta be a hooker and they're all drunk and they stink with money. I've got this Fred or Ed or Ted all set up, and he's a architect. Here's the story I told him, so that when you come down—"

"C'mon, Kristal. I'm falling out. What're you talking about."

"I'm *talk*-ing about do you want to make some money."

"Whafor."

"You need a lot of capital to gamble in Vegas, believe me, it's the only way you'll beat the house."

"I'm not gonna gamble in Vegas. . . ." I began to slur off.

"He wants to meet you." My breathing was regular. "All right, I'll tell him we'll have breakfast with him tomorrow."

". . . you can't beat th'house. . . ." The door was always locked.

She hung up.

"I'm a widow, myself," said Kristal, to Al the architect. "I love this jelly. What is it. Mixed fruit? I'll give you one of my strip pictures if your wife won't mind."

"I won't show it to her," Al laughed. "What about you, Randy? Are you married or are you just running wild?"

"No." I had been aloof all through breakfast.

"She's single," Kristal intervened. "She's got that innocent face, but don't let her fool you. She does things sometimes that turns me *crizzum* red."

"Really? Like what?" Al grew rakish.

He was quite good-looking, though not my type. "I sit on her nose," I said. Kristal stifled laughter, but she was very upset with me later, after Al saw us to our door. "You were very rude," she stormed. "You turned him right off. And he was all set to spend plenty more money on us."

"I can buy my own breakfast." I tucked my toothbrush into my suitcase. "Why didn't you invite him into the room? I would've left you alone."

She was scandalized. "You got to be a crazy fool. Never invite a man into the room—that's how chicks get raped. While you're with me, no man gets in. Jesus, you don't know the first thing about watching out for yourself. And stop packing, cause we're not splitting. We're goin to Port Huron."

"Where," I sighed, my back to her. My eyes snapped her face in the mirror, then dipped stealthily down to a pile of her strip pictures, in the open drawer before me.

"It's about an hour north of here. Port Huron's a border town, right near the Canadian line. Nothin but men. I used to strip there at the 402 Club. There was four girls on stage and five bar hustlers, and about forty-five, fifty men in the audience—we made out like *champs*. . . ." The photos were all subtitled "KRISTAL BALL, The Hungarian Tempest." The top one showed her crouching on a mess of tulle, her black hair teased up to a two-foot crest, her expression immodest, nipples covered by little silver cones. Her breasts held their own, but her hands were cupped underneath in case they fell. She wore studded bikini underpants and shiny mules with spike heels. ". . . It's nothing but factories up there, automobile parts and crap, and the guys are either single or they can't go home til weekends to be with their families here in Detroit. It's like in the Old West, no women except the strippers. The men have all this money and nothin to spend it on except a show."

"So?" The next photo had Kristal cornered and snarling on a tulle-covered stool, and wearing the same underpants plus a lamé Merry Widow top festooned with jingle bells. ". . . I'd like to see the old haunts and check out a few friends, that's it. And maybe we'll trip over a little money without any strain to ourselves—god damn it, all you got is jeans and formals. I forgot to get you a nice casual look, like this pants suit." She sucked in her breath. I traveled from the eight-by-ten glossy back to the Tempest in the mirror. She labored with the zipper on her red pants.

She was older than her photos, and puffier in odd places, as if her whole body had been on a crying jag. The small teeth and the grin between the uppers and lowers were the same. The double-dare starpoints, in the eyes' gleam, were sharper.

"You're a size nine, you wear this suit," she exhaled. "I ate too much breakfast."

She continued her lecture on bulk capital in gambling as she drove north, under the freezing sun. All I knew was, red made me look loud, and the shaggy wig made me feel criminal.

"So, you *should* look somewhat whorish in this town. And if anyone asks, you're a nightclub singer. I always say I'm in a whorish line of work. I'm a stripper, or a bunny, or a madam. Something to the effect that he thinks I can hardly wait to open my legs for him. But you never *act* whorish, cause you're lady-like inside. Never bring up sex, let him. If it comes to it, say you're a virgin. Or you're not a virgin but you're very old-fashioned. It's possible to have a whorish job and still be pure. . . ."

To our right, Lake St. Clair's shore appeared. Fishing shanties were scattered over the white ice. On our left, a snowmobile shot through the entrance of a trailer park.

"Okay, Kristal," I said. "What are you really trying to get through to me?"

"How to attract men. What else."

"I never had any trouble attracting men."

"Course not. You don't know any other way to attract men except by lettin them get you into trouble!" she scoffed.

"What the fuck does that mean?"

We passed billboards warped and bowed by the winter blast, closed-up Dogs 'N' Suds, Big Boys, boarded-up Victorian summer homes lining the lakeshore. "I'm not some pawn in your plot to overthrow the world," I added as an inspiration.

"Whyn't you shove yourself up your cunt! Christ! You'd think I was tryin to molest the morals of a minor!" She slammed the palm of her hand on the steering wheel. "I'm only tryin to give you a little technique, a little style, so you'll never have to worry about money again, and so no one can ever take advantage of you the rest of your life! 'What the fuck does that mean?'! I'm doin it for my health! For my high blood pressure! Hey, bitch! You got it better with me than you ever had in your mother's stomach!"

It was the last time for a long time we had this boring argument.

Making brazen U-turns in the midst of traffic, Kristal drove up

((143))

and down the same block on Broadway, the main drag of Port Huron. "I know this is right. I swear. The club's here—the same spot as that crummy beer bar. Watch out for cops, I'm gonna make another U-ey."

While she chased her tail, I had an opportunity to study the town. It didn't have the frontier atmosphere that Kristal had described. The men on the street didn't look famished for pleasure. I didn't see any prominent hard-ons. But then again people were bundled up too cozy to tell.

"This is pe-posperous." She parked, and we ran shivering into the Kresge's five and ten. She propelled me toward the cafeteria. "I'm hungry. Grab a tray. Have some of that Italian dish." The waitress poised a spoon over the sink where steam was escaping through the cracks in the thick red scab which protected the spaghetti.

"Coffee, please," I said.

"That's all?" Kristal pushed her tray briskly down to the stuffed peppers. "One of those, some bread and butter, and a diet cola. Is there a yellow pages and a phone in here?" The waitress pointed to the back of the store. "Here's a five, Randy, get us that booth over there."

Minutes later she returned, sat down to her lunch, and snapped open a compact mirror from her purse. "Is it the fluorescent light or do I have too much makeup on?"

"You don't need all that black liner. . . ."

"Got to keep your eyelids warm, up in these parts. Long as we're in this store, I'm going to buy some of that natural-look junk. . . . What's all this food for?" She pushed her tray across the table to me. "You know what? The 402 Club isn't listed in the phone book."

"Are we going back to Detroit now?"

"Not so fast, kiddo. It must have changed names and moved to some area of town where there's more luxury. Miss?" she called to the elderly cashier. "What happened to that night club that used to be across the street?" Intrigued, the lady approached our booth. "Luxury type entertainment—the name was the 402."

(((144)))

"Well, I haven't lived here s'long. There's the Rat Shack cross Broadway there. Sort of a get-together bar. It has dancing, I'm told, and a nice band."

"That's the place. Thank you so very much."

After the cashier retreated, Kristal bared her teeth. "The *Rat* Shack? Anyhow, it's the 402, all right. Wait til you see the inside."

We waited at a table in the Rat Shack for two hours, when the regular crowd began to show, and "The Dodge Boys," the house band, was due to play.

"See that? We're gettin cruised right and left," Kristal said under-breath. "Stop chewin your hangnails, it's so ugly. You're nervous. Stop drinking coffee and order a drink."

"I'm trying to stay awake for the strippers."

"Okay, smartass, so it ain't a burlesque club any more." She ordered me an Irish coffee. "That's an up and a down at the same time, because you need to shape up."

The tables were filling up with stag girls, and the few un-escorted men casually started to play the field. Kristal and I certainly looked exotic. Almost everybody else was young, wore jeans, and drank beer.

"I know just who to call," she snapped her fingers. "This guy I was engaged to for a couple of weeks. His mom's Hungarian, she loves me. Joe'll know where the club moved."

"Ask him if there's a commune near here. I want to do some sightseeing, too."

"Don't have no more of that drink. It's makin you sarcastic." She sped off to find a pay phone. I ordered a second Irish coffee. The half maraschino cherry and the scoop of Reddiwip on top was deposited to my empty stomach, and the whiskey and coffee went towards my sarcasm. The band jump-started into their first number. A strange finger twirled into my curls.

"Is that a wig?"

Under the man's neatly clipped moustache, white light shafted from his teeth. He wore suede nicely. I gathered he was the town Omar Sharif. Several tables were full of girls glaring at me.

He sat down and put his lips to my ear so he wouldn't be forced to shout over the music. "My name's Barry. I've never seen you in here before."

"I just blew into town. Name's Wiggy."

He laughed, "The skinny girl in red with the wig-hat on," and ordered a round of drinks. "I'm an unlicensed chiropractor. What do you do?"

"I'm a night club singer," I answered, forgetting exactly why I had been instructed to say this. God help you, I addressed myself, have you become *warped*.

"What sort of music do you sing?"

I wobbled out a few bars of "Raindrops Keep Fallin' on My Head" as my third Irish coffee arrived.

"You're funny," he grinned. "I like you." I scarfed the half-cherry and buried my muzzle in the whipped cream topping. "That's attractive . . . I'm hurt you didn't ask me if I wanted your cherry."

"I'm still sittin on it. You don't want a cherry that's been sat on by the Lord knows who. Do you?"

He laughed again. "Then at least you'll allow me to kiss your white moustache off. Because I just hid your napkin."

I pulled my wig off and wiped my mouth on it. ". . . I lied. I'm not a singer. I'm a clown."

"You make me laugh, you're different. Whatever you are— hey, you've got dynamite hair," he shook it loose from its pins.

"Here comes my friend."

He watched Kristal approaching with little interest. "How'd you like to slip away and spend the night with me? I've never made it with a beautiful clown."

"You don't come on strong, do you?"

"You seem like the kind of girl who doesn't like beating around the bush anymore than I do. And I think you're attracted to me."

"You've got me all wrong, I'm not that kind of girl," I said loudly. "Barry, this is Kristal. I was tellin him how old-fashioned I am."

"Usually she never lets a man buy her a drink," Kristal sat

down and expertly picked up my untidy line. "One of her friends got raped by six rednecks that way, so either you're lucky or you must have some kind of charm. Now what are you gonna do? You've got two girls on your hands! One wild, and one innocent."

Barry propped my wig over his empty beer glass. "And one clown. What do you do, Kristal?"

"I'm a stripper. I used to play engagements right here in this club."

"Sure," he consoled her, "and she's a night club singer."

Kristal frowned. "That's right, that's what she is."

"When you walk through a storm . . ." I yodeled over the band's guitarist who himself had just gone into a bad skid.

"I just invited her to spend the night with me. She knows all my old favorites," said Barry. "You're welcome to come along."

"Well, you're just a lifesaver in disguise, because we've got this problem," she rattled off a new story listlessly, as if her heart for this hustle had deserted her, "we checked into the Algonquin Hotel cause I was meeting my fiancé Joe to get married here, with Randy as my flower girl, but Joe and me had a fight so the wedding bells are off. And he had the balls to leave us high and dry with a big hotel bill and no money. My friend here the flower girl was ordering up filet mignons and champagne breakfasts three times a day so you can guess what the bill is, and they won't let us back into our room—"

"—Enough of the bull," said Barry. "There is no Algonquin Hotel and since I moved here I've never heard of a striptease joint in Port Huron. Want a drink?"

Her eyes slit. "I am not a liar."

"I know, you're a clown." He was being very diplomatic, all things considered.

"That's a hell of a thing to say to a lady!" She leapt up and escaped to the bar. I was alarmed to see a sorrow shading over her face as she left us.

Barry pressed my arm. "I'm really not into these head games. Can't you get rid of her? We were having a good time before she came along."

I would always remember my first Irish coffee overdose. It was like being lashed to the nosecone of an unguided missile. I turned angrily on Barry. "I've tried every way I know how to tell you I've got gonorrhea."

"You girls are very depressing, really." He picked up his beer and departed.

Kristal was disappointed he'd split, because the bartender had confirmed her version of Port Huron. The 402 had closed, the Algonquin Hotel was an apartment building now, and "everything's changed," she said. "It's progress. You can't hold the clock hands back. This place used to be a hole in the wall. Now it's all residential, and discotheque, and . . . that guy was just a swinging single. He wouldn'ta spent a nickel on you, he just wanted a piece-a ass. And I found out Joe is dead. Eat something, you're loaded." She tossed a bag of beer nuts she'd bought at the bar over to me.

"Oh shit, I'm sorry, Kristal. I thought you made up Joe." She was staring at the wig on the glass as if it was graveyard plunder. Ashamed, I tried to replace the curly brown scalp on my head. "No wonder you were acting so weird."

"That's nothin." She snatched back the bag, tore it open, and shook nuts into her palm. "He was leaving home to follow me to Ohio, to Youngstown, where I had a contract to dance. And a truck hit him. When I told his mother it was me on the phone, she cursed me out in Hungarian. 'The devil will sit on your head!' and whatever have you." She spilled the nuts on the floor. "Let's get out of here."

We were silent during the drive back to Detroit. Once, she tried the radio dial. "Nothin but religion. Sunday crap." Snow began to fly at us. "Goddamn it. I know I'm not lost, but I can't see a fuckin thing."

I was unable to help her—infernally stoned, infernally awake— as the white storm caked up the lanes behind us.

I woke at noon. The only item in focus was my nose. On my way to the bathroom I stepped in Kristal's breakfast tray. The bacon fat washed off in the shower. A caffeine fit gave my hangover a serrated edge. No candyass cocktail that looked like a sundae was going to lay me so low, I vowed. "Coffee for four," I barked into the room phone, "and scrambled eggs, very dry. And two beers."

According to her note, Kristal was out ruthlessly raping another Sears department store so that she could leave Detroit in a better frame of mind. She returned with hair appliances, makeup, and a complete new wardrobe in size eleven, including a short and snappy fox cape. She willed to me her size-nine gear. "I'm pleasingly plump. Anyone doesn't like it can keep skinny eatin shit. No offense."

She had a couple of presents for me. One was a gold chain necklace with an Aquarius waterbearer charm on it. "I peeked at your ID to get your birthdate." The other present was a new ID, which would transform me into Kriska Ilka Mellkas, 5' 3", hair black, eyes black, thirty years old, permitted to get smashed in the state of my choice. "I want you to have it," she said affectionately.

Breakfast had gentled me. I begged to take the wheel when we checked out of the hotel, and nosed the station wagon south to St. Louis. I even started the conversation. "What's your sign?" I asked.

"Libra," she answered remotely.

"Justice and truth, protection of the weak against the strong . . ." I recited with ardor.

"Don't count on it."

She needed to be drawn out a bit. "When did you quit stripping?"

"I got married. Nine years back." She was in no mood to counterfeit. I was startled to realize that the husband she'd stitched into so many tales was a genuine. I waited for her to locate the place where she wanted to begin. ". . . I was stripping at the Tough Kitty in L. A. This was right before New Year's, sixty-six going into sixty-seven. I was staying at the St. Jerome Motel. The owner was a court physician whose son was a M. R. They let him run the desk—"

"A what?"

"A M. R.? A mentally retarded. He was in love with me. I threw this big party for all the strippers and comics and musicians, and I charged it to my room. I had this big hotel bill I couldn't pay. So I told the son I'd elope with him. I got married to him and then we drove back to the motel. I made him rent a car, it was a sixty-seven Fury, so no one would recognize us and wreck the honeymoon. I was using my Hungarian accent. 'Dahlink,' I says, 'now you must carry me over the trash-hole.' We're parked in the rear, so he has to run around to the front to find out if the lobby has a threshold. In the meantime, I take off in the car! and I never went back."

"That—*he* was your husband?"

"Hell no, that spaz don't count. I'm gettin to the part about my husband if you'll keep your tits on."

I got off work about 2 A.M. that night, and I drove to a different motel to score another room.

I hear this moaning and groaning in back of me. I look around—and there's the ugliest guy you ever want to see in your life. His hair hasn't been brushed since they invented Adam, he's drooling all over his beard, he's got clothes on that would stand up by themselves if you put them on the ground, his glasses are swinging off his ear, he sits up and feels around the air with these grubby hands and says, "Who the fuck are you!"

I said, "Who the hell are *you?*" Here was this drunken filthy loaded-out-of-his-tree Hells Angel, in the back seat of my new Fury.

He starts calling out the names of his buddies. He didn't know where he was, because the Angels had never left him alone before. What happened was, the cops had been chasing them out of the Valley, and Beau was so loaded he couldn't pack. Couldn't stay on the back of a motorcycle. Therefore, the Angels pulled into the Tough Kitty parking lot and dumped him in the first car whose doors was open. Later they came back to collect him. But they forgot where they put him. They were loaded, too.

He's sick, he says, he's a poor little lost guy. He talks me into driving him home to Cucamonga. I never heard of this place Bongo-bongo but I said, okay. From this point in the story on, ask me no questions why I said or did anything which made no sense.

After twenty miles on the Berdoo Freeway I got very scared. Beau offers to drive. We switch over and he starts driving: toward the oncoming traffic, then toward the shoulder. He drives another fifteen miles in this zigzag manner.

"Are you all right?" I asked. "I mean, you're pretty loaded, aren't you?"

"Well," he says, "I'm loaded, but being loaded doesn't affect my driving. I'm blind."

It turned out, he could make out light and shadows at least. When he rode with the Angels he'd follow the taillights of whoever was in front of him. At this hour, however, there were no cars to follow, so he'd drive toward the lights in the middle of the freeway, then as soon as they got closer and brighter he'd turn the wheel and head for the lights on the shoulder.

I ended up in Cucamonga at this huge ranch with an iron gate, where the Berdoo Angels live. "It's Mole!" he yells. On account he was blind, the Angels called him Mole, or sometimes Bomo, although his name was Beau, for Beauregard Pace.

The gate opens, and I see this character with a double-barreled shotgun, a preacher's hat, white socks and sandals, and otherwise buck-ass naked. He's walking guard, with a bottle of wine. "My God," I said, "dig the crazy sentry." Who was called Reaper and used to be a priest. The Hells Angels were having a gang bang with a couple of chicks once upon a time, and the preacher who's trying to talk them out of it ends up joining them instead. After he fucked the little fourteen-year-old girl he blessed her. They decided he'd make a good Angel.

Beau drove past the gate to this mansion. By the time we got a few hundred yards there were about nine bikers sitting on the hood. When we got out of the car, Beau made sure to hold my hand, because I was shitting. And when this one called Hully-Gully asked me "Who're you?" Beau said, "She's with me."

"Oh hi, brother," says Hully, and gives Beau a handful of pills. Reds.

"Thank you, brother," says Beau, and swallows the whole handful.

Then Hully yanks my dangley rhinestone earrings right out of my ears and goes off to try them on his old lady.

Beau says, "Listen, the place is getting rough. Tomorrow is New Year's Eve and all the different clubs are coming down." I didn't know what the hell he was talking about. But what he meant was, different chapters besides the San Bernadino chapter were there at the ranch, and some of them were not on the best basis with some others. ". . . I'm gonna lock you in my room," he says. "That'll be the safest place, because in about half an hour I'm going to be out to lunch." Again I didn't know what the hell he was talking about. But what he meant was, he was going to pass out from all the dope he'd just swallowed and then he wouldn't be available to protect me.

Then I turned to look back, before we went in the mansion where they all had their rooms. The Fury was half gone. In two minutes, they've got the fender off, they've got it jacked up, the wheels are disappeared, the battery out, and somebody had thrown the back seat onto the ground and was jumping up and down on it. Beau didn't see this, of course, on account he was blind. But I freaked: "That's a brand new car!" I didn't mention it was also stolen.

He says, "Boys will be boys," and locks me in his room, goes outside and boards up the window.

Here I am in a white minidress with long princess sleeves and slits and bows on the side, and white boots, in this lovely room with one greasy-grimy mattress on the floor and one putrid electric blanket with no cord, and a dresser, at five o'clock in the morning.

Beau crashed for about fourteen hours, then around seven-thirty the following night he came by and tried to open the door. But he'd lost the key to the padlock. I heard him go off again. Then the rest of New Year's Eve all I heard was screaming, and coyotes.

Next morning I hear this "BOOM!"

Beau shot the padlock off the door with his gun. I was pissed. I hadn't shown up for work at the Tough Kitty on New Year's Eve of all nights, so I knew I'd been fired for breaking contract. And my new car was in smithereens. "Don't come near me, motherfucker," I told him. "I'm from strict gypsy upbringing and I'm a virgin. I'm saving it for the man I marry."

He was tickled pink, because no one ever dared talk to him in this way. Beau was one of the most vicious Hells Angels of all. If you said hi to him, and he was loaded, he'd cut you, for no reason special. He rode his bike on the sidewalks in Riverside. The townspeople got to walk in the street. Marlon Brando once asked him for his autograph. Everyone looked up to him and respected him. When Kit the Kite was a prospect he thought so highly of Beau he said, "Mole, brother, you name anything of mine you want and I'll give it to you." Beau said, "I want your pinkie, it's got a nice nail on it." So right there in the bar, Kit took out his knife and cut off his little finger. Beau wore it on a leather thong around his neck. It always grossed me out.

But around me, Beau was the gentlest, most generous man on earth. And nobody knew it. He abided my wishes: he never touched me til the night we got married. If he had I would have blown his head off with his gun.

. . . Beau sits on the mattress beside me, and I move away. He says, "Why don't you like me?"

I said, "Because you are repulsive. You haven't taken a bath in a year and you smell like a sack of niggers."

He went away.

After a while I started crying. How was I going to get back to L. A.? Suddenly this handsome dude opens the door and

((153   ))

walks in. He had long, wavy blond hair, and the clearest blue eyes with sexy dark eyelashes, and clean clothes, and the thick glasses. It was Beau. It had taken him over an hour to scrub and shave and comb himself. I didn't recognize him til he spoke. He said he was taking me home.

He couldn't start his Sportster, so he took some parts off it to fix up this three-wheeler in the garage that had been laying around so long the chickens lived in it. I heard this unearthly noise. Up rolls Beau on this tractor job with chickens flying from it. "Get on," he says.

He drives me into Riverside and phones up his mother. Beau was one of six sons and they were all going blind from retinitis pigmentosa. R. P. is the slow type of blindness that takes a long time before it shuts your eyes down completely. His mother wires him a hundred dollars, anyway, and we take the Greyhound into Hollywood. I picked up my stuff from the St. Jerome. Nobody said nothing because they saw me with this gruesome fierce dude in a Hells Angel jacket. I loved that. Except, there was no hotel that would take me *in,* either, when they saw Beau with me: "Sorry, all the rooms are rènted." Now I have no job and no place to live.

Beau says, "Pack up. Come back and stay with me. I won't bother you. Besides, as long as you're with me no one'll hurt you."

I said, no way.

"Well, in that case, why don't you marry me." He goes on to say he's shooting heroin, and if I don't marry him I'll be the person responsible for him becoming a hopeless junkie.

I said, okay. I'll go back with you.

I lived with him at the ranch for three months. All the Angels liked me, and everybody just couldn't believe the way him and me got along real good, constantly kidding each other . . . We slept together but he never laid a hand on me. Then, one time he cheated on me.

I'm very jealous. I don't know why, because I wasn't fucking him, certainly. I suppose he got so horny sleeping with me.

There was this girl around the ranch who was epileptic and very ugly. He screwed her in Chuckie-poo's room. I called him Chuckie-poo because he was my favorite of all Angels.

They'd locked the door from the inside. I said, "Come out of that room."

I heard Beau say, "Oh—my—God—I left my gun on the dresser in my room!" I started shooting at the doorknob. Him and the chick went out the window.

Then I informed everybody, "I'm not mad anymore. I'm going to cook dinner." I put the gun away, and I cooked up an enormous kettle of paprikash. Which consisted of five cans of dogfood and whatever that rat poison is that has mercury in it. It doesn't kill you, it gives you the shits.

They all sit down. Chuckie-poo takes a bite. "Best hash I ever ate," he says. It was Calcan. Beau shows up for dinner, then. He runs in screaming, "Don't eat her food! She's a crazy Hungarian! She just tried to shoot me!" Chuckie-poo is already grabbing his stomach and racing for the toilet. I was running to get the gun out. But Beau had disappeared again. So I climbed up a tree to wait.

The little epileptic mama walked by and I took a potshot at her. Beau opened his window and yelled, "Now, god damn it, honey, stop that!" Playing the big protector.

"Honey my ass!"

I stayed up there til two in the morning. Now I'm very tired, and hungry, and cold. So I forgive him. But I have a problem. I can't get down from the tree. Beau is asleep. He goes to sleep early on account of the reds he took. And the little chick, she's with Chuckie-poo in his room, because they all screw her on the ranch.

Reaper helped me down. I walked off the ranch, through two miles of woods, and wearing nothing but short shorts and a halter top. On Route 1, I finally accepted a ride from a guy who looked trustworthy. He was a bearded freak, an intellectual who had gone to college and then moved out to the West coast and settled down to the business of being a freak.

He let me stay in his house in Santa Monica for a few days without touching me. He was just thrilled to meet a real Hells Angels mama. He even drove me back to the ranch.

Reaper was the first to see me. "Mole ain't himself," he said. "You shouldn't do this, cause he's never had a steady girl before. He's gone crazy without you."

I slammed the kitchen door. Beau hollers out from his room: "Who's that?" I didn't say nothing. I know he saw me from his window. "Hey, you scaggy bitch, where's my dinner!" I went in and took a look at him. Big crocodile tears start dribbling out of his blind baby blues. Then he held me. Things got tender, and he said, "You leave me one more time and I'll kill you."

I loved him. He was somebody that needed me. His strength reminded me of my father. Not that he was strong physically. Just, he was so mean. I liked the feeling of being with a man that other people fear. He didn't believe in God. He thought Hitler was great. I'd get pissed: "Hey, man, he killed my great-grandfather." Beau said, "Here he was, an asshole and a faggot, and he fooled the whole world! an idiot, a nut . . . he killed his own niece after he discovered he was impotent. . . ." Things Beau said made a lot of sense after you thought about it. But I changed my mind about marriage when I got to the courthouse. The judge started with the spiel, do-you-this and do-you-that, and I couldn't speak. He thought I must be a wetback. Finally I nodded.

That night, our honeymoon, was the same night I opened in El Centro. Beau was nervous. He had never seen me dance. Before I went onstage, while I was hustling drinks, he took my flashlight and shined it on my tits to see how much I was showing.

He saw my act from the front table, but he got upset. While I was dancing, I took his glasses off his face and made believe I was cleaning them on my crotch and then put them back on him. After the show he came backstage and threw me over his shoulder.

That was the last time I ever stripped. He wouldn't let me. He got embarrassed very easily. By this time, he couldn't tell day from night, but he hated to be treated like a blind man. He would rather walk into a wall than have you hold him back.

"Here's the Hilton. Look, they've got a Trader Vic's! Christ, I hope they have sweet and sour pork. That would just make me so happy."

She couldn't stop talking, that first night in St. Louis. In Trader Vic's, she ordered a five-course Polynesian dinner and triple shots of cognac. She made me eat all the food while she drank and sputtered on about blackjack, poker, keno, how to beat the house, and businessmen with jet lag. "We're bein cruised left and right," she declared. This time it was true but she was uninterested. She seemed to have some kind of personal troubles that she had her own way of battering into submission.

Determined to stay awake until she got to sleep, I ordered three Irish coffees when she asked room service to bring up a bottle of Courvoisier and a can of diet cola.

She held the uncapped bottle between her thighs like a powerful glass boner, as she sat on the edge of her bed. "—What nationality are you?" she interrupted herself once, distracted by the sudden movement of my elbow when I drained my second drink. "Oh, right, you don't know, you don't have no parents. You can be whatever you want to be whenever you want. Like me. Shit, I can be anything. I don't walk, I don't crawl . . . but if the law's after me, I run like hell. Where was I?" I wondered if I should have the bell captain send up a claw hammer, to pry the bottle out of her lap, and to pound her head into the pillow. "You can fool . . ." she paused to organize her lips ". . . alla the people . . . alla the time. *One at a time.* You got to do them one at a time, that's why it's a life's work. My philosophy is this . . ." she rocked, both hands clutching the bottleneck, and shouted, ". . . FUCK YESTERDAY. AND I'LL MAKE SURE

TO MAKE ENOUGH TODAY . . . TO SAY FUCK YOU TO TOMORROW." Her fists whitened around the bottle, which I thought was going to ejaculate. "Because . . . the world is a *joke*." She cackled persuasively. "Everything around you is just *air*. You suck it in. And you suck it out. That's all. You can be anything. I can be anything. I can even sound like Judy Garland. Listen." She huffed up her lungs: "Some-WHEEEERE—"

The walls of the room lurched. She shut her eyes tight.

"Some-*WHEEERE*—"

Water swelled between her lashes. The tears never brimmed over but clung to her eyes like hardening glue.

"Some-*WHEEEEEERE*—"

She kept up the "somewhere," slugging away at the Courvoisier, until the quaver in her voice slowed down and faltered to where she actually did sound like Judy Garland. By the time she got "over the rain-BOOOOOOW," the house detective knocked.

I lugged her to bed. As I was putting her red wig away in her suitcase, I saw the vial of diet pills. In eleven days since the date of the prescription, she'd taken nineteen tablets. I flushed the remaining twenty-one down the toilet.

Happy size eleven, don't mention it.

She never mentioned it.

Amphetamine eats mettle, strips the thread right off your screws —I let her sleep the sleep of the undead all the next day. I had a bad night myself, from Irish coffee nightmares, hugging myself down close inside my tiger cage and listening to the bombs sizzle overhead, never daring to raise my head above ground until daylight began to bleach my lids.

I quietly picked up the phone and ordered up eggs and a beer. Then I went for a walk in downtown St. Louis. The air was soft. Bewildered by strollers persistently smiling at me for no reason whatsoever, I kept looking back over my shoulder, also to keep an eye on the distant Gateway Arch, a monument to the opening of the Golden West on the Mississippi's bank, a brilliant twister lassooing the sun's pale warmth for a forgery of gold. So I'd smack into another shopper, who'd smile erroneously at me, and the whole thing would begin again, til the beer wore off and I went back to the Hilton.

"I like this city. It has a nice feeling," I said to Kristal. She was eating lunch in bed and watching game shows on television.

"It's a pretty good place to operate, except for the god damn blue laws," she griped. "Everything shuts down at one o'clock. The waiter told me the niggers have sent the whole city down the toilet. But some racetracks just opened across the river, so something must still be cookin. I'm gonna call my agent. He lives here, he'll know where there's money for us. . . . I'm sicka talkin. Every time I open my mouth, I yawn. I don't know why I'm so tired. Run downstairs to that gift shop and get me a pack of Marlboros, will you? I'm gonna start smokin again. And some magazines."

By the time I got back up from the lobby she'd crashed again. I turned the TV off but she hollered at me in her sleep to leave it on.

She woke again at nightfall, as I was closing my diary, and she remained glumly awake through a room-service dinner. "You ever been on television?" she asked, pushing her tray to the foot of the bed while I changed channels for her. "I been on 'Let's Make A Deal' about sixty-seven times. I never sent in for tickets cause that takes six months. I'd just drive onto the studio parking lot by giving out the name of Monty Hall's producer that I memorized from off the screen. There'd be buses there, unloading the audience—grown men dressed in diapers, their wives with black eyes painted on—the most asinine carryin on. I'd be all cuted up in, like, a white and green Hungarian costume, with puffed sleeves off the shoulder, with my bosoms all bunched up. Real colorful. The guy passin out the tickets'd go by and I'd say something to the effect of 'hey stupid' and hit him over the head with my rubber chicken. And he'd hand me a ticket."

"Did you ever win anything?"

"You have to get them to put you in the middle, or on the aisle. I never got a good seat, except once. I took Beau with me. I dolled him up in one of those short-pants outfits, you know, with the hat and the bow under the chin and the blue boy collar and the lace—Little Lord Fairy-Fart. You never saw a Hells Angel so *sourful*. They picked him to be number four on the aisle for Monty to make a deal with. . . . The fat man, what's his name, comes out and warms up the audience: 'If nobody wins anything, we'll all go over to Monty's house for dinner.' I've heard this joke sixty-six times and I'm biting my chicken in half for him to get the hell off the stage. Then we hear, 'fifteen seconds . . . ten seconds . . .' and Beau jumps up and shouts, *'Fuck this, she ain't makin me do it!'* and drags me outa there by my tail. I was dressed in one of my old strip costumes, as a black pussycat. The lady next to us got picked. She won a camel! . . . Beau had a big pride."

"Are you still married?"

"We lasted about eight, nine years," she burrowed under the covers. "Up til last year, matterfact."

"Why—"

"—go back to your colorin book. I'm sicka talkin."

She snored, I read magazines, til midnight. I got down to the hotel bar just before last call, ordered a flying wedge of Irish coffees and beer, and signed it to the room.

"Randy. What's this?" Kristal prodded my arm and yanked my hair. "You put this fifty-dollar bill under my pillow. Did I lose a gold tooth I should know about?"

I tried to grasp the question, but it had a bad bounce. I'd been sleeping so hard I was too exhausted to chase after the unmatched words and pictures scooting around like dead tennis balls in my head.

"Operator? This is room eleven-sixteen. This is very important. Please place a wake-up call every five minutes for the next twenty minutes til my bridesmaid gets up." She hung up. "Okay, Randy, it's now seven-thirty. You better be down in the dining room by eight cause we're having breakfast with my agent, and it'll be very dumb for your future if you don't show."

"Fucked up," I mumbled.

"You can go back to bed afterwards." She left.

By the third wake-up call, the hotel operator was on to me: "Miss, how'd you like me to send up one of my Valiums with the bellboy? Would you like me to get room service to rush up with some coffee? Have you ever tried soda with bitters?"

"Beer . . ." Why was the pillowcase rumbling?

"We can't serve alcoholic beverages before noon—hold on." I waited on the line, then dropped the receiver into the cradle.

The fourth call woke me up. A man's voice through a toxic southern accent: "Hah, aynjil-cakes," for starters. "Lo? You there nah? This's yer room ten-o-nine undying love an' devotion."

"What timezit?" I knew he was some kind of distant relation to the fifty-dollar bill.

"Ten to eight ayem, for your incredibility. We got a breakfiss rawndyvoo. If Ah drop mah knahfe, you have t'promise to meet me under the table, hah hah hey. See you in ten minutes?"

"Can't."

"Ah get it, your sister-in-law's in the room list'nin. Okay, Ah'll still meet you tonight as originally planned. Take care, pretty lawng-leggy wishbone."

I hung up, got up, and went through the motions of getting dressed. It must have worked, because I arrived fully clothed in the dining room, only fifteen minutes late. Kristal was sitting with a translucent old man. As I approached, she dabbed specks of oatmeal off his chin and lapel with her napkin, and shone me a bright sickly smile. "Sid, this is Randy. Isn't she gorgeous? Don't get up, Sid."

He had risen from his chair, and stooped forward to take my hand. He must have been stocky, once. His belt had gathered so many pleats to his diminishing waist that his pants flung out like a square-dance skirt, and the belt loops cluttered up on either side of his fly like counting beads. "My dear young lady . . . you'll forgive me if I don't quite remember your name. It's been a long time. You were a good little dancer."

"This is Randy," Kristal repeated.

"And a darn good gal with the jokes. Randy." He sat down

again after I slid into a chair opposite. "Randy. Well, Vera has the memory. She remembers all the girls' names. They still call her up with their problems."

Turning her face away from him, Kristal interpreted under her breath, "Vera is Sid's wife. I can't figure out if she's died, from what he says. You're right if you think he's senile." She discreetly tapped a finger on the side of her skull, indicating that her agent had the Forever Hangover. "We were just reminiscing about the old days when you came in. Right, Siddie? Remember Madame Sex? Sid booked me and her as a feature. One thing she could really do was via-brate her butt, but I got the standing ovations. All I had to do was stand on my head and throw out my ass! Well, she had silicone in her boobs. You could see it when they threw the black light on her, half the boob went black, hard as a base-ball—"

"—I handled two hundred eighteen of the exotic dancers," Sid fluted, "and I feel very happy and proud I never brought any scandal into the field. I'm not ashamed to take my wife anywhere, anytime, and I don't think any one of the girls would say I ever made a pass at them. Course, when you called yesterday, I couldn't remember, but Vera told me who you was. Here I've got your message," he unfolded a bit of paper from his breast pocket, Kleenex lint floating off it, "says here 'Kristal,' and I couldn't . . . this is my wife's handwriting . . . and I handled all the exotics from Honolulu to . . . Japan."

"Sid had the teletype machine goin twenty-four hours—" Kristal urged.

"—that Western Union facts machine—"

"—and always the coffee on the hot plate and ten phones ringin, and Sid was always so strict: you had to *behave*—"

"—I screen every one of the girls—"

"—no pubic hair, no rubbin your jugs, everything clean. And I lived up to it. *Class.*" She paused to light a cigarette.

"Then," Sid noted the light change and eased once more into first gear, "the go-go dancers came into style—"

"—they up-surped the business," Kristal fumed out white smoke and shot past the old man's heap, "I mean, burlesque is a class entertainment. I only come out at two, three thousand, with a guarantee for a personal maid, you know?"

"The operators don't want talent . . . a revue . . . it's a sad situation, there, they want something sixteen years old they can go to bed with, if you'll pardon the expression."

Kristal grinned suddenly. "Sid? You always called me a 'good kid.' Why'd you say that?"

". . . I never tried to steer anyone wrong. I don't ask for troubles. Now . . . Kristal, you want me to book you in town here? The Silver Garter?"

"Oh, Siddie! You mean the Garter's still around? With Jack running it? And the same band?" He nodded. "Man, I'd love to see him, you call Jack and tell him it's the gypsy girl with the forty-six-inch boobalas that was the first to ever dance on a piano, cause I made him more money than he's seen in his whole life. I don't want him to make me get up and dance, though. Even as a special added attraction. Unless he starts talkin four figures. Cause I'm on my way to Vegas."

"He might want you to mix, then."

"Sure, we'll mix." I looked up from the menu. "A mixer is supposed to mix," she explained, "with the customers, and get them to buy drinks. All they serve is a carbonated grape juice, tastes like wine, strictly nonalcoholic, cause Jack don't have a liquor license. That way he can stay open as late as he wants. And we get a percentage off the drinks. Don't look at me like that."

"All I want is a beer," I whined.

"I'll be getting back to the office," said Sid. "I'll be taking my leave of you two lovely girls. I'm retired now."

"Okay, Siddie," said Kristal. "Give my love to Vera."

"All the girls still call up asking for her. She listened to their hang-ups. I never know what to tell them, now. . . . I may be a great-grandfather soon." He peered down at the table surface and rapped it with his knuckles. "Can't tell if that's wood, there."

"There must be some way," I said after he left, "you can convince them to serve me a beer."

"I can't. It's the law. Shit." She was tearing the scalloped edges off her paper placemat. "He was like a father to me. I feel a hundred years old. Anyhow, at least we can go by the Silver Garter. I know lots of people there. . . . Now tell me about this fifty-dollar bill. And don't act feeble, I've had enough of it for one morning." I shrugged. "You don't remember, do you?"

I recalled a businessman from Kentucky bullying me in the bar, singing country-western songs in my ear, dumping his blues on my lawn ("Mah problem is, sex is just too . . . impo'tant. Ah spose Ah'm not the irresistible species of sexual magnificence a woman'd tahr her clothes off for. An' mah nex' problem is, Ah've had . . . few too many beers."), and jamming his finger on the "CLOSE DOOR" button in the elevator, until I was forced to tell him I was traveling with my sister-in-law, an alcoholic trying to go on the wagon, whose birthday was the next day, and if I only had the money to buy her a magnum of the best champagne, she'd break down and get juiced, pass out early, so that I'd be fancy free to enter Room 1009 for an evening of fleshly jubilation. I bullied him out of a fifty-dollar bill, that's all. I'd been chewing the inside of my mouth. Blood, whiskey, and coffee fueled my revenge.

"Thank god," said Kristal. "I thought you might have screwed some guy for the bread. Not a bad hustle, for a drunk. Soon you'll be hustlin in your sleep!" The ends of her mouth drooped. "That guy, Sid . . . ten years ago, I swear he handled *alla* the big names. If burlesque was really all that dead, I wish somebody'd had the guts to tell me."

It was a false alarm, because Kristal found the Silver Garter in the yellow pages, under "B" for Burlesque, still alive.

"I don't believe it," she handed me the phone. "They've got some chick with multiple orgasms answering their number."

I put my ear to the receiver. "—Oo, ah, oh, have we got thrills for you, unh-*hunh,* don't be alone tonight; we've got live onstage

((164))

young vivacious and topless lovelies and hysterical comedians for your special enjoyment," a tape-distorted woman's voice croaked, "Ah! Ah! continuous thrills until one-thirty A.M., and our girls will be so very glad to really give you a show to remember. Thank you for calling the Silver Garter."

"All I get is that recording," said Kristal. "Jack won't mind if we just turn up. That son of a bitch would ream himself just to have me back in the show. Let's take a cab. I really want to make a star entrance. How's my fotch?"

She'd reverted to the black-striped Panther Woman eye job, and even sprinkled a little gold glitter in her frosted blond wig. Her tits butted against the nipple-high neckline of the white gown, the pink aureoles rolling like leery peepers as she swung her fox cape over her shoulders. I shivered in a black and silver spaghetti-strap design from my friend's former size-nine collection. I didn't even have my fluffy blond armpit hair to keep me warm any longer, because she'd make me shave it off. "Not in a night club you don't, not with me, not with that hippy-drippy gardens hangin down. You'll like mixing—it's very social. Anyway, it'll keep you off the booze for one night. I don't like how cute-assed you get when you get shit-faced." I'd woke up from an afternoon nap feeling unusually helpless. "If we leave now, we'll get there before the first show starts. Do you think I look like Mae West? Guys in the audience used to say that. I'd want to look like her. Judy Garland was a sorry bitch, but Mae West came through it like a queen. I always wondered if it was true she's actually a man in drag." The phone rang. "Hello? . . . Who? Room 1009? Are y'all from Texas? . . . Oh, you're the kind gentleman that sent me the beautiful magnum of Mumm's, for my birthday today, and I thank you so very much. Our husbands have just joined us and we're going out to take in a show, and then we'll come back and drink your wonderful gift. . . . Yes, I'll tell her, and thank you again."

She tossed me her purple rabbit coat. "Here. Get set to drink a hundred gallons of grape juice."

Once inside the Silver Garter, we staggered over our hems,

((165))

heading for the single light source, a yellow bulb clipped to the cashier's desk. Jack slammed the register drawer shut. The low-down threat of disco music from the theater beyond pulsed around our ankles.

Jack was used to the dark. He waited while our pupils enlarged, observing us with his own global yellow lynx eyes. "You used to work here," he said to Kristal.

She flung her cape back from her shoulders and casually rested her chest on his desk. "Shit yes. You gave me the stage name of Klover Honey." Bubbles of heartburn popped behind his lips. "You oughta remember me. I put you on the map, financially speaking."

"Can't remember my own name, doll, you're talkin back fifteen years."

"*Nine* years, Jack. You were makin that girl Ginger strip in her eighth month—she had to dance with her back to the audience to keep her stomach hid! Do I know you, or do I know you?" She covered her naughty naked teeth with a curling wet tongue.

Jack leaned possessively on the cash box. "Klover, huh? Just dropped in to see us on your way somewhere? Is Klover still your name?"

"No, Kristal. And this is my friend Sandy." He nodded at me. "We're on our way to Vegas where I'm opening at the Turkish Room. We thought we'd mix for you, for a few nights, and bring some class to this establishment."

"Naw, babe, no," he tapped his pencil eraser on a page of his accounts book, "we don't hire temporary girls. Only if they're permanent, and they gotta perform in the show. That's the rule."

"Are you kidding me? All I'm asking is to make you money which you know I can do by the truckload, Jack. I'm not fresh to this business."

He shook his head. "Just girls who work steady year after year. The other girls . . . we like'm, but they fuck themselves up by gettin too damn cute for their own good—" He glanced warily at me, then past my shoulder as the street door opened. "You gals are welcome to stay and watch the show."

"Are you open?" asked a man's voice. Kristal drew me aside. A couple of customers felt their way towards Jack. "Can't see."

"We're open, sure," Jack chuckled. "You're inside, ain't you? Three dollars plus a soft drink is four dollars."

"Bankamericard?"

"Any kind, fellas," he pumped the credit card through a press and tore off the receipt, "go right inside. The show's not on for another half hour, but the girls there will give you your soft drink and tell you anything you want to know."

"You go inside, too," Kristal whispered to me. "Jack's uptight cause he don't know you. I'll join you in a minute."

I sat in the back row of tables before the stage. Two girls in harem scanties were bending over to chat with the fellas in the front row. The theater smelled familiar: the deep-fat odor of the Royale Ballroom. On the small stage, some peculiar props were set up before a blue curtain: an armless chair, a big soiled plush dog, an umbrella stand containing two ostrich plumes, and a street sign, askew, indicating the major intersection of "Pleasure Place" and "Fun Freeway."

"We're gettin outa here." Kristal's breath scalded my ear. "But I ain't through with that prick yet. You just stand by me and agree with anything I say." She plucked up her long white train and swept back into the lobby with me, the bridesmaid, lockstepping behind.

Jack stood his ground calmly as Kristal inhaled. The two breasts lifted, aimed at his chest, and cocked for a stick-up. "All right, Jack. I'm gonna be straight with you. I'm on the make. The airline lost our luggage, and we don't have the sixty-two dollars to get out of the Hilton, where we been staying, and into a cheaper hotel. If we can pay the bill and get out tonight, we want to work here. Sandy too. She does whatever I do and goes wherever I go." I agreed.

"You mean you'll stay on indefinitely? Oh, love to have you both."

"And you can put us in that hotel down the street?"

"That's a halfway house for narcotics now. You're still living ten years back, doll. This area used to be all white. Now it's all black. They don't hurt anybody, but people think they do. . . . I'll set you up at the Weston. It's the cheapest hotel, about three minutes from here. I'll start you tonight. The salary's one hundred dollars a week, to mix, and to be in the show."

"I make better than that doin nothing!" she protested. "Jack, I oughta kill you! You used to *father* me. . . ."

He sweetened up a touch, and the two leaned into each other to make rapid sense in low voices.

JACK: "—*plus*—one hundred to two hundred dollars on the side. Everything's changed. Here's how we operate. You don't hustle drinks no more. You do anything but."

KRISTAL: "You mean jerking off under the tables? . . . No? Then where?"

JACK: "Each girl has her own private room back there. What about Sandy here?"

KRISTAL: "We've screwed before. Can't wear it out! What if we get busted?"

JACK: "It'll never happen."

KRISTAL: "Okay, but I'd rather French than fuck. How much does a dude pay?"

JACK: "You got to do it both ways if he wants it, and you get forty for the hour."

KRISTAL: "We get forty, you get sixty! I know you, right? How many times does he get to get his rocks off?"

JACK: "In an hour? Ho ho, leave some time to talk and bullshit with the fella first. . . . Here's ten dollars for the cab, and fifty to get you out of the Hilton—"

KRISTAL: "—I need $62!"

JACK: "Get off my nuts, doll. . . . Hi, there! This way, fellas!"

A cabdriver, who had just delivered two out-of-towners from the Holiday Inn, was enlisted to drive us back to the hotel.

"Drive slowly," Kristal told the driver. "I have an upset stomach ache and a hemorrhage from seein the filth that's happened to St. Louis."

The driver nodded enthusiastically. "You see, those black people come in and knocked the hell out of the prestige."

"I'm talkin about the Silver Garter has no class anymore. When
I was there nine years ago—"

"—used to be a first-class joint, I know it. But you see, the
blacks—"

"—I know it, the place is fulla niggers, that's it."

"Right." He saluted her in his rearview mirror. "And the local
people is afraid to go out of doors. But now, these conventions,
at the hotels downtown, the men don't care what they pay for entertainment, or what the neighborhood's like. So we've got the
Silver Garter, it's the only strip joint in town."

"It's not a strip joint, it's a *whorehouse*," she snorted. "There's
a big difference." The driver emitted a rising passage of giggles.
"What nationality are you, anyway?"

"I'm Indian. Creek, dear."

"You got an accent—are you sure you're not Hungarian?"

"No, they call me Dago, sweetie. Dago Jerry. Now, what makes
you say all the girls are turnin tricks back there?"

"Oh, Jack talked to me very frank, believe me." She lit a
cigarette, then fumed up the cab with bitter reproaches. "Nine
years ago, that place was so packed with guys you couldn't close
the goddamn door! And you didn't have to strip the whole way,
and they had a complete live band. Now each girl has a tape, she
gets up and does a little titty dancing, a guy picks her, then they go
down to the basement, which used to be for wardrobe. Now it's
sectioned off and each girl has her own cot. And they *fuck*." Dago
Jerry's giggling reached a kind of plateau. "The only reason I'm
running my mouth is, I'm in a state of shock. Jack used to take
care of his girls. Now they're just pieces of asses to him. Well, he
must be takin dope and can't cope no more."

"No, now, Jack's on top of it," said the Indian, "he's doin all
right. See, he gets a lot of square girls in there that never danced,
never hustled before. He turns them out right there in a night or
two. And it's a legal front. He don't serve liquor, so he can go

late as he likes, and he gets some big-time spenders—I've had guys go over there for all-night parties—"

"—hats off, okay? I mean, very good, you know? But it's not for me. I'm shocked and abhorred at him. I'm a big-name star, twenty-five-hundred-a-week exotic dancer with a personal maid, and Jack has the balls to get me down here on contract and then tells me to fuck in the back room!"

Dago glanced in his mirror again. "You're not taking the job?"

"When my pussy freezes over, I'll take that job!" He started tittering again, this time on a high note in a descending pattern. "I mean, he takes sixty dollars and the chicks gets forty, for a whole hour! Listen, you have to buy me a new . . . Roy's *Royce!*" she spluttered. "And maybe then I'll fuck you! . . . But he doesn't have anything in that place I'd want to put my dick in if I was a man."

"Well, you can't say that." His laughter idled pleasantly in middle range. "You don't know men. They'll screw anything. Ooo, baby, it's true. Men are terrible."

Kristal had us checked out and on the road barely a half hour later. I'd been needy of an intravenous taste of black caffeine, bum whiskey, and plaster of whipped cream—but she only allowed me the coffee part, in a cup, and then handed me the wheel and the map. "You drive. You had the nap this afternoon."

"Why are we going to Kansas City?"

"It's got a nice club called the Satin Slipper."

"Kristal," I sighed, "why don't we quit stopping off at all these shitholes that only depress you? Why can't we get on a plane and fly straight to Las Vegas or L. A.?"

"No." The station wagon shimmied as I passed a bus. "Not unless you want to buy the tickets." I stole a look at her. She was glowering. "I'm all out of money, myself."

The awesome spatula of life flipped me over, to sear me on the other side. I had been on "bad trips" before, but so far as I could remember they had all been in my head. She heard the gasp. "I only left New York with about a hundred dollars. I had to get you the best doctors, and luxurious drugs, gourmet meals, Hiltons the whole way . . . how the hell do I know where it all went. So, I miscalculated. I never figured on a hippie having such expensive tastes."

"Gold!"
That's where her money went.
The hotel operator had rung our room phone for an 8:30 P.M. wake-up, ending our day-long sleep. Kristal went to the bathroom. I switched on the table lamp between our beds and propped myself up on the pillow, trying to decide what city we were in. From my years of hitchhiking, I was used to waking up in strange rooms. By my third Hilton, however, I still wasn't used to waking up in rooms that looked the same but were actually different. Kristal had left open, at the foot of her bed, a makeup case. From under its lid, a tantilizing yellow glow beckoned me with its song.

"What's your beef?" Kristal adjusted her wig in the bathroom mirror and once again brought off her transformation into a blond celebrity. She refused to get dramatic over my discovery of two bracelets and one necklace of gaudy new gold coins, now weighing in at a couple of pounds on my trembling wrist. The Gold Exchange in New York City was located right around the corner from the Royale Ballroom. A seven-thousand-dollar garnish. ". . . I wanted to look my best in Vegas. I get jealous when I see the other cunts flashing their artillery around the casinos."

"But what will you do for money?"
"I was gonna hustle you out of your money." Her hand with the black eyeliner was steady as an old master. "I go for the nearest buck. . . . Not funny? Well, lose your paranoia. I promise I won't touch your money."

"Kristal, I'm begging you. Let's go straight to Vegas. I'll pay for everything. I've got about twenty-two hundred dollars."

"You could never afford me," she sneered, untangling the fringe that trickled off her cleavage and smoothing her white gown. "Is that what you're wearing to a night club? Jeans and a sweater?"

"But you're broke!"'

"That's when I start to *cook*, kiddo. I can hustle my own god damn plane fare. Get a move on, the blue laws in Kansas City are as bad as St. Louis. The hookers turn to pumpkins at one o'clock. You comin? You can watch."

"You can help," she added, as we got out of the taxicab, "by shuttin up. Not matter what I do, stay shut up."

The curtained window of the Satin Slipper was decorated with shabby stickers, barely readable by blue bulbs: "Thrills Galore," "Girl-O-Rama," "Hilarious Comics." Next door the pink-bulbed storefront of the Po D'Swah, a female impersonators' club, advertised "Beautiful Girls," and "Hilarious Commediennes."

Kristal steered me inside the Satin Slipper and stopped at the bar. The feature strip act had just begun onstage. "I'd like a Courvoisier with a Seven-Up chaser, and a Irish coffee for my sister."

"May I see your ID?" the bartender asked me. I was mesmerized by the dancer, who had removed her green elbow-length gloves and now paced restlessly around an elaborate boudoir set.

Fishing my ID out of my purse, Kristal explained to the bartender, "She's deaf, my sister. You have to face her so she can read your lips. Are you the owner, too? This is a nice club, I've heard about it everywhere. It's a pleasure to see good dancing." She removed her fur cape and draped it over her arm. The stripper let her evening wrap slide to the floor, revealing a green satin formal with an explosion of green tulle at the knees. "Is she gonna show pubic hair?"

"Nah, it's against the law," the owner answered. "She'll go down to a G-string."

"I'm so glad you're not a whorehouse." The dancer's entire gown fell away somehow, and she stood in a green spangled bikini, garter belt, and green net stockings. "I'm on my way to open at the Turkish Room in Vegas, and every club I stop off at has changed over to whores."

"Now that's a shame. What's your handle?"

"Kristal Ball, the Hungarian Tempest."

"Are you a dancer, or a comedian?"

"Yes, I'm a funny girl. My sister here does my wardrobe."

"Jeez, Miss Ball, don't pull your shoulders back," he laughed.

"You ain't seen enough bosoms in this joint yet? Listen, I gotta let'm out, they need sunlight to grow. . . . Don't tell me that's the end of her number. She's got a nice tight little body."

"This is where she gets in the bathtub."

"Oh yeah, blowin bubbles. I used baby oil with the black light in my act, until the stage manager had an accident in the stuff I spilled. Look, my sister's in love with your stripper! Make her another drink."

"That's a shame now, she can't hear the music. Pretty girl, too. You don't look like sisters." The dancer bowed. I clapped along with the men at the tables.

"Oh, she's deaf allright, but she ain't too dumb. Watch." She closed my hand around a steaming glass of Irish coffee.

"YOW!"

"See? I'm so awful to her sometimes. . . . Be seein you." She dragged me away from the bar and sat us down at a table across from a man wearing a gas station uniform. His head had the classic rodent's bone structure, bracketed by two huge pulpy ears. "Hi, Doug." The name was stitched across his breast pocket. "I'm Kristal, and this is my stepsister."

Mean miniscule eyes glittered over the glass of beer tipped toward his mouth. "You sellin something?" He pronounced his s'es with spikes on them.

"Shh! Cover your mouth with your hand like I'm doin. She's deaf, but she can read lips, and I don't want her to know what I'm sayin to you. She's very innocent and I'm her idol, right? I'd just like . . . to get away tonight, you know? I wanna fuck."

He examined me, sucking down his beer noiselessly. He cupped his hand over his mouth. "She wanna fuck, too?"

Maintaining a blank face, I looked down at my lap, absorbed in watching my hands sweat. As long as I couldn't be deaf to this dialogue, I had a right to be blind.

KRISTAL: "No, dumb-ass. She's just a kid. We've got a room together at the Holiday Inn. I'm not hustling you, I don't want

((173))

money, I don't want a drink, I can buy my own drinks. I'm no good in bed if I drink. But I've been getting *her* drunk so I can put her to sleep soon. Then I want to take a cab and meet you somewhere."

DOUG: "I'll pick you up at the hotel."

KRISTAL: "No, I don't want her to know I'm with you."

DOUG: "She'll be asleep."

KRISTAL: "She's deaf! Her eyes'll be closed but she can still be awake, and I can never tell! What'm I gonna do, shout 'Are you asleep' in her ear? No. I'll tell her I'm goin out for a bite and she'll see me gettin in a cab. Where can we meet?"

DOUG: "I'll call out to the house, see if she ain't home. She's getting a divorce anyhow."

KRISTAL: "Who?"

DOUG: "My wife."

KRISTAL: "We'd better go to a Travelodge. I wanna ask you something, though—do you eat pussy? That's the only way I get hot. Keep your hand over your mouth."

DOUG: "Okay, yeah . . . I like it that way. Shit, I like to tear it apart with my hands."

KRISTAL: "Oh, *beautiful*. Now, I'll need cabfare. Don't let her see you. Pass it under the table."

DOUG: "I'll give you ten, allright?"

KRISTAL: "We're all the way out at the airport Holiday Inn!"

DOUG: "You better be levelin . . . is twenty dollars enough? I'm gonna fuck you good and hard like you want it, so you better not be fuckin with me. . . ."

After making a big display of phony hand signals for the deaf in front of my face, she got my attention, blew Doug a kiss, and whipped us out of there. "Pshew! That guy was just a regular bowl of snakes!" she panted outside on the street. "For twenty bucks he'd rather slit my throat than eat my pussy."

"Did you see those carbuncles all over his neck?" I breathed. "Look, there's a taxi."

"We're going next door. And you can talk this time."

She really had it in for me tonight. She was determined to shove my nose in the scummiest nickel-dime hustles she could scare up in this burg. I sat on a toilet lid in the Po D'Swah ladies' room. Kristal had dealt me my instructions and a fresh glass of Irish guess-what, and dispatched me to wait in here for half an hour.

I left the door ajar so I could listen to the stage show.

"Here he is, *Mister* Showbiz, René Kildare!"

A black man in a white organdy gown trotted out of the men's room across from my stakeout and I heard his high heels pecking down the hall to the stage entrance. I sat through a rendition of "The Way We Were," and afterward two white transvestites did fifteen minutes of lip synching to a tape of "Julie Andrews And Carol Burnett At Carnegie Hall."

Then I reckoned it was time for my big scene. I stood up and stretched my shoulders, one-foot-six by five-foot-ten-and-a-half. The third drink of the night had given me a false fierce sense of purpose. I put on my best volunteer fireman's swagger and walked back to our table, where I surprised a fragile dyke whispering in Kristal's ear and sliding an arm around her.

I coiled my fists and growled, "Listen, Kristal, I've had enough of your shit! Now, you're my fuckin *wife!* If that bitch doesn't get her hands off you I'll blow you both away—"

"Honey, don't hit me!" Kristal shielded her face, while her friend with the stuffed crotch shrank away.

I threw Kristal's cape at her and roughly pushed her toward the exit: "Just wait til I get you back to the hotel, you fuckin whore, I'm gonna kill you. . . ."

Back on the street, Kristal praised me effusively for my performance. "How much did you get?" I asked, unable to prevent my mere chest from swelling with pride.

"She was a factory worker, didn't have much on her. I got forty-five dollars for cabfare and a hotel room where we could safely eat each other out. Then when you came on, you even got *me* scared," she stroked my arm and mewed, "would you have punched her? Would you have defended my honor?"

"I was more looking forward to beating the shit out of you in front of everybody," I replied.

"Shut up, twat, cause we're goin back into the Satin Slipper now to call a cab. So you're deaf, remember."

"Hello, girls!" A young man in denims staggered out of the Slipper, followed by a taller, bearded man in a plaid lumber jacket who was guiding his buddy with one hand and dragging a backpack with the other. Denims bore down on us: "Can we give you a lift somewhere?"

"He can't hold his mud too good," chuckled Backpack.

"Oh my god!" I quailed. A short distance behind them came Doug, leaving the club for his powwow with Kristal.

"Run!" Kristal grabbed Denims' arm and I grabbed Backpack, and together we forced them into a serious gallop. We heard Dangerous Doug bellowing, "Hey, you dirty cunts!" and then the patter of rubbersoled workboots as he pursued us.

"You've got to save us, he's a maniac!" Kristal shrieked at Denims, "Where's your car!"

"Around the corner," his legs pumped obediently while his face glazed over with shock and booze—we all turned right— "It's the great white monster up ahead. . . ." He dashed round an obese white van, vaulted into the driver's seat, and unlocked the opposite door for us. Backpack graciously extended his hands to help Kristal up.

"I'm not gettin in that thing!"

"Just lift your leg," he smiled.

"I'm not a goddamn dog—"

"—Hey, Doug's stopped following us," I tugged her gown.

Denims pumped on the gas pedal, flooding the udder of the monster; the engine mooed frantically.

"PUBLIC HEARING TEST, MOBILE HEALTH SERVICE UNIT," Kristal was reading the side of the van by the light of the high beams on a beat-up Valiant heading for us at redneck speed.

"That's your pal," Backpack said, and heaved Kristal up onto the hump between the seats. He jumped after her and hauled me onto his lap, slamming the door. Denims pulled away from the curb.

Luckily we were pointed downhill, so the van picked up a little momentum. The Valiant tailgated us, as if willing to give us the handicap until we reached a decent speed for a chase. Denims made a few attempts at sudden hairpin turns but the cow wouldn't corner. And Doug, after blinking his headlights for encouragement, finally made a contemptuous U-turn and disappeared.

"That was close," Kristal said with disdain.

Denims was panting, nevertheless. "Who was that guy?"

"A horrible maniac," she fanned her face, "with concubines all over his neck—look, that restaurant's open. Pull over, we're starved. We'll even let you buy us dinner."

The van lurched into the restaurant parking lot. Backpack assisted us girls down onto the ground, then Denims backed into the street and trundled away into the night. Kristal was insulted. "Your friend just stranded you."

"I don't even know the cat," Backpack said cheerfully. "I met him in that bar and he said he'd give me a lift to I-35."

"Oh, you're a hitchhiker." He bowed from the waist. "Well, you ain't freeloading no free dinner off us."

"I'm not into an eating bag just now, thanks all the same. But I was thinking, maybe you two chicks'd like to get high out here before your evening meal. I've got a Thai stick we could smoke up between us. In fact, you'd be doing me a favor. Then I wouldn't have to worry about getting busted for carrying it in my pocket. I could just worry about the other five sticks in my backpack."

"No way. Grass makes me crazy."

"Me, me!" I piped up, raising my hand.

Kristal tried to wither me with her eyes, then decided to go on inside the restaurant and order. The Backpack and I lit up, in a pitch-dark corner of the lot, and passed the weed back and forth in silence.

((177))

"Warm enough, baby?" he asked softly, after a while.

"I wouldn't know," I blew fragrant smoke in the direction of his voice, "This is great shit . . . I can't see your face, but you have a very musical voice."

He laughed. "Can't carry a tune, but I can talk in B-flat. That's the most laid back key. . . . You're beautiful. Have I told you that already? No? I could swear I told you that, six, seven times in the past second. Must have been rappin to myself."

"How many fingers am I holding up?" I made a peace sign. "Fifteen."

"You can't see me, anyway, it's too dark."

"Yes I can. I can see you, and I know you're beautiful." Our fingers climbed together in the glow of the reefer as I passed it to him. His other hand caught mine and led it to his face. "This is how you can see me. Now say, 'Hi, Cody' . . ."

"Hi, Cody—is that your hair?"

"Right. Long, brown, and wavy."

"And this is your beard."

"That's the beard. We've been through a lot of fights over the past five years, my beard and me, ever since we got together. Used to be, you couldn't walk into a bar without some cracker crankin up a chainsaw and tellin the same, same, same old joke: 'Hey, hippie! How come you grow on your face what grows wild around your asshole?' "

"It feels like a pussy," I laughed. "Very silky."

"A pussy, huh. Well, some day I might let you taste it, then. Now . . . if you travel that hand north—don't poke out my eye—there you go. Those are the eyelashes. Cody's pride and joy. Spread your hand and I'll give you a butterfly kiss." I felt long sleek lashes flickering like wings on my palm. "I'm going to light a match now, so you can get the whole effect. Our dope just went out."

In the brief miracle of fire I glimpsed a good face, a face you could hang your hat on and call home. If you didn't care for green eyes under a rich awning of lashes, you could slide down polished tanned cheekbone bannisters and land in the supple snare of ferns, and if you parted the fine frond hairs of this beard, you would

((178))

see the most gentle smile, and if you placed two fingers on the swell where the lips are pinkest, they also would part, and you would see the tongue, a glistening carpet unrolling the way clear through to the core of the earth, or thereabouts, wherever it is a kiss ends. "Oh, wow—!"

The entire matchbook had flared up when the one match burned down, and Cody threw it to the ground and stamped on it. It was a pretty good time for me to stop kissing this stranger and get the hell into that restaurant so I could sober up on some real food. This was where I came in nearly three years ago: shared reefers, hitchhikers, and sleeping bags hastily undone from backpacks. I should be taller and wiser by now.

Kristal had finished her meal and was stabbing at my cole slaw. "I ordered you the fish of the day. What's the matter with your eyes?" she demanded.

"Ain't you ever seen her happy?" Cody grinned, sitting down next to me and plucking a french fry off my plate.

"She looks like she had brain surgery." She frowned at me. I ignored them both, and fell to devouring my breaded catfish and anything else in sight that I could lavish my appreciation on. "You sure got her wasted. For god's sake, Randy, use your fork and knife. . . . Well, so how's the hitchhiking racket?"

"Aah, it's been a real bringdown," he drawled, lighting a cigarette. "I just came down from Alaska where I'd been working on the pipeline for a couple of years, and nothing's changed. The pollution, the ecology . . . the pigs still pullin over on the highway to hassle me about my long hair, while these huge mother station wagons and Caddies scream past us doing eighty, burnin up seventy gallons to the mile, destroying the ozone . . . and here's me, just stickin out my natural thumb and, just diggin on bein free in the open air and the land—" he turned suddenly away to cover his mouth, coughing globules of nicotine and rare cannabis up from his throat. Kristal rolled her eyeballs and made a dreadful grimace for my benefit.

"Listen," she handed him her water glass, "if it's such a drag for you to hitch rides, I have a proposition to make that will save us all fuss and bother. How'd you like to drive our car to Vegas? Are you going west, too?" He crunched ice cubes and nodded energetically. "See, Randy and me were driving this brand new car that we won on 'Let's Make A Deal' across the country to our Beverly Hills home. We wanted to see the sights, you know? Take our time. But we're both bored to death now with driving and we'd rather fly the rest of the way. We also won a trip to Vegas, so we're gonna be living it up there for about a week. You can meet us there."

"You mean—you sure you don't want to make the rest of the drive? I could take the wheel. If you're bored with the scenery, there's some hot towns for boogeyin on the road. Oklahoma City ain't too shabby, it's got a lot of good action—"

"No, we're anxious to gamble," she waved his mouth shut. "We'll give you the name of our hotel and everything. We trust you cause you're a hippie."

"Far out," he said.

My head reeled with drink, food, grass, appreciation, and thanks for Kristal's generosity, thanks for the break from our dismal touring routine. I picked up the dinner check. "My treat!"

"I don't believe it," said Kristal. "Must be our anniversary."

"Well, it's past midnight, so it's Friday the thirteenth," said Cody.

"I wish you hadn't told me that."

He couldn't be expected to understand about doom days, or to heed the gypsy nerves quivering under her skin.

After Kristal made our Las Vegas reservations from the room phone, I skipped down to the Hilton parking lot with the car keys for Cody. "Solid," he said. "I didn't think your girlfriend dug me at first."

He started the station wagon, then got out and stood over me while it warmed up. "She comes on very strong, on the outside, but really on the indoors she's got a very big heart," I said.

"Oh indeedy, she's a fox."

I kicked a tire. He watched me. I gave him a folded note.

"Here's the name of our hotel and the names we're registered under. . . . I guess I'll see you in Vegas."

He pocketed the note, and his hand came up with a white pill. "This is what we'll do, just between you and me." He broke the tablet in half and dealt one piece to me. "It's a Quaalude. When we meet in Vegas, and if the two halves fit exactly, then we'll drop the tab together and have some fun. But if one of us didn't hold out and already ate their half, or if the halves don't match, then the romance is off."

"Fair enough." I tested the pill with my tongue, and swallowed it. "That was good. Now what do we take?"

His laugh was equal parts protest and admiration. "You've been around, haven't you. You're beautiful. I don't want you to think I like you or anything." My hair was blowing over my mouth; he draped it carefully, like a doting father, behind by shoulder. "Say, 'G'bye, Cody' . . ."

"Bye." I turned back toward the hotel.

"Not even a little kiss?" he called.

"I'm not that kind of girl!" I kept walking.

I stopped smiling to myself the instant I hit the lobby. Why had I wasted all that time teasing him? Protecting my piss-poor virtue from men had got to be a sick habit which must have sunk in somewhere between the Royale Ballroom and the Midwest. I ran back to the parking lot to get my kiss, but the car was gone.

Kristal was in bed, snacking on several bags of vending-machine shrapnel when I returned. "Did that asshole drive off okay?" she inquired.

"He was very nice."

"All right, did that nice asshole drive off okay?"

"Yes, and you're full of shit, because you liked him, too. It was dynamite of you to trust him with the car."

She ripped open a bag of potato sticks. "All of a sudden I'm an angel from the Lord if I'm nice to a hippie. One of *your* kind, hm. If you think you're in the same class as those dumbbells, you've got a pretty low opinion of yourself. I wish you'd fuckin make up your mind whether you want to hang out with stupid people, or the smart ones."

It was impossible for her to quench my nonexclusive warmth for humanity, now that the Quaalude had kicked in. "You're so full of shit," I sat beside her and hugged her neck playfully. "There's plenty of room for everybody. Some people are just simple and natural and straight. Why should they have to be smart, too?"

"Because," she brushed off salt that fell from her lips onto my encircling arm, "it hurts to be stupid. As for instance that dude will find out sooner or later. I just never could understand the point of being a hippie. I mean, why sleep with your head in the dirt, if you're not listening for anything?"

I got up and seized the hairstyling wand she'd plugged into the lamp socket. "From now on, if I hear another word against hippies *or* freaks, I'll curl your face for you with this thing."

"Oh honey, don't hit me!" she giggled and covered her face. "Jesus, you make a good butch."

I advanced, pressing a button on the wand so that it spat hot steam.

"I won't, I promise! I swear! On my mother's dick!"

"We're in the wrong ticket line," I pointed out to her, the following afternoon at the Kansas City airline terminal.

"No we're not." She crossed her eyes, fussing with the bangs on the brown shag wig she'd taken back from me because I didn't "appreciate" it. "I could only hustle enough money last night to fly to Oklahoma City, so that's where we're goin."

"Oh, get off my ass." I had slept exceptionally well. "You're trying to make it seem like I forced you to run around town picking small change out of the gutter. Of course I'll pay your ticket to Vegas."

"And what'm I sposed to gamble with? You know, the pink in that dress becomes you very much. My pants are killing me. I went and ate two breakfasts for lunch. Why didn't you stop me?"

"Why do you want to go to Oklahoma?"

"I'm sicka goin to places I already been."

I grabbed a handful of her cape and endeavored to pull her off the line, "It's my money and I say we're going to Vegas, or I'm going to L. A. without you!"

She yanked her cape free, and snarled her lips back from her teeth as if biting on a blade: *"We're going to Oklahoma City."* She leaned into me: "Keep your voice down. You're in this, too. We can't go to Vegas for a couple of days yet. Not until the state police pick up that hip—hitchhiker. If he tells them we're in Vegas and we're not, they'll know he's a liar—*don't yell*, shh! Boy, are you a nut. You don't keep track of nothing. That rental car was sposed to be returned to New York two weeks ago! How long did you think we could keep driving it around? I had to unload it on someone. So I called the police and the rental agency this morning and reported it stolen—oh, guess what. The agency said they'd already contacted Graham in London, and he said he'd pay whatever the bill was, whenever you turned it in. . . . He must still be completely bonkers about you. I told you to marry him. You'd have made a good wife. Except you went bad—yes, sir, two tickets to Oklahoma City."

"Wait"—I pawed desperately at her furry back—"then we can meet Cody and the car in Vegas! We can still turn it in, if Graham's gonna pay for everything—"

"It's too late," she hissed, "and will you shut *up*. I already placed the stolen report with the cops before I found out about Graham. You go ahead and do whatever you want. It's your god damn name on the rental contract, not mine. Save your asshole hitchhiker. You go to jail for grand larceny." She turned and chattered with the ticket agent in order to avoid the sight of my colorless face. "Yes, sir, that was one one-way to Oklahoma City."

She was right. I hadn't kept track of anything. I'd pretended it was just a free ride. I hopped a storage car, free airconditioning and no windows, and let the slinky rails wipe me off my feet, didn't count no station stops, or how many hustles had linked up like sidecars to our ass-end . . . oh yes, I was in like sin. Every dollar in my pocket and every stitch on my back was hustled. "Same for you?" asked the ticket agent. I nodded submissively.

"First class will be sixty-four dollars, do you have your money ready? You have only a few minutes to boarding. . . . Thank you, sixty-four out of one hundred."

And oh yes, it pained. I could bear the gangrenous torment of turning criminal, because if you're riding with the hoboes, you can get used to any odor, any color, even decay, and even green. But hoboes shouldn't mix with hitchhikers, a sweet and innocent tribe, shouldn't give a well man a leg up into a boxcar noxious with crime, and "wait another fuckin minute, I do not have to shut up" (I knew better than to say this outloud), "I can go round Kristal and call off the cops as soon as we get to Oklahoma City, say the car was never stolen, my sister-in-law is an alcoholic and forgot where she parked it last night when she was plastered . . . unless she made up the part about Graham paying, and the car really is too hot to touch, because she does that sometimes, decorates the truth with as much as twenty percent horseshit scrollwork, and she isn't even aware what she makes up and what she doesn't—"

That, anyway, was my train of thought as it began to cross the crazy rapids. There were those on board who bet the bridge would never hold.

"Hurry up," Kristal said, "we still have to get through the purse inspection."

Kristal's complexion was ghastly. "I want a Harvey Wall-banger," she told the stewardess.

"Can it wait til we're in the air, ma'am? We're about to take off."

"I have to have it *now.*" Kristal had just seen the other late arrival to first class take a seat across the aisle from us. It was Cody.

If he was surprised, too, he was not the type to dwell on it. He caught the stewardess's sleeve as she bent to serve Kristal her drink. "Is this plane going to Las Vegas? No? Good, cause I don't want to go there."

The plane positioned itself on the runway. Kristal choked on her drink, trying to swallow it whole. "Aw, *SHIT!* Hey, miss!"

The stewardess, clamped in her own seat for departure, feigned not to hear. "Hey *bitch!*" The woman scurried forward as Kristal rose from her seat. "Get me a needle and thread, I just split my pants." She locked herself in the lavatory.

After the seat belt sign was turned off, Cody pounced across the aisle, sat in the vacated seat next to me, and pulled a tobacco pouch out of his backpack. "I had to tell you you're beautiful, because I forgot to when I saw you last." With bewitching flourishes, he rolled a cigarette. I began to laugh, in a jumbled fashion. I declined the stewardess's offer of unlimited free cocktails.

"You seem nervous." Cody passed me half a white tablet, which I dropped into the armrest ashtray. "You're interesting," he said. "You're different. I never know what you'll do next. Most chicks are so predictable I just skip ahead to the ending and then throw the book on the floor." He looked down and thoughtfully laid a hand on my thigh. "That's the longest leg I ever saw. Goes clear from here to Tulsa. Prob'ly have to have to wrap it around my neck three times before we might get down to business." My leg slid out from under. "I was hoping you could tell me what Oklahoma City's like. I'm going to a town called Chickasha, just south of it. There's this girls' college there. I'm gonna fall in on this chick." He stretched himself, the pointy toes of his cowboy boots yearning up. Removing the plaid lumber jacket, he scratched ardently under the collar of his flannel shirt. ". . . So far, I haven't got you jealous, and you won't let me get you stoned. . . . This outfit sure is hellfire on sensitive skin. . . . Well, this chick in Chickasha means nothing to me, anyway. I never even met her. She doesn't know who I am. She doesn't know I'm coming. . . . I got onto her through the *Mother Earth News* classified section."

His voice was getting to me again, the way it had last night in the parking lot: as if he were narrating a sweet dream, bowing the low strings, blowing a bit of smoke into the cradle's mainsail to make it sway in time with your lazybones and your crickets.

". . . Usually I don't like to resort to the ads." His hand was back having a siesta on my thigh, "But I partied away every last dime last week with a chick in Puerto Rico. At least I got airfare to Chicago out of her before I kissed her off, but I had to bust myself on a cold, cold highway gettin to Cincinnati where my buddy lives. He's the one that answers all the *Mother Earth* ads. He never wants to meet the chicks, he's armless, writes with his teeth. I look over his correspondence to see if there's anything that's got a trust fund. Sure enough, I spot this one little lonesome bird with a paper-towel fortune. Now, I can tell from reading her letters that she responds to the rugged outdoors ramblin man type. So I borrowed this weird Boy Scout rig"—he chuckled, patting the backpack—"and got some rough sort of . . . ecology-conscious shirts and things from an Army-Navy store. I figured I could pick up enough dust on the turnpike between Oklahoma City and Chickasha to give the effect of having hitched down from Alaska: 'Hi there, my pal in Cincinnati told me I should look you up if I happened to be wandering through' and you know the rest. I can't decide whether to have her take me skiing or to Mardi Gras. I'm not talking over your head, am I?"

There he was, my first fancy man. He caught me looking at his crotch, what appeared to be a tidy bundle but nothing like the rock of ages. And then I looked up at his face, where the eyes were waiting for me. You could almost hear soft brown lashes rustle in the tradewinds like in a good travel brochure: "escape" . . . "explore" . . . "exotic overgrowth" . . . "fabled clear green waters, calm, untroubled, and guiltless, the offshore kiss of, the whispering breath of" . . . "your heart's content" . . . damn, he was scary.

"Another Harvey Wallbanger," Kristal ordered as she passed the stewardess.

"Pardon me." Cody stepped into the aisle and put a hand under Kristal's elbow to guide her into her seat.

"Get your hands off me, thank you."

"Why. You got any loose parts?" He smiled goodnaturedly and sat on her armrest. "Well, I thought there was so much rapport going down between us three that we could have us a little party. You don't often run across folks in the same line of business . . .

((186))

one of your own kind, you know. I wasn't sure about her," he inclined his head toward me, "but you," he tipped toward Kristal, "I spotted straight off. Not that you're obvious to square people, understand. Only to me . . . because I'm in the same game as you, ma'am."

"He's a hustler, too," I said.

"What do you mean, 'too'!" Kristal exploded. "Mister, you're talkin to a lady, and you'd better treat me like one in case you ain't carryin a parachute in that knapsack which you better get out of the aisle, and then I'd like to know what you've done with our brand new car!"

"You're a lady, huh," he smoothed his beard pensively. "And here I thought you was a honky." He stood up to allow the stewardess through with Kristal's cocktail.

"Two more of these, and some brandy if you don't have Courvoisier—a double shot." Kristal waved her away.

Cody relaxed back onto the armrest. "You were asking about your car. Now . . . that's the hot rental station wagon? Well, there's this rich chicks' college in the St. Louis suburbs. And I drove out there last night and fell out in the back of your car, right on the edge of campus. Comes the morning sun, you see me laying about the grass reading a book of poetry, with a sign in the car window, 'Help Must Sell For Tuition $500.' And along comes some horny little French major and I take her for a ride to her bank, and we get back to school in time to lay about the grass and eat Quaaludes til her pants are so charmed she forgets to ask for the pink slip on her new station wagon. Well, I had to catch a plane. But I stopped over in Kansas City just to make sure you two got off safely to Vegas. I was hoping to tell you in person how grateful I am you helped me when I was down. Because I prefer to fly first class, when I'm able."

"You're most welcome, asshole," said Kristal. The stewardess set three more drinks down on her tray. I was flopped over my tray, laughing with my head buried in my arms.

Cody shrugged. "If you snooze, you lose."

"Asshole," she repeated, knocking back the double brandy, "get your asshole off my elbow rest. Now you've finished with your lovely story, go sit on your face."

"Listen, I have nothing but respect for you. I won't blow your scams. Honor among thieves, you know?"

"There is no such thing. Unless—you aren't gypsy, are you?" With each Wallbanger her complexion and her confidence and her curiosity improved. Cody and she began to circle, watching each other across the equidistance, glancing away only to measure the loyalty of my position. I simply gazed out my window, enjoying the superior view, and occasionally I'd smile for my own reasons.

"My mother's Mexican, my dad's Scotch. Grew up in Watts. That's a ghetto, L. A. area."

Kristal was unable to think of a racist epithet for Mexican-Scotch. "My late husband and me used to live on the Hells Angels ranch in Berdoo."

"That's not too close. Now, I had a chick once who was dancing topless for me, and she worked with some of the Angel mamas. I used to hang out at some of their bars. The Sandshark, Santa Ana—"

KRISTAL: "—right, with the fireplace, were you there the day the Straight Satans came down—"

CODY: "—right, we had a chick turned out on the pool table, we were runnin a line on her the whole day til we had to move her into the shitter when the Satans—"

KRISTAL: "—no, it was the Gypsy Jokers—"

CODY: "—about two hundred showed up—"

KRISTAL: "—and this great big axe comes through the fuckin door—"

CODY: "—partner of mine cut one of the Angel's heads almost off, he was a Satan one-percenter—"

KRISTAL: "—and the Angels killed seventy-two of'm, or put'm in the hospital anyway—"

CODY: "—kind of a big party. Right."

KRISTAL: "What club did you ride with?"

CODY: "I didn't. I don't need any of that brother shit, just so I can ride a bike."

The stewardess was passing by; Kristal reined her in. "My girlfriend wants coffee with cream and sugar, and a little bottle of Scotch."

"I didn't hear her say nothing," said Cody. I could feel his green eyes wash over me. His lashes dipped down to mop up the spill. "She's a quiet one. . . . Or are you shy? Mm?" He blew a little dart of air at me, rippling some strands of my hair.

KRISTAL: "Her name's Randy."

CODY: "Is she in the same gig as you? To tell you the truth, I still can't tell."

KRISTAL: "We're together and that's all you need to know."

CODY: "Now, you two remind me of the poem:

The fox knows many tricks.
The hedgehog only one.
One good one."

KRISTAL: "What's that?"

CODY: "It's a poem from—"

KRISTAL: "—no, what's the hedgehog's trick."

CODY: "Oh, yeah. You roll up tight in a prickly ball, and the stampede goes around you."

KRISTAL: "Where'd you get your college education?"

CODY: "I didn't. I'm a one hundred forty-six IQ. I guess I can become anything I want to be if I set my mind, and my heart, to it. But I won't. I've got this problem. I set a goal, I achieve it, then I let it go. I like to start at the bottom all over again, start something new. I'll be a poet for a week, if that's what the particular chick requires. I write songs, too. And . . . I did a lot of reading in the joint."

KRISTAL: "I have never and will never go to jail for nothing I do."

CODY: "Well, my old man touched me for this job when I was young—he had a printing press stashed up in Idaho. Used to print up checkbooks. I got caught passing one of the checks in a deli—

pretty stupid. Now I try to stick to hustling chicks. It's safer, more fun, and rewarding, too."

KRISTAL: "And you get to sleep with them, don't forget."

CODY: "Right. That, too."

KRISTAL: "Well. We have never been near a jail and we travel first class, Hiltons the whole way, and we never lay down with nobody."

CODY: "Oh. Are you two gay?"

$\begin{cases} \text{KRISTAL: "Yes."} \\ \text{ME: "No."} \end{cases}$

"No," I repeated. "He won't fall for that, Kristal." She emptied a miniature bottle of Scotch into a cup of coffee. "I don't want that."

"You'll drink the fuckin thing or I'll shove it up your cunt," she blared. "I went and ordered it special for you." I sipped the improvised Irish coffee, the potion that would give the nearest hustler certain powers of persuasion over me.

Cody winked at me. "I can see who wears the pants in this gang."

KRISTAL: "She's lyin. She was a lieutenant in the Navy before they kicked her out for ballin a huge old bull dyke admiral."

CODY: "She's not gay."

KRISTAL: "You want a show? You didn't pay no entrance fee! It's five hundred dollars! We don't do anything spectacular, though. I come off in three seconds and she rolls over and jerks herself off."

CODY: "You're right, that is not a show."

KRISTAL: "Look, now she's furious with me. Okay, we're not gay. I have to say that, or she'll beat me up when we get off the plane and she won't let me eat her pussy tonight. . . . Well, it's true that we're dry, though. We don't fuck."

CODY: "I get out of it if I'm not attracted to the chick, now, or if I can't get into her head. Even on a rooked gig. I give her some slick jive instead. I tell her she's unlike any other woman I've ever known: she turns me on *spiritually*. I say, 'I'm feelin weird about you. You make me think about things like, what it'd be like to

((190))

settle down, raise a family—this is fuckin up my head. I want to go off alone to make some sense of it.' So I sleep on the couch. Or better yet, I disappear for two days. Then I come back and dangle it some more: 'Hey, I went out with twenty chicks and all the time I was diggin on you, Sally or Sue, you're fuckin up my head. I'm not used to this, I got to get away again to think.' So she buys me a new camper, or a jeep, she's tryin to show me how our lives can come together without the loss of my mobility. She understands my mobility is as important to me as my mojo. She knows I'll disappear for two days into the woods again, but I'll come back because I'm so hung on her. *But,* I don't. To me, a chick is like a dog. Cmere dog, cmere dog! . . . Dog won't come. You start running towards the dog? It runs away, man, it don't run to you. But if you say, 'fuck you, dog,' and turn around and start walking back alone . . . here comes the dog, right? . . . Randy's different. She's got her one good trick, which I still can't figure out. She's the smoothest hustler I've ever met. She keeps her face smooth. She's a peach with features."

KRISTAL: "She's the type men fall in love with. I attract men with money."

CODY: "I guess I'm in love, then, cause all I know is, I'd do anything she asked me to."

KRISTAL: "Okay, give us back our five hundred dollars."

CODY: "I would, but she's got to be the one that asks me to."

"Well," I said, "I won't."

Kristal tried to order me another drink, but the plane was landing.

Cody strapped himself into his seat, then leaned over the aisle again. "By the way, one more thing. Are those your own tits or is that a wig?"

Kristal's eyes ignited. "I've got a cold and my chest is swollen," she said grimly. "You're really an asshole. You could've got way more than five hundred dollars for that car. . . ."

"I did," said Cody.

"I need some money. Now, please," Kristal whispered as we

joined the deplaning passengers. "Don't let him see your wad." But Cody had already spotted it as he was delicately craning over my shoulder, to lob into my purse some miniature Scotch bottles he'd snitched. My green "wad," fat as a roll of socks and eager to play, clamored all over my hand as I skinned a hundred dollars off.

Kristal jostled me away and we headed for the baggage-claim area. ". . . And give me something smaller, like a ten . . . Randy, I know you dig that guy but you got to lose him, fast. He has a knife in his boot." That was not an unusual accessory for a hippie hitchhiker, which Cody wasn't. "He's a bullshit artist, he's seen your money, and we don't need him tagging after us any more'n we need our heads examined." I was a touch terrified of Cody anyway. To him, a chick was like a dog. Or, still more poetic, like a hedgehog. He even seemed to know I was in heat. "Just don't talk to him. Shine him on. Make as if you're in a big hurry, get our bags in a taxi—oh, and if the redcap or somebody asks for our baggage tickets, you point me out over there, at the courtesy phone, and say I got them and keep walkin."

No sooner had I left her when Cody appeared, to help me hoist a suitcase off the baggage carousel. I ignored him, and signaled a porter, who finished snagging the other six pieces of lugage. "You're not hurtin for costume changes," Cody murmured.

I handed the porter a fiver, and followed his cart out to a waiting cab.

Finally, the driver parked and turned off the engine, as I paced in front of the terminal where I could keep an eye on Kristal, still busy inside slavering over a Holiday Inn hotline.

"I'm happy I got you outside. You're always much friendlier to me in parking lots." Cody fell into my stride. "Must be the pollution. Don't frown, you'll get frown lines. . . . This wind throws a mean curve, don't it? I'm not anxious to be stranded on a turnpike by my lonesome tonight. I'm not so all fired up to get to Chickasha so fast. I'm not so joyous to leave you on your own tonight. Ain't you ever heard of the buddy system? Don't smile, you'll get smile lines. . . . Guess you have to get back to work tonight, to keep your girlfriend in furs and Hiltons." He didn't mind doing all the talking. He must have strolled serenades through the bitterest weather conditions you could imagine. "How come you're afraid to break up the team? Do you owe her? Afraid to cut her loose because she'd starve without you as the pretty young bait? Is that the team? You're the brains, the beauty, and the slickness, and she's the fuck-up? You should dock her a week's allowance for the nice try at rippin me off with the rental car. What if I'd been an honest creep?"

I halted.

"No, no," he said. "Don't spoil it by apologizing. I'll lose my fatal fascination for you. Can you and me spend the night together? I promise I'll keep your hands to myself. . . . Don't shake your head." He placed his palm gently on my head to stop it. "Puts stress on your neck, saying no. And all I want to see marked all over you is the good news, after I make love to you." His hand then stroked down my hair.

My eyes were measuring the breadth, overall tone, and comfort of his arms, in case they decided to foreclose on me. "I can't," I said.

"You're . . . not afraid of me, are you?"

No, I'd buttoned down my fear of him, under my coat, close to my breasts, where it warmed, nursed, and fretted.

"Then are you shy? Or married or in love?"

"I don't trust you."

His face went tender with concern. "That's sweet of you. Of course we can't trust each other. That's why I thought we got along so well, cause we feel the same way about each other. We both know all the lies, so what's the point in runnin riffs? How many chicks do you think I'd ever tell all my tricks to? . . . I've got this crazy little crush on you. Don't ask me why. Maybe because you're the first chick I could be honest with, or maybe because I'm a bouncing baby fool for beauty. . . . I want to lay down beside you tonight."

His hands began to search around my waist. "I can't, Kristal doesn't like to have men in the room. . . ." The dizzying plaid of his lumber jacket drew near. I was being sucked into the red and black crosscurrent.

"You always so hasty to pass up your pleasure? 'Whoops, here comes some fun, better lock my door!' We deserve a little time off together. Don't you ever leave the hustle-bustle once in a while, to treat yourself to something finer than a Hilton hotel room with a color TV and a fat roommate? How'd you like to score something a few doors down the hall, so we can hear if she starts crying?"

I smiled inside his arms. "Who's paying?"

I had thought it was a joke, but the question apparently posed a serious ethical problem for Cody. He released me, grinned ruefully, started on another compliment about how slick I was, but couldn't come up with an answer before Kristal cleft between us and scooped her share of me into the taxi.

"Catch you later," he called, rather lamely.

"I'm sorry I took so long," Kristal said after the cab got rolling. "I hope I came just in the nick of time."

"Thank god." I was referring either to small favors or big disappointments.

I watched the bath tap gush. Daddy Water was a poor sort of romance to be purling round my knees, but I gladly settled for the calm. At least that man Cody had talked some wisdoms into me before thumbing a lift out of my life and back into his, leaving his characteristic trail of broken dreams behind him.

I'd learned that Kristal was no major witch. Her spells over people were the cheapo kind that stalled the minute you got into traffic. In one more day I would be walking away from her, yielding her to be looted and dismantled probably, by Vegas vacant-lot vandals, while my plane smeared the sky to Los Angeles.

I felt somewhat sorry for her now. Ever since we'd left New York, I'd seen her freaking in the face of deterioration. She was losing her looks as rapidly as she was losing ground. It was the changed land that was giving her back her empty promises. She ranted, drank, swore, took pills, ate anyway, escalated dress sizes, changed wigs, sweated fotch, hunted down her past by the moon and fled its debris by dawn. . . . Her sole lucky charm was me, the bashful stray she's shoved into front-line duty. Her strip pictures were outdated, her tits were outsized, her stories were outrageous, her skin was breaking out, and now I'd outgrown her. She'd been outhustled by a *man,* a man whom I'd left practically begging to sleep at the foot of my bed. Even if he did mistake my deaf-and-dumb act for slickness, Cody had given me my very own pride, pride of profession almost, pride of belonging with the brigands at last, after nearly month of Kristals. I felt confident to face the future alone. I could not conceive of being ever again strapped for money, or abused for sexual purposes.

Maybe these lessons were very precious, and I still owed her a little. Maybe I should throw my full support behind her until we reached Vegas, so that she'd have plenty enough capital for gambling. I knew she was wanting to hustle tonight, because she'd been collecting room keys from each of the three Holiday Inns we'd visited before arriving finally at the Northwest Hilton.

Three different bellboys had told us that a dangerous wind was barreling up throughout Oklahoma, but it was nothing, I thought, compared to the funnel force of Kristal. The humiliating encounter with Cody, the shame of having to depend on me for funds, and the hail of Harvey Wallbangers, all had galvanized her into a rage for hustling. As soon as the bellboys deposited our luggage in one room, she'd bellow for another: "More class! More luxury! More room! More expensive! Better bedspreads! I'm a lady, not a refugee!" After parking our bags in various choicer rooms, right on up to a bridal suite and a parlor, she'd develop an allergy or an aversion to the towels and we'd make a violent exit from the hotel. She was like one of those flash twisters that came on and disappeared inside twenty minutes, leaving the management too numb-struck to ask for the return of the room keys. They jangled together like a tambourine in her pocket.

The same diversion had gotten our suitcases out of the airline terminal without our surrendering the baggage stubs. Turning off the bath water, I could hear her wailing on the room phone: ". . . my whole trousseau, all my money, my credit cards, my identification, were in those bags. That makes me pretty stupid, doesn't it? Here I am with just fifty dollars to my name and no ID—I could be Harry Belafonte callin you up, right? Except I don't resemble him, my measurements are forty-six twenty-two thirty-eight! I'm laughin on the outside, cryin on the inside, right. My wedding dress was handmade by my aunt from Czechoslovakia, raw silk, unreplaceable . . . no, my fiancé can't be reached, he's in the Air Force in Honolulu, he thinks he's meeting me in Vegas for the wedding. I was gonna get off here to take the sightseeing bus the rest of the way, but now I'm stuck here in the Hilton gettin all horny and everything . . . and your name is Joel? . . . Cramer, right. You sound so sexy, maybe I'm makin a mistake with the marriage. . . ."

By the time I got out of the tub, she was toiling with the airline's New York Office: ". . . I'm just a nervous wreck. Listen, do you have the same president as about four years ago? I used to go with him. He had gray hair . . . Parkins, that's him, I was his playmate. Yes, I'm an entertainer. My entire wardrobe was in those five suitcases. I'm stuck here and I've already caught such a bad cold my chest has swollen to forty-eight inches! Well, I want to send him a telegram about my predicament but I need an address from you, darling. It's night where you are, isn't it. Better make that his home address. . . ."

"What're you getting all dressed up for?" she demanded after hanging up.

"We only have about four more hours til all the bars close up." I fished a cocktail dress out of the size nine suitcase.

She was a bit stupefied by my efficiency. "But I ain't eaten anything since lunch."

"I thought you always performed better on an empty stomach."

"I said, a empty *wallet*."

"Same difference. How's my makeup?"

* * *

"I'd love another drink," I said. "Don't pay any attention to her. She's mad because she knows I dig cowboys."

"You do? My good fortune." The gentleman sat down at our table. "Please don't hold my hat against me, miss," he smiled politely at Kristal. "In Santa Fe where I'm from there're folks enough that wear cowboy hats aren't cowboys. I'm a gun dealer, myself. There's an antique convention this week here—are you staying here at the Holiday Inn?"

"Yes," she said, "we have a room together."

"She's trying to let you know she's my chaperone," I sniped. I had finally gained mastery over Irish coffee. The only noticeable effects now were a kind of viciousness, and a spotty memory the next day.

"When two women are drinking alone in a hotel lounge," said Kristal, with much enunciation, "it so happens most men assume they are whores. I am trying to let you know you're in the presence of ladies. Even if my baby sister-in-law here doesn't carry herself like one."

"No, now," the man wagged. "I would not have sat down if I thought you looked like hookers. I've found I can go through life without payin for that kind of thing and I'm still breathin in the morning. I am sure you are both ladies."

"Then take off your god damn hat, sir." Kristal airily rearranged her neckline.

"It's my vanity," he apologized. "Y'see, I'm a little short on hair—"

"Then by all means, leave it on!"

"She knows I'm crazy for bald men," I explained.

"Sir, let me tell you something about this girl." Kristal laid a silken hand on his arm.

"Call me Brad."

"I'm married to her brother, so I know her. She's had a few drinks so she likes to act wild, but really she's very innocent. Matterfact, she's only been in love once, and that was with a much older man like yourself. She won't even look at the nice boys her own age. And last week, my husband caught her trying to run off with this older man who looked a little like you. Well, the man lost the use of both arms and his neck after my husband got finished with him—"

"—she's lyin, my brother never hurt anyone—"

"—and he had me take Randy away on a sightseeing vacation so that she would forget this older man. Now you can understand why I try to keep her out of trouble."

"They treat me like a teen-ager." I laid a younger, more silken hand on his other arm. "I'm twenty-one and old enough to know what kind of men I'm attracted to."

"You're old enough to get sent straight to bed this very minute!"

"Ladies," Brad grinned and petted both our hands, "let's us toast another round of drinks to world peace and no more conflagration between the sexes. You have nothing to worry about, cause I would not dream, anyway, of conducting myself in a dishonorable manner. I just respect the hell out of women. I believe in that woman power. Fact, I think men are just like putty in a woman's hands."

"Glad to hear it," Kristal appeared mollified. "Then I can trust you alone with Randy while I go to the toilet."

After she left, Brad asked, "Do you two scrap like that all the time?"

"I've been so, so miserable," I moaned. "This is the fourth Hilton I've been in since we left Virginia last—"

"—This is the Holiday Inn, honey. Maybe you better go easy on that ice cream you're drinkin."

"I don't care where I am. All I know is, here I am in another strange city, with nothing to do, and my sister-in-law is a big fat drag, and I'm hornier than I've ever been in my life."

He cocked his head so that his hat brim hid his face, but from the look of his neck I could tell Brad was a blusher. "No wonder she's so cautious about you," he laughed.

"I wish you hadn't promised her you'd behave."

"Would you think me," he stroked the frost off his beer stein, "less of a gentleman and a scholar if I told you I have been known to break some promises?"

"I'm goin out of my mind. This is the fourteenth cocktail lounge this week where all the band knows is 'Love Will Keep Us Together,' " I moped.

"You're too young to be so cynical."

"Shoulda known you'd treat me like a kid, too. Do you always make fun of young girls who're turned on by you?"

"Well . . . maybe you've got me all mixed up with that other fellow you were in love with."

I removed my hand from his sleeve. "Maybe. Except that he respected me and listened to me as an equal. You don't understand. I'm not an animal. Sure, I've got my needs, my desires. I'm a grown woman now. But also I'm very romantic to a fault. I've only ever slept with two men in my whole life. I don't care if you believe me. I'm not the type that can just sneak off to some man's hotel room and *screw*. If I was going to sneak around, it'd have to be the right man and the right—a special place, someplace romantic. Like, the bridal suite!" I laughed. "Do you know the manager at the desk said nobody's in it tonight because it's Friday the thirteenth? Would you believe couples are that superstitious? . . . And tomorrow night was booked a year in advance, cause it's Valentine's Day."

"You think it's still available?"

"Stop teasing me. . . . You don't understand, like I said. You don't know what it's like, not being experienced at my age, when you're so curious about sex and everything. Still, it has to be a special man."

"I will! I will! I will! I will!" cried the singer.

Brad eased his hat back on a youthful tilt. "Oh, I recall something like what you describe. I'm only eleven years older than you."

"That's why I *crave* an older man. How else can I learn to be a good lover? Would you believe I've never given a man *head* in my whole life?"

His exposed face gawped and flushed. ". . . Wouldn't think a gal as pretty as you'd have a problem locatin a volunteer. . . . Sugar, you're almost as pretty as you are a little crazy."

"You're right," I giggled. "Forget it. Now I'm gettin embarrassed, too. I really don't like to be aggressive. It's just that I like you." I squirmed restlessly, looked around, and stood up. "Let's dance. How tall are you?"

"Hold on." He pulled my chair in close to his, and had me sit down again. "Would you like me to get that bridal suite and meet me later on tonight?"

"Are you kidding me? It costs fifty bucks. And we'd probably have to tip the bellman another ten to shut him up. I'm sure a hooker'd cost you less."

"Now you're doing the teasing. Here's . . . one one hundred dollar bill says I'm serious." He pried apart the rawhide lips of his wallet so I could peer in.

"Jesus, I've never seen one—don't do that, my sister-in-law might see us!" I snatched the bill out. "I'll get the room—you tell her I've gone to the desk to check for messages."

"Good girl. That's spunky."

In the ladies' room, Kristal clanked through her keys until she found the right bridal suite for the right Holiday Inn. ". . . I don't like that you were the one who brought up sex. I told you to always let the man go first."

"Times have changed," I twitted.

Later I stealthily passed the key to Brad under the table.

"Where's my change?" he whispered to me out of a blind corner of his mouth.

"What?" Kristal fumed. "Do I have to put up with this secret lovers language? Has she been makin passes at you?"

"I'm a consenting adult!" I shot back.

"You're a *disgusting* adult. Go to your room."

"Ladies . . ." Brad begged.

* * *

"Don't we have time for one more hustle tonight?" I wobbled after her through a lobby.

"We're back in the Hilton now," said Kristal. "I wish I hadn't got you started on that Irish crap. You're ridiculous, you don't remember where you are from one—"

"—one more . . ."

"One minute you're a scared little mouse and the next you're just the eagerest miss beaver—you drive me nuts with these moods of yours. Look, the bar's still open."

We were in time for the last call. Kristal made me order a Fogcutter to calm myself. "Shit," she said, "don't look, but here comes another case of jet lag."

"How's business, girls?" A visiting vice-president of sleaze sprawled all over a chair and most of our table.

"Standing room only," Kristal replied. He held an executive wallet to the candle and flipped drunkenly through his credit cards, evidently searching for his identity. "Put your money away, sir, you can't afford the prices. And get your hand off her, she's not pro. She's straight."

"What's this deal here?" His face stormed over with loathing. "I make more money'n you ever dreamed of, how much y'think I make in just one year? Sixty grand. Sister, I can buy your whole family."

"And I make three times that, mister, in a recession. You happen to be speaking to a very expensive callgirl. I'm used to bein treated like royalty in Washington. Right now I'm on vacation, so put your damn wallet away before it melts. This lady already offered me one hundred dollars and I turned her down. The only reason I'm havin a drink with her is I feel sorry for her. She's very frustrated."

"My husband's impotent," I confessed. "I've been married three months and I'm still a virgin."

Her eyes glimmered approval. "Yeah, he's seventy years old and she's still savin it for him in case he gets it up before he croaks. The old fart is asleep upstairs. All she has on her is a hundred dollars cash, and she figures if I eat her pussy she isn't really being unfaithful to him. Hair-raisin, ain't it?"

The v.-p. suddenly remembered how to exhale. "Sheeesis!" He blinked and smacked his head.

"Well, tough tits, I'm off duty, you two. About the only gig I'd feature is a three-way scene. I really get a kick outa a guy and a chick makin me at the same time all over the bed and the floor."

"You're torturing me," I breathed, sliding Brad's hundred-dollar bill under her cocktail napkin. "Please let's go." She shook her head. I turned desperately to the v.-p. "She just wants more money. Could you cash a personal check?"

"I think I want in on this," he said softly.

He chipped in another two hundred dollars toward the sale of another Holiday Inn key. "Wait a minute, I have to catch an early morning flight," he complained. "Why can't we go up to my room here at the Hilton?"

"Why?" she jeered. "Have *you* got three joints, incense, a black light, a magnum of champagne, and Old-English-Leather-scented bubble bath upstairs in *your* suitcase? Sir, I'm an artist, that's why I command the higher prices. You want references? Now I gotta catch a taxi back to prepare my room. You two give me twenty minutes head start."

She left. "Should we trust her?" the v.-p. asked.

"I do. At this late hour I have to," I sighed.

"Are you Mrs. Parkins?" called the bartender. "Phone call."

I returned, wringing my hands, to the v.-p. after getting off the bar phone with Kristal. "Rats, my husband's awake. Here, you take her key. The money doesn't matter to me. Enjoy yourself, you lucky dog."

When I got back to our room, Kristal was still on the horn. "Yes, hello. I want the number for Western Union in Manhattan . . . thank you. Here, Randy."

I blithely refused my half of our profits. "Save it for Vegas."

She shrugged. "Whatever you say. I'm thrilled to see you havin a little fun with the game for a change. It's like a whole new you."

"Not bad work if you can get it," I pranced off to sit on the can.

I could hear her through the closed door: "Hello, Western Union? . . . No, I'm callin local from New York, we got a bad connection . . . Don't I know it's five A.M., my boss woke me up to send this telegram to some little cupcake of his that's stranded in Oklahoma City. Men just burn me up sometimes. . . . Let's you start typin and I'll dictate, cause I wanna go back to bed. . . ."

The bathroom parquet fluctuated. Suddenly, I was depressed. I was wishing Cody had been there tonight, to see me operate. I might as well have been, for all the world, a natural.

In the morning Kristal received an awesome telegram.

DEAR MRS PACE I AM SORRY FOR YOUR INCONVENIENCE IF YOU WILL PRESENT THIS WIRE TO MR JOEL CRAMER AT THE OKLAHOMA CITY AIRPORT I AM SURE HE WILL BE MOST HELPFUL IN HELPING YOU ON YOUR WAY WITH ALL POSSIBLE SPEED AND EVERY POSSIBLE FINANCIAL COM- PENSATION FOR YOUR CONSIDERABLE LOSS AND EXPENSES AT THE HILTON MY VERY AFFECTIONATE REGARDS AND ALL POSSIBLE BEST WISHES ON YOUR WEDDING IN VEGAS FROM THE DESK OF B B PARKINS PRESIDENT

"Which dress makes me look the saddest? The gray one or this green?" She was rushing to catch the courtesy bus for the airport. "I've been buyin my outfits too tight. They give me a pain in the stomach. I'm gonna buy a *Brides* magazine in the gift shop to carry under my arm. You know, they have to pay you minimum five hundred dollars per bag they lose? Help me rumple the skirt. I'm not sposed to have no other clothes."

I spent the afternoon waiting for her return and growing agitated. Neither the local TV newscasters nor the room-service waiters seemed to have a trace of devotion for Oklahoma City. The room's windowpanes clattered whenever the wind threw a punch. There had been a sudden outbreak of tumors on all the soap operas. When I opened the curtains once, nothing was visible save a clay-colored blowing chaos of dust, snow, and lightning.

Later that evening as we stepped out of the hotel, the same funnel winds shredded Kristal's blond wig, whipped her off her new platform shoes and onto her ass. She sustained a malignant black bruise, and we had to abandon our plan to bring sunshine to a couple more Holiday Inns. Thus we were forced to hustle the cocktail lounge in our own hotel.

But, throughout, Kristal was radiant. Her skin had cleared overnight and was so incandescent she skipped the fotch. Her breasts lilted, buoyant above the graceful jersey tide of a blue dress, part of the new size thirteen wardrobe she'd brought from a Sears store on her way back from the airport. The looser fashions concealed the storage of past double brandies and double brunches puffing around her waist, and she was free to enjoy comforts like heavy breathing and the chocolates she'd given me for Valentine's Day. Then she discarded her blond wig and heaped the thick black rummage of her own hair down onto her shoulders, and the darling tongue kept racing out across those pretty little teeth, and some kind of vagabond twinkle kept showing up in orbit all around her.

She looked like the whole idea behind a wonderful broad or a big terrific doll.

Due to tornadic conditions, no flights had left Oklahoma City since noon, so the hotel was crawling with giddy, hysterical, held-over businessmen. Kristal was the belle of the bar. I just vanished into the shadows behind her tits, which changed our basic act to Kristal as the merry widow and me as the insufferably prudish sister-in-law. Yesterday, how could I have thought her a white elephant or a has-been? She trumpeted right back in, on her second wind, Saturday night and she didn't need me for a loan. I was awash in Irish coffee bought by men trying to get me lost so they could get at Kristal.

She told a great "cream-their-drawers" story. She said ladies had to be wary of men in hotels because a very respectable woman friend of hers was enticed into a hotel room and raped repeatedly by a bunch of psychiatrists from a convention. Afterwards they were sorry. She didn't feel a thing anyway, because she had an unnaturally huge snatch. So they introduced her to a colleague who couldn't fuck because he had this problem: his abnormally giant dick. Matterfact, his friends called him "Rope." After a suitable period of courtship he married her.

I pretended to be mortified at this story and fled to the ladies' room. Kristal came in minutes later for our basic ladies'-room consultation. I sat swaying on the toilet lid and emptied my purse onto my lap. "Was that a true story? It was gettin me horny."

"Except for the rape part, and it happened in a massage parlor."

"Far out." I clawed through hotel keys. "Hey, we can't sell'm one of these—how is anyone gonna expect to get to a Holiday Inn in this weather?"

"I'm usin our key. I want to split in about five minutes. We'll put up the chain lock inside our door."

"What're we quittin for . . . I coulda hustled all night."

"We can only do one hustle, cause we're stuck here," she said faintly. "We can't go to no other bars. And I've got a stitch in my side. You're not holdin up so good either, kiddo."

As soon as we got to our room she threw up and went to bed. I passed out.

During the night, I heard a key turn in our lock. We'd forgotten to chain the door. A man whining for Kristal faltered toward our beds.

I sprang up, utterly naked, grabbed a handful of curlers from the nightstand and pitched them at his head, screaming "How dare you! RAPE!" After he ran out, I slammed the door so hard it shook the hallway, and I slid the chain to.

Kristal mumbled in her sleep, "This's the worse city I been in my whole life."

"Say 'good morning, Sunday.' " A man's voice woke me from

dreams of death's door battered upon by merciless erections . . .
enflamed hotel conventions . . . strangers in the night.

But I had chained the door.

"Say, 'good morning, Cody.' "

He was sitting on Kristal's unmade bed. A towel covered his
genitals sort of angelically. He rubbed his wet hair with a second
towel. The phone rang. I bashed it. The receiver scrambled onto
my pillow next to my ear.

"Happy birthday!" cried Kristal's voice. "Did you forget . . .
Are you there?"

"Um . . ." I couldn't stir enough saliva up in my mouth to
swallow panic. ". . . How many keys'd we sell last night?"

"I let him in. It's your birthday surprise. The weather's much
better. Just be sure you're out of the room by one. I'll meet you
downstairs, that gives you four hours. We're checking out and
movin to the Airport Hilton, cause it'll be another day before the
airline gives me my money so we can split for Vegas. . . . hell,
you're not list'nin. Just make yourself decent. Room service is on
its way. Bye for now."

Death by dial-tone throb. The receiver won't set down in the
cradle so I shut it in the nightstand drawer.

"Hope you're not planning to operate. Your hands ain't too
steady," said Cody slowly. "And how old are you this morning?"

Everyone, even I, always forgot my birthday, with all the excitement spent on Valentine's Day. I helped clean up the red
construction paper and the doilies. "Nineteen."

"Too bad. That's the last year you get to be a teen-age alcoholic."

I began to whimper.

"Such a hurtin head, my-my baby, don't you cry, I'll stay by
your side," he soothed, and handed me a yellow pill and a can
of beer from his backpack. "Might as well not prolong your
hangover, pain's something you don't have to learn to love. Here,
speck of Valium and some warm suds. Whup it down, baby,
that's it."

Why was he nude? How and when did he get here? Why did
Kristal, who disliked men and Cody, and wouldn't allow either

in our room, suddenly betray me, betray her, on my birthday? What had I done between the ages of sixteen and nineteen? I had a lot of questions but they seemed perfectly happy playing by themselves without me disturbing them. Knock knock. "Room service."

"Hold that beer can steady—" Cody quickly secured a tuck in his loin-towel, gathered me up in a riot of bedclothes, and overturned me in the bathroom. "Run a hot bath on those nerves and you'll feel better. I'll sign for the breakfast."

After ten minutes of absently scrubbing my pussy in my cloudy litle pond, I heard Cody rap on the door. "Can I come in?"

I reached a pokey arm up to the rack, for a towel to cover myself. The white cloth flopped into the water, and I dragged a sodden edge up around my neck. "Okay."

He entered, taming down the brown satin waves in his hair with Kristal's brush. Then he shook his head briskly, the wet ends snapping on his bare shoulders. "I tried to keep your eggs warm, but they were gettin things kinda greasy under the blankets. . . . Well, happy birthday. You didn't tell me this'd be a formal occasion." He sat on the tub rim and tugged at the skirt hem of Kristal's white evening dress which was undulating on the surface of my bathwater. "I should've reminded you to wash the tub first. That's three days and three coats of native soil makin that pink-color ring around. . . . But you don't care, do you?" he grinned. "You look much more peaceful now. Almost like you were still alive." He picked up my foot. It sank like a rock to the bottom again when he let it go.

I noticed some vague blue scribbles on his arms. "Are those tattoos?"

"Yah. Don't mean a thing. There's nothing else to do in the joint, so we'd tattoo each other. And we weren't too good at it. Except this señorita here on my elbow, that's professional . . . and this one." He showed me a blue question mark on the middle finger of his right hand. "I get that renewed every couple of years, cause I keep chewin it off. Nervous habit." My head lolled back on the ceramic slope of the tub, knocking over

((207))

the empty beer can, which fell into the water and drifted til it snagged in weedy dress fringe. "See how careless people pollute our natural heritage."

"Did you hitchhike up here, in the storm?"

"Had a car this time. A bitchin little Spitfire."

"Ah. From the Chickasha chick."

He began to dab mascara off my cheek with a washcloth. "Lighten up, now. I'm a skilled laborer like anyone else. Do I ask who buys you these fancy ballgowns you wear in the bath?" I was now staring at the white ray of his bare hip, underlined by a swimsuit tan, where his towel was slipping its waist tuck. "You were pretty easy to find. There's only two Hiltons in this city. I admire someone who registers under their real name." I couldn't see the upper part of his body anymore, because my sedated eyelids mourned, observing a day of pleasant stupidity, at half-mast. "I have to get back this afternoon so she don't get suspicious. It's not my fault. The whole time I was with her I was diggin on you in my head." I yawned. "So happy you missed me, too. I think you'd best come out of that pudding and have some coffee with me. Just to be sociable." He yanked the drain open, and left the bathroom.

To follow our eggs and sausage, Kristal had indicated on the menu a wedge of chocolate cake. Cody lit the birthday candle on it. I blew it out.

"What did you wish for?"

I sat on the edge of my bed, beside him, with the spread wrapped several times around, under my armpits, and with my gaze fixed on the tablecloth, silent and agreeable as a collision dummy. I'd made out a blank wish. Always one to be safe, that Randy, young hedgehog.

"What are you thinking, baby?"

I shook my head slightly, smiling.

"Well, okay. Is it all right if I just look around for a while?" He pointed his finger at my breastbone and pressed, passing down

slowly, until the bedspread loosened away from my tits. He bent
his head and tasted just a tip. The pink puff focused into a small
berry nub. The flanks of my cunt sucked together for an instant,
as his tongue rode up over my chin and slid between my lips,
ducking under the teeth before ripening inside my mouth. His
sorrel lashes closed the green eyes like an underwater sundown.
A hand twined up into my hair and cupped my head as I sank
back onto the sheets.

"What a good boy am I." He leaned over me. "Handfuls of
peaches and a mouthful of cream. . . . Can I ravish the rest of
you? . . . I know you don't like to waste time talking, so we'll
say three blinks means yes. . . . Wait, that was four. Four gets
me worried."

"Okay," I murmured to the ceiling. I'll just not move, I thought.
I'll have a little nap while I get laid. It's my birthday and I don't
have to stir for nobody.

He pushed the bedspread up under my breasts. His towel gave
way against the brunt of his cock—it arched, like a sturdy carmine
handle, and tapped his belly softly as he sat back between my
knees. I could see it was royal hemp, this upward cabling of
muscles with the ruddy crown. He rested his palms on my thighs.
The thumbs slid down til they found the nook where the thigh
cords tether to the furry lips, and he stroked, and he rowed my
legs apart.

My cunt clutched for its supper, buttering itself. . . . Cody
stretched onto his stomach and lowered his parted mouth to the
spoon.

"You don't have to do that," I said helpfully. ". . . I never
come the first time."

He looked up. "That's interesting. I always do." He raised
himself, sitting back on his heels, the good cock bumping against
his waist again. "Jesus! The things this kid says when she finally
opens her mouth! Well, listen." He heaped the bedspread across
my ribs as a barricade, so that I couldn't see my own pussy.
"Me and her are havin a private scene." He asked it: "Tell me,

do you believe in sex as a way of getting acquainted? . . . She says yes. Three blinks. Does my prick agree with that?" His cock nodded jerkily. "Okay. We think you should just butt out, up there. If you get bored, I'll get you some magazines. But all the fun's down here. We got puppet shows. . . ."

"Okay," I murmured to the ceiling. I'm going to get my pussy eaten, I thought, and I'm not supposed to take it seriously.

He needn't have bothered. I felt his tongue doing its field-trip number—forging upstream, chasing over roots and moss, fingers tilting the stones, prying off the bark, a question-marked stick poking at holes—but it was all too distant, far, far inland. I was nowhere near. I was swooned off on a smooth white beach, under a sky like a polished blue lens.

A breeze, strange, stiletto, whistled up the sand. I scanned the horizon, and saw the straggling thread of a twister. It cast its livid canopy over the sea, spinning to shore . . . the sky turned all colors of a bruise. Birds wailed and spiraled in rapture.

The palm leaves broke out in sweat as a pungent humidity set in, and the pluming squall bore down its darkness.

All the wildlife fled inland. Horses bolted, shuddering the ground.

I grasped a mane and slung a leg over. My knees failed to grip. Screaming, I was hurled about on the rampaging spine, as the storm's funnel force roared in, engorged, contracting, and, contracting, "oh" it burst.

I twisted away from Cody's mouth. My cunt was afterflashing. My knees dropped away from his ears but my hands remained clenched in his hair.

"Didn't know you could cry like that," he said, reaching up to wipe the damp hair off my stunned face. His beard smiled through the pearly wet I'd rained on him. "I like the way your little peach mouth opens up when you come. Think you could try it again?" He dipped down.

"Again?" My fists tightened in his hair.

"Why? Are you shy?" His tongue poured onto my hysterical clit.

I gasped, my hips shaking: "No no maybe you better not, it's too much, it—"

"Look, I'm very busy and I can't have any more of these constant interruptions."

"Okay," I reasoned with the ceiling. He doesn't have to chew me out, I thought, just because I'm not as brave as I should be.

My clit was rigid with alarm. His gentleman tongue petted it patiently until my cunt melted, opened, broke out the rare wines. . . . I didn't know where all this juice was coming from, it kept streaming down his chin, pooling between my cheeks.

His tongue started to jab, roughly, muscling in, and his fingers felt like a wild mob of hands now, clamored up and down the slit, seizing my ass, plundering my twat, my asshole, and I began to come—too sharply. He locked his arms around my struggling thighs and hung in, riveted to my cunt, til the climax shot down my spine like jagged fire. My back hooked, my pelvis tipped the great bone ladle and, under a blazing clitoris, flowed radiant lotion over his mouth.

"I keep trying to make you happy, and all you do is cry," said Cody fondly, although my eyes were the only dry part of my otherwise sobbing body. "Come on, let go of my hair so I can try again."

I tensed my hold. I hauled him up onto my bosom. I wanted his company now. I was scared to be alone any longer, with my cunt prowling around loose down there. "Fuck me," I said.

He laced his fingers in mine and gently pressed my arms, elbows crooked, back onto the sheet. His legs climbed onto mine and, as he lavished his tongue into my mouth, I realized he had me pinned, perfectly, with his weight, matching his limbs against mine, and he was going to complete the final assembly by inserting his hard penis into my tender slot.

The cap of his cock wavered at the rim of my cunt, nudging the moist fur aside, fishing in the hot slick, stretching a long weekend with his eyes closed in a deep kiss tangling this girl down so she can't move or cry out, perfectly natural . . . he centered his cock for the shot, and plunged in, dead on, then enjoyed long leisurely strokes, from the tip to the base of his joint, arching his ass, gliding in on a curve, the tough head smudged across the womb's end as his pubic bone shoveled up against my clit. I had given up fighting for an edge. I let him.

He speeded the thrust, until he was driving me like a stake into the mattress, and quickened more when he heard me coming, as the soft loam furrows closed over my face, a low marshy orgasm, the stoned sunken lowing of bones plowed so down, deep, and dirty, that the last rapid hammering sent me below for good, to death and disappearance.

"Are you there?" He rapped his knuckles on my forehead. I nodded, only for purposes of show. "Good, cause sometimes I worry about you."

He waited, then rolled over, lifting me out of the hopeless shambles of my body to float what was left, feathers and flotsam, on top. He watched. He smiled as my long yellow hair swept to and fro on his chest, as he skimmed me back and forth on his cock, dreamy descant moans vaporing up from my throat. "Angel, angel," he sighed. I was something flown, while he guided the twine, and the coming of the whole soul, released, and really divine, fluttered my thighs in its wake as it passed.

"At least you smile when you cry," he said, and set me down again.

I felt very well traveled. I decided to bring him home with me.

He planted a knee between my legs and began to saw me cross the grain. My hips romped around as I snuck a hand underneath and caught his balls. They slapped in my palm, and I inched one finger up the thick back root to creep into his asshole.

He paused, hissing in his breath. I fastened my cunt around his joint and kissed it hard. He coiled, choked, I felt his cock leap inside me. He jolted, unsprung, butted one last time against the roof of my quaking vagina, and jetted sperm up, aiming for the heart.

"What did you do," he groaned at length, raising his head. "I came too soon. And all you can do is laugh . . . well, what do you know." He touched my eyelashes. "Tears. Weird."

* * *

He buttoned his dusty plaid jacket. "I won't swear to it. But I do believe I love you."

My nipples burned under the sweater. But I wouldn't empty a reply into the silence. Clenching my teeth, I ignored the maudlin lyrics my mauve labia were sending up to me. I read off the address from the piece of paper he'd given me. "Til March, Jackson Hole, Wyoming. Ski café, bottom of Rendezvous Mountain, or Million-Dollar Cowboy Bar." I squeezed it into my jeans pocket and reached for the doorknob, to let him out.

He caught two hanks of my hair, reined me back, turning my face. "Try to make it, baby. I want something with you. I don't know what. A something . . . a relationship, I guess."

Love, love, thump, thump, the word flung itself against my locked teeth. Help, I am a prisoner in this girl's stubborn coward mouth. "What happens if you don't call me tonight, or if I can't make it to Wyoming by the end of February?"

"Then we have lost, because we have snoozed. I'm not gonna stick around waitin for your mother to approve. Because she won't. Kristal's hung up on you."

"What do you mean?"

He smiled. "You're beautiful. Say goodbye."

"I was just havin our reservations made for Vegas," said Kristal, when I met her at the front desk in the lobby.

"I . . . might not be going with you."

"Okay. You're a grown-up now." She handed me the hotel bill to pay. "How was the cake?"

"Wonderful!"

That evening at the Airport Hilton, I also assumed the bill for an elaborate candlelight dinner, just the two of us. Kristal asked the pianist to play "Exodus." "Cause my father wrote it," she told him.

"Another Courvoisier?" I signaled the waitress.

((213))

"But this is your birthday. And you're not stuffin yourself with anything except Irish coffee."

"We're celebrating your latest hustle."

"I've got'm eatin out of my *girdle*," she crowed. "They think I've got some sort of scandal on the president that could ruin the airline."

I let her order a flaming dessert. Then I got over the speech I'd been dreading.

She said, delicately, afterwards, "It doesn't seem like a so very charming arrangement. Either way he'll be spending most of his time with this college chick."

"Only until he can get enough money off her. If he calls tonight, it means we can split tomorrow for Wyoming for a couple of days alone, before she comes up, while she takes her exams or something. If he doesn't call, it means it isn't cool for him to leave her right now, so I go to Vegas with you and then fly up to Jackson Hole after a week, which gives him time to ditch her."

"That's just so romantic." She shoved her dessert plate aside so she could lean forward. "He may be the greatest fuck since Adam, Randy, but he's nothin but a bullshit artist. He's not an honest person."

I'd been waiting for this. "At least he was honest enough to say so."

"If he wants to go skiing so bad, and he wants to be with you, how come you don't ski away with him on your money?"

"Because I'm special to him," I said weakly. "If he wasn't honest with me . . . or he asked for my money . . . I'd know he was out to hustle me."

"That kind of logic will get you in deep trouble. Take my advice, and you let him spend a lot of money on you until he thinks you trust him enough to start chippin in some of your wad —then split. That's the way to hustle a gigolo." I went all mushy with horror. "Oh, forget it." She tossed off her brandy and swayed festively to the piano music. "You gotta live your own life and learn from your own decisions. If you really dig someone, then you gotta turn the other cheek and just hope and trust in them, come what may."

"It's the only way," I agreed, relieved.

"It don't make any difference to me if you come to Vegas or not. . . . You and me are almost at the end, anyhow. I was thinkin that, this morning. By the way, are you still gonna go find your foster parents in Long Beach, to tell you about your real mother?" I nodded. "Good. Because that's more important than finding a new boyfriend, kiddo. Well, Vegas isn't your type of town anyway. I'd be in the casinos the whole time. Once I start to gamble you can't get me away for love or money."

"Then where will you go?"

"I told you, I got a room at the Paydirt, on the Strip. Right across from Caesar's Palace."

"No, where will you go after Vegas?"

"I told you, I never know where I'm goin till I get there. You know me." She grinned. "I'm not responsible for my actions."

The Irish coffee had given me that nasty craving again, for a scam, and I stopped off in the cocktail lounge while Kristal went to the room to pack.

My catch of the evening was a scientist, in his mid-thirties, divorced, and highly paid for building lasers. He had arrived that day from Miami for a military conference he was unable to discuss. He talked fondly, instead, of some kind of therapy whereby people with above-average incomes and intelligences could be "up front" with each other. He had an idiotic imagination.

I mutely sipped my drinks and almost started crying. I knew Cody would call tonight. And I knew I would never see Kristal again. I didn't actually want to see her again. But I *cared* whether I did.

"Laser" thought I had an air of sad mystery, and thought I should talk it out with somebody. He offered to pay all my hotel bills if I moved into his room. This would save us both money, since the Army was paying for everything.

I hovered over him with a "cream-their-drawers" story and a

room key for sale and a kick in the head, but it was too lonesome, operating alone. Fuck this, I thought, I've got seventeen hundred dollars socked away in my suitcase and I don't need the petty cash from this turkey.

I visited the front desk in the lobby for the third time. The night manager handed me the note I'd been waiting for. "Mr. Cody called. He'll meet you tomorrow morning. Stay put."

Kristal had wedged a note, too, in our door, telling me not to turn on the lights and wake her up.

I tottered inside and struggled off my clothes. Then, when my eyes were used to the darkness, I lurched toward my bed.

I could see the shape of her, mounded under her covers. Book on the shelf. Put it back. We had come to the end, her and me. Good lady, goodbye. I bent to kiss her hair and fell on top of her.

"Goddambish," she whapped my face in her sleep, "you're hurtin my stomach."

In the morning, I was furious that she'd cleared out of the hotel without waking me. That she could be so easily gone. I would not have gone so easily. If I were her, I would not have let me get off so easy. I would not have let me go.

I lay in the bathtub and eyed, covetously, the water splurging from the tap. My knees began to creep forward. No, I thought. Not today. I'm savin it for my man.

PART

III

She wasn't in her room at the Paydirt. I waited on the line while they paged her in the hotel casino.

Another fit of sobs shook my aching rib cage and I fumbled around the lumps of Kleenex on the bedspread for a dry shred.

"Yeah?" said her voice. I could hear the slot machine orchestra, an endless finale, jangling in the background.

"It's Randy." I gasped for more breath for longer sentences.

She yelled at someone, "Don't take my seat, bitch! You see the chips, you see the drinks, I'm only gonna be on the phone a minute —sir? This broad is crazy . . . Randy? I got to make it fast. Where are you, anyway?"

"Ok—Oka—Okla—O . . ."

"Are you throwin up again? . . . You're cryin." She paused while still another whooping wave of tears dashed against the receiver and gurgled away again. "Don't tell me you're still at the Hilton. You oughta see it here, it's one of the biggest weeks of the year, the whole city's lit up like a king's ransom twenty-four hours. I never heard you cry so much."

Finally I was exhausted. Snot flowed peacefully into my mouth. "Can I come stay with you?" I asked, snuffling. "If I take a plane tomorrow?"

"What happened to your Romeo cuntstrummer?"

"He was supposed to come this morning, but it's midnight."

((219))

"Well, maybe something came up and he can't get to a phone. Maybe he got his tongue caught in something."

"He's not going to show up, Kristal."

"I told you he was a bullshit artist. Worse than that, I knew he was a troublemaker—I'm sorry, don't start cryin again. You come on along, sure, if you really want to. I gotta get back in this game, though. I'm not winnin, I'm not losin, I'm drawin aces and threes, I'm just so hyper. Maybe this phone call will bring me good luck. Cause if I get bad luck I'm gonna blame that on you, too. Take it easy and I'll see you tomorrow—now what?"

"Kristal? Why did you let him in the room?"

"So you'd find out what you were dyin to know."

I hung up, wiped my nose on a knuckle of tissue—except it was Cody's note. "Stay put," it said. Since morning I hadn't left the room. The phone only rang once. It was the front desk, wanting to know if I was staying an extra day. After twelve hours had passed I opened up my suitcase to get out the deodorant and the toothbrush.

I'd given him my heart and my lap. I'd have waited a week in that room for his call. But I knew he wasn't coming when I discovered that my wad of money was missing from my suitcase. Then I called Kristal. I knew she'd rag me cruelly when she heard he'd stood me up. That was enough. She didn't have to also know he'd drugged me with beer and Valium, dropped me in the bathtub while he pilfered my suitcase, then fed me birthday cake and fucked me five ways.

So why did he leave a note telling me to stay? Kristal answered, "That's what pimps do. They kick all the legs out from under. Then they come back and fuck you six more ways and holler for more money. He doesn't care how you hustle it—dry, wet, sideways —because he is too occupied to care. He's too busy hustling *you!* It's one hand screwing the other."

I didn't want to listen to that. So I didn't tell her he'd robbed me. I didn't even really want to see her either. But it gets drafty under your skirt when you got no more legs left, and you need someone to push your little tray around til you get used to the weather down there.

He'd left my purse alone. I had enough cash for the plane ticket to Vegas but not enough to settle the hotel bill.

The cocktail lounge was closed. I called up the Laser's room. The scientist asked me why I was crying.

Something had happened to me in the hallway.

I could be up front with him. He could come to my room. I could come to his room. These group therapy people eschew public places and sunlight, which might destroy them.

When he opened his door and let me in, I was even more upset. It had happened again, in the lobby, the same god damn thing that happened in the hallway outside my room when I went out to get a soda. Men . . . were offering me money . . . to come to their rooms! A shudder cruised through my persecuted limbs.

"Why is everybody in such a hurry?" I asked sadly.

"Takes all the pleasure out of relationships," nodded the Laser.

Not just the pushing and the shoving, but the flashing of cold cash. Besides, I would never enter an utter stranger's rooms for no money you could name, if I didn't feel he was trustworthy. A friend of mine had been raped in a hotel room once, by a hippie hitchhiker who looked perfectly innocent.

But, if I like someone, if he takes the time to talk to me, to relate to me as a person, there wouldn't have to be this yanking out of fifty—even hundred-dollar—bills. We could just act like two people who dug each other, and who happened to be spending a few days in the same hotel with no one looking, and who decided to have a good time together, in this go-lucky whirlygig world. My eyes smarted from weeping and I swallowed the yawns bloating behind my lips.

The Laser agreed completely. I rose to leave. He urged me not to. I thanked him for listening to my heartaches. He asked me how many days I was staying on in the Hilton.

I was leaving in the morning, unfortunately. I was driving a car

((221))

west to L. A. for my sister-in-law. The family thought the sightseeing trip would be good for me, so that I might forget something that happened to me. Don't ask—something a man had done. So far the sightseeing had been nothing but expensive for me and I couldn't afford these unkind hotels.

"You seem so sad and mysterious." The Laser reached out to stroke my face. I flinched. "Jesus. Someone really has hurt you, haven't they."

"I'm sorry," my voice broke over an honest heartache. I opened the door. "I wish there had been time to get to know you better. You're one of the nicest men I've met in a long time." I begged my eyelashes: go on, once more, and then we'll turn in. Bat, bat, bat. Thank god something still works around here. A thin tear was released onto my flushing cheek and I turned away shyly.

He marched me to the front desk, announcing I would be staying on in my room two more days and that the total bill should be transferred to his bill. It was unthinkable I should go through life missing out on all the fun I clearly deserved, fun like getting to know intimately a man who wouldn't harm me.

In two days, his conference would be over, and if we continued to have a good time together . . . if we just let whatever happened happen, maybe we'd even drive to New Mexico for a few days and he'd take me skiing. He wanted to know more of my story. He wanted to get into me. He was sure I'd feel 100 percent better in the morning.

I didn't. When I checked out at dawn, I left him a message telling him to stay put, I'd be back for dinner, and then I took a taxi to the Oklahoma City airport, where I waited for the next flight to Las Vegas.

I'd hardly slept. All night long I hauled my shame around the mattress, dragging the bedclothes after me, groveling for sleep or for dying. I'd rather be dying any day than dumb. I'd rather be weary from loading up a pile of good sense on the smart gang. And my period had just begun. I'd rather my thighs toiled for a proud pain, but all the tampons in the world would not sop the blood of one so dumb. I was really fucked.

* * *

I got out of the taxi from the Las Vegas airport to the Paydirt Hotel and stood glowering down the Strip, at hectic bulbs on the marquees for clubs and casinos, their pale electric commotion in the daylight and the cool gritty desert wind. One hand was in my pocket, strangling and unstrangling my last $2.88.

I sent the bellboy with a dollar and my suitcase to Kristal's room, entered the casino, converted $1.85 to change at the cashier's cage, and played the nearest slot machine until my paper cup was empty of nickels. Then I dropped my remaining three pennies into the sand of an ashtray. Good, I thought. Now I'm really fucked.

Kristal had left word at the desk that I could find her at "poker, craps, or twenty-one." I wandered through the quacking throng of gamblers, not knowing what color hair or what dress size I should be looking for.

It was gold on white that finally caught my eye, as the crowd around a craps table shouted and gave way for a losing toss of the dice. Kristal shrilled a Hungarian oath, scooped up her chips and swung around. Her blouse was unbuttoned to release the rolling white mounds, and the gold chains and coins and charms which clanked like an escaped chandelier when she bumped into me.

"It was you!" she yelled. Black wig curls were sealed to the sweat on her brow. "You ruined the toss! You better stay away from me, go play the slots til I have you paged and then we'll have dinner."

"I don't wanna gamble."

"Then go to the god damn lounge and have someone buy you a drink." I scowled at her. "What are you, five years old? Go find something to do, go up the street to Circus Circus. They got free trapeze artists and a elephant—what's the matter?"

"I got cramps."

She softened. "Oh kid, I'm sorry. I told you, I get crazier'n a sack of snakes when I'm gambling. You go to bed and order up anything you want. Try some tea with lemon and rum and drink it while it's very hot."

I ordered up three Irish coffees and gulped them down before they could cool. Then I pulled the covers over me and roiled in hatred.

The larceny swelled in my heart, gouging a deeper hole for itself. Cramps lunged down through the wound.

The room grew dark. I fainted into sleep, strangling and unstrangling any hapless man that stumbled into my dreams.

Kristal woke me with a tray of food, and changed the blood-spotted sheets. "Is this your first day? Is it always this bad?"

"Just the first and the second."

"Wish you could get money for donatin this stuff."

"I hate chopped liver."

"You're losin iron with all that blood. . . . Meanwhile, I'm winnin a fortune out there! I got the house all worried. I'll see you later."

The instant she left, I phoned room service for a hamburger and two Irish coffees.

Later I wept, pawed through my suitcase in search of loose change. I wept some more, and thrashed in all of Kristal's luggage, but couldn't find any money. She was wearing all her jewelry. I uncrumpled Cody's other treacherous note, the one in my jeans pocket, and I glared at his handwriting sample, the ski resort address. Notice the way the R's on Randy and Rendezvous Mountain swipe like claws—I threw a lamp on the floor and called up the Million-Dollar Cowboy Bar in Jackson Hole, Wyoming. "Is Cody there?" I hollered.

"He left bout a half hour back!" a man hollered back, over a band playing country music.

A stunned pause on my end. "Cody? Long brown hair and long green eyes and, and, a beard?"

"Sure! Cody! Don't think he's coming back tonight! It's snowin pretty hard! Aren't you the same gal called for him five minutes ago?"

"I'm his widow!" I slammed down the receiver.

He was actually where he said he'd be.

Was he daring me to come after him?

I'd do it, then. My imagination began to climb the road to revenge, oblivious to the thickening snowstorm, til it found Cody high in the Rockies. There, I slowly looted his pockets, his backpack, his girl friends, and fucked him eleven ways before the eyes of horrified cowboys frozen in their tracks. When it was over, I was not satiated. I added extra punishment. I made him fall in love with me like he said, and never leave my side so long as he remained handsome and wonderful. That would finish him. That would finish both of us. I was tired, and fell out with the light still on.

Kristal closed the door and sat heavily on her bed. I opened my eyes, trembling with hangover. It was morning. She stared dully at me. "It's all gone," she said, pulled her wig off, unlatched the waist of her beige slacks and let the zipper drift down her belly as she sighed deeply.

"Gone? Not all your money?"

"Everything." She picked up the phone and dialed the front desk. Her voice drawled out now in her Hungarian accent: "Yoo-hoo, tell me who is the meneger off your casino. Mike . . . Corchran? Is that Armenian? Ah, Irish. I vish to speak vith him, thenk you dahlink." She put her hand over the receiver. "How's your period this morning?"

I bunched a pillow behind my back and sat up. "Prob'ly still goin strong."

"Good—ah?" She snapped back to the phone: "Mister Mike Corchran? Is it you heff such a vahndervul sexy woice but your casino is vull of problem, mattervact I em shocked end wiolated at the treatment by your monkey goons who are not gentlemen and treated me like dirt betveen the toes, yes. I em Mrs. Pace in Suite four-oh-three end you end me should speak *frenk*. Ve know the score, okay? I em not tourist sheep lemb, dahlink. Effry year I visit vahndervul Paydirt casino because I loff to gemble. Alvays I brink twenty thousand to lose end alvays I heff such a good time to lose, ha ha! That is the vay the score goes! I don't care about the money,

I heff plenty more. I em a vidow, no husbend to fuck or tell me vhat I spend—but. I em used to treated like a lady. Shills, Mister Corchran, shills! Six o'clock this morning I'm vinnink sewen-card stud end they vallpaper provessional shills all around my table. . . . Good, I'm so heppy you know vhat is a shill. So I lose, lose, lose. Okay? Then the pit boss giff me *teb* to sign. Okay? Still I em not get med. I'm through, I say. I go to bed. Oh no, these bestards say, you pay right now. They shoff me into the beck ovvice. They von't let me go in peace and pay after I sleep—end I em a guest here! . . . Yes, they call me blenk-blenk-blenk names end vun men vants to greb my tits! Vell, I can't blame him anyvay. I em vighting off hends end they make me pay this teb . . . Yes, it is a insult end I neffer received rough stuff in all the times I heff stayed here—no. I em not sayink I vant my money beck. You vould not giff me beck, okay, ha ha? I vas the stupid head, I did not see the shills, that is Las Wegas. I only vant to complain! I em a nervous shook-up! Neffer heff the Paydirt try to tear my dress off in beck room for lousy two grend dollar marker! . . . Vell, that is kind. I only haff dinner vith you because my niece heppen to be in loff vith you. She vatches you vhile I gemble but I send her beck to the room because she make all the men horny she is so gorgeous vive-voot-ten yellow curls down her beck—but me, I don't speak a vord to you I em so mad."

I suddenly noticed why her chest wasn't shiny. All the gold was gone. Even her hand was naked of the coin bracelet, and the ruby-spray ring. "What happened to your jewelry?" I gasped, after she hung up the phone.

"Do you believe it?" She was seething. "I had a straight flush. All my money was down but I didn't have enough to stay in. I'm going to bed, I said. Oh, but you got the winning hand, they said, sign this tab and you'll get all the money after this hand. . . . But they'd dealt a full house to the little old lady on my right, who was a pro! And now they got this piece of paper says I owe'm two grand, and these . . . ugly thugs take me to the office and threaten me. They won't even let me leave to hock my jewelry, no! Two guys are guarding the door, and the pit boss opens a closet—full of mink coats, sable, chinchilla! He opens the desk drawer—

crammed with diamond rings and gold necklaces! . . . They took every piece I was wearing for that marker. . . . Well, mouse, here we are."

I waited breathlessly for her to ask me for money.

"Randy?" She tilted forward, hands clasped. "I need you to help me with this hustle. It's the biggest I've ever done. But they got my gold—" her fists redoubled in gypsy tantrum "—and they *insinuated* me and I wanna make'm pay."

I nodded, relieved.

"We're gonna have dinner with Mike Corchran and he's a big big dude in this city. Don't let the Irish name fool you. We're dealin with the *mob*."

Far out, the mob. I didn't care. I was just as broke as she was, and three times as suicidal.

"But I need you for this one, all the way, Randy. If you come through I swear I'll never ask you for anything again as long as I live. And you get half. And I'll do anything you ask afterwards."

"Don't worry, I'll do it," I promised. I gleamed inside. One good burn, and she'll owe me another. Kristal's going to help me get Cody. Where was I, though? Nevada. "What time can I get a beer in this state?"

She yawned. "You can get one sent up now. They relax on the rules here."

She slept til late afternoon, then we began our "twalette." First, she slung a leg over my neck and plucked my eyebrows. "They been drivin me crazy ever since I first saw you."

"Ow. You're takin my face off!"

"I went to beauticians' school, I'm followin the shape of your bone structure."

"What else am I sposed to be, besides your niece?"

"You're a well brought-up teen-ager who's tryin to act grown-up and worldly wise. I think that pink ruffles dress from Bloomingdale's would be right on the nose."

"Shit, no. It's too little-girl. I should wear your black chiffon gown. Then I'd look like I'm tryin to be glamorous."

She sat back on my waist. I grunted. She considered my eyebrows and waved the tweezers dangerously. "Since when do *you* know what you're doin?" We glared at each other. She decided this was no time to alienate me. "You just shut up and keep bleedin down there."

"Wha—why?"

It so happened, the hustle depended on it. We rehearsed the fine details while she sewed her black dress down to a size nine.

"Thank God someone in this family still has some jewelry left," she lamented, fastening the gold chain with the Aquarius and the Valentine charms around my neck. Then she petted into place the black chiffon off-shoulder flare, with its silk-screened scarlet poinsettia. "Don't hike up that skirt for no reason, so he can't see how your shoes don't match the dress." She frustrated herself for another hour making long sweet ringlets in my hair with the styling wand. Then she circled me. "This guy's got showgirls and whores comin outa his ass but I bet he don't see much young pussy in Vegas. I mean, from a good family. You look . . . innocent . . . and behaved . . . but also ready for adventure. I like it. Remember, don't you dare have a drink. They don't respect girls that gargle in booze, they see too much of it. You're a nice Catholic hotpants. Remember, we go to Mass every morning."

"Ve hed such a nice *Mess* this mornink," Kristal warbled, "at the church. If Rendy's parents should see how I'm lettink her run loose in Las Wegas they would haff me excommunicated. Her uncle is a big priest in Vashinkton. All the Kennedys, dahlink . . ."

"Yeah? I wish I could get my daughter to go to church more often," said Mike Corchran, glancing at the Keno scoreboard above as it flashed green numbers for a new game. I was penciling in numbers on my complimentary card by the light of the table candle. Our voices mingled with the distant tintinnabulation of slot machines, their levers pumping, their fruit spinning, in the adjoining casino.

"I vorry I em the bed invluence on Rendy. Since she hess come here she is all mix-up vhether she vants to be a nun or a showgirl!"

He focused on me for the first time that evening. "Well, sweetheart, you're tall enough. Finished?" He beckoned a Keno hostess, who scampered off with my card. A waiter whispered in his ear and he disappeared from the table again.

We were almost ready for dessert and we still hadn't been able to nail the little man down for more than two seconds of conversation. He materialized to sit down for each course long enough to make sure we were happy with the food, then his name would be paged, or a note handed to him, a word whispered. . . . Waitresses nipped around in abbreviated bums' outfits with gold trays, dressed as cheeky panhandlers, in keeping with the Paydirt theme which I think was either the Gold Rush or the Depression. "Don't touch your food," Kristal hissed, "he said he's got a daughter! *Daddy* him! I'm goin to the ladies room to leave you two alone, this may be our last chance."

A few minutes later, Mike glided into his seat and spun a fork in his linguine. I concentrated on him. His face was a good middle-aged practical square, lined with boxy corrugations, his tough brown hair shorn square; one ear was cocked for business on the wind, his movements were skillful and spry; his eyes skipped around just like roulette balls; I bet he could beat me up with both arms tied behind his back and both legs and his head chopped off. "I hope your aunt's feeling better about that incident," he said. "Unfortunate. At that hour of the morning everybody gets tired, the staff can't tell the difference between the screwballs and the respected guests, and these bad mistakes get made—you haven't eaten anything."

I looked away, pouting.

"Aren't you having a good time in Las Vegas?"

"No."

"A pretty girl like you?"

I smiled slyly. "Do you think I should have anything to do with most of the men here?"

He grinned and shook his head approvingly. "I wish my daughter was as smart as you. You're about the same age. Here, taste this steak of yours. . . . Every damn rock group comes through here she's out of the house. I'm afraid of her getting in with the groupies, with all the VD going around."

"I wouldn't know about that." I nibbled on the meat he sliced for me.

"Course not, you seem like a good girl."

"Well, I don't go out with people my own age, it's a waste of my time. I only like older men. Older men with power."

A waitress bent down with a house phone. He listened, said "All right," and hung up. "How old are you?" he asked.

"Twenty-one."

"Yeah? I thought you were younger."

"I'm a junior in college. Why, did you hope I was younger?"

He laughed. "I'm a family man."

"I'm a French major. Does that mean I should give up on jumping you?"

"Oh, Jesus." Still laughing, he rubbed his rectangular forehead. "They'll wear me out . . . always getting me into trouble."

"Are you sick of college girls?"

"No, sweetheart. I'm just busy. Finish your steak."

"Make me."

Kristal flounced back down on her chair. Her eyes were narrowed with desperation and from peering at the Keno scoreboard. "Guess he didn't fix it so you'd win. They got a new game up. Where'd that prick go?"

"He had to leave. He left us two free passes to the show. . . . I tried, I swear."

"A show! All we need now is to sit around watchin French whores and acrobats! How'd the Daddy crap work out?"

I thought. "I got a little rise. Mostly he just laughed at me. He said if I was still up around two, when things were quieter, to come by and he'd give me some chips to play on the house."

She brightened. "Then it worked."

"No it didn't, he's just not interested."

"You got to keep at it," she urged. "The 'Oh please Daddy,

let me stay up, just one more story.' I'm tellin you that's his weak points."

At two o'clock, Kristal renewed my ringlets in the casino ladies' room, and scored a sanitary napkin from the vending machine. "Lose your tampon now and stick this in your pants."
"I walk like a duck in those things."
"You better not. And no drinking. Remember, even if you can't see me I'll be watching."

As I waddled fetchingly around the blackjack tables, I could feel Mike Corchran's eyes on me. Whenever I turned, he broke into a short-legged trot, a flash of brown polyester, vanishing behind the tuxedoed ranks of the pit bosses and henchmen.
Several guys tried to pick me up. "I'm with Mike Corchran," I demurred.
Later, the head hostess shot up like a golden gusher beside me: "Mister Corchran sends you these chips with his compliments. I mean, regrets. He's very tied up the rest of the night and he thought you might enjoy one of our games."
"No, thanks, I don't gamble," I replied.
"Could I bring you a drink?"
An abdominal cramp prodded me. "No, thank you."
I did a few more laps around the casino, then leaned against a pillar outside the red velvet rope surrounding the baccarat table. The croupier kept glancing eerily at me, over the shoulders of the players. I thought I'd never seen so many people in a place so deserted. Everybody's mind was off behind closed doors, while their eyes prowled around outside like Dobermans.
"Where's your aunt?" murmured a voice that came up to about my chin. Mike Corchran whistled tunelessly next to me.
"Oh, hiya. She went off wherever she goes every night . . . she gets loaded, picks up some man in the casino, and doesn't come back until morning."
"Yeah?" Concerned, he stopped cracking his fingers and grazed

them over his balls, dying to scratch. "Did you see the show that's on in the lounge? Couple of good kids."

"I thought you might wanna come tuck me in."

"Oh, Christ. You're a pain in the ass," he groaned, smiled, and motioned me toward the elevators.

I turned my key in the lock and opened the door so he could see past me that the room had no aunt inside. "Good night, dear." He adjusted my elbow so that I faced in.

"Aren't you coming in to read me a story?"

"No, sweetheart, I was just teasing you."

"Oh." My curls drooped. "I wouldn't seduce you, unless you wanted me to. I'm just feeling so lost in this place."

The corridor was empty. He brushed me inside the room and left the door slightly ajar. "Tell you what. I'll ask them to bring up a couple of drinks, we'll talk, you'll get very sleepy, and then I got to go." He sat down briskly in the armchair across from the two double beds, picked up the extension phone, and dialed two digits. "Who's this? . . . Peppy, this is Corchran. Let's see, what room am I in. Uh . . . Suite four-oh-three. Send up a double martini right away. And a Coke for me. Some kooky kid wants her bottle before beddie-bye. . . . You're shitting me. Tell him I'll be down in fifteen minutes. . . . Nah, nah, fuck off. This is Winnie-the-Pooh time, I told you. Hurry it up." He hung up. I pulled back the bedspread, propped one pillow against the headboard and hugged the other against my waist as I sat down, tucking one leg under me and dangling the other over the side, rubbing my heel against the valance until my shoe, which was the wrong color for my dress, slipped off and disappeared under the bed. He sighed. "I've got two daughters, one seventeen and one nine. They're both a pain in the ass."

"Could I have an Irish coffee instead of a martini?"

He laughed helplessly. "No, sweetheart. That'd keep you up all night with nightmares. Why'd you think us micks invented that shit? . . . So tell me about school. What're you going to do after you graduate, get married and raise kids?"

"I'm gonna do volunteer work for politicians, and some modeling. When I think about getting married . . . it'd have to be a real man. Someone who commands a lot of respect. Someone I feel safe with." I tried not to think about Cody. "You don't get to meet many of those, if you sit around and wait." I wondered what a martini tasted like.

He mulled me over, up and down. Kristal was right: he was getting interested. "Well, you're not a pain in the ass. I was kidding you. You're kind of refreshing." His hand groped in his inside coat pockets, pretended to scratch his ribs, and withdrew. "Anyway, thanks for getting me away from all the pressures down there for fifteen minutes. That's why I always appreciate my home, my family, my wife."

"But," I mused, "do they appreciate you?" He stared at me. "I mean, I'd love to have a father like you. I always did wish for somebody strong. Not a hypocrite."

"You're very sweet." He was very moved. "I'm going to use your bathroom, all right?"

"Take your time. You can use my toothbrush, too," I giggled.

"No, dear, I'm not staying the night. Jesus."

"I only meant you have garlic on your breath."

He grinned, shook his finger at me, and closed the bathroom door behind him.

My heart puttering, I yanked back the bedcovers, pulled up my skirt, shoved my underpants down to my knees, and planted my ass on the pillow. I clutched my scalp with both hands, clotting my ringlets with sweat. Then I leapt up again and examined the pillowcase. There was a perfect crimson vagina-print on the whiteness.

I hopped my buttocks around the sheet underneath, smearing a little reddish rumpus around, then pulled up my pants. I silently ran to the door and closed it, after slinging the "MAID PLEASE CLEAN THIS ROOM" sign around the outside knob.

When Mike came out of the bathroom he saw me braced against the door, my eyes wide with panic. A key was turning in the lock, and the door—"My aunt!"—shuddered against my back.

"Rendy dahlink?" Kristal squeezed her head around the jamb. She saw Mike Corchran. "AI-EE!"

The shock sent her flying back into the corridor as I slammed the door and, hands shaking, I slid the chain-lock into place. "She'll just murder me, you gotta believe me!"

We heard voices of alarm outside. Mike forced me aside, unchained the door.

Kneeling on the carpet, several hotel guests had hoisted Kristal to a sitting position, to plunge her head between her legs. Her slacks creaked, and she revived. Mike hooked capable hands under her armpits and dragged her inside as she stumbled to her feet.

I had shut myself in the bathroom. "ENIMAL!" I heard her cry. "Vhere is she? Vhat haff you done? Ah, God, my heart! She vas a WIRGIN!"

"A what?"

"A FIR-gin! You heff attecked a innocent sixteen-year-old firgin!" She burst into tears.

"Mrs. . . . I haven't touched your . . ."

"Liar!" I pressed my ear against the door as she lowered her voice. "Do you know vhat you haff done? Oh, vhy did I leaff her alone vor two minutes! Vhat big story did she tell you, how she is a big college girl, she is a model, she is tventy-six? My God, you couldn't see how she vas pure end so young end her parents vill put us all in jail?"

"Kid," Mike called, knocking on the bathroom door.

"Security," someone was knocking on the room door. I emerged in time to see Mike admitting the house dick. Then I pitched forward onto the rug because I only had one shoe on. Kristal screamed and grasped a patch of her blouse under her left tit. The jungle population on the silk print heaved up and down with her bosom: "You think I don't know vhoopee vhen I see it? Vith her hair a mess en vun shoe missink?"

"He didn't," I quailed. I was permitted to tell the truth from now on.

"Liar, you heff alvays lied!" Wheeling, she made for the phone on the nightstand between the two beds, "I em callink your father in Vashinkton—" and she saw the stained pillow. "Ah God, God!" It slid out of its case, which Kristal raised incredulously. Then she grabbed a corner of the bottom sheet so that it shrieked away from the mattress, and she held it aloft so that the three men could see the red grief trail.

"I got the curse last night," I protested feebly, then broke down. It was no great relief to be telling the truth, because it was the losing side. I was under enough strain as it was.

Mike looked from the wailing aunt to the linens, to the weak-stomached waiter, to the sobbing pile of teen-age frustration on the floor, to the embarrassed detective, and made a "shhhh—" noise through his nostrils. It was the sound of his final disappearance.

I had my own reasons for crying. When I looked up, he had been replaced by a strange diplomat, a man with keys, in a coal-colored suit, with a sleek and jaundiced face. Kristal had regained her breath and was bawling Hungarian contracts. She tore the pillowcase repeatedly until she was left with a precise patch of blooded evidence. The man sat on the other bed and protected the phone with one hand. "I vant a doctor!" Kristal ranted, flailing the bit of sheet. The waiter unwisely remarked that Sinatra could get ten grand for that size shred of his athletic support. The waiter was replaced by a wider man with chins. "—I vanna lawyer, I vant police, I vant to call Vashinkton!"

"I don't think," said the diplomat, "you want to create that kind of trouble for yourself."

"Ah God," Kristal sank onto the opposite bed, "there is no dollar sign on her prizeless purity end I em in the middle of dogs . . . no, I vanna drink. I vant to vorget." Her head bowed. Mascara babbled down her cheeks.

"Good girl," the diplomat signaled, and the house detective unveiled the double martini from the tray near the phone, "and then we'll talk about sensible solutions." I was too young for even a beer.

I don't know what special affection Kristal had for the number fourteen. They offered ten, and I could tell they'd go as high as fifteen.

"Bestards," she hiccoughed, wiping her face with the pillow-case and crumpling it onto the tray. "Ah, God," the sadness. We were both very shaken by the experience. The long hours of sobbing, hurling reproaches at each other, at God, at gangsters, tugging on the small white cotton square with its picture of an angry mouth, the humiliation, the meat prices—they hadn't made it very easy. We expected that. What they didn't know was, we suffered every degradation we pretended to suffer, and then there was nothing left. There was no filling the emptiness in our throats after Kristal changed the fourteen thousand-dollar bills at the casino cashier and we checked out.

At a downtown hotel, breakfast was pushed around the plate along with hopes for sleep. The money burned our pockets, our stomach lining crackled, went up like celluloid under a match.

We changed flights in Salt Lake City.

As our plane climbed the sky and Wyoming's Rocky Mountains crashed like petrified breakers, Kristal really spooked. "This is the stupidest, craziest, most asinine fuckin idea you ever had. Whoever lives on those things must be nuts."

"I don't think anybody does," I leaned over her, saw the rapture outside the window, and my intestines gawped. This might be too high for me. "Anyhow, it's a better idea than goin to Reno where you'd just lose your money all over again."

"I didn't lose no money." She smiled grimly.

I motioned impatiently for the stewardess to bring me more coffee. "I know you," I sniped. "You'd play, and if you were winnin, you'd win til you lost, so that you could turn around and start to win again. And if that didn't happen soon enough for you, you'd run to the next town. I don't call that a living. I don't even call it a life."

Her eyes bugged. "Here we are chasin a cuntlapper bullshit artist up in the North Pole, just cause he ripped you off for peanuts, and you have the balls to criticize *my* life?"

"I wanna *get* him," I muttered for the hundredth time, and scorched my tongue on my cup.

"And I believed in you, in what you wanted to do. You were lookin for your real mother. You were gonna find your home." My mother was furthest from my mind, where I had kicked her. The plane hit an invisible wintry turbulence and I sucked down my fear of finding my home. "And now you just made a whole seven thousand dollars and all you can think about is tearin back to the same god damn dude that rolled you, so you can get laid and get rolled all over again, which is just what he will do."

"You were sposed to help me," I said in sudden distress, "so it won't happen again."

"I promised, I know. But I don't have to like it. Where's the barf bags?"

"Use your purse."

"Now I know why I never missed havin friends," she muttered. Her hand gripped a patch of monkeys on her blouse, that same place under her left breast, some kind of local pain. "I know my life is a buncha shit. But it's hard work. And I'm a widow and a orphan." The airplane plummeted for landing in the Grand Teton Mountains.

We'd landed too close to the sun. Its chill blaze shellacked the sky and the white peaks to a radiance fatal to the gaze.

As we disembarked in the tiny airport, Kristal and I stooped, blindly hugging ourselves. Our furs seemed no more than gauze in the cold, and the glistening pure air was stropped like a razor to cut fine.

The other passengers strode around in dark goggles, feather-weight parkas, and quilted pants, shouldering ski equipment from the baggage claim. They beamed wordlessly at each other, full of mutual trust, and emited breath similar to bleached steam.

It was a good thing neither of us could inhale the stuff. The other folk would have noticed the breath of an undesirable element. This obscene shit-tinted gas would come fluffing out of our mouths, and they would have smelt nighttime, cocktail lounges, strip clubs, malodorous men, empty promises, the caffeine, the liquor, and the larceny.

Against the snow, our skin looked the color of greasy gunmetal, like we were sloppy mutants coughed up on Heaven's impossible shore. Our lungs were collapsing, dying for the lower stratospheres of the lower species, and the dark toxic sleep of crooks.

A courtesy bus deposited us at Teton Village, a small resort complex at the foot of the ski slopes. It was twelve miles from the town of Jackson Hole, where Cody was cooking, but it had a Hilton and the Vegas travel agent said Rockefeller built it, so I thought Kristal might be mollified.

She was, once she got her second wind.

"Fuuuck," she said, in awe.

We were standing with our luggage in the snow, waiting for the Hilton bellboy, a huge ruddy hippie in woolens, with ski-tow tickets stapled all over his behind.

The beautiful white hump of Rendezvous Peak tilted back over the darling collection of hotels, shops, chalets. Occasional specks skied into view, down the crests, down the deltas, into the lap of Rendezvous where others just as prosperous were waiting for the lift to swing them to the top again.

White people with red faces on vacation, and the silence was soaring, all over the firmament. "Wall to wall suckers," Kristal opened her arms, unmindful of the cold, "this place is so exclusive I'm gonna come in my pants if I don't freeze first. Oh, fuuuck."

I knew what she was trying to put into words. Here was a virgin community untouched by human hustlers. You could just savor the elegant chilled farts. And we were the first pioneers. This was the land of the free, America. A simple phone call to a travel agent could accidentally deplane you on the upper crust: so rich, so innocent, so *ours* . . . because the only property of money is that it changes hands.

"Hoooly fuuuck," said Kristal, and then the French heel on her boot encountered a patch of ice. She plunged into a snowbank.

The desk clerk advised her to buy some wiser boots, with cleats. "I need a whole wardrobe," Kristal agreed, animatedly signing the register. "Can you tell me which shops to go to? And can you cash a personal check?"

At a central shop in Teton Village, Kristal tossed parkas, down-filled coveralls, hats, mittens, soft dense sweaters, long-johns, turtlenecks, socks, and scarves onto the sportswear salad she was growing on the counter. She listened fastidiously to the advice of the cherry-cheeked girl who waited on us. "Well, of course I want her to be warm," she petted my butt, "but sexy. I gotta find her a rich husband in a week."

The girl laughed, "There's plenty of rich people around, for sure, but all they do is ski. We're not a real swinging place."

"We are not," replied Kristal evenly, "swingers."

They arrived at a lemon-yellow outfit for me, topped by a pink stocking hat with a spectacular pompom. "Who do I make the check to? Can she wear that rig outa here? . . . Randy, go up near that steam shovel and find out about ski schools."

The steam shovel was the chair lift outside the window. I pulled her aside. "I ain't here to learn skiin," I seethed. "These are just warm clothes, that's all."

"You wanna 'get Cody,' I was under the impression," she said smugly. "You think he'd give you your money back if you walked into the Cowboy Bar and started hollerin? No, you're gonna walk in on the arm of some rich dude and start off the hustle by shinin him on. Now, if all the rich guys here are skiin around the mountain, that's where you go to find one."

"But that could take days."

"Maybe," she shrugged. "That's your problem. *I'm* not goin up there."

I enrolled in an afternoon novice class, by which time I figured I'd be fully awake the next day. When I returned to the ski shop, the girl said Kristal had gone to the jewery boutique. "Oh, you must mean Mrs. Florentine," they said in the jewelry store. She had gone on to the souvenir shop. In the souvenir shop they said Mrs. Florentine had left. I half-skated down the icy bank leading to the Hilton and snuggled into a stool at the bar.

Kristal plucked the Irish coffee out of my hand. "And while we're on the subject, you're not touchin the booze no more. I'm puttin you on milk from now on. Listen, if you're out to hustle another hustler, you have to be on your best smarts at all times."

We ate in the dining room, the silence between us marred only by Kristal's lips smaking on the rim of her brandy snifter. She was taunting me.

Just wait, I swore into my cocoa, I'll be out there tomorrow and inside three hours I'll come back with a rich turkey.

As her hand raised her glass again, I noticed the subtle glimmer of jewelry. Native Indian rings and bracelets covered her fingers and wrists. If there was no gold in Wyoming they sure stocked a pissload of silver.

The mountain air had fairly whomped us in the chest, and after the hot milk and the Courvoisier at dinner we both rowed ourselves to bed. Before dropping off to sleep I mumbled her name.

"What?" her voice wobbled in the darkness. "You gettin the DT's already?"

"How're we gonna get Cody?"

"You're gonna be actin like the money he took from you meant nothing whatsoever to you, just pennies. And when he sees you with a rich dude he'll think you're hustling him and another shipment's comin in. So he'll be tryin to get close to your good graces again, so he can be there when your rich dude starts pilin the diamonds and the pearls all over you. You can even let'm fuck you again."

"And then I'll rip him off." I smiled and began to count sugarplums.

The change in altitude must have puzzled my ovaries, because in the bathroom the following morning I found that my period had stopped.

It was 8 A.M. and I let myself out quietly so as not to wake Kristal.

The mountain dissolved upward into a dim fog. Only my face strove through the cold, while the rest of me got off easy, sealed by my new fashions. Except for my pink lid, I felt lemon and yellow through and through, and with a tummy full of egg yolks and armfuls of rented ski gear and a sunny body temperature, I trudged to the chair lift. Good morning! how are you! P. S., I have a gun! I felt like shouting to the pleasant people, my new friends, and future in-laws for the outlaws . . . but to get on the chair tow you had to put your skis on. I'd already forgot the instructions given to me in the rental shop, so I bought a ticket for the aerial tramway and climbed aboard.

Apparently, reformed alcoholics enjoy a false euphoria for a short time. It was over for me the instant the tram door closed me inside the small gondola along with twenty-five euphoric skiers, palpitating with health, and we were hoisted into the sky. My breakfast crowded my unborn screams. My eyelids sank, my eyeballs rose.

The one time I peeked, we were passing a forsaken rock ridge that tripped and swooned down four thousand feet. Altogether, the vertical drop was 4,139 feet. I learned a lot from keeping my eyes closed and my ears open. There were those on board who called this mountain "Mean Big Mother" and it was up America's largest ski slope I was heading. Someone nudged me and described what I was missing, saying I should wait to go back to sleep til we got to the top, which took twenty minutes, not too bad for two and a half miles.

Outside the tram, I laid my skis down and leaned back on my heels and tried to adjust my organs to the scenery. The sky was a dazzled blank blue, and the ground hurtling down and away from my boots was so white it was like a war between the stars. But a thick fogbelt obliterated the mountain's waistline. Behind me was a lodge. I had only three hours to wait til beer flowed. In there I could shanghai rich bachelors before they went off the precipice.

As if aware they would have to go on alone, my skis began to slide, picked up speed quickly. Some ways below a gentleman stopped them with his pole and motioned me to hop down and rescue my equipment.

I forgot the lodge and stumbled down the hill leading to the trails. Lucky for me Fate ain't wasting her time, I thought. Lucky for Fate, cause I ain't the patient person I used to be. And look, he's handsome, too.

"If a runaway ski gets going down this giant, someone gets decapitated," the man said cheerfully. "Let me help you with your bindings."

"I'm sorry, I'm just such a nervous wreck," I began, after he'd secured my boots to my skis. "My sist—"

"You'd best go over there if you're nervous," he laughed, pointing a glove. "That's the easier slopes—in fact, follow the girl in the green jacket with the red hat. That's my old lady." A distant red-green figure waved a ski pole and vanished over the rise. "Just keep her hat in sight, she's taking all the laid-back trails." He poled off in the opposite direction and sailed off a cliff, which was the expert trail.

I pretended I was not conscious until my skis had glided me to the brink of the "easier slopes." Then I found I was okay, spiritually, so long as I didn't move. The only way to stop heading downhill was to sit down.

Skiers whisked past me, making swift curtseying turns. Because I was sitting in the snow, so many patroling medics halted their run to examine my bones that I taught myself to stand, lounging against my poles and leaning away from the ravines.

The fog drifted upward, shook off a light snow, then faded. Now I could see clear down to the bottom of Rendezvous Peak. Teton Village was so tiny I could have reached out and squashed the Hilton with my thumb. I could have saved this white land from crass gypsies bearing rubber checkbooks.

And then I met Mannheim.

He was sweet, he was innocent, he was good, he was good-looking, he was rich, he was a patsy, and he helped me get to the bottom. It took four hours, so I had plenty of time to spin a story, while Mannheim showed me how to inch, slide, scrape, and finally to ski to the foot of the Mean Big Mother.

What *was* this stupid girl doing poised on top of the awful mountain, with no prior experience in freefall?

Well, it was the only place where she could get away from her sister-in-law. But the story begins further back. A couple of years ago, Randy ran away from home and fell in with the hippies. All the livelong day and every day, she screwed around, smoked dope, lived for the moment, until she got involved with heavier drugs and drug traffic. Then her boyfriend flipped out and she got scared. She ran back home to Virginia to stay with her brother, who took her in and helped her clean up. And now that she has recovered she's not sure what to do with her life.

Now, her brother recently married a former stripper and B-girl who made no secret about her affection for his money. In fact, if she weren't such an outrageously comical character there would be no living with her. Anyhow, his new wife got it in her head that Randy should solve her problems like she did: go forth and marry a rich man. So she decided personally to drag Randy from one luxurious resort to the next and train her canny eye for wealthy bachelors. Randy doesn't give a fuck, she knows it's a waste of time. She just enjoys going to all these fancy places. But she's starting to wish she could find a way to sneak out and have some fun. Unfortunately, her sister-in-law never leaves her side and cuts short the advances of any man who isn't obviously wealthy and eager to get wed.

Next week they're going to Honolulu. Randy is hoping to learn how to make it on a surfboard with some beach bum, because doing it on skis looks out of the question.

"You mean, if we had dinner tonight we couldn't be alone?" Mannheim asked, with his faint melodious German accent. He was head anesthetist for a Chicago hospital and preferred to be called Mark. "Why don't you tell her I'm a rich man who wants to marry you?"

We had just slid in front of the ski café at the foot of the mountain. I glanced at the rosy huffing mob of cocoa drinkers on the open-air terrace, and wondered if Cody was there, and if so, if anybody was warding off the weather with two simmering spoonfuls of his risky green eyes. "Careful," I warned Mannheim, "it'll cost you plenty."

"I hate to see a blond go to waste . . ."

"You wouldn't want to waste Kristal, either, she's a gypsy brunette with giant knockers and—oh, what am I saying." I shook my head ruefully. "Here I'm sposed to be a cleaned-up decent person and all I can think about is orgies. Listen, she's going to show up any second, and it's not worth the hassle for you, cause I'm sure there's loads of dynamite chicks here for you to party with. You're kind of easy to look at."

He had taken off his knit hat and goggles, revealing wispy brown hair, modishly long, and tender gray eyes with rays of crow's-feet, and dimples, all those scars of kindness and breeding, and when he turned his chin you could see he had a quality profile. "How do you know how I get my kicks?" he persisted. "Maybe I like dangerous situations. Maybe I could sneak around to your room tonight and hook up the chair lift to your bedroom, and away we go. Ever make it on a chair lift?"

"Ever have a chick throw up all over you while you were makin it?" I laughed. "Okay. If I come with my sister-in-law for dinner, and you lavish money and pretend you're just all bent out to make me your fiancée, in a couple of days she'll not only be leaving us alone, she'll stay in her room and toast us with champagne and stay smashed the rest of our vacation."

"Sounds like a bit of a gas," he chuckled. "And I have another idea. I'm sharing a room with an old friend who's very good with the ladies. I'll have him come along. He'll take her off our hands in no time. That's it—pull that piece there." My bindings snapped open and I jumped free of my skis. "Where do you want to put your gear?"

"I'm takin it back to the rental shop. I don't need this crap no— anymore. I just found my future husband!"

"Another Randy," Victor groaned, as our drinks arrived. Beyond the windows of the Alpenhof cocktail lounge, that steep ivory fang Rendezvous launched into the deepening twilight. Around its root, floodlights shimmered the icy path linking the Teton Village hotels.

"Oh right," remembered Mannheim. "Vic had a Randy a couple of weeks ago at Snowbird. Randy One was a real drag."

"Very possessive chick," said his friend. "After only two days, she was demanding everybody change rooms around so she could get to my body more, and all kinds of shit. Wanted me to leave my wife." A short, husky real estate broker, burnished and swollen from the neck up by an obsession with the outdoors and heavy drinking, Vic had been mowing down the Mother all day. He and Mannheim were on the last week of a month-long stag tour of great slopes and selected chicks, after which they would return to Chicago.

Earlier that afternoon, after leaving Mannheim, I'd flailed down the path to the Hilton, to tell Kristal about my conquest. On her bed I found a note saying she had gone into the town of Jackson Hole to shop, which reminded me to call the Million-Dollar Cowboy Bar.

"Cody? Not here," a man shouted over a jukebox attack. "Try the Great Western, that's where he stays. Is you the same chick was here last night with him? You left an earring, silver turquoise thing."

"Just throw it out, I got lots," I hung up. That was all I wanted to know: he was still in town. I left a long note for Kristal which detailed the con and where and when she should show up.

"I'll get her drunk, we'll have sex, and she'll forget all about you two," Vic rattled his bourbon and rocks belligerently. "Her tits had better be as big as you describe. I want to get to bed early."

"Oh, I don't think so," I said.

"She won't fall for his charms?" asked Mannheim. "He keeps telling me they're considerable."

"I mean, I don't think he'll get her drunk."

"Watermelons," Vic muttered, as Kristal's sweatered chest bore past the hostess in the doorway.

"My sister-in-law, Kristal," I said.

She looked at me, at Mannheim's hand on my leg, at the steaming goblet of Irish coffee in front of me, and at Vic, who stood up. "I am not," she said to me, "your god damn sister-in-law."

"This is Vic," I said.

She twirled a red wig curl contemptuously. "Good evening, potato-nose."

Vic pulled out a chair for her. "Right this way, cow-jugs."

"The hell I will." She sat. "Hey!" she called to the waitress. "I want a triple Courvoisier." She plucked up my glass and sniffed.

"My sister-in-law thinks she's my mother," I said.

"I'm her nurse," Kristal snapped.

"I'm confused," said Mannheim.

"No wonder," she arched an eyebrow. "Randy's a psychological liar. I'm her nurse cause she has a drinking problem, so no more of this," she set my cocktail back on the waitress's tray as her cognac was served.

"She used to be in vaudeville," I explained nervously, retrieving my drink. We glared at each other. Her eyes were opaque. I couldn't understand why she was trying to scotch the con. "She'll say anything to scare off any man who doesn't seem serious."

"Oh, I'm serious," said Mannheim. "Randy is my ideal girl that I've been waiting for."

"I don't give a shit who she screws. And neither does she." Then she smiled vivaciously. "Her and me is opposites. Randy's fucked hundreds of men and only one woman in her life. Me, I've fucked hundreds of women and only one man."

"Who was the man?" Vic demanded.

"Who was the woman? Her?" Mannheim asked me.

"I told you she was a character," I kicked savagely at Kristal under the table.

"Honey, don't," she whimpered. "She beats me up in bed, she's so vicious."

"Who was the only man?" Vic insisted. "Why only one?"

Mannheim grinned. "Come off it, Vic, she's goofing on you."

"I've only ever met one real man," she said airily, "and that was my late husband, who was a Hells Angel."

"My brother," I prompted desperately.

"Your brother, my ass." She signaled the waitress. "Hey bitch! Another triple!"

"They don't have a table for four available in the restaurant downstairs, so you and I will be dining separately," Vic informed her. "And then I'll introduce you to some real manhood, the genuine article. We'll get just as kinky as you like, how's that? I'll tie you to a snowmobile instead of a motorcycle—"

Kristal interrupted: "Randy just wants to get a rich dude to take her to the Cowboy Bar in town so she can make this jive artist she's in love with jealous. She'll never fuck you," she told Mannheim.

"Have another drink," he replied, "you're too intense. We're going to dinner."

As we left Kristal and Vic alone, I saw only a look of the most passionate dread on her face before I turned away.

The maitre d' seated us in the restaurant. "You poor girl," he sighed. "Vic loves that sort of thing, but I'm too sensitive. Those games are all right for a minute, but after that I like people to talk straight. I don't know how you stand being with her."

"I didn't have no choice," I said, hoping I wouldn't overhear. "You can't pick your relatives," I said, hoping I would go on not understanding anything. "But" I added, "you don't have to take a lot of shit from them."

"Or you can have another drink."

"Yes."

I don't recall hearing anyone mention the dangers of drinking at high altitudes to me. The blood is thinner, or something. Kinships wane. I don't remember.

Then I was outside in the snow. I heard the trebling heartbreak of the wolverine. She is in exile, and sings about how she is deeply sorry. She sways and weeps in the snow, under the full moon. She pleads with the desolate mountaintops for just one little kiss.

Mannheim held me close. "Cry it out, poor darling," he murmured. "It's only the moon . . . we have so much water in us, that the full moon pulls it out just like the ocean tide, it pulls the sorrow out when it's too big to keep inside . . . now I'm starting to cry, too, poor girl." Beyond his shoulder, the phantom wisdom peaks gnashed the stars. "It's my fault, I shouldn't have let you drink so much."

"Randy!" Kristal's voice echoed among the distant lights of the hotels. "RAN-DEEE!"

I slipped on the icy path outside the Alpenhof as I tried to escape the sound.

"She's mad," he said.

I grasped his fur-trimmed hood, "Help me, I'm so scared, I don't know where I am anymore," and my arms sought his thermal lining.

He bent down, inquiringly, then kissed me. His tongue hunted salt, in the delectable swill of tears. I wanted him where only a man can do. I wanted him inside, right where it hurt.

When we ducked into his room, Vic had already returned. He was stretched out on his back with his eyes closed and his meathooks gripping the edges of the bed. "Mark?"

Mannheim pulled me inside, put his finger to his lips, and quietly shut the door. "*Ja,* it's me. You look like you took a few too many punches to the head."

His face was green under the sunburn which came out a thunderous gray color. "Damn. First time I ever got the spins since college."

"What happened to your lady friend? Didn't you get any?"
He moaned. "For a while there, I was afraid I was. Oh God, I
thought, she'll kill me. She'll fuck me to death. Then we got into
a hassle over the ring she wanted me to buy. So I bought it, and
then I wouldn't give it to her. I paid for it, so it was mine. So
she grabs my nuts. 'Give me the ring,' she says, 'or I'll twist
them off.' So I gave her the ring and split. But she wasn't through.
She attacked the desk clerk downstairs. Made him sell her everything he had, which was just postcards and stamps, and she
charged it to our room. Then she came up and hammered on the
door for a while, screaming that I was raping that kid, what's-her-
cunt"—his eyes had unstuck and now he saw me,—"Jesus Christ,
Randy Number Two." The phone rang. "She's not here," he
barked into it, and hung up. "She calls every five minutes for you.
This time she called from the Mangy Moose. She's still drinking.
Jesus Christ, I've never seen a chick drink so much. I thought I
was far out, but she—Mark, don't stand there like that. If you
think I'm getting off this bed and leaving the room so you two
can laugh and scratch all over the place . . . no. I'm dead." He
closed his eyes again. ". . . She's a *savage.*"

After I let Mannheim out, I crawled back into my ravaged bed,
curled up onto my side, and read the wall's blank lesson. I left the
light on for Kristal.
I heard the door slam. "Randy. Are you awake?"
"Yes." I didn't bother to roll over to look at her. I'd seen her
enough times like that, sitting down on the edge of her bed, un-
hinging her waistband, kneading her stomach, staring at me with
that strange famished glitter in her eyes, looking desperately for
trouble, or expecting it.
"My stomach's murderin me. I called the room ten minutes ago,
why didn't you pick up the phone?" I didn't answer. "I was here
in the Hilton, at the bar, I made two hundred bucks off some rich
old hag and her gigolo who were celebratin this guy, this friend
of their's birthday. I happened to be showin my strip pictures to
the bartender and the gigolo comes over and wants to buy me for

a surprise birthday present for this friend—he wanted me to take the guy's key and sneak into his room after he went to bed, but I said, 'I'm not a whore, I'm a lady.' Randy? Are you list'nin? What's the matter, are you sore at me?"

"You tried to blow the con tonight," I said wanly. "Why."

"I didn't like the dude you were with. Besides, we gotta move out of here pronto in the morning. You know my sense, the one that knows when the shit's gonna start to come down? I'm tellin you, it's time to run."

"Go ahead and run. I don't care."

"You're a stupid fuckin smartass," she yelled, stung. "You don't care you're gonna wind up in jail?"

"I haven't done nothin. Not since I been here. I don't care if you want to leave."

"I don't like your tone." I could hear her slinging her clothes around the room. She paused suddenly. "Did you fuck that guy?"

I didn't answer.

"Where, here?"

I didn't answer.

"You know, you haven't changed one bit. You're still throwin it away on the worst kind of jerks I keep tryin to warn you about—"

"I don't need you anymore," I interrupted. "He's taking me out for breakfast tomorrow, we're going skiing, then in the evening he's taking me into town to the Cowboy Bar. I know what to do from here. I'll tell him you had to leave because of a sick— because the sight of him made you sick. I don't care. I don't need you now."

She turned off the light. I heard the bedcovers rustle.

We lay awake, listening to each other's unrest.

"Randy. Are you awake?"

"Yes."

"Please don't stay mad at me," she wailed. "You'll get into trouble if you don't leave with me tomorrow. You're not gonna get Cody. You'll get burned again."

"Go to sleep."

"I'm lonely. You're hurtin my feelings."

My face began to burn in the silence. I couldn't leave her. All my life, I'd had these trick blood ties. My foster parents had played my parents, and I walked away from that. Kristal had played my sister, my aunt, my in-law, my wife, and my mother . . . but there was something more in the room, and I couldn't leave her before finding out what it was. The silence now sputtered like a furnace.

"Randy? I'm sad."

I felt my bed sag as she climbed in behind me. Her arm crept around my waist, and she reeled herself in, crooking her body to fit. Her long big breasts milled around my back. Her stomach billowed against my ass. Her pulse seemed all over me, or maybe both of us were so afraid.

Her hand left my waist, meandered, found the ledge of my little bosoms. "You're drunk," I said, though she was not.

"My mother used to rock me in her lap, no matter how old I was, whenever I was blue." Her mouth worked out the words against the skin of my shoulder. "You don't fit inside my body like two soup spoons," she whined faintly. "You got a nice body but you're too big, you know? Like stackin the soup spoon on top of the sugar spoon. You have to be the one that's the spoon in the back, cause you're bigger. You'd have to turn around and hang onto me, so we'd fit."

I didn't answer.

Her hand traced slowly down, over my rambling ribs, over the twist of my navel, down the soft dip to the brake, my muddled curls, and the trembling little clit trying to draw the peat over its head. "Don't," I whispered. "Stop. I mean it, please."

"Okay," she murmured. "I know you get horny and that's why sometimes you get unhappy bein with me. . . . Makes no difference to me, cause I don't like sex, I just need you not to be mad at me—"

"Don't," I said. She got up and packed her bags.

I waited. Still I was unable to leave her. I knew there was more.
"I wasn't goin to fuck you," she blurted. "I could've fucked

((251))

you a long time ago, back in New York, when you didn't know your ass from your rear end. I've fucked a hundred women. It's a snap. I have other kinds of strong feelings about you. I don't know what they are. You're like—to me, you're—you don't know the whole story . . . *I wanted to have a kid by you.*"

I rolled over, faced her with wide moronic eyes, and waited, as the whole story, of how Kristal had divided her love among the needy, unraveled as fast as a pulled thread on a blind hem.

Now, I never could resist a cry for help, on account of my great big stupid heart, but we've already gone into that.

Felice was my first love. There she was, sitting on the street corner and crying because her girlfriend had thrown her downstairs. Felice was supposed to be the butch, but she also had a habit of taking lots of aggravation.

I'd just got out of work at the Royale. It was four in the morning.

She was sixteen, the same age as me, a poor skinny thing, pretty, with long straight black hair and huge arm muscles, and she hadn't had a thing to eat in two days.

I marched her into a all-night Colonel Sanders. Hey, I says, I bought a whole dinner in here last night, and when I got home the Cokes had spilled all over the chicken, and so forth. Shit, I could have afforded to buy it, but I wanted to show my little friend how the first place you should never have to go is hungry. So they gave me a new order, and Felice ate it.

I let her stay with me at the America, and then after a while we got an apartment together with all the trimmings. She was very spoiled, went to fancy private schools, her parents gave her everything her whole life til they found out she was gay. So I had to provide her with much luxury, I can certainly tell you.

The first year was great. The sun shined on us. We fucked every night. I cooked and took care of the house and worked at the dance hall. The only part I didn't dig particularly was the sex. It was the way I was brought up.

After the first year, she was lucky if she got me every three months. Also, she was very jealous. And not just about my customers. She'd want to punch out any woman who looked sideways at me! And she meant it, she was fierce. She was dressing and acting more butchy, too, black leather jackets and boots and zippers. You know, this was '63, when everybody was trying to look like Brando. She let her moustache grow out. I bleached it. It came out red. Of course I could not bring her home to my parents in Connecticut. The one time I tried, my mother chased her off the lawn with a broom.

Felice ate me, I didn't eat her. I think in all the times, off and on, we were together, I ate her pussy maybe ten times. She had a bad smell about her, even though she did keep herself clean. Sometimes she'd go to fuck me and cry, "God, I wish I had a dick." So she brought home a dildo and I hit her over the head with it. But we made up. She got a tattoo on her arm muscle that said "KRISTAL IS LOVE."

She was so jealous, she tried to get me fat so no one would look at me. That only made my titties bigger. Then she started working at the dance hall with me. I put a wig and makeup on her, and made her tie her shirt high so her cute little navel showed, and we were a great team. But she was so possessive that one night she beat up one of my customers, who turned out to be one of Frank's friends from the mob. So Frank fired me. That's when I took up stripping really big. I went out on the circuit, just to get away from her.

We broke up all the time. She never took it seriously til I showed up married.

She came to Hollywood, called me up, invited over all her gay libber friends, and decked out her whole apartment with my strip pictures, photos of us from the dance hall, and she blew up to six feet this stupid picture I took in one of those coin booths where I pulled my tit out—her pad was nothing but a mausoleum to me. I hadn't seen her in five months, so while she's telling all these girls how fantastic I am, I'm a stripper and a vestal virgin, whatever have you: I walk in with this grubby Hells Angel. I kissed him with my tongue and they went "yuch."

Felice almost puked. They all hate men. So did I, but Beau, I have said before, was somewhat of a special person, and I loved him.

After I married him, the Angels all hated me, because I made him go inactive. I wanted to have a house and kids and no hassles. Whenever the Angels used each other's houses for meetings, it got hairy. Once they got fucked up, they had no respect whatsoever for people's property, they'd tear the place down. If somebody was already in the bathroom, they'd piss on your couch or chair.

So Beau became a woodcutter, felling timber once a year in the High Sierras, and we got a house in Riverside so he could be near his old haunts and go get wiped out once in a while. The first year was really nice. I cooked for him, I cleaned for him, I fucked my head off with him because I wanted kids. It was a phase I was going through. If I was horny, I jerked myself off while he fucked me.

One time he said, "Honey, give me some head." I never have sucked a dick in my whole life. But I was drunk and I got down there. You know the little hole a man has on it? I swear it winked at me. I got sick on it.

It has a certain kind of odor, too. It's my mother's fault I would notice that.

After a while, I just didn't want it. I figured he'd only touch me if I wanted it. But three or four times a year, he'd get hot. Or there would be an occasion, like a birthday. He tried to eat me a lot of times but I wouldn't let him do it. I felt it belonged to Felice.

I wanted to love him like a brother. We had a mental telepathy thing, I always knew where he was going every time he walked out on me. He always knew I was with Felice when I walked out. Although once I flew home to my parents. They never met Beau but from his pictures they hated him.

That time my mother was dying. Hold me, Mom, I said,

and she always did. Then she cursed me, on her deathbed.

She did it to upset me. She knew I was getting all her gold jewelry anyway. Pop tried to make me stay. He still hoped I'd settle down and go to international law school. Fuck her gold, I said, and split. But I took the rent money. My dad chased after me as I jumped into the cab. That's a crazy man after me! I yelled to the driver, run him over! If he'd been alive the next time I came back, we would have sat around and laughed about it. You think some things will always be funny.

I went back to Beau and we got down to the serious business of fighting again. That was our relationship. He would never hit me because he was too strong. He choked me, that was better. But he put a stop to that when I put a knife in his ribs. Once, I shot at him by accident with a submachine gun while he was setting up a target in the yard. Then I had to go to my beauty appointment. Beau came in when the hairdresser was taking the rollers out and asked me if I was ready. Why, I said.

He said, I think some of the bullets went in me.

The queer hairdresser wanted to finish styling me the next day because he was freaked out, Beau's shirt was all bloody.

Beau says, if this thing's costing me six-fifty, you finish it now. And he read a magazine.

Of course, once we got to the emergency room at the hospital, he made a big noise about the pain, oh God! I'm in pain! Because he wanted them to give him a fix.

If he wasn't getting a fix, like the time he had his cataracts removed, he didn't want any anesthetic, he wanted to feel everything because he thought the operation was interesting.

Then the last two years, I was putting my foot down hard as I could, I didn't want the sex, I'm very small and it hurt me. If he touched me, I wouldn't have a headache—I'd have a heart attack! One time he touched me I got so sick I went to have my gallstones taken out. It seemed every time I did let him fuck me, I got pregnant. People we'd run into would ask, what happened to her? and Beau'd answer, I just poked a little fun at her and she took it seriously.

Three times I had miscarriages. The doctor said I was psychosomatic.

The last time me and Beau broke up was Felice's fault. I went to stay with her, we had a fight, and I threw her out of her place in Hollywood. The phone rang and it was Beau. He loved me, he wanted to make up.

I asked, what happened to that chick I heard you were with?

He said, I only went with her cause she looked like you.

I says, well, how could you *see* she looked like me? He was blind as a bat now, from the R. P. And he was crying. He said he'd admit to being legally blind, he'd go to school and learn Braille, and even Felice, he says, if the bitch makes you happy, I'll sleep in the other room.

I'd never heard him like this. It's all right honey, I said, she's out of my life anyhow. Right then Felice walks back in the door.

Is that your *dick?* she yells. He heard it. She grabs the phone from me and says, forget it, man, she's mine, and hung up.

He called back again. He was loaded. Don't hang up on me this time, he says. How come you lied? You said she was gone. You know what, bitch? I'm gonna come back to cut your throat.

Then he hung up.

I don't know why he shot himself. He was the bravest person I ever knew. Felice didn't feel any remorse. He was nothing but a dick. I stopped loving her then.

I couldn't show up at Beau's rite. The Angels would have cut me.

For a week all I did was walk into L. A. gay bars and holler, who wants to *fuck?* And I'd let any woman with the balls to answer take me to her place and eat me. When Beau shot himself, I thought, he did it because I'm gay. But I hated it. So then I didn't care what sex I was. Felice was back home trying to slice off her tattoo with a Schick injector blade, but

I didn't care. All I cared about now was being afraid of the ghosts, Beau's ghost coming back, like the ones that used to touch my father's neck at the dinner table.

I called up my father, but his number was disconnected. I thought he would always be there, but when I flew back I found he'd died. He left everything to me, but in trust. Because he didn't trust me. He put all his land, and the jewelry, and the house, everything in a trust fund for *my* children, so they'd become international lawyers. Just when I was thinking of coming back to him because the last thing I ever wanted to do was screw anybody ever again in my life, which you have to do to have children and lawyers.

So all love was dead and I went back to work at the Royale. You know, my whole life I never could figure out nothing about sex for myself, but I could rap about it like a champ and make a fortune. It's all talk. It's easy for me because I put no value on money.

Money talks, but talk's cheap too, especially when you have fucked up on love.

I thought how it was funny, afterwards, how what I'd loved best about love was fighting it. Then losing it, and fighting for it. I lived for the moment when people came back, when the person says, I can't live without you. Anything else about love got on my nerves. All I ever wanted was for someone to need me so much they'd die without me.

A baby is one of those. When I found out I was three months pregnant, I could have laughed.

I tried to leap out of bed, but a thick ferment of cocktails sloshed over my reflexes, and I sank back on my elbow.

She laughed, sitting on her bed across from me, pulled her sweater up from her slacks, and petted her tummy, which rose like a foothill from her panty elastic, between the ridges of her open zipper. "Thought I was just a fatso, right?"

"Whose baby is it?" I gaped.

"My husband's, of course—Beau's!" she yelled, scathed. "What the hell kind of a person do you think I am!" Relenting, she lowered her voice, "And stop staring at it like I was a roast beef. . . . It's Beau's, because before I left him that last time I let him fuck me, it was somebody's anniversary or something, I don't know. I didn't know I was pregnant when he shot himself, I didn't know it when I left Felice and balled every butch on Hollywood Boulevard, I didn't know it when I went to Connecticut and saw my dad's will. . . . I didn't find out til I was back at the Royale, a couple of days before I ran into you barfing all over your narcotics in the john—I'd just gone in there to barf myself! And you were in my way."

I glimpsed her now, as her life crossed mine in the back view mirror: tumbling like a bombastic weed down the passing lane. The charmed circle whirled by, on the force of a seventh sense, on the pain of labor, fighting its center, careening, fighting for its center, the eye of itself, the strange and tempestuous pussy where a baby turned round inside. And how did I belong in all this?

". . . I'm four and a half months along. I thought I'd miscarry and lose it like all the other times, and I thought if that happened, at least I'd have you left, cause you were like a little dope too. But then you got smart, and we got so close, and the baby just kept growing like there was no today, and I changed—I felt like it was *our* kid." She gazed at me with some kind of evaporating sadness. "I'll be okay. Only, sometimes I don't want it, I don't want to see its face. I'm scared of seein Beau. I'm afraid he's comin back to slit my throat, like he said before he signed off. Gypsies are most superstitious. And then all these movies they got now about devil children. I've see the coming attractions on TV and it scares me, you know?"

"Why didn't you tell me?" I stammered.

"You were too young . . ." her voice bristled as the dawn approached and she regained her old self, ". . . to understand the facts of life. You'll learn now, after I split. That was my big beautiful mistake with you, tryin to keep you so you wouldn't get hurt. Boy, what you don't know," she shook her head scornfully. "Guess what I did. I was the one stole your money in Oklahoma City. The seventeen hundred dollars you thought Cody pinched.

I did that and I left you that note from him tellin you to stay put."

My expression became tangled as my eyes flew up from her belly to her lips, where more words were forming neatly.

"I took it cause that's what he would've done to you anyway, sooner or later. But you go with him now, by yourself, and see. By the way, I put the money back in your roll. You should count your money more often."

"No . . ." Helpless anger made a swipe at me, and missed. "Son of a *bitch*," I breathed, in helpless admiration.

"Yup. You think that's terrible? Look what else I did. I've had your mother's address ever since we left Arlington, but I hid it from you cause I didn't think you were ready. I knew you wouldn'ta been taggin after me if you wasn't scared of facin her." She plunged her hand into her purse; combs, compacts, mascara wands, hot jewelry, and false IDs clacked together as she sought something. "I got your foster father's number from the Long Beach naval base, and then I talked to Inger. She said he'd retired and went back to Baltimore to live with his mom. When I tried to get the adoption crap out of her, we had some big drag-out cursing. I told her I was your probation officer. You remember when you were in the bathtub jerkin off? That's when I was talkin to your real mother on the telephone, I finally got to her." She handed me a crumpled sheet of Holiday Inn stationery. "She's married now, to some guy who's not your father. That address is in Culver City—that's in L. A. See, I'm not so bad. I was pointin you to California all along." My eyes rummaged along the penciled letters "MRS. DERMOT CHATHAM," as if, unscrambled, they shaped a face, a pair of arms, a rocking lap, or "COME HOME."

"I didn't get much on her, just the address and the number and she wants to see you. She did a ton of cryin her eyes and thankin the Lord, and then I heard you croakin in the bathtub, so I hung up. . . . Well, it's all yours, now. You've got your bullshit artist and your mom, and I'm not gonna worry about you no more, mouse, cause I taught you how to hustle your way."

"Uh-uh," I pledged out loud, to my penciled-in mother, "I'm not going to hustle anymore."

Kristal hooted. "*Boy,* are you dumb. I'm takin your blue ribbon back. You don't understand fact one in the facts of life. You'll just stop, right? Hell, you don't even have a trust fund, like me." She petted the wad bulging in her womb again. "Just, overnight," she snapped her fingers, "you're an angel, just like that, stop, right? . . . Miss Saint Moron. Wait'll your ma sees her devil baby."

"You're a cunt, you know that," I summarized.

And she preened. "Hundred watt."

I could let her go now. Refolding my mother's name in precise well-mannered creases and pressing the beloved paper between the pages of my diary, I laid away my angel wings for use in the morning. Now I could sleep. "So . . . you're going?"

"Naturally. I'm not stickin around for the shitstorm."

Through the curtains, a pearly arctic dawn and a feeling of snow overwhelmed our lamplight.

"I don't have nothin else to say," she shrugged absently, already leaving me.

Except, I wondered, "Does it move?" I stretched out a hand to her belly. "Can I feel it?"

"You get away, god damn it, you know I can't stand bein touched!" She batted my hand off. Then her teeth gleamed in a goodbye grin, like a saucer of dawn.

After she left, I was able to sleep all day, although there were many interruptions.

Each time I was woken up, I was full of the weird lucidity that comes from being abandoned by gypsies after drinking too much in a high altitude. It was not the moment to mess with me, because sleep was a deadly mission.

"Who is it?"

"Mark."

I wrapped up in bedclothes and opened the door.

"You're not ready for breakfast," he peered past my head, "are you alone?" He stepped in, clumping white flakes off his boots. "The snow's not supposed to let up for a couple of hours, so there's no skiing. Where's your crazy sister-in-law?" He kissed the corner of my mouth.

"Um . . . let me put something on. She's out visiting a friend . . . all day." I opened the closet and searched frantically through the pockets in my coat. "Might even stay overnight." My hand found my wad. I kept my back to Mannheim, who sat in the chair by the window.

"Great, then we have the room to ourselves. Vic's still not himself today, I don't think he'd move out of his bed for any money on earth." I counted eight thousand seven hundred and some singles. "Maybe she'll get caught in an avalanche. If money won't move Vic, maybe it'll buy a good avalanche. I don't know how you stand her. I don't think I could go through another night like last night."

"I'm sorry about all that crying and hysterics."

"Poor girl, I couldn't blame you. I thought it was lovely . . . and I'm your friend . . ." His voice trailed off. I turned. He was reading from a piece of notepaper that had not been destroyed.

Dear K—

Score! 2 rich dudes, 1 doctor + 1 real estate, dinner at Alpenhof 6:30. Real estate's yours. You're married to my brother and you took me in when I was a hippie on drugs. You're trying to find me a rich husband at posh resorts, next week Honolulu etc. You're *super*-strict and used to be a stripper. I learned to ski! See ya

—*R*

"That's a funny sort of thing," he said, smiling hopefully at me.

"No it's not." I sat beside him. "And I could tell more lies to cover it, but I like you. You deserve the truth." My skull felt strangely liberated from my neck. I laid it on his shoulder and told him the whole story.

I tried to make it amusing. I left out Cody, and I ornamented the role of Kristal with villainous touches, but basically I told him the true story. ". . . So she's gone, and it's all over." I laughed. "I don't need your money, I have plenty. I want to get some sleep, and when I wake up I want to be any old happy girl fuckin around, on vacation, no more hustles, no more booze. I can be honest now."

He was silent. His mind spiraled away in confusion. I recognized the veil over his face. One day when Kristal had told me too many lies, a humid fear came over me and I no longer could trust my mere five senses to tell me what was true in what she said and what was false. The answers had been torn from the back of the book. So I let her leave me.

I think Mannheim liked the original story better, the one I told the day before on the slopes, because that would be the only time he would ever believe I was honest. I could talk a thousand truths now. And he just wouldn't know.

". . . And that's the truth, I swear." Nothing remained for me to swear on, since there wasn't nothing I held sacred.

"And you want to take a nap now?" he asked vaguely.

"Yes. But we'll have lunch, all right? I'm payin, it's on me!"

I kissed him efficiently at the door and went back to sleep.

I dreamt about the truth, a land made up from scratch, where some things are sacred, and look exactly like other things enchanted by lies. Well, I wandered about, putting down giant poker chips shaped like Valiums, placing my bets on what would turn up a winner.

Now, I didn't belong anymore to Mannheim, that innocent tribe of squares who shiver like dodoes in their frail fraying nests, in their hideouts in the mountains, on their penthouse battlements, suffering the vertigo before extinction.

But I didn't belong either to Kristal, to the burgeoning underworld. I hadn't undergone the final rites. And my crimes so far had been invisible ones. I had abused words, like abuse of magic: invisible.

The room phone rang. It was a woman asking for Mrs. Florentine.

"She's not here."

"When she comes back, could you ask her to drop by the front office? The manager would like to speak with her."

"This is her roommate, can I help you with something?"

"No, this would be a matter between the manager and Mrs. Florentine."

I slept.

The third interruption was another phone call. "This is Vic. Mark just left. He told me your colorful history, and now he's gone up to the slopes hoping he'll get himself a merciful concussion—look. I don't care if that fat sidekick of yours cost me a day of skiing, I'm a big boy. But Mark's too nice a guy to ask you to leave him alone, he's quite scared of you in fact, and you're ruining his vacation. The man leads a somewhat sheltered life or maybe he's just good-hearted, he doesn't understand how to deal with street types. But I do and I'm offering you one thousand dollars and I'll cover your hotel bill and a plane reservation on the next flight out—that's tomorrow morning." He waited for a response. His breathing seemed rapid. I think he was quite scared of me, too.

"Huh," I said softly.

"*Fifteen* hundred, and not only do you *not* join Mark for lunch, cocktails, or dinner, but you stay in your room until you leave. I'll make up some story to tell Mark, and I'll walk over right now to settle the billing arrangement with your hotel manager, and I'll leave the fifteen hundred dollars in an envelope at the desk. I hope you don't mind travelers' checks. And if you have any hesitations, let me tell you something about Jackson Hole. They don't see too much crime up here, and bunco won't seem like such a light offense to them. Up here they lock you up and throw away the key. And let me also tell you what I think of you—"

As he pelted me with insults, I began to hate him with an honest angelic hatred. After all, this hustle was his idea, not mine. I was no common or special criminal today. I was a whole new you. It was enough getting my neck used to the larger head. "Pay up and shut up," I interrupted, in a tone suitable to his worst fears.

"—you're a very smart young lady," he wound up quickly, "we have a deal. Goodbye."

I slept.

The fourth interruption was a phone call from the manager, confirming that a Mister Victor Botsford had laid his credit card on the line for all my room expenses, and had also left an envelope in my name at the front desk. And where was Mrs. Florentine?

"She left, this morning."

Oh, ah, well. There was the matter of her checks. Would Mister Botsford assume those costs as well, because Mrs. Florentine had been cashing checks for cash at the desk, and according to hotel policy her bank in Hollywood had been notified this morning, at which point the manager had been advised that her account had been terminated many months ago. Several shops in Teton Village had also been calling him, according to their policy, to vouch for Mrs. Florentine on some sizeable checks for jewelry, fashions, and bric-a-brac.

So that was the shit Kristal's seventh sense saw coming down, a light brown drizzle. I apologized. Mrs. Florentine had a small drinking problem and probably packed the wrong checkbook for her vacation. I should have kept an eye on her eccentric mathematics but I was off and away skiing so much of the time. I offered to drop by the manager's office later and cover the amount of her booboos, with some travelers' checks. I went back to sleep.

"Who is it?"

"Say hi."

I clawed the bedclothes to my chest and threw open the door. "What are you doing here?"

Cody shook snow off his new ski clothes and hopped inside. "Well, say hi first," he laughed, and closed the door. He flung his knit headband onto the chair, tossed his brown hair, "Can't say hi, huh?" and fell to his knees. He swept aside my sheets and kissed my bush. "How's tricks?" he asked it, then sniffed it twice. "Someone's been sleeping in my puss." He peered up at me slyly. "Thought you was a *dry* hustler."

"What are you doing here?"

He stood up. "Getting shot down by you, for openers. Cause I know you got here yesterday and you didn't even call me at the Cowboy Bar. Hey, I been waiting for you to fly in from Vegas like we decided. . . . Well, you were easy to find. There's only one Hilton in Jackson Hole."

I swam into his arms, good old lagoon.

He licked the craggy sleep from the corners of my eyes and

my mouth. "Cmon, peach," he lifted me up wholly, and carried me into the bathroom, and ran water on me in the tub. "Actually," he said, perching on the tub's rim, "I saw you yesterday at the bottom of the mountain. But I didn't come up to you because I was with that chick—the same one, from Chickasha—and besides, you were with some dude." He mussed the soap in my pubic hair, then teased the slippery bar up and down the long way of my slit. "And if you're like me, you don't like to be bothered when you're workin."

"I'm so happy you're here," my thighs squeezed his hand. The blue tattoo question mark on his finger spangled in suds, and slid in and out of my cunt. "So good to see the peach smile," he said. "takes years off baby's face. Okay, here's the soap, here's the washcloth, and now you know what to do with it. Wash yesterday's dude off. He looked like a safe bet, too. How much *dinero* did you shake off him?" He eased down the toilet lid, sat on it, and leaned against the tank. He let his head sink back and closed his eyes contentedly.

"I didn't fuck him for bread." I started in between the toes.

He snapped back for a moment. "No? For fun? You tryin to make me jealous?"

"If it was for money, you wouldn't be jealous?"

He chuckled, relaxed again. The green eyes rolled back under the complicated lashes. "No, baby, it don't matter to me. I was even married once to a hooker. Good-hearted working girl. Funny scene. I don't know whether she played me or I played her, but the fucking was dynamite. We'd be takin a nap, middle of the afternoon, or she'd be up washin dishes, and she'd get a phone call. 'Be back in a while, sweetheart,' she'd say, out the door, into the car, off to a date, and an hour later she'd walk back in the door and finish the dishes."

"How long were you married?" The water was crinkling my hands. Small pains in my ribs signified a bad crush inside, heart still cramping for this smooth man, what a sweet thief.

"That one was . . . I better wake up here . . . two years? I don't know. Been married three times. My last wife said I got

((265))

married just like gettin in and out of the shower. Well, it's true. They make it so easy to do. Don't think I ever divorced her. We had a kid runnin around somewhere. He'll be one this year. Actually he's four years old, but the silly sucker had to be born on Leap Year, so this year's his first birthday"

"And you don't know where they are?"

He began to hunt around the pocket in his electric blue parka. "She could be anywhere. I can find anyone if I want to. Most folks ain't that good at gettin lost."

"But why get married at all?" I sloshed onto my knees to scrub my buttocks.

"I loved'm. That's all." He smiled vacantly at my ass. "I'm a romantic. . . . Either that, or I'm a bouncing fool. There's a poem goes, 'The head chooses the way, but the heart is a stargazer, and together they make up a natural fool, who turns in place, under the moon.' . . . There was a lot of craziness last night in the Cowboy Bar. Always is in any bar, when there's a full moon. One poor hard-on got thrown out into the snow, and there was no one out there to beat up on. So he tried to beat hisself up. Did a good job, too."

"You made that up." I sawed the washcloth against my back.

"I don't think so. I was wasted at the time. You want a Ritalin?"

"What's that?"

"A mood elevator pill. You seem depressed. No? How about a downer?" His hand emerged from his pocket and opened; he sorted among the pills in his palm with an index finger. "Try a Mandy, it's all the rage at women's colleges. Been takin'm all morning."

"No."

He selected a tablet. "I'm gonna wash this down with you," he cupped a hand under my head and raised it up to his mouth. His tongue plumbed around mine until he had enough juice, then he let me go, inserted the pill between his lips, and swallowed it down. "What happened to your partner, anyway? The fat fox with the giant jugs."

"We had a fight this morning. She left."

"You catch her hand in the till?"

"Something like that. I'm sure I'll never see her again."

He laughed tenderly. "Don't count on it. People like that always find a way to get back in your life. Only way to stop it is, cut them off totally. If they're talkin trash, cover your ears. If a little trash leaks in, you're finished. No matter what that dyke does, you just shine her on and keep walkin." I rubbed at my throat, my overburdened neck. "When I was in Morocco last year, I found out the police have a unique system for punishing their criminals. They cut off the o-ffend-ing mem-ber. Like, if they bust someone stealing chickens, they cut off the hands. That's what you got to do with scam artists. Chop her off right at the wrist." His head fell forward, his eyes flew open briefly when his chin jounced against his new Indian silver necklace. "Shit, I got to *nod.*"

"How'd they go about punishing whores?"

"Huh, let's see. If you chop off the offending . . . if you amputate the cunt," he cackled to himself, "it only leaves a larger hole, don't it? System's not much good on peach-face hustlers, I guess."

I finished polishing my face. "I'm not gonna hustle anymore."

He hauled up his eyelids again. "So you got wet just once. You take a bath, dry yourself off—poof, you're a dry hustler again, if that's what's bringin you down. I won't tell nobody."

"You don't know anything about me."

"You mean, where you were born, your mommy and daddy, that stuff? 'S not important, baby. Sure you don't want a Ritalin? You're too sad. Man, I know exactly how you feel, all the times I've woke up and said, I'm gonna stop."

"I am not going to hustle anymore, unless I have to for some reason."

"And that," he wagged an unmarked finger at me, "is why I go back to doin it. Cause you have to. There's always some reason. You're just depressed. What you need is a new partner. Will you marry me?"

My soap sank. His head tilted, resting his temple against the towels draped from the rack behind him, he was smiling. Framed by his soft coppery beard, his face gazed at me through a sort of holy contemplation, or just fatigue.

"You're beautiful," he lilted. "And I only marry for love. Or would you rather go steady. You can take me to Mardi Grass, and then we'll go to Acapulco, cause we can really cook in Mexico this time of year. We'll synch up our wristwatches, split up, I'll get the heiresses, you go after the heirs, we'll meet back up in Aruba, catch some rays, hit the casinos, run some scams on honey-moon couples . . . wife swappers are the funniest ones . . . they even got mistress swappers and hooker swappers there . . . and if you want, the hustle just as dry's an elephant's eye, my baby . . . cocaine's eleven bucks a gram—"

"No."

He rocked on the toilet seat, laughing silently, in delight. "Oh, I love the way she says no. You give the best no of anybody I ever knew. You been saying no to me since the first time I met you, and I'm still not tired of it. You're beautiful. Can I spend the night?"

I remembered my deal with Vic. "I'm leaving tomorrow."

"Then you don't have much time, do you, to make up your mind about bein my official squeeze. I'm splitting the next day or so, myself. I'm working on scorin a truck. If she gives me any more clothes and jewelry I'm gonna look like a blazin faggot boutique." He got up and stretched, swaying a little. "I better call the office and let'm know I won't be back tonight."

He left the door slightly ajar. As I toweled off, I heard him ask for a room number. Then I heard him reel out a familiar serenade, a tune that had been running in my head for days. I had to stand in the doorway to catch all the words.

"Say hi . . . Don't you be shittin me, valentine, just say hi . . . I'm with a chick, yeah. . . . Cause I think I'm in love with you, that's why. And I need my space. I thought I'd dig on a little foreign pussy and forget all about you. Well, no such luck for Cody. . . . Cause I kept diggin on you the whole time, valentine, thinkin about your beautiful legs and your beautiful mind, so I couldn't get behind her at all. It's never happened to me—no, I'm not gonna ball her. I'm goin out to get drunk instead. You're too much inside my head. It's too different for me, I don't like this feeling. . . . No way. Not this night or any night. I'm not comin around you til I get completely stoned and I figure out what the hell you're doin to my life. Shit, I don't even know why I called. You're cramping my whole style and the worst part of it is, I dig it. I don't like it, but I dig it. . . . I love you, too. No I don't. You know what's on my mind, girl, when I put you out of it? I'm picturin myself in a truck, red color, panel job, flat out in the third lane, heading for New Orleans. Like I planned before I met you. Now, I don't see no red-haired valentine in the seat beside me, cause my life is not your kind of life. You couldn't stand all the changes, all the adventure, it's too rugged. If I had the truck, that's what I'd be doin right now, instead of bein trapped in the mountains with a warm, soft valentine from Oklahoma who's playing numbers on my head. . . . No. Say goodbye. . . . You're beautiful. And I'm crazy. Catch you later."

He dropped the receiver into the cradle.

"Don't you know any other songs?" I asked.

"Some grind," he sighed, shedding his waterproofs and woolens onto the carpet. "I'm whipped. Gonna come lay with me? If I fall out, get the hotel operator to wake me up in a couple of hours. I think I better go back tonight and shake her down. Yo," he yawned, "don't know how'm gonna get m'dick hard tonight, with all them Mandies. . . . Cmon, peach, don' make me lonesome." I left my towel behind. "Beautiful," he said as he nuzzled his head into my pillow, although he wasn't looking at me; his eyes were out appreciating some lunch. I flapped the bedclothes over him and got into bed. He rolled onto his back and included me in his arms. ". . . So nice, bein with someone with something happenin 'sides sex and head games." He felt for my face, pulled it up and kissed it fondly, then patted it down onto his chest. "You and me got something . . . spiritual." Cmere dog, cmere dog.

Minute yellow hairs rose all along my spine.

"Cept you're trouble in my head," he mumbled. "I think we better go our ways and I'll dig you later." So you turn around and walk away from the dog.

"No you won't," I said distinctly.

"Sure I will." His hand slipped up my thigh. "Unless you chop off my hands." Three, then four fingers tucked into my cunt. "Go ahead. I dare you."

Tears sweated in my eyes as I clenched my fuzzy mouth down there. I didn't make even a dent in his hand. I only got wetter.

I passed my hand to his leg. "Cody?" His cock was slumped over his thigh.

"Want some head?" he slurred.

"Fuck me." Come back.

He blindly kissed the distance between us, and passed out. He began to breathe through his mouth. Certain of his teeth were false. Abuse of words, abuse of magic.

I unraveled myself from his arms and attended to some of my new responsibilities.

I picked up my envelope at the front desk. It contained $1,500 in travelers' checks and $250 cash for airfare. Then I visited the manager, who presented me with Kristal's bad checks. Vic's travelers' checks barely covered the total amount of her illicit wardrobe and jewelry, but she had in the past dressed me from tip to toe against the cold front, so we were quits. I received in return the little stack of bouncy daisy-dappled checks with their peculiar title: FELICE FLORENTINE. On the backs were clerks' notes from her ID—the third I'd known her to use. Her purse had looked a lot like Cody's wallet, which I'd examined after he fell asleep. These people could be any age and any origin, depending on which ID you picked. "What nationality are you?" I remembered Kristal asking. "Oh, right, you don't know, you don't have no parents. You can be whatever you want to be whenever you want."

Back in my room, I sat for a while, staring through a moist veil of confusion at Cody asleep in my bed. He might mean everything he said he meant. And I just wouldn't ever know, you see. His body was curled in graceful illegible script, the sound of distant surf rasping in his open mouth. Then I packed my suitcase, and, when I went to lock up my money wad between the covers of my diary, I extracted the paper with my mother's name and address before stuffing the book into my purse.

I ate a long and thoughtful supper in the Hilton dining room. The sun had gone down, and drowsy skiers toasted each other. Their children discussed the slopes and the weather forecast with the assurance of politicians. No wonder they were all called squares. They went up and down, and back and forth.

Cody spoke of bright southern climes, of tossing the squares high as confetti, leaving no trail. We'd be ageless bandits, his hand in my pocket and I guess mine in his. But I had been on that thruway with Kristal. I could see that trail well enough, of hotel rooms fastened one to another, scam upon scam, miles of tufted barstools, fizzing snifters, and the reckless clash of wits, sexual advances, house drummers, beady new nights, new faces for the fleecing, new places to hide the wad, ransacked embraces, binges, blackouts, and surrender.

Dear mother, I've just hustled myself right to the bone. We've been flocking and padding that new freeway, with a white-line stitch, and guess what, it thins down to nothing when it reaches the gaunt horizon. Here I am, chapped, travel-sore, rattling my regrets: so reach down to the foot of the bed and hoist your perfect patchwork of squares up over me.

I'm sick, really out of it, in my mother's house. She is a dense, caring shape all around me. She tends me hour after hour. She tips milk into my mouth, licks my ass clean, gives me reasons for living in singsong. I sleep night after night in the same room. One day fastens to another. She gives me sandwiches. She gives me placemats. She gives me linoleum, and math. God damn, even the mesh on the screen door is so square, you can hear the gypsies preparing their tatters, blocks and blocks away.

* * *

"This is Randy your daughter." I was nauseous with fear, and clutched the spiraling cord on the telephone.

"Who?"

I looked over my shoulder at my bed and raised my voice. "This is Randy." Cody didn't stir. "I'm your daughter."

"Miranda?" The woman's voice wavered up, wonderfully slow, as if searching for a higher harmony part.

"Yes, it's me." Doubt leapt like lava in my throat. "I hope . . . you're not in the middle of dinner or anything."

"Dermot!" she shouted away from the receiver. "Oh, praise God," she whispered tremulously to me. "A woman phoned a few weeks ago and said my baby was looking for me and then when I heard nothing—Derm! It's my daughter! It's Miranda, get on the other line!—dear, I prayed so hard I had to go to bed, and my husband said I was going overboard about it, but here you are—here he is, here's Derm—"

"My father?" I asked.

"Hi, Miranda! Where are you!" a man boomed on another extension.

"No . . . dear, he's not . . ." her voice stalled. "Dermot, talk to her, I'm making such a mess of myself . . . Miranda, say something so he can hear you . . ." she burst into muffled sobs, "Derm, she's being so sweet. . . ."

"Hello?" I called to her. "Mother?"

"Hi! Where are you, honey!" the man repeated.

"Wyoming, uh. Can I—do you—" I was panting now. "Mother? Do—can—do you want to see me?"

"Oh, please," came the sweet watery words, *"please come . . ."*

We both wept softly.

"Sure, come on down, there's a guest room upstairs." The man's voice barreled like a foghorn over the tears lapping on either shore. "Just us chickens here, you know. Just Sue and me, and some of that California sun if you need tempting. Boy, I thought, that's Sue's baby kid on the phone, but I guess you're all the way to college by now, aren't you, must be around your vacation. Tell us a little bit about your life, honey."

"Is that my wake-up call?" Cody bounded out of bed, naked, back in business.

I hastily got off the phone: "I can't talk anymore. I'll come soon. I don't know when but I will, I'll call you sometime soon."

I hurried past Cody into the bathroom, where I buried my unforgiveable face in my arms and cried to the bottom of the bitter mug. The two voices, my mother and her husband, were gusting about my head, and me grasping like a moron at the winds, all this fuss that I started in the lives of some simple normal people who were expecting a perfectly formed unsmudged do-right child at the screen door. And not this corruption. This twisted itchy pup arriving under a swarm of larcenous urges.

But, I had to see my mother, just for a minute. I'd make Cody wait around the corner in the new red truck while I visited her. I'd pretend to be a college girl on vacation. Then I'd drop her postcards, from exotic resorts, boasting about my grades.

I emerged from the bathroom when I was ready to announce our partnership to Cody. He was all dressed. "Some hotel," he commented, his thumbs gently brushing at the smudges of tears on my cheeks. "They wake you up, and make you cry. Good morning, Miss Bates, time to get up, you have two more weeks to live. . . . Not funny? I got something for sniffles."

A small bottle and a tiny spoon appeared from his parka pocket. He scooped out a hit of cocaine and steered the spoon at my nose.

Fuck it, I thought. I've come all this way to spite my face, so here's to that. I snorted. The white dust shot up the grand canal to my brain, where it spat its two cents' worth.

A mighty shakedown began, the changing of one's mind. I trembled, and stared into the tunneling hazel of Cody's eyes, those twin nooses. His arms cinched around me.

Fuck these arms, I thought. I got my own arms. Fuck this shit. I got my own shit.

My bowels pressed to evacuate. I returned to the bathroom, closed the door, sat on the can, and voided the past. Fuck it, I thought. I belong now to my mother, I'll make it home. I'll be true. I'll go to college. I'll take tests, and then vacations. I want like anything a regular rhyming lullaby and a face that matches mine, that will sing *Oh please, please come,* and no more felons, with their room keys, their tricky zippers, and their spooky jive.

Cody knocked on the door. "Say goodbye. I got to split."

"Gbye."

There was no response at first. I could picture him outside, waiting for the tall blond fraud within to set up a sudden wail and break her leash to follow him. And I might, so I dared not open the door again until he was gone forever.

"Will you be here tomorrow?" he called, hesitating.

"I'm leaving."

"Goin where?"

"Visit my mother."

"Where does she live?"

"San Francisco," I lied.

"Need a ride?"

"No." I ground my teeth, sanding them down to a grim determination.

I heard him laughing. "Later, peachpit."

The next morning, it wasn't from the cold I was hunched down inside my coat at the Jackson Hole airport. It was suspicion. Even on the plane, I continued to peer, from time to time, over the matted sheep curls on my collar in case my lawless friends had pursued me. I was unsettled when no hoyden hollered for Courvoisier and no gigolo was there to dodge his tongue into my ear. I could still feel their derision. They said you couldn't just snip a hole in the page and fly out. If they let me do it, it was just another illusionary trick. All along I was only moving sideways, pawnishly, while they pursued me.

When I arrived at the Los Angeles airport and disembarked into the grainy desert warmth, I acted quickly to change my appearance. I took a taxi to a used car lot, where I paid cash for a Nova, '74, inane, and blue. I used the bathroom on the lot to change into a simple pink and white striped wraparound dress. Driving into a gas station, I bought a map and X'd my mother's street in Culver City. Then I drove onto the San Diego Expressway, north, rammed the accelerator, and rushed into that lowering goody-goody California sun.

I overshot the Culver City exits. I doubled back, and missed again. The sun went down. I'd lost my pursuers, and humbly took the correct offramp.

Like all the other houses on the block, my mother's was some chalky pastel color, with a stiff square of lawn like a carpet remnant, and a green spotlight shafting through palm plants.

All I asked for, from that small stucco house, was not answers, not home, but one brief audience with a giantess: an overwhelming bosom, a burrowing lap, miles of arms, and thorough fingers picking off those little grudges that clung to me like burrs and sparkled so nastily in lowlit hangouts across America.

Someone was standing on the porch and another shape hovered around in the corner of a picture window. A Cutlass was parked in the driveway. I locked my suitcase in the trunk of my car, then crossed the lawn delicately on my high heels.

The figure on the porch turned out to be a painted wooden Jesus who came up to my shoulder and seemed to want to lean on it. The hem of his robe was surrounded by planters in the shapes of rabbits, elephants, dwarfs. A vandal had taken a red pen and sketched bloodshot veins in his eyes—"That's Clyde," said a man, swinging open the screen door and stepping under the porch lamp. "He's supposed to scare snails out of the garden. Need help? You look lost." Sizing me up and down through a friendly lens, he raised his beer can to his lips. The robust belly flexed underneath his yellow polo shirt when he swallowed.

"I'm Miranda."

"God—dog—damn!" he laughed in surprise. His beige toupee slid back obediently with his scalp as his eyes widened. "I pictured you pretty as your mom, but I never thought you'd be a big young lady! I'm Dermot. Sue's husband."

"I'm sorry I didn't call."

"Now, I wondered who that might be, parked in that car, giving the house the once-over. I'm sort of sensitive to things like that, being a police officer," he chuckled. "And then I saw you walk up and I says, just like the Communists, to send me a beautiful spy on my day off and the old lady's out. Step around Clyde, honey, and come in. . . . Sue won't be back for a couple of hours. She's on this religious kick and goes to prayer meetings all Sunday, but that's when I'm watching football anyway. . . ." I was following him inside, through a narrow hallway, over cream carpeting, through a small dining room that sagged with the weight of an immense crystal chandelier, past corner cupboards full of virgin plates, and into the tiny living room. Derm timidly gestured me toward a morsel-size chair in turquoise brocade. "Make yourself comfortable. The TV's on the fritz, so I was just laying around by myself listening to the Victrola. Can I get you something? A soda?"

I touched the white tulle curtains, silly crinolines, and turned to look at Derm's eager face, tanned and coarsely lined like clawed tree bark, at his can of beer, poor sweet guy, I guess I'd interrupted his high. I could see the pit in the cushion of the chair were he'd been sitting, the one man-measured seat in this lingerie department. "I'll have a beer, too," I said.

"A full grown lady and she drinks suds," he rejoiced, flipping over the record of movie themes in the stereo. "I'll be right back, I'll get you one of the good glasses from the kitchen."

While he was gone, I scanned the mantelpiece quickly for a photo of my mother, but there was nothing behind the file of china cocker spaniels and Swiss weather clocks. The "Theme From *The Magnificent Seven*" pranced boldly out of the cabinet speakers. Dermot turned the volume down as he reentered.

"Here you go," he handed me a glass of beer, and lowered himself unsteadily into his armchair. I sat opposite on one of the eggshell jobs. "I guess you want to wait for Sue to come back before you tell us all your news." Our eyes met anxiously as beer swirled down our throats. "Promise me you can hold your own on that stuff," he begged, "otherwise Sue'll murder me and be doing prayers all over you."

"Don't worry," I said. "I'm a pro."

The record player started "The Theme From *A Summer Place*," the beer crooned along, and suddenly I was as much "at home" as I ever could be on the map. It was one of the songs on the Royale Ballroom jukebox. "Tell me about you," I said, leaning forward.

"I worry and wonder . . ." sang the "Theme From *Moulin Rouge*."

"I worship women," Dermot sighed next to my ear.

". . . but where is your heart," I sang with the record.

"That's why I stayed a bachelor so long, so I could worship as many women as possible."

We danced, swaying slowly, deep in thought, the two of us in some alcohol tidepool where nostalgic shells open and umbrella. All the empty beer cans were shoveled under the skirt of Derm's armchair.

". . . Sue and me were always completely open with each other about the past . . . so you'd think I could understand better . . . change of life . . . this last year, all the Jesus crap . . . women are something else, I'm telling you . . . I mean, how could I get uptight about anything she did twenty years ago, when I see such a pretty girl as you, with Sue's eyes and Sue's hair . . . Jees, Miranda, I'd be proud to be your real dad. . . ."

"I bet you'd be really strict," I teased, tipping into my mouth the beer can I'd perched on his shoulder. "I bet you'd spank me every chance you could get."

"You and Sue both!"

Feeling his hard-on increase, I stepped back slightly. "No you wouldn't, you're really a softie underneath. . . ."

The song ended. "You're right," he said. "I just worship them . . . I forgive them everything they do."

We heard a car door slam and somebody humming in a quavery soprano. "Whoa, that's Sue." I chugged down the rest of my beer and toed it under the chair as Dermot turned the record player off. He tossed me a breathmint and popped another into his own mouth. "I'll head her off before she comes in and tell her who's here. Go easy on her, honey," he cautioned. "She's got kind of nervous these days."

I stood with my back to the mantel and cleaned up my posture.

Nobody had ever looked like me before. I hadn't even thought of imagining the jolt of seeing someone share my face. Through the weathered salmon-colored makeup on the face of the little lady clinging to Dermot's belt was the same look of pinched innocence that had won me so many customers.

She wore a white gown with lacy parts, and her yellow hair was crafted into a steep beehive. Derm held her steady against a trembling excitement that might fling apart her tiny structure. Her eyes screwed up and she began to wail. In an instant her cheeks were drenched in tears. I had frightened the pretty thing, with my gaping awe, which she mistook for horror. I saw her like a mother sees the firstborn: perfectly formed, and minuscule.

I crossed the room in three strides and gathered her into my arms. I felt the delicacy of her body and the helmet shapes of her bra cups. "Mom," I whispered, sucking in my breath, afraid to break her. "Bless God," she wept. I cried a little, but they were the jumbo tears of the giantess who can only put her big eye to the window of a fragile home and imagine herself inside it.

My mother tottered, her head between my breasts, and I released her. "What a nice dress," she gasped. She'd left a splash of cosmetics on it. "I want one, too. Have you seen all my thingies?" She flew to the mantel and fussed with the position of a porcelain leprechaun.

"Let's all sit down and get our bearings," said Derm. "Miranda, you take my chair—Sue, no . . ."

She was on her knees next to an ottoman, her hands clasped in front of her, her chin lifted bravely. "Yes. I've got to speak my heart," she smiled, "before I forget. Tonight at the church, there was a hush after the prayer line, and everyone was saying what a sweet hush there was, and Brother Scully picked me out and said if I proved God in the offering I would be rewarded. And I never felt surer of anything in my life, so you can call me cracked, but I want to say a final prayer, here and now, to thank our Lord for sending me back Miranda, and I don't care what you think. Miranda, dear, please join me. Derm, go to the bathroom or something."

He cast an entreating look my way, and left. I knelt obligingly beside her. She closed her eyes and began, "Lord, bless this thy servant Sue and . . . thy servant Miranda, um . . ."

I waited. Finally her eyes opened. "All done," she said. "Sometimes it's easier to finish it inside your head." Her attention fastened to a perplexing design in the lace on her sleeve.

"Mother?" I sank back on my heels. "Who was my father?"

She searched my face with her eyes, bending forward in her effort. "Oh, dear, I wish I could tell you. But you look at bit like all of them. I liked them tall, and blond." Her laughter burst into fearful panting. She grasped my wrist, and faltered on: "I was what was known as *fast*. We lived in Annapolis, near the naval academy, and I didn't care a flying fig for my reputation. They wouldn't show me your face when you were born, but now I can see it wouldn't have helped me, to guess, you know, because really you look a bit like them all. But I was punished, I can tell you. I can see you had a better upbringing and more opportunities than me, but don't ever be tempted to be a good-time gal. Your body is the temple of God. And if you aren't careful, they'll come around later and have it *cut out*."

"What?" I recoiled.

Dermot had returned and was leaning down to help her up. "That's all she needs to know, Sue," he soothed. "You've said it now."

"A hysterectomy," she said triumphantly, ignoring him. "And I'm not even forty yet. They took the whole thing out. If I hadn't found my faith—"

"—you're just the same, Sue, you want some sherry?"

"I am *not* the same. Yes, a bitty glass, and some for Miranda."

"No thank you."

He left the room again. My mother lifted herself onto the ottoman at the foot of his armchair. "Derm thinks hormone pills are the answer but they scare me. Stay on the rug if you like, dear, it's vacuumed—look at my new stockings, quick." She hiked up her skirt so I could see a delicate trail of flowers woven up the calf. "Whoops, here come the men." She accepted a glass of sherry with a maraschino cherry in it from her husband. "Sit down, sit down, you funny old cop, Miranda's going to tell us all about college and all the young men who're after her." She bit off the cherry and sucked on the stem between sips of wine.

"Oh," I said, "I'm just a French major."

"Isn't she lucky? Can you picture me with spectacles and books and a college degree, Derm?" She laid her head in his lap.

"Nope," he grinned. "Not this dolly princess."

"Go on, Miranda. And pull your dress over your knees, Derm goes crazy for young girls. He reads all my *Mademoiselles* in the john."

"Maybe you're tired," I suggested.

Dermot nodded fondly. "Sherry knocks her right out. Come on, Sue. Let's get you ready for bed and then you can come down and say good-night." He wrapped his arm around her tiny waist and lifted her up.

"And then we'll talk some more," she assured me, gracefully concealing her boredom with a wink. She turned and giggled up at her husband. "I have to take him with me cause he always puts the toothpaste on the toothbrush for me."

"I don't mind waiting," I said, "Sue."

I followed them through the dining room and watched them go upstairs. Then I stole lightly back to the livingroom, grabbed my purse, snitched the bottle of sherry from the kitchen, and broke into a canter as I emerged onto the front porch.

I raged onto the freeway in my Nova, swigging from the bottle, and missed the intersection with the route headed north. Again and again I snapped through the cloverleaf whip, double eights, north, east, south, west, til I had looped, knotted off, and cut loose the cord. The tart's cervix winked goodbye. I had to struggle on, in life, hand over hand, on a rope of empty promises, not daring to look down at my origins below, because all the bloodlines were poorly maintained, rarely traveled, washed out.

When I woke, on some Hilton mattress on the California coast, the dawn was arching over the Pacific. I ordered a beer from room service. I wasn't mad anymore.

It was my fault. Kristal had warned me about tooling after answers, but I was a lockpicker from way back.

I didn't lack for a home, anyway. She'd helped me forge one that packs easily and travels everywhere. If I belonged anyplace at all, it was on a portable private road where truth has adopted lots of little lies in order to make a good home for a loner such as me. You see? I was learning to stick with the stories, the tooled loveliness of imaginary facts. They were my friends: they let me be anything I wanted.

Kristal said, "Nobody needs to know the truth half the time cause it's gonna be a pain in the ass if they do. Nobody needs pain. It's sick persons who want it."

There's this friendship, between emptiness and promises, like the sisters charity and larceny, joined at the hip since birth, who've practiced their three-legged gait til the limp is imperceptible.

I'm not saying this is any kind of a life for you and you and you. It's for us freaks of nature, vagabonds. The wad's gone, the story's tired and thin, we're cleaned out, and we start from zero again, over and over this happens. It's like an appreciation of the way things are, of sunup and sundown, of the imperfect egg-shaped rolling of orbits. . . . We get some kind of screwy pleasure from the beauty of empty hands, and then hands filling up, and then hands overturning.

But I'm skipping ahead. On this morning I was not nearly down to nothing. I still had seven thousand dollars and one trashy mother, and I was pretty eager to lose them both so I could start over. I was driving away, north, to find a city where I could spend my roll as quickly as I'd earned it, and then I'd walk through the polished skeletal arching of zero, because on the other side I could be anything, anybody's guess.

PART

IV

———

"Pluto Studio," I answered the phone, which was part of my job.

"So," the woman's voice coughed politely. "You're fuckin nigger photographers now, I hear, Miss O'Neill. What kind of a name is Tracy O'Neill? It hasn't got no more class than your last one."

"It's perfectly legal," I retorted. "I'm makin an honest living."

I should have acted more surprised after four months of peace and quiet, except I knew jive artists are loyal fans of drama, they love turning up unexpectedly like they have some kind of corner on magic. They're unable to close the book, even if you chop the hands off, new ones grow back with fresh sticky fingers.

"How'd you find me? Where've you been?" I asked.

"Never mind." My guess was as good a story as an answer. "When do you get off today from blowin your boss?"

"Don't you come around me," I lowered my voice. "I'm his hired assistant and he thinks I'm frigid because of a traumatic accident."

"I don't like your snotty tone. I'm not askin you to come out and hold up a bank. I came all the way to San Francisco because the baby's due any day now and you promised you'd be there when it's born."

"I *did?*"

*   *   *

"Was that call for me?" Pluto stuck his head out of the dark-room.

"That was my"—I was about to say sister-in-law, from force of habit, when I remembered he was under the impression my whole family had been wiped out in a blaze the firemen had failed to put out. That was how I got the job— "godmother. She has some news about my baby." He also thought I was working to raise enough money to hire the best lawyers to get my baby girl away from her foster parents. The child was the result of a rape and I'd been talked into giving her up for adoption. That was how I got a raise, and why he was paying me cash, so I wouldn't have to declare my income. I was not anxious to declare my presence to any government, anyhow.

These stories were much more satisfying for Pluto than fucking me, but he didn't know it.

Kristal had checked into a Hilton, then set about finding a hip obstetrician. She insisted I be allowed in the delivery room with her.

"She's my husband," she twinkled at the doctor. "We're gay. What can I say, I love the bitch."

"Sure, I guess that's no problem," he shrugged. "We'll have to have a talk," he said to me, "if you can make an appointment some time with me, I'll run down all the things you should expect when the baby comes, Mister . . ."

"O'Neill."

On July 23, 1976, at 7 P.M., Kristal broke water.

The white maribou on the neckline of her negligee fluffed over my fingers as I guided her wheelchair down the hospital corridor. Her humungous belly strained and peeked out all the wrong parts of her peekaboo nightie. "You certainly seem pleased with yourself," she remarked. "You look bigger. More well-rounded."

"It's the Pill."

"I knew you had to be fuckin somebody to look so smartassed."

"No, nobody. The Pill's for just in case."

"Then you must still be a bathtub nympho," she hooted. "Do I know you or do I know you?"

She was in rare spirits for a while. She busied herself cutting a triangle off one of the five wigs in her overnight case, after the nurses shaved the woolly hair off her cunt.

So this is where Cleopatra is, I thought, gazing at her secretive face. So this is where the Nile queen is going to have to tough it out to the end of the reincarnation.

Then she went into labor. You can imagine how she hated that, since she wasn't used to steady work.

"Cocksucker!" she screamed at the doctor in the delivery room. She had refused any anesthetic.

"Now, Mrs. Pace, push again."

"Horse dick up your mother's ass!"

"She's got to stop fighting it," the doctor whispered to me. I hid a grin behind my surgical mask. I knew she liked fighting it and would keep on fighting it after it was born. Anything to get a rise. It was her way of saying "I love you."

"Pant like a little dog," urged the doctor.

"What *shit!*" she bellowed.

As the doctor held his hands ready under her heaving pussy, I was waiting to see all the cognac, fast foods, and flaming desserts I'd seen go into that belly gush out again. Instead, out came a perfectly decent human being in a beautiful vivid jelly.

As the doctor held it aloft by the ankles, my eyes flew to the square knot in its crotch.

"Hey Kristal!" I cried hysterically. "It's a dick!"

Our reverent laughter climbed the walls along with the baby's wail.

Of course, I was the baby boy's godfather, so for months I showered it with gifts, mostly water pistols, which he preferred to pacifiers for sucking, but not more than his mother's long sloping tits.

Then in the fall, they both disappeared.

I discovered one of my checkbooks missing, and Pluto started to notice fraudulent charges on his credit card statements.

It was getting harder for me to disguise my restlessness. I was bored with my new name and wanted to vanish, too, to some new city where I could spend all the money I'd accrued, and then start over. It was, as I have said, what I considered an honest living, and it suited me, I thought, so long as I avoided known criminals and definite crimes.

There was a knock on the door of the darkroom. "Pluto's not here," I called, waggling a print in the developing bath.

"Say hi, peach." I heard the tail end of a laugh that started six months ago.

"Oh, no!" I clasped my cheeks as they flared up in the amber light, and my heart went all agog at the sight of the outrageous stars in my eyes. "No, no, go away!"

"Don't tell me this old world is too small for you. Come on out."